A SCALY TAIL OF MURDER

A FRANKIE CHANDLER MYSTERY

JACQUELINE VICK

Copyright © 2022 by Jacqueline Vick

all rights reserved.

No part of this book may be reproduced in any form or by any electronic or mechanical means, including information storage and retrieval systems, without written permission from the author, except for the use of brief quotations in a book review.

Cover Art by GoOnWrite

ISBN: 978-1-945403-51-4 (Paperback)

ISBN: 978-1-945403-47-7 (eBook)

To Al and Bev, my heroes.

Special thanks to Clayton Ray Bradish, III for your help with the story details involving massage therapy. Any deviations are my doing.

ONE

The woman who stared back at me from my bathroom mirror had nice eyes. Hazel, with more green than brown. They sat under natural brows somewhere between pencil thin and caterpillar. Auburn hair that hung past her shoulders curled inconveniently from an overabundance of cowlicks. Slightly full lips. Enough to notice she had lips. Not a classic beauty, but not an ogre.

Leaning forward, I studied the light creases edging my eyes. They couldn't be laugh lines. Not with my disposition. Now that I was in my thirties, I had to stop squinting. And frowning.

I fought off disappointment. Silly, I know, but I thought my recent engagement to Detective Martin Bowers would show on the outside. My face. Or my posture. I thought I'd look different. Peaceful. Glowing. Ready to break into song.

Straightening my shoulders, I let one drop in a relaxed pose. My left hand crept up to my cheek like a pale spider.

"Oh," I said, affecting surprise. "This?"

When I wiggled the fourth finger on my left hand, my engagement ring didn't sparkle because it was a pull tab from a can of soda. Bowers had taken the morning off to whisk me away on a quest for the perfect symbol of our love. Not having worn a ring since I'd won a plastic ruby at the fairgrounds—I was seven—I thought I should practice.

Lowering my voice to a sultry level, I puckered my lips. "Darling. You shouldn't have."

I sucked in my cheeks and ran my fingers through my hair. The tab caught, and it took five minutes to work it free. With a long, loud sigh, I moved back to my bedroom and hung up the clothes piled on my bed, all discards in my quest to look like the perfect fiancée. Or at least a grown up.

Bowers, dressed for work, would most likely wear a suit, or at least a sports jacket and tie. At six feet tall, with short hair a shade above black and deep-blue eyes, my fiancé could wear a gunny sack and still make pulses race. Not that he was metrosexual or obsessed with hair products. He was rugged enough to be manly without overdoing it. Not the kind of nut whose idea of a fun date included hiking Mount Everest or paddling the English Channel.

PE, or Pre-Engagement, my go-to outfit was sweatpants and a t-shirt. Maybe jeans. However, if we walked down the street holding hands, I wanted the people we passed to think *What a lovely couple*. Not *That's one seedy customer Detective Bowers is hauling to the station*.

For today's grand event, I'd settled on a short-sleeved royal blue blouse with white polka-dots, beige slacks, and leather sandals with low heels. Open-toed sandals. Should I have attempted to paint my nails? Did I own a bottle of nail polish? No need to go crazy.

I moved back to my home's combination living room/dining room for a quick assessment. After a sniff, I sprayed an evergreen aerosol to mask Emily's cat odors. Then I sprayed again. Once I'd straightened the mismatched pillows on the blue-and-white plaid couch donated to me by my parents, I tried to see my home through impartial eyes. Well, not impartial eyes. Bowers' eyes.

Would he be surprised by the watercolor of a Gambel's quail that now hung above the couch? I'd brought her home last night. Painted by a local Wolf Creek artist, the picture gave me a rush of joy every time I gazed at it.

I frowned. She might be lonely. The rest of my standard off-white walls were bare. Then the arrangement of dried flowers on the end table next to the lamp caught my eye. That counted as a decoration.

As I considered the rest of the room, my excitement died. What had one painting and a vase of crummy flowers accomplished? I'd created a glaring contrast to the rest of my home.

Boring off-white. Like the curtains covering the sliding back door that led to my patio and my dingy old carpet. Pedestrian, like my second-hand furniture, which included a marred dinner table with a row of divots that made me think of a bear mauling. And the coffee table that reminded me of Grandma's house. Who was I kidding? My home's interior resembled an indifferent safehouse.

At least it was neat for once. Everything in its place. Except my bra. Right where I'd dropped it last night on the floor between the couch and the torchiere lamp. As I tossed it into my bedroom, I wondered if I'd have to give up comfortable habits like discarding my clothes on the floor after we were married. Closing the door behind me, I sniffed my armpits and ran my tongue over my minty-fresh teeth.

Ten minutes to go before Bowers arrived. Excitement and nervousness battled for control. Excitement over what engagement ring shopping meant. Nervous for the same reason. And I had little experience with jewelry. Not that I hated jewelry. It just wasn't on my list of priorities.

Nerves took the lead.

Stepping out my back door for a change of scenery, the heat immediately settled on me like a wool blanket worn at the beach. Tricky thing, the Arizona sun. While it allowed you to remain free of sticky sweat, luring the uninitiated into skipping sunscreen and loitering outdoors, it sucked the liquids from your body until even your eyeballs were thirsty.

The morning trills of a Lucy's warbler brought me to the stone wall that looked over the dry creek bed behind my house. Straining my ears, I waited for the comforting three-part call of the Gambel's quail that frequented the shrubby area near the bank.

When I set my hands on the wall, I heard a metal ping. I'd forgotten the pseudo engagement ring. I twisted the pull tab off my finger. It left behind an indentation. Mortified, I rubbed the skin until it looked like I'd frolicked in ragweed. Better Bowers should think I had allergies than know I'd been prancing around the house pretending to show off my ring.

Finally, the quail called out. A good omen. If she could make her home in the overgrowth that had reclaimed the creek, surely, I could establish an inviting environment for Bowers and I to live in with my credit card and a few decorating magazines.

I stepped inside. After closing and locking the sliding door, I pulled the monotonous off-white curtains shut to keep out the heat.

Bowers would be here any minute.

Returning to the bathroom mirror for one last critical

review, I forced out a reassuring nod. *Frankie Chandler, you've come a long way.* Since fleeing to Wolf Creek, Arizona, two years, eight months, and five days ago, I'd slowly rebuilt my confidence and carved out a new life.

I was engaged to the man I loved. A man who at one time feared touching me after I'd transmitted an image of an angry cat to him while we were holding hands.

My best friend lived a few miles away, and I saw her for breakfast at her bistro almost every morning. My pet psychic business, which I kept subtly tucked behind an animal behavior storefront called U-Behave, had grown to where I didn't have to buy my parents a tin of popcorn for Christmas.

When the doorbell rang, I straightened the collar on my blouse and ran a hand over my slacks. Bowers was just as lucky to have me as I was to have him. I'd have to repeat that mantra a few times, but it would stick. Eventually. Especially after we married, and I discovered his faults. I walked to the front door and swung it open with a bright smile on my face. It wasn't Bowers.

The man on my front stoop stood over six feet tall, wore a tight-fitting white t-shirt over his muscled torso, and his smile showed off straight white teeth. In one hand, he held a dark-green gym bag. He ran the other hand over his short light-brown hair in a self-conscious move.

I couldn't remember how to breathe. I shouldn't need instructions, but the natural mechanics of pulling in air escaped me.

"Jeff?" I croaked.

And then the room swam.

TWO

"Chauncey," I muttered, pushing his snout away from my face. He made a shushing noise, which was an odd sound to come from a dog. I wrinkled my nose. He had rolled in something musky. Funny, but it was pleasant, unlike the usual smells my dog brought into the house. My brow wrinkled as my logical mind fought through the haze. How did he get outside? Or inside? My ginger mutt no longer lived here. "Chauncey?"

My eyes flew open. Instead of my pup wanting to play, Jeffrey Ross, my ex-boyfriend from Loon Lake, Wisconsin, leaned over me as he unbuttoned my blouse.

Shocked into motion, I slapped at his hands.

Unfazed, he tugged at the third button from the top. "You need air."

"Stop it!" I shrieked.

In response, Jeff flew up and backwards, a look of surprise on his handsome features. Mid-air, his body twisted and slammed to the floor, face down. Bowers pressed one knee into my ex's back as he reached for his cuffs. I scrambled off the couch and stared in disbelief as a tsunami of anger slammed into me.

My worst nightmare had just walked into my home. I felt violated. This was the scumbag who had cheated on me. This was the oaf who had forced me to flee Loon Lake after he'd shared my secrets with a buxom reporter, telling her how I'd faked my psychic appointments. Back then I'd had to fake them because I hadn't yet discovered my ability. The scandal made the front page.

I blame what happened next on shock.

With Bowers balanced on one knee, I easily shoved him aside with a two-handed body slam, toppling him.

"Frankie!"

Before he could recover, I straddled Jeff's back and pummeled his solid shoulders with my fists. "How *dare* you?" I shrieked. "How *dare* you come into my home? How *dare* you show yourself to me?"

My verbal assault lacked creativity, but I continued in that vein.

"How *dare* you, you rotten son-of-a—"

Two muscular arms clamped around me and lifted me to my feet.

"No fair hitting the cuffed man."

Keeping my arms pinned to my sides, Bowers carried me to the couch and dumped me there. He pointed a finger at me.

"Stay."

He returned to Jeff and yanked him to his feet. My ex winced.

Spotting a stray catnip mouse under the coffee table, I picked it up and winged it at Jeff's head, earning me a stern glance from my fiancé.

When Bowers leaned in to take a closer look at my ex,

Jeff raised his chin and held a pose. I'd call it *Honest Man Faced with Adversity*. He looked the same. Square jaw. Roman nose. A few more lines around his eyes, the light creases contrasting with his tanned skin. Plenty of muscles without reaching football player status.

Bowers sent his gaze back to me. "You know this man?"

Years of good-girl training kicked in, and as I stood, my tone morphed into polite sweetness. "Martin Bowers, this is Jeffrey Ross. Jeffrey, this is Martin, my fiancé."

Bowers raised one brow. "This is Jeff?"

The accused grinned at him. "You've heard of me?"

My fiancé, the detective, shook his head in wonder. "Do you want to press charges?"

Jeff snorted. "For what? You dropped like a rock. I made you comfortable and was giving you some air." He looked to Bowers for approval. "That's what you do, right?"

"It is." Bowers crossed over to me and angled my body. He now had both of us in view. Resting his hands on my shoulders, he peered into my eyes with concern. "Are you all right?"

Still panting, I wiped my hand over my face because I was pretty sure there was spittle around my mouth. "Fine. I was just...surprised."

Bowers jerked his head toward the grinning man in my living room. "Because he showed up, I assume."

I blew out a breath, willing myself not to hyperventilate. "Yep."

"Uninvited."

"Absolutely."

Bowers turned to him. We might have rehearsed it as we said in unison, "What do you want?"

Jeff turned his back to us and waggled his hands. After

Bowers removed the cuffs, my ex rubbed his wrists. "Not very hospitable. What would your mother think, Frances?"

After the article came out, public reaction forced her to wear sunglasses and a hat every time she left the house. "I think the last time she mentioned you, it involved castration."

He looked shocked for about two seconds, and then he laughed, showing a dimple in his left cheek. "Beverly Chandler would never use that word."

I held up my hands. "Okay. She didn't say it, but she meant it."

"Yikes." He examined my sparsely decorated living room with wonder. Jeff plastered his apartment with sports memorabilia, trophies, beer signs, and framed prints of animals. The kinds he liked to hunt. Wisely, he didn't comment except to say, "Aren't you going to invite me to sit down?"

Crossing my arms in a classic defensive posture, I said, "If you're joking, I don't get it."

He put on a martyred expression. "You're still mad about the Buffy thing."

"The Buffy *thing*?" My arms dropped. "Are you referring to the times past clients harassed me at the grocery store? Or did you mean when teenagers prank called me? Maybe the death threats left in my mailbox." I snapped my fingers. "How about Father Jakius and his many visits begging me to come to confession."

"You're being dramatic."

I clutched Bowers' jacket lapels. "If he's in my house, I can shoot him, right? Let me borrow your gun. Pretty please? I'll give you fifteen children if you do me this one favor. How about it, Bowers?"

He wrapped his hands around mine. "Why don't we get rid of Jeff and give you a minute to cool down?"

"Wait." I peered around Bowers' shoulder. "We don't know why It's here. That may be valuable information to have when they discover the body."

Bowers sighed. "Mr. Ross, why are you here?"

My ex got up, strolled to the sliding glass door, and pulled back the curtain. "Call me Jeff. I was in the area and knew Frances had moved here, so I looked her up." Over the wall and several miles beyond, Four Peaks, part of the Mazatzal Mountains, stretched out, forming a majestic backdrop. He gave a low whistle. "I could get used to this."

"No, you couldn't." I yanked the curtain out of his hand and pulled it shut.

He grinned down at me. "So, when did you get engaged?"

"Recently." I kept it brief because I didn't want to tarnish my special moment.

Jeff laughed. "Weird. You didn't seem the marrying type."

He'd never asked. And why would he after I'd moved in with him and let him test drive me like a used car? My chest felt tight, and I had trouble getting the words out. "How did you know I lived in Wolf Creek?" I answered my question. "You called my mother."

"She didn't sound mad at all."

Why didn't she warn me the minute he hung up? Maybe she was in shock. He was right. I'd better call her later.

"What's Penny up to?"

My best friend didn't like my ex even before we parted ways. Another point in her favor.

"She's married," I mumbled, still wrapping my head

around having a conversation with Jeff after all this time. In my fantasies, the first time I saw him again, I murdered him. Slowly. Painfully.

"Anyone I know?"

"Kemper Mohr. You've never met him."

"Good for her. Now *she* seemed the marrying type." He glanced at Bowers. "You're a cop?"

"I am."

When Jeff lifted his hand for a shake, Bowers responded in kind. I pushed my fiancé's arm down and turned on my ex.

"You didn't come here to catch up with me. What do you want?"

His forehead wrinkled and he gave me his puppy eyes. "Frances. Is that any way to treat an old friend? I came all the way to Arizona to—"

When he paused, I narrowed my eyes. "To what?" A possibility leaped into my head. I gasped. "Is Buffy here on a story? Did she send you?"

Jeff drew himself up. "Buffy and I are over."

Frowning, I tried to work it out. "You broke up with Buffy and came to Wolf Creek to see me? I don't believe you. Exertion isn't your style."

"Well, I didn't come all the way just to see you."

"A-ha!" If I knew Jeff, another woman waited in the wings. "Who is she?"

"Charity. Charity Samuels." Instead of the broad grin of a man immersed in a passionate affair, his lips twitched out a spiritless smile. Something smelled, but I played along. I clapped my hands together.

"Tell us about her."

Bowers darted a concerned squint at me. I patted his arm.

"Really. I want to hear everything about her. What does she do? Where did you meet? How long have you been going out?"

My ex wandered to my couch and sat down. "It's a new relationship."

"Exciting." I nodded several times. "She must be *special*. I can tell from the deep emotion in your voice when you said her name."

He slipped me a suspicious glance. "Right. Well, she's a masseuse. They like you to say massage therapist. We met in Milwaukee at a convention. She lives in Glendale but works in Wolf Creek."

"And you fell passionately in love," I cried, delighted. "What a *charming* story."

"Frankie," Bowers murmured.

Holding my hand out toward my fiancé like a veteran crossing guard halting the kiddies in the face of certain death, I told Bowers he was out of his league. "Jeff belongs to the Order of Liars, First Class. You've interrogated thieves, arsonists, murderers, and activists. You're no match for him."

My ex beamed at what he considered high praise. My fiancé's expression shifted into neutral, but I caught the glint in his eyes, sensing a challenge. I stormed over and loomed above Jeff with my hands on my hips.

"Tell. Me. The. Truth. Why are you here?"

Jeff did what he always does when cornered. He ignored me and stood. "I should get going."

He moved to hug me, glanced at Bowers' expressionless face, and decided against close contact. "Good to see you again."

Since I couldn't say the same, I said nothing.

Once the door closed behind him, I grabbed the evergreen air freshener and fumigated the room of Jeff's presence until Bowers removed it from my hand.

"I'm not that fond of pine."

My legs shook from the adrenaline coursing through my body, so I dropped onto the couch. Bowers took the spot next to me.

"That was interesting."

Leaning forward, I ran my fingers through my hair. "Glad you enjoyed the show."

"I didn't."

Covering my face with my hands, I mumbled, "I'm so embarrassed."

"You *did* lose it for a minute there." About to add something, Bowers patted my shoulder instead. "We can reschedule if you're not in the mood."

I swiveled my head. "Reschedule? You mean let that jerk ruin our big day? Not a chance."

Grabbing my purse, I headed for the door, with Bowers trailing in my wake of fury.

THREE

By the time Bowers parked the car in downtown Wolf Creek, I'd had a private talk with myself.

Get a grip, Frankie.

Jeff. Stupid lout. Showing up unannounced. A not-so-gentle reminder of my past. How humiliating to have my greatest mistake step into my present and flaunt himself in front of my fiancé. Bowers knew about my ex-boyfriend, but now he would see exactly what kind of idiot I'd been to fall for Jeff's charms. Unwilling to chain himself to a woman who lacked taste and common sense, my fiancé might reconsider our engagement. Stupid, stupid Jeff. He'd already muddied my past. He would *not* ruin my future. Didn't I deserve a second chance?

Okay. It wasn't an upbeat pep talk, but it helped. Right then, I resolved to break the hold my prior error in judgment had over me. I'd embarrassed myself this morning and covered a special event with a patina of yuck. Bowers hadn't deserved that, and nothing, *nothing,* meant more to me than his happiness.

He deserved a strong fiancée. One who dared anyone,

including her ex-boyfriend, to cause her confidence to flounder. One who didn't bother to brush off difficulties because they weren't worth the effort. One who laughed easily at life's quirks and didn't have a care in the world. Confident, Imperturbable, Carefree Frankie. Carefree Frankie for short. My new persona.

Bowers said, "Ready?"

Blinking against the blazing sun, I nodded and got out of the car. The stores on this block of Main Street were quaint representations of the artistic community that had taken over Wolf Creek after the last financial slump. Bebe's Bakery, with signage in Desert Rose script and a baguette in the logo. A Good Throw, the pottery store and workshop. All the oes in the name had cracks, like eggs.

When I glanced at the front of Wilhelm's Jewelry Emporium, I learned transforming into Carefree Frankie wouldn't be that easy.

I'd passed this place hundreds of times and only thought *It's Mr. Wilhelm's nice little store.* How had I never noticed the Gothic gold lettering on the window to the left of the door? What blindness had kept me from seeing the mannequin heads propped on pedestals covered with silky white fabric, each wearing a sumptuous necklace and matching earrings? Wilhelm's Jewelry Emporium looked like the place where women in ball gowns came to die. I didn't belong.

The nod I gave Bowers resembled that of a woman who had just steeled herself for the final walk to the electric chair. I was having a panic attack. If the detective, trained to observe, noticed, he said nothing.

As he held open the glass door for me, the battle between my excitement and nervousness ended in a knockout blow. Nerves won.

Maybe Bowers was right. We should reschedule. After ten minutes with Jeff, the ensuing flood of memories his appearance brought had knocked my self-confidence on its keister. When I'd imagined picking out an engagement ring with Bowers, the scene reeked of joy. Giggles. Even girlish shrieks. Not stomach-churning uncertainty and shame.

No. Jeff would not ruin this moment for me. I straightened my shoulders and stepped inside.

Everybody in Wolf Creek referred to Wilhelm Baumgartner as Mr. Wilhelm. He stood behind a glass case that came up to the chest of his beige three-piece suit, his black glasses pushed down to the tip of his pointed nose as he examined a pair of earrings for a sturdy older woman in a peach denim jacket, khaki pants, and aqua sandals.

Soft white carpet covered the floor and dared our footsteps to ruin the room's ambiance with clicking heels and clomping soles. Glass cases filled with sparkly things formed an upside-down horseshoe along the back and sides of the room. In strategic spots throughout the main floor, display cases beckoned clients to kill time admiring special items that were above mingling with the other trinkets.

A few people, a single man and a younger couple, browsed the wares. While we waited, Bowers steered me to the closest display case filled with an arrangement of jewelry made by local Yavapai and Apache artists.

It wasn't hard to get excited over the hand-crafted finery, even for a woman who thought bracelets were for prisoners. I set to work massaging Bowers' ego with my feigned love of girlish adornments.

"That's gorgeous." I pointed at a charm with a pattern of lines etched into a flat, green stone. "Such detailed work."

Bending to get a closer look, another piece caught my eye. If I ever took to ornamenting myself, I would choose the silver cuff with unevenly placed turquoise stones wrapped in a silver spiral. The price tag caught my eye, and I stumbled back against Bowers' chest. "Yikes."

A young woman walked up with a tray of champagne glasses. "Would you like a beverage while you browse?"

Grabbing the closest one by the stem, I threw back the bubbly and returned the glass to her tray. Bowers raised a brow.

I choked on the final tickle. "I'm nervous."

His smile said he expected nothing less. "I can see that." Since he'd be on duty directly after our adventure, he sent the girl away without taking a glass.

Time to bring out Carefree Frankie. My smile broadened into a grin so wide I thought my lips would crack. "It—it's just so exciting to be here." What did carefree look like? Twirling in circles with my arms spread wide seemed like overkill. Instead, I giggled until I snorted.

From behind the counter, Mr. Wilhelm removed his glasses. "Madame, I will have your earrings ready in two weeks. Like new."

"And they'll match?" The woman's tone expressed doubt in Mr. Wilhelm's qualifications. I knew she had money because she was the only person in the place who wasn't whispering.

"I promise. You will not know the difference."

As she left, he tucked a box under the counter and raised a finger in our direction. "May I help you?"

I pointed to my chest. "Me? I mean, us?"

Even as he nodded, I jabbed my finger at the single man and the other couple. "They were here first." Instead of a polite gesture, it sounded like an accusation.

"They are deciding."

From the pained expression on the young man's face, a

direct contrast to the dreamy smile his companion wore, his choice was between walking out of the store, and running.

Bowers took my hand and pulled me to the counter. I sent a desperate glance around the room, but the champagne lady had gone into hiding.

"We'd like to see your engagement rings."

Here we were. The decisive moment.

The old man beamed. "Congratulations. I'm honored you would come to me for such an important purchase."

"Important?"

Yikes. Important sounded like my decision would impact orphans and widows.

"The most important you will make in your life. Aside from your fiftieth anniversary ring."

"I'll have to go through this again?" Panic seeped into my tone. One jewelry purchase gave me enough stress to last a lifetime.

Bowers squeezed my hand. "Let's worry about that when we make it to fifty years."

With him close to forty, and me in my thirties, we might not live another fifty years. The thought calmed me until I remembered the weighty decision still facing me. Important also sounded expensive. The subject of Bowers' salary hadn't come up, so it was a mystery how much he made. However, I didn't want him to take out a loan for a piece of jewelry.

"I don't typically wear rings." I wanted to make it clear that something simple would do. Simple and cheap.

"But you will wear this one, no?" Mr. Wilhelm chuckled. "And the other of the set."

"A set? That's more than one, right? I have to decide on two rings?"

"Typically, you will have an engagement ring and a

wedding ring," Mr. Wilhelm explained with the patience of one used to dealing with jittery women. "After you are married, we can fuse them together if you like."

"Oh." I tittered and placed a hand on my chest, where I could feel my heart pounding. "Of course."

The jeweler slid over a flat display box covered in royal-red velvet. When he peeled back the cover, I resisted the urge to put on my sunglasses. About twenty rings twinkled, beckoning me to look and admire. Lumpy gold that resembled the skin of that action hero, The Thing, competed with 14 carat gold bands and even light gold bands that looked like silver. But these were only the modest wedding bands. The brilliant engagement rings shoved them offstage like understudies grabbing their big break.

Diamond chips, square-cut diamonds, and the ever-popular solitaire stole the show. With my limited knowledge of jewelry, I classified them as small, medium, and *I can't lift my hand*.

Bowers placed his palm on my back. "Do you see anything you like?"

My shoulders tensed. Asking me which ring I liked was like asking a dog which flower he preferred to sniff. Or wee on. Anything would do. I couldn't even make an educated guess since the rings didn't have price tags.

Was I expected to choose a costly piece to reflect the colossal value Bowers would receive by marrying me? I knew fools who were impressed by the expensive tastes of their partners, proud of living paycheck to paycheck to support her addiction to clothes, shoes, or whatnot. Not my style.

But if I picked a less pricey, practical ring, would it show I was cheap goods and not worth haggling over? Sweat broke out on my upper lip as I contemplated nuances I couldn't begin to decipher.

Think, Frankie. Think. Choosing an engagement ring should be a simple task. If I couldn't do this right, the rest of the marriage would topple like a row of dominoes.

"It sometimes helps to try one on." Mr. Wilhelm being helpful. He gently removed the simple band with a solitaire and took my hand, sliding the ring over my knuckle.

"It feels cool against my skin." I glanced at Bowers and giggled. "Kind of a surprise, like how I expected snakes to feel cold and clammy but found them to be warm and soft." Wiggling my eyebrows in Mr. Wilhelm's direction, I added, "Kind of cuddly as long as they aren't attacking you."

"Er, yes."

As I moved my finger to pick up the light, Bowers nuzzled my neck. This ring would be a symbol of our love. Forever. It was up to me to choose that symbol and never, ever change my mind. I couldn't even pick from a breakfast menu without regretting my selection.

I would wear this ring until I died. They would bury me in it. Unless Bowers wanted it as a keepsake. And if, God willing, I got pregnant and fat, I wouldn't be able to remove it at all. It would stay there, wrapped around my finger in a stranglehold I'd never break.

With a shaky breath, I tugged off the ring and shoved it back at Mr. Wilhelm.

"Perhaps you see something you like better?"

"No, no. That's not it."

"Do any of them appeal to you? Just to give me an idea what you like?" Bowers' voice had an edge to it.

I stared at him, panicked. "You pick."

Mr. Wilhelm gasped.

My fiancé studied me before turning to the jeweler. "It's

my fault. We didn't discuss the ring before we came, and I think you've overwhelmed her with so many beautiful choices." When he smiled, he hid his disappointment, but I knew it was lurking behind his deep-blue eyes. "Why don't we come back with a game plan?"

I nodded without speaking.

Fortunately, Mr. Wilhelm, the professional, said that was the best suggestion he'd heard in years.

Once outside, Bowers said, "It was a mistake to do this right after Jeff's appearance. You're still keyed up."

I turned to Bowers and clutched his jacket. "I haven't ever thought about a ring. I've never thought about wedding dresses—. Oh, poop. I'm going to have to try on wedding dresses, aren't I? I can't even find a t-shirt that looks good. Or wedding cake! What if nobody likes what I pick? What if *you* don't like what I pick? And what about the reception. What if everybody gets sick from the food? Or *dies*? People can die from rotten food."

"You're hyperventilating. Take a deep slow breath."

I tried, but I choked. "I saw how stressed Penny got planning her wedding and she had dreamed about it for ages. All these things that come naturally to women, I don't think about. What's wrong with me?" I sobbed. "Maybe Jeff's right and I'm not the marrying kind."

He put his hands on my shoulders and squeezed. "Frankie. It's okay. I've never been engaged before, either. We'll take it one step at a time. There is no right way. There's only our way." He set his lips in a grim line. "And our way doesn't include Mr. Ross' opinion."

I rested my head against his shoulder until my breathing returned to normal. "I'm sorry I'm such a lousy fiancée."

Holding me away from him, he gave me a gentle shake. "That's the only thing I won't put up with. You beating yourself up. You're my fiancée, and I think you're perfect."

He shifted me so his arm was around my shoulder. "It's like my sister's sweet potatoes at Thanksgiving. They're a tradition. Everybody loves them except us. Would you like to eat sweet potatoes every year just to fit in? Those gooey marshmallows, and—"

"Stop." My shoulders shuddered. "Some things are too terrible to contemplate."

He kissed my temple. "I've got to get to work. We can talk about it after dinner tonight. Okay?"

"Thanks for understanding."

While I appreciated the reprieve, I didn't think those few hours would help.

FOUR

Bowers dropped me off at home.

In a frenzied desire to make up for my failure at Wilhelm's, I spoke three words that should never come out of my mouth. "I'll make dinner."

It was the right thing to say. The corners of his lips twitched in a pleased smile. "That would be nice." Or maybe he was holding back a laugh.

I waved at the receding car until it turned the corner. Once it was out of sight, I sprinted for my front door. The first thing I did when I got to my kitchen, panting, was to pull open every cabinet as well as the refrigerator door. Emily, my black-and-white cat, stepped into the pantry and settled onto the case of water bottles where she had a better vantage point from which to mock me. And she had reason to expect entertainment.

At first glance, my shelves revealed a box of saltine crackers, peanut butter, a few apples, and some instant rice. The large flat of Raman noodles had appeal, but my ability to boil water wouldn't impress Bowers.

The last time I'd cooked for him had been Thanksgiving

dinner. If he hadn't arrived with a cheese plate, and a pie, and a side dish, and taken over the turkey preparation, my guests would have ended the night struggling to hold up their heads, weak from hunger.

I could run to the store for some frozen Chinese. Or frozen Mexican. It seemed a shame to have a perfectly good microwave and not use it. But that wasn't good enough. I wanted to be a supportive, caring wife. One who could make a house a home. One who could serve warm cookies to the kids when they returned from school. A wife capable of whipping up a nutritious and delicious meal for her family.

Gack! Did I say wife? My mother was a wife. Penny was a wife. I, Frankie Chandler, was going to be a wife. I leaned against the counter until the lightheaded feeling passed.

After blowing out a huff of air, I straightened my shoulders. It was time to woman up and make dinner. How hard could it be? The Thanksgiving turkey, a large unwieldy bird, was an exception. It had been a mistake to venture into the cooking arena with a holiday meal.

Bowers loved Italian food, especially lasagna, so after a quick phone conversation with Penny to get the recipe, I returned to the pantry.

The ingredients were all there. Well, most of them, but that's why God created grocery stores. One hour later, I returned with the items missing from the list—lasagna noodles, mozzarella cheese, Italian sausage, ricotta cheese, Parmesan cheese, pasta sauce, and canned tomatoes.

Using a paper towel, I blotted the sweat off my face. The exception to Arizona's dry heat came with the monsoon season when the weather toyed with Arizonans, sending humidity, sprinkles, light showers, and wind until, just before we gave up on ever being comfortable again, the rain would come. And when it came, it came in torrents.

Not even a deluge of rain would save me from my commitment to make dinner, so I grabbed the recipe, written on scratch paper, and got to work creating my first culinary delight.

Though I struggled a bit getting the Italian sausage out of the casings, soon the sauce simmered, and the noodles bubbled in the water. This wasn't difficult at all. Kind of like making dog food from scratch.

While I waited for the pasta to finish, I called my mother. She answered on the first ring.

"I'm counting stitches, so make it quick. Remember this number. Seventy-two."

Mother, the consummate craftsperson, crocheted, knitted, beaded, sewed, and wove her own fabric. Her handmade gifts were a treat. Her grasp of complex situations like my relationship with Jeff were not.

"Why did you give Jeff my address?"

"Oh, raspberries. I moved my hand. Now I have to start the row over." She sighed. "Why do you think? He asked for it."

"Just because someone, like my evil ex-boyfriend, asks you a question, you don't need to answer it."

"What's the big deal?"

"Wha—Don't you remember what he did?"

She laughed. "Old news. That was ages ago. You need to let these things die or you'll get indigestion."

"Why didn't you just tell him you didn't know how to get hold of me?"

"Can you imagine what the neighbors would say if they thought we'd lost contact with our only daughter?"

"You didn't need to tell the neighbors. Just Jeff."

"That would have been a lie. Lies catch up with you."

Setting my tone on Pained Martyr, I said, "Well, thanks to you, he came here." No response. "To my house."

"That's nice."

"No! It wasn't."

"What number did I give you?"

"Seventy-two."

"Okay. This sweater won't knit itself. Love you. Bye."

The call disconnected. I didn't have time to mull over Mother's lack of sympathy—or interest—in my trauma. A hiss alerted me to water boiling over onto the burner. I'd forgotten the noodles.

I grabbed the pot by the handles, immediately dropping it back on the stove. It sloshed over the counter. And my recipe.

"Darn, darn, darn."

Alternating between blowing on my hands and dabbing at the soggy paper with a kitchen towel, I wound up with red palms and a Rorschach test. Forced to improvise on the remaining steps, I felt confident by the time I popped the pan into the pre-heated oven. It looked like lasagna.

I still wore my outfit from the jewelry jaunt this morning, so I only had to set my glass kitchen table and I could take a break. By the time I finished, I was humming.

Take that, Donna...Donna...the Donna that always played the mother on television. All I needed was an apron and I could accept my award for Home Cook of the Year.

"Now for your din-din," I sang out.

Emily's ears twitched. She sauntered to her food bowl and stared at it, waiting for food to appear. Which it did. As it always does.

At least my cat would forever appreciate my skills with a can opener.

FIVE

Once I iced my palms, I took a cup of coffee to my backyard, which was more of a cement patio with a border of pink rocks and shrubs. Time for a mental regrouping before Bowers arrived.

After raising the umbrella on my green-and-blue tile patio table, I slumped back in my wicker chair and reviewed this morning, trying to put my finger on why I'd transformed into a harridan at the sight of Jeff.

It wasn't spurned lover syndrome. Any feelings I'd had for my ex in that arena were long gone. I'd experienced a wave of rage that left me exhausted and...sad. Sad over what I'd lost? Maybe. And what had I lost? My innocence. Not innocence as in virginity, although there was that. I struggled to find the answer.

"My confidence," I whispered. "My ability to trust. My self-worth." A tiny thought bored into my psyche. Could my past mistake mark me for life? Was my error in judgment visible, like permanent eye liner? Behind my back, would people say I wasn't worthy of Bowers? Living with Jeff hadn't felt like a life-altering decision at the time.

When I'd foolishly moved in with him, ignoring my conscience, my parents, and my parish priest, I felt I was taking a grown-up step. A late bloomer, I'd never been in a serious relationship, and here was someone who wanted to play house. Play being the operative word.

I'd already established myself as an animal communicator after fixing a few pet problems for prominent people using animal behavior knowledge, the cold reading techniques of the best Las Vegas mind readers, and common sense. It amazed me how people couldn't find their own solutions, but I was happy to take their money and considered it a win-win. Their problems disappeared, and I made a decent living.

Then Jeff betrayed me to Buffy Beaumont, reporter extraordinaire. At least in her own mind. After Lois Lane's exposé wound up on the front page of *The Loon Lake Local*, telling everyone I was a charlatan who took advantage of innocent people concerned about their pets, my life in Loon Lake was over. Never mind that I had helped those people.

When I confronted my live-in boyfriend, he pointed out that we didn't have a serious commitment like a marriage license. In shock, I moved back in with my parents and attempted to weather the criticism and threats. Finally, Penny, my best friend from childhood, urged me to move to Wolf Creek, Arizona, and live near her. She didn't have to ask twice.

What was it that made women like Penny hold out for the right man? I supposed Penny's group had more faith in themselves. Me? My middle name was deference.

Only one piece of cake left? You take it. Please. One seat remaining in the lifeboat? I'm sure your loved ones need you more. Take it. I had nothing special planned for my life. I'll just curl up on deck and make friends with the fishes while they nibble my toes.

I thought I'd moved on from guilt and shame, but my reaction to Jeff said there were still issues I needed to deal with. The words of Father Jakius, my mother's parish priest, came to me. *When you forgive someone, they lose all power over you.*

Could I forgive that lying, cheating twerp? I didn't know, but I had to pull myself out of this morose mood, and soon.

Just as I finished my coffee, a White-winged dove landed on the corner of my stone wall. Suddenly, a male landed on her back. In three seconds, the mating was over, and the male flew off. Jeff in a nutshell.

I stood and leaned against my wall, absorbing the scenery.

Dirty smoke created a haze that blurred my view of Four Peaks. Squinting, I realized it wasn't smoke. It was dust carried across the desert by high winds. The call of my Gambel's quail broke the silence, and the hen skittered between shrubs with her babies scurrying to keep up. I counted ten.

We'd had a light sprinkle during the night, and the fresh rain smell of creosote made me long for heavy showers that would bring the desert plants to life. Heavy, but short of a flood.

When the monsoon rains hit, the simplest dip in the road, like the one on my street, would fill with tumbling, dirty water deep enough to carry away cars. It only took twelve inches. Fortunately, city crews had marked most dips with signs like *Turn Around, Don't Drown.*

Turn around, don't drown. The fates were waving a flag

to stop me from following the course set in motion by Jeff's appearance.

As usual, I ignored them.

SIX

Bowers showed up at my door with a bottle in one hand and two wine glasses in the other. He still wore his navy sports coat, white shirt, and jeans.

Tonight was a test of my ability to provide my future husband with those things he would crave after a hard day's work. A good home-cooked meal. Relaxation. Maybe a little fooling around. We weren't off to a great start.

"Wine?"

"It's sparkling cider, but it bubbles. It's a special occasion." He grinned. "You cooked."

"You shouldn't have," I said, nodding at the glasses.

He held them up by the stems. "We drank from coffee cups at Thanksgiving. A novelty, but not one I want to turn into a habit."

"No. I mean you shouldn't have brought a corked bottle. I don't have an opener."

Handing me the bottle as he stepped inside, he said, "It's a screw top. Hey. You bought a painting."

Foolishly pleased, I dragged him over to admire my new picture. He gave me the appropriate number of compliments, but as he gazed on it, his expression held something other than admiration. Maybe I'd stunned him by finally doing something about my bare walls.

We took Bowers' mini bar into the kitchen, and once we'd emptied our hands, he pulled me in for a kiss. I ran my fingers over his shoulders. "You must have been a cute scout."

He cocked his head. "Cute?" He planted his lips on mine for a healthy kiss. When he stepped back, the first thing he did was open the oven to peek at dinner.

"It looks good." He cranked the temperature dial down to warm. "Let's have a glass of cider first."

Before he poured, he removed his jacket and hung it over the back of his chair. He left his belt holster on, but I'd gotten used to a man walking around my home wearing a gun. What really freaked me out was how I actually considered one of my kitchen chairs *his*. If that wasn't proof of permanence….

We took our glasses and moved to the living room. As Bowers sat, he leaned forward and tugged at his shirt to unstick it from his back. "I wish it would get it over with and rain."

Joining him on the couch, I asked, "How was your day?" stopping short before I added *dear*.

He grimaced and held up his glass. "Because I got in late, I'm going to have to return after dinner to catch up on paperwork. Hence the cider. I hate to eat and run…."

"No problem." Hiding my disappointment, I broadcast Understanding Fiancée instead. I leaned my head against his shoulder and curled my legs on the couch. "This is what it's going to be like after we're married."

Butterflies fluttered in my stomach on the word married.

He adjusted his position to get his arm around my shoulder. "It is. Are you up for it?"

"Absolutely."

He sipped his cider. "Are you feeling better? You were awfully upset this morning."

"I think they used to call it a brainstorm."

"And it was just the shock of seeing him?"

How to explain? "Imagine if your most humiliating mistake walked into the room."

"It would be a surprise."

"A surprise? That's too nice. The man ruined my life."

He hesitated, choosing his words carefully. He might have been testifying on the stand. "I hear what you're telling me. And I can see how it might have felt that way at the time. The betrayal. Losing a great deal and having to start again someplace new. His sudden appearance stirred up those feelings, and—"

"Stop it."

His brow wrinkled. "Stop what?"

"You're using your *detective talks to hysterical witness* voice on me." I wiggled my fingers at him in a hypnotic motion. "The soothing, calm voice and validating words. *I hear you.*"

He nodded. "Okay. I'll be direct. You were upset seeing him. Understandable. And I'm not dismissing what he did to you or how you felt about it."

"But?"

"Your life isn't ruined. Is it?"

"Well, no." Just this morning I'd been grateful for so much. How had I forgotten? "Definitely not."

"Good. Glad to hear that." He gave it a decent interval before he set his glass on the coffee table and changed the subject. "We haven't talked about where we'll live once we're married." He stroked my arm to make it a casual question, but I pulled away.

"It never crossed my mind."

"We can't live in two separate houses, Frankie. I plan on sleeping in the same bed with you."

"I should *hope* so. It's just, I hadn't thought that far ahead. I like my house. I know where everything is."

He sent an amused glance around my living room. "There's not a lot to lose track of."

"Ha-ha." My laugh had a hollow ring. "I bought a painting."

Glancing over his shoulder, he said, "We can take it with us. I'm sure there's a spot on my walls. In fact, as soon as I saw it, I thought of just the place for it. My spare bedroom."

"But, and don't take this personally, your place would make me feel like a visitor."

He leaned forward and rested his elbows on his knees. "If you don't want to pick one or the other, we could always buy a new house."

"You mean our own?"

He smiled. "That's the idea."

"But what if Emily doesn't like it there?"

My cat sprawled across the couch next to Bowers, belly up. "I'm sure she'll adjust."

"Or what if Chauncey runs away from your sister's farm and comes back here. I know it's miles and miles away, but dogs have done it before. We'll be gone, and he'll be lost."

"I don't think he'll leave June's. He seemed pretty happy there."

I sighed. "He did."

"We don't need to make a decision right now. I just want you to start thinking about it."

He rubbed my knee, and I leaned in and kissed him. As I sunk into his arms, a gust of wind rattled my back screen. Bowers got up and closed the sliding door, and when he returned, we occupied ourselves with more smooching until the timer went off.

When I removed the pan from the oven and set it on the stove top, I indulged in a pleased grin. The cheese had browned to perfection. Smells of garlic and onion danced around me, begging me to savor my first bite.

While Bowers poured more cider, I served us each a slice of lasagna, which was difficult with the way it slopped off the spatula, the ricotta cheese pouring out the sides. Maybe I should have used bowls.

He lifted his glass. "Bon appétit."

"Back atcha."

The top layer of Parmesan crunched as I bit into it, the sharp nuttiness overwhelming my taste buds. That made up for the sickeningly soft, tasteless noodles and watered-down sauce. The tough sausage added another texture, as did the firm tomatoes under the cheese.

I covered my mouth and coughed. "You don't have to eat it."

His smiled strained at the edges as he kept chewing, and he winced as his teeth encountered a hard piece of Parmesan. I heard the crunch from across the table. Once he swallowed, he said, "It's your first attempt at lasagna."

"But I wanted dinner to be perfect." I swished my noodles through the ricotta cheese. "This is inedible."

"It's fine. How many eggs did you use in the ricotta?"

Did he say eggs? When he slurped another mouthful, I

noticed he'd switched out his fork for a spoon. He glanced at my expression and said, "It's fine."

I might have believed his mediocre endorsement if he hadn't slid the serving bowl of salad closer and started to eat directly from it. After a few minutes, he cleared his throat.

"There's something I want to talk to you about."

His expression was so serious I set down my fork, which was a blessing. Keeping the panic from my voice, I said, "What's happened?"

"Nothing, yet. But it's something that *may* happen. I hope."

"So, it's a good thing."

"A very good thing. Especially if we want to start a family." He grinned. "Maybe not a family of fifteen, but still, a larger income would help. You do want children, right?"

The sexiest words in the English language are *I want you to have my baby*. They meant real commitment. A total giving of self, holding nothing back, that resulted in a life. I remembered that much from my high school catechism because it made an impression. I leaned across the table and squeezed his hand.

"You remember Randy from the Christmas party? Randall Dahl. Tall guy. He's retiring at the end of the year, so they're on the hunt for his replacement. A sergeant."

"And they asked you? What would that mean? Would you work longer hours? Would you be out of danger forever?"

"Several of us have gone through interviews, and the results, along with our experience, will help the committee decide. I'll still be a detective, but I'll coordinate the investigations."

"Naturally they'll pick you. Who else is there?"

"Smitty is up for it."

I remembered Smitty as a grizzled man, kind of a slob, who had outgrown his beige sport jacket.

"And Juanita."

Detective Juanita Gutierrez. Bowers' sometimes partner and always competition. The first time I met her was at an office function, where I discovered her nickname. Python. I'd felt she was up to no good, so I talked Bowers into letting me drive home. He'd had a scotch. I'd had iced tea. Halfway home, an innocent patrol officer pulled us over. She'd received a call about a drunk driver. When she saw who was in the car—and smelled my breath—she assumed it was a joke. I didn't.

"You'll still get it. You're the best cop in Wolf Creek."

Though he joked about my bias, I could tell my positive response tickled him. Bowers wanted that promotion. Bowers *deserved* that promotion. I'd have to find out who was on that committee. Maybe I could invite them to lunch and remind them of my fiancé's finer points. At a restaurant, of course.

"Will I have to salute you?"

He got up, came around the table, and wrapped his arms around my shoulders. "No, but you'll have to learn to follow orders."

A tingle ran through my shoulders as he kissed the top of my head.

"I'm sorry. I have to run."

"Have you got enough time to hit a drive through on your way back?"

Concerned Fiancée. Always looking out for Bowers.

SEVEN

Five minutes later, I'd ruminated over my disastrous dinner and worked up enough self-pity for chocolate. Just as I'd unwrapped a single mini crunch bar, the doorbell rang. I should have brought the bag with me when I answered the summons.

My ex slipped inside before I could react. He'd put on a hunter green Milwaukee Bucks windbreaker and left it unzipped.

"I didn't want to talk in front of your guard dog, so I waited until he left."

"You mean my *fiancé*."

He wiggled his ring finger to indicate that mine was bare. "Not yet, he isn't."

I pointed at the doorway. "Leave."

"Frances, hear me out."

Did I hear an appeal in his voice? Was he prepared to grovel and beg my forgiveness? Father Jakius hadn't mentioned groveling as a prerequisite to forgiveness, but it worked for me. Still, I remained suspicious. This was, after all, Jeff.

"Why should I?"

"I know you're mad at me—"

"How insightful."

"Come on. We have history, and not all of it was bad. You must have liked *something* about me." He grinned as if his finer points should be obvious.

I pressed my lips together and he waited.

"Frances?"

"I'm thinking."

"I can tell. You're making faces. If you can't remember the good times, I can. And I remember what a—a noble person you are."

"Noble." Even saying it out loud, the description didn't fit.

"Sure. How you always jumped in to help others no matter the cost. Unlike anyone else I know, you're selfless."

"You mean a doormat."

Tilting his head, he brought out his Sad Eyes. "Being angry, it's not your natural state."

"Okay. We're agreed. I'm a saint."

"I wouldn't go *that* far." Something in my expression made him take the shortcut to his point. "I'll lay it on the line. I'm in trouble, and I need your help. The Frances I know would at least hear me out. If you don't want to help after you've heard my story, you can toss me. Okay?" He rubbed his shoulder, reminding me of my loss of control this morning, and his eyes pleaded with me.

My heart twitched, which was merely a sign I wasn't dead.

One thing about Jeff. He understood me. He knew I had a soft spot for stray dogs and orphans. Goading me into helping him wouldn't be difficult. Even as my brain screamed IT'S A TRAP, I asked, "What kind of trouble?

And why would I care?" I added that last bit to salvage my dignity.

I let him take a seat on the couch, but I didn't offer him coffee, or cider, or one of my candy bars, and I stuffed the decorative pillows between us.

He sniffed the aroma of garlic and onions that hung in the air. "I don't suppose you have leftovers."

Even if I hadn't stuffed the sorry remains down the garbage disposal, giving him the opportunity to mock my cooking skills wasn't part of my plan.

"I cooked for two. You have five minutes."

"It might take longer." He removed the pillows and scooted to the cushion next to me. When I bared my teeth, he scooted back.

"Talk fast."

He took in a deep breath followed by a mournful sigh. "After Buffy left me, I wasn't in a good place."

"Time's ticking."

"I was at a job fair in Milwaukee, and there was a massage convention next door. They were giving away free massages. That's how I met Charity. We hit it off, and she said how much fun it would be if I lived in Arizona."

I held up a hand. "In one half hour—maybe forty minutes—you got to know someone well enough during a massage that she suggested you relocate?"

"Well...it wasn't just a massage."

I froze. "You had sex with her in the middle of a convention?"

"They had a screen up. It made it more exciting."

Blinking rapidly to chase the image out of my skull, I stuttered out a response. "You're—you're a mutt. I can't believe you."

"But that's not the problem."

"The fact that you don't see that kind of behavior as a problem *is* the problem."

"Can I finish my story?"

Assuming the bad part was over, I told him to continue.

"As soon as I arrived, I went to see her at Friendly Fingers."

A guffaw slipped out.

"It's the name of the spa where she works. She was... surprised. I may have misunderstood. My head wasn't on straight. You know. Because of Buffy. It seems she was making small talk. She didn't mean for me to move out here."

After a few seconds, I threw back my head and laughed until my sides hurt.

"That's not very nice."

The final giggle petered out. "Nice? It's perfect. Your hound dog ways have finally gotten *you* in trouble." I stood and held out my hand. "Thank you for that. You cheered me up."

"Frances! This is serious. I don't have the money to get back to Loon Lake. I spent it all on airfare. I thought—I assumed I'd stay with Charity until I got on my feet." He spread his arms. "I'm stranded. Not only that, I left my keys at Friendly Fingers and—I don't think she wants to see me again. I hoped you could stop by and pick them up for me."

"You're driving a rental car."

"Yeah. So?"

"How are you driving it without keys?"

"I'm talking about my personal keys. My Loon Lake keys."

"I'm not in the mood to meet any of your girlfriends."

"You don't have to talk to her. Just ask at the front desk. I know it's awkward for you to meet her—"

My eyebrows shot up. "Awkward?"

"You know. After what we had."

"I could give two figs about your girlfriends," I said, contradicting my earlier statement. "I could stand in a room filled with your girlfriends and the only thing I'd feel is boredom."

"You'll do it?"

Too late, I recognized the corner. It's one I've backed into on many occasions. "Fine. I'll get your stupid keys."

He grinned. "Thanks a lot." He glanced around the room. "As for tonight, I could sleep on the couch."

Pummeling him had tired me out, so I took a different approach. I smiled broadly. "You can leave now."

"But Frances," he pleaded.

"Ding. Time's up." I stood, and he reluctantly followed suit.

"I suppose I could sleep in my rental car."

"You could."

"You don't know of any isolated places around here, do you?"

"The desert."

"I mean someplace I could pull off the road without being bothered by carjackers. Or thieves. Or cops. I can't afford a ticket."

A gust of wind sent my outdoor chimes into a tinkling frenzy and my imagination into overdrive. I could see myself in the car at night, listening to the coyotes make a kill. The screams of the victim. No streetlamps around to give me warning if shadows approached the car as I slept. Not that I would see them if I were sleeping. But if they tripped, they might wake me up. I'd know there was someone out there but wouldn't be able to tell where they were, which is worse. I could turn on the headlights, but if they weren't in front of the car, it wouldn't help. And if they hadn't noticed the car, I would alert them to my presence.

A wicked idea bumped this frightening scenario aside. I'd thought of a fitting way to get back at my ex. Father Jakius' plaintive voice came to me. *Frances, revenge is not part of forgiveness. You must put aside petty desires and—*

I told the imaginary priest to take a hike.

"All right. I'll help you."

As he grinned down at me, I detected a hint of smugness. I'd soon wipe that off his face.

"I know just the place for you."

EIGHT

"You want me to spend the night in your store?"

I'd led Jeff to the U-Behave entrance off Maricopa Drive and took my time unlocking the door, leaving him standing in the light rain that started falling on the drive over.

I flipped on the lights and paused to admire my shop. Penny had forced me to clean up the old bakery attached to the Prickly Pear Bistro—the one she let me use at no charge—and she helped with a few alterations. My glass counter now displayed stock instead of dust bunnies. Mostly treats I sold or gave to client's pets along with CBD oil chews for anxious animals. Across the countertop, I'd placed food bowls filled with clickers, ID tags, and other trinkets. The dishes themselves were for sale, too.

Sturdy leather leashes hung from one wall, and in the far corner, I'd stacked beds according to size. My store looked great. Maybe this gag wouldn't count as cruel or vicious. He should have come three months ago.

"I change my mind. This place is too good for you."

Sensing his last chance to sleep indoors slip away, he said, "I'll take it."

The smells of country fried steak and spiced apple fritters seeped through the cracks around the door behind the counter that led into the bistro. The staff were closing for the night. I could hear the faint clatter of dishes as voices joked and chattered, free from the restraint of customers.

When Jeff stepped inside and wandered my shop, he tracked water across the floor. About to complain, I kept silent. Maybe he'd get up during the night, slip, and break his neck.

Unable to resist some sarcasm, I gestured to the dog treats. "As you can see, you have everything you need."

He picked up a spiked dog collar. "That depends on what we're doing."

"There is no *we*. *You* are staying here. Alone."

"Where am I supposed to sleep?"

A couple scurried past the front window with their shoulders hunched against the light downfall. They glanced through the glass as they passed. Jeff waved, and they picked up their pace.

He dropped his hand. "I'm exposed. I can't sleep if people are watching."

"Keep the lights off and no one will see you." I pulled a soft blanket covered with bunnies from the shelf. It was too nice to waste on Jeff. I shoved it back into place. "It's Arizona. You won't freeze."

He shook his head sadly. "What happened to you, Frances? You've become a cruel woman."

"You're kidding, right?"

"Buffy wanted to help."

When I realized he believed it, I gaped. "My word. You might be more naive than I am."

"It started out as a fine article. She was going to get you into the *Local*. Free publicity." He scratched his ear. "At least at first. By the time I saw what she planned, it was too late."

"You mean you were already sleeping with her." I cocked my head. "Wait. Are you telling me she got the hots for you and decided to sabotage *me* to win *you* over? That she ruined my life so she could have you? Incredible. She should have just asked."

I held up a hand to stop his answer. "It doesn't matter. You repeated things I told you in private because I trusted you. The two of you giggled over me and publicly humiliated me."

"I never giggled."

"And you cheated on me. You took every ounce of self-respect I had, and I admit I didn't have much back then, and you trampled on it. You made me feel cheap. I got prank phone calls and threats and I couldn't go outside for fear of running into an old client. But it was my own fault. You're... who you are. I should have known better."

"It got out of control."

"It doesn't matter." I gestured at the area behind the counter. "There's a cushioned mat on the floor. Sleep on that. You'll be out of sight."

He strolled across the room and stood so close I could feel his body heat. Though I refused to retreat, I leaned away and came dangerously close to tipping over.

"What about my keys?"

"Tomorrow morning, I'll pick up your keys from Friendly Fingers and bring them back here. After that, I don't want to see you again. Understood?"

"Deal. Just go to the front desk and ask for them. Anyone can help you." He grinned. "They're friendly."

After taking one last look around the shop, I flipped the light switch off. The streetlamps, acting as night lights, made the interior glow.

My desire to humiliate Jeff left a bad taste in my mouth. Even minor cruelty didn't come naturally to me. But he deserved it. However, spending the night safely tucked away in my shop, though uncomfortable, lacked the punishing aspects of, say, a public flogging. I'd aimed low, but it was the best I could come up with on short notice.

A voice came to me out of the shadows behind my counter.

"Aren't you going to tuck me in?"

"Fat chance." I took a deep breath and words passed my lips that I thought I'd never say again. "Goodnight, Jeff."

NINE

When I rose early the next morning, instead of throwing on sweatpants and a t-shirt, I showered first, then chose a clean pair of jeans and an unwrinkled top—a peach blouse with a round collar that set off my auburn hair. Look at me. Establishing new habits.

At the thought of meeting Charity's coworkers, I added a swipe of lipstick and applied moisturizer to the tiny crow's feet that showed up when I squinted.

I'd looked up the spa online last night. Technically, they opened at nine, but the Welcome section mentioned early morning appointments were available as an accommodation for people coming off night shifts. That meant someone would be there, either a manager or a single masseuse who had drawn the short straw. I preferred to get this favor over with.

At ten minutes to eight, I parked in a space in front of Friendly Fingers Spa and turned off the engine. Why did it not surprise me Jeff's girlfriend worked at a place that begged for a police raid? The sign above the door, written in bold purple, was bookended by pairs of eyes with long lashes.

As I got out of the car, a hot breeze sucked the moisture out of my face, making the sprinkles from last night a misty memory. The only other vehicle in the lot was a black pickup truck parked in the back corner.

A large planter with a blooming orange-and-pink lantana blocked my direct path back to the sidewalk. Each shop entrance boasted an identical wooden planter and plant. I skirted around it, and a few determined steps brought me to the entrance.

Standing in front of the glass doors, I fluffed my hair and gave my reflection one last look before stepping inside. Jeff's plaything might not be here, but it would help my self-esteem if her friends didn't let out a derisive snort when they met me.

Human beings have a need to pull on door handles even when the sign says closed. It's a declaration of impatience and—in a weird way—optimism. I didn't expect the door to open. It did.

The lights inside the lobby were off, but the strong morning sun flooding through the front windows made them unnecessary. In the waiting area, a plush violet couch and two matching armchairs were arranged around a glass coffee table on which rested magazines I would never open. *Healthy Today*, *Yoga Fanatic*, and the ever-popular *Colon Cleanse Monthly*.

On the pale-blue walls hung photographs featuring women in skintight outfits holding yoga poses on beaches. The only time I'd tried yoga, the flaky instructor had put the class in a pretzel position and forgotten we existed while she nattered on about a mind-numbing experience she'd had with a rice cake.

A polished wood counter guarded by plexiglass protected the receptionist from any deadly diseases emitted by the exhales of the clientele. Farther back, behind the counter, a modular wall blocked my view of what lie beyond. I assumed it hid a workspace where the owner counted her cash.

I called out. No one answered.

To the left of the counter stood a door that hadn't closed all the way. When I peered inside, a hallway of thick ice-blue carpet led past several open doors.

Once I passed through this portal into the land of masseuses, I was committed. Even if Charity didn't have an early appointment, what if she liked to show up hours before she started her workday so she could stretch and chant mantras and do whatever massage therapists did to warm up?

What would I say if I found her here? *Hi. You don't know me, but I've come for Jeff's keys.* Would she think I was yet another of his conquests? The competition? A sudden thought kept me rooted to the spot. Did she know about me? Would she make snide remarks and laugh? *You're the fool who took six months to figure him out. It took me half an hour.*

Grandma always said to eat the burnt parts of life first. I think that was her way of tricking us into eating her charred pot roast without complaining, but we took it as a challenge to get life's yucky stuff over first.

If I were alone at my workplace, I would view strangers with caution. So, as I stepped into the inner sanctum of Friendly Fingers, I called out again in a cheerful, nonthreatening voice.

The air in the eerily silent hallway smelled like a schizophrenic woman getting ready for a date. Peppermint, sweet flowers, and nail polish remover mingled together and threatened to give me a headache if I stuck around. Water trickled from somewhere nearby.

Glancing into each room as I passed, I noted the variety in setup and decor. A manicurist's room with comfy chairs, rolling carts, and colorful paintings on the walls. Other rooms with massage tables as well as side tables covered with CD players, CDs, and assorted bottles. One room, in addition to the massage table, had a chair that gave me a flash of my last trip to the dentist.

The last massage room on the right was home to a tabletop fountain, source of the trickles. The room across the hallway, plastered in island photographs, held a surprise, and not just the wrinkled sheet tossed over the massage table. A large terrarium rested on the side table along with the masseuse's tools of trade. Curious, I crossed the room to take a closer look. Though crowded with rocks and fauna, including a branch that rested against one glass wall, no animal lurked inside that I could find.

The click of a door closing reminded me I didn't belong in here. As I moved on tiptoe toward the hallway, I stopped short when something half under the table caught my eye.

A cell phone. When I picked it up, the movement activated the screen and showed an unfinished email to the Arizona State Board of Massage Therapy. After Charity Samuel's name and license number, it said *I have something very serious and urgent to tell you. Contact me as—*. That's where it ended.

Dang it. Charity was here. If she caught me snooping in her room, it might set the wrong tone. I set the device on the side table and peered both ways before stepping into the hallway.

The corridor ended at an exit door. There weren't any

signs warning me alarms would sound if I left this way, so I depressed the push bar and peeked outside at the cars in the lot. No people. I let the door swing shut.

To my left stood another door marked LOCKERS in purple lettering. It opened into a room with benches padded in lilac and matching lockers with keys on spiral wristbands dangling from the locks.

This room needed one of Grandma Chandler's famous airings out. The strong smell of chemicals, used to anticepticize the area against foot fungus and things I'd rather not think about, couldn't mask the smell of damp clothes and sweat.

Farther back stood showers without doors. And Bowers wondered why I didn't go to spas. At least the bathroom stalls on the other side of the room offered privacy.

I assumed the wicker basket in the corner was to hold used towels. No matter what difficulties I ran into with my pet psychic business, at least I wasn't in charge of used towels.

A light splash came from behind a curtain of plastic sheeting hanging at the far end of the room. Just a small swish that didn't repeat. I walked over and peeked around the plastic, immediately regretting the impulse.

Friendly Fingers was getting a hot tub. One that was still under construction. The edges surrounding the basin were unfinished concrete, but decorative tiles with swirling patterns of various shades of purple and blue covered the rest, including the steps down and the bench that lined the inside perimeter.

The hot tub wasn't empty. Construction workers must have tested the seal. That explained the water. It didn't explain the blond woman, face down in the tub. The edges of her hair floated in long strands around her head, so she resembled a flower.

"Hey, there," I called out, hoping she was the source of the splash. "That's not good for you." She didn't respond. When I reached the edge, it became apparent the woman wasn't capable of any movement, and I rushed to her aid.

My foot slipped on the second step, and I landed hard on my knees next to her. Grabbing her shoulders, I turned her on her back and wished I hadn't. Full lips parted as her jaw dropped. Even more unsettling, her green eyes stared, surprised. Drowning hadn't been on today's to-do list.

Unable to find a pulse, I put a hand over her mouth and nose to see if her breath tickled my skin. It didn't, so, with tense shoulders and a clenched jaw, I started CPR.

Was it three breaths and ten compressions? It had been ages since my last first aid class, but I went with three and ten. She could scold me later if I was wrong.

After a few frantic minutes, pumping and blowing seemed pointless, as already her skin felt cool. But I refused to give up. How many times had the *breath of life* brought a victim back from a reunion with great-great-grandpa because the rescuer had persisted? Continuing with new energy, a small movement caught my attention. I gasped in surprise and sat up.

The most beautiful lizard I'd ever seen watched my ministrations from the nearest edge of the hot tub. A pattern of blues and green bordered by black covered his thirteen-inch body, including his tail, and small crests ran along his back. His eyes resembled wooden buttons with black centers, and his nose and mouth were dusted with yellow, as if he'd been chewing on pollen.

Desperate, I tried something new. After quickly

connecting to him, which made his head jerk up, I rummaged through his immediate thoughts, hoping to find a memory of what happened. Maybe she'd choked on a jawbreaker and needed the Heimlich maneuver. Or she had an allergic reaction. He could point me to her medicine. Along with images of lush foliage and humidity, a feeling rushed over me. One of release. Freedom.

"Who are you?"

I jerked my head to find a petite young woman dressed in black stretch pants and a sleeveless aqua t-shirt that looked fabulous against her dark skin. She wore her curly afro pulled into a bun at the nape of her neck.

Touching the body on the shoulder, my voice became defensive. "I found her like this. She's not responding."

The woman rushed forward and dropped to her knees beside me. "Charity? Wake up. Come on, girl. Wake up!"

It *would* be Charity. "That's not helping. You call an ambulance; I'll keep going."

"What's happening?"

A woman in her fifties wearing a lavender suit rushed over. She already had her shoes off and tossed them aside before she jumped into the tub and pushed me aside.

"I was a nurse," she said, taking over my efforts with an expert hand. Her black pageboy covered her face as she went to work.

Relieved to take a break, I pulled out my cell phone and dialed 9-1-1. The younger woman sat frozen in place. She gaped at Charity, willing her to sit up and say, *"Surprise!"*

As soon as the operator answered, I said, "There's an injured woman at Friendly Fingers Spa. At least, I think she's injured. She was face down in a pool of water."

"Give me that."

The woman in lavender told the operator there wasn't a hurry. "She's dead."

Still staring at the body, the young woman moved her frozen gaze from Charity to me. She whispered, "What have you done?"

TEN

Yes, I did consider leaving the scene, especially after the paramedics came and insisted we call the police. No one knew my name or my purpose here. However, they could always jot down my license plate. Or there might be security cameras. Also, the employee who first discovered me wouldn't let go of my arm, and she had better muscles than I did.

Detective Juanita Gutierrez was first to arrive. She wore a tailored black suit with a white silk blouse that popped against her medium-brown skin. Her high heels would mean my death if I wore them, but I had no illusions. I'd seen the detective sprint in those babies without breaking a sweat. Today she wore her long, dark, curly hair loose.

She aimed her photo-ready face at me, flipped open her regulation notebook, and frowned. Not that her frown resembled mine. She didn't get a line between her thick eyebrows. Nothing puckered.

"It doesn't look good for the fiancée of a Wolf Creek detective to discover a dead body."

We stood by the showers in the locker room. Technicians had removed the plastic sheeting, so I had a clear view of the hot tub and the crime scene people doing their job.

"Maybe I should go. I don't belong here, and my presence might cause unnecessary complications." I shared a sympathetic smile with her, but the detective rejected it.

"Oh, no. You're staying."

Drat.

"Why are you here and not Bowers?" I asked.

She raised her perfect eyebrows. "You need him to hold your hand?"

"No-o-o." Gutierrez was giving off vibrations like an animal. A tense, angry animal. Since she was the only person I'd ever encountered who did so, she made me nervous. I adjusted my answer. "Maybe."

"I'm Norma Hinkle," said the woman in lavender. "The owner of Friendly Fingers Spa."

The detective turned her attention to the young woman who'd discovered me discovering Charity's corpse. "And who are you?"

"My name is Alberta Schweitzer." She spoke in a whisper but offered a small smile. "Everyone calls me Bertie."

The corners of Gutierrez's mouth twitched as she jotted down the name, and Bertie felt the need to explain.

"My parents are into the sciences."

"And you?"

"Let's say they aren't thrilled with my career choice."

A flash of sympathy crossed Gutierrez's features. It never occurred to me the Gutierrez family might not be thrilled with their daughter's decision to become a cop. Dealing with dead bodies.

My gaze wandered back to Charity. Curious, I took a slight step forward to get a better look at Jeff's temporary girlfriend. She had on black stretch pants and a matching tank top. Her slack expression didn't do justice to her pert nose and full lips.

Since I'd told Gutierrez I'd found Charity face down, and I'd already moved the body to try to save her, the ME didn't worry about fiddling with the corpse. He had the massage therapist on her stomach to get a better look at the back of her head.

Charity would never treat another client. She'd never see her parents again, or get married, or have kids. Or work out. I couldn't help but notice that, even dead, the woman was fitter than I'd ever be.

"Are you checking out the corpse's butt?"

I slipped Gutierrez a guilty glance. "What? No!"

"Stop it," Bertie said. "She was a human being." Her eyes narrowed in my direction. "And this person killed her."

My legs shook. "I did not," I hissed, doing my best to impersonate an irate woman who is trying not to lose her temper.

Fortunately, Gutierrez didn't like anyone telling her how to view her suspects. I knew she was fuming by the rattle in my chest, but on the outside, she turned uber-professional.

"We're not yet sure how the victim died. Do both of you confirm this is definitely Charity Samuels, your coworker?" Her tone implied Bertie didn't understand anything about police checklists. Identify body. Check. Take statements. Check. Collect samples and data. Check. All steps that must be completed before the accusation throwing event.

"She wasn't a co-anything," Norma pointed out, her voice tight. "She was an independent contractor for my spa."

Bertie stared at the corpse. "That's her. For sure." Turning away, she gasped. "Oh my gosh. Is that Stripe?"

The iguana peeped over the lip of the closest shower floor. Bertie approached him cautiously, and when he didn't run, she picked him up, though she held him away from her body with undisguised revulsion. "I need to put him back in his terrarium."

Sweeping a hand toward the exit, Gutierrez told Bertie and Norma to wait for her in the reception area.

My shoes squished as the detective led me out of the spa and down the hallway to an empty massage room that contained a large vase of glass flowers in unnatural colors. Several folded sheets and a blanket rested on a chair in the opposite corner.

Moving the linens off the chair, I wondered at their softness. At home, mine felt like steel wool.

After I got everything arranged, I sat down, folded my hands in my lap, and looked up. On the wall over Gutierrez' shoulder, a poster of a serene woman stared back at me. Written in the sand at her feet was a saying that encouraged me to love my, er, female parts. I hoped to never meet the owner of this room and angled my chair, finally asking the detective if she would mind changing places.

Gutierrez had rested her firm butt against the massage table. With a honeymoon looming in my future, I was suffering from derriere comparison-itus. She glanced over her shoulder, turned back with a slight smile, and decided she liked me uncomfortable. She stayed put.

"Why were you here? Were you early for an appointment?"

Her gaze took in the rest of the room. She didn't bother to hide her distaste. If Gutierrez went for a massage, it would be at a place where they bundled you up in robes made from the wool of baby lambs and served glasses of champagne. The real stuff.

For a minute, I thought about telling her I'd simply dropped by for a massage and found the door open. Unfortunately, there were too many obstacles. I'd never gotten a massage before. Why now? If I lied and it came out, Bowers would get mud on his badge. "I came here to see Charity Samuels."

That got her attention.

"You knew the victim?"

"No. Not exactly. I knew *of* her, but I didn't know her."

"Then why did you want to see her? Did you have an appointment booked?"

Did they keep records of appointments? Of course, they did. I could say I dropped by on the off chance she had a free spot, but why would I have asked specifically for Charity?

"No." I really, *really* didn't want to explain why I came here. In fact, I would do anything to avoid telling Gutierrez about Jeff.

The detective rolled her eyes. "Tell me this doesn't have anything to do with the iguana."

And suddenly, I didn't need to come up with a good lie.

"You got me." I shrugged. "She called me about the iguana."

Gutierrez slapped her notebook shut. "Spare me."

"No, really. It was behaving oddly."

"Oddly how?"

"Um, we never discussed that part."

"The victim's iguana was behaving oddly right before she was killed. Maybe the animal is psychic."

Lady Luck had shown her face and kissed my forehead. The iguana belonged to Charity, so all my lies gained credibility. Not to be rude, but a dead woman couldn't contradict me.

Juanita Gutierrez had seen a sample of my pet-reading skills. Enough that she couldn't dismiss me as easily as she wanted to. She ran her hand over her mouth. Surprise, surprise. Her perfectly applied mauve lipstick didn't smudge.

She stood. "Come on."

I stayed put. "Where are we going? Are you arresting me for something?"

That made her lips curve into a fiendish smile. "No. You're going to help with the investigation."

Reluctantly, I followed her into the massage room with the iguana. She stepped aside and motioned toward the terrarium.

"So, talk to it."

Pursing my lips, I studied the situation, searching for the hitch. "What do you want me to ask it?"

"Surprise me."

Up close, the lizard's branch was obviously fake. Rubber, or even plastic. I wondered if he minded. I'd soon find out.

Animals usually give off a unique signature wave, such as static, or buzzing. Tuning in to one animal was like tuning the nob on a radio to better hear your favorite station.

This one sent out a hum that vibrated so slowly it was more of a pulse. Medium in pitch. Soft in volume. I imagined a highway of light traveling between the iguana's mind and mine. Don't ask me why, but it works.

As I did so, the briny smell of ocean water and taste of pomegranate filled my senses.

About to bring up an image of Charity, I paused. At my one meeting with the woman, well, she hadn't looked her best. Glancing over the items on the table, a set of keys caught my eye. I reached without thinking. Gutierrez sprang forward and grabbed my wrist.

"Don't touch anything."

I wiggled my fingers at a small photograph in a silver frame. "You can let go now. I just needed to see Charity, well, not dead."

She stepped back, and I bent closer and peered at the couple. The woman was Charity. Perky nose, deep dimples, full lips, and blond hair done up in a ponytail on the crown of her head. The guy with her wasn't Jeff. He had facial stubble, dark hair, and more muscles than anyone had a right to.

Standing straight, I sent the image from the photo to the iguana. He responded immediately.

As the buzz in my head amped up to a roar, the iguana's blue-green coloring bled into a deep green. I covered my ears. Since the noise was inside my head, that didn't help. Anger flooded me. My pulse raced, and my chest tightened. Throbbing, hot, rage, and all directed at the image of Charity with her boyfriend. Gasping in air, I feared either my head or my heart would explode. It was only a matter of which one gave out first.

A brave—or more inquisitive—psychic would have stuck around to see how the anger developed. Or which body part gave out first. Surrendering to my cowardice, I broke the connection. The effort sent me stumbling back, and only the detective's quick reflexes kept me from landing on my kiester. She caught me under the armpits and shoved me to my feet.

"What is it?" Gutierrez demanded. Unwilling to lend credibility to what she considered a performance, the detective decided I got my jollies ribbing dangerous, armed ladies. "Here comes the punchline. Is he missing mommy? Feeling lonesome in his cage? Or did he whisper the name of the killer. Interfering with a police investigation, even as a joke, comes with a penalty."

"No." I drew a deep breath and released it. "He—that is I think—"

She decided I wasn't faking my trembling hands and quavering voice. "Just spit it out."

I glanced at the iguana one last time. His coloring had returned to normal. "When I showed him an image of Charity, well...he *hated* her."

ELEVEN

I heard Bowers' voice right before he stepped into the room. He wore a chocolate-brown blazer, a cream-and-brown checked shirt, and black jeans. His gaze paused on me and roamed down to my legs, wet from the knees down, before he slipped Gutierrez a questioning glance.

"She found the body in about three inches of water. In an unfinished hot tub."

Since he was on duty, he refrained from pulling me in for a hug, but his voice held concern.

"What are you doing here? Are you all right?"

Drat. A direct question. Bowers and I had an agreement that I'd never lie to him. That put me in a tricky spot.

"To answer the second question, I'm fine. Detective Gutierrez hasn't broken out the rubber hoses. Not yet. I feel a little queasy from touching a dead body."

"You touched her?"

Gutierrez answered for me. "She attempted CPR."

Bowers hadn't removed his gaze from me, and his eyes filled with the light of approval. The flash of pride that tingled over me didn't dampen my determination not to answer his first question. But he remained where he was without any indication he wanted to leave us to look at the dead body. Weren't corpses the detective's version of catnip? Unfortunately, he had more pressing concerns.

"Why were you here at all?"

Cornered, I rubbed my eyes. "I was looking for Charity."

He gave me a long look, one that had me squirming. "Why?"

Slipping a glance at the other detective in the room, I said, "Can we talk about it later? It has nothing to do with… this." I hoped to high Heaven that was true.

Detective Gutierrez saved the day. "She was going to work her voodoo with the deceased's animal. In fact, she just gave me a demonstration." She gestured toward the bored iguana. "Apparently, the animal hated his owner. Maybe *he* killed her."

And that's how I got out of lying to Bowers. Gutierrez did it for me.

Since he knew what I did for a living, my fiancé accepted this explanation with a nod. Step one accomplished.

Now for step two. It would be more difficult to keep Jeff out of this mess, especially as Bowers knew all about my ex's relationship with the massage therapist. The question of the moment was would Bowers share his information with his fellow detective? The answer came swiftly.

He turned to her. "Could I speak with you privately?"

I backed off a few feet and pretended to confer with the iguana, leaning in and tapping on the glass. As I lowered my hand, I palmed the set of keys.

"Frankie, honey, could you leave us?"

"Oh. Sure." I jangled the keys, indicating they were mine. "I'll wait for you in the lobby."

"Thanks."

As soon as I stepped out the door, I held up the keys and studied the little rubber Gumby hanging from the key chain. On his backside, someone had written a phone number. My phone number back when I lived in Loon Lake. I was certain Jeff had kept the rubber keepsake because it was Gumby, not for my phone number. Either way, these were Jeff's keys.

An irritating thought chewed at my brain. Could Jeff have anything to do with Charity's murder? He wouldn't have sent me here to retrieve his keys if he'd killed Charity.

The next possibility left me light-headed. Maybe Jeff had learned to master his emotions. Maybe he was mad about the way I attacked him and thought of a way to get back at me. I chuckled. Jeff, mastering his emotions. What a joke. Also, he was sound asleep at U-Behave.

Then I got angry. Every time I had anything to do with Jeff, my life tumbled into a bottomless pit. He was my bad luck charm. He was my curse. He was the boogie man with great abs.

When Bertie Schweitzer called out to me, I followed her voice through the open door into the lobby, where several people dressed in a variety of casual clothing whispered in funereal voices.

The lone man—medium height, medium build, and medium blond hair—seemed the least affected by Charity's death. He stood, dry-eyed, in blue medical scrubs, taking in the reactions of his fellow employees. It was difficult to gauge his expression behind his retro handlebar mustache.

Bertie and Norma were there, too, as well as a statuesque woman, close to six feet tall, with light-brown skin.

She also wore loose medical scrubs, though hers were a bold shade of burgundy that matched the ribbon that held back her curly, dark hair.

No one was using the couch, so I sat down.

The front door swung open, and a pale-faced brunette thin enough to be a stick figure walked in. From her black exercise pants and loose, mint-green t-shirt, I gathered she worked at the spa. The patrolman outside, arguing with a thick-necked woman, heard the front door close and turned his head, but the woman tugged on his sleeve and distracted him again.

The stick figure adjusted the carryall on her shoulder and said in a surprisingly rich alto, "What's going on? Why are the police here?"

Mustache Man's eyes gleamed with the strange excitement that comes over people on the periphery of murder. "The queen has been dethroned."

"Queen? Talk sense, Fred."

Bertie, after shooting Fred a chastising glare, approached her and rested a hand on her arm. "Brace yourself, Gazelle. Charity is dead."

Gazelle goggled at Bertie for ten seconds before her face crumpled. Her gathered eyebrows, on the thick side, and the upside-down smile formed by her thin, wide mouth reflected anger behind her tears. Was she mad at the killer, or Charity?

She rummaged through her carryall. Instead of a tissue, she pulled out a handful of dead grass tied with a string. Clutching it seemed to comfort her. Gesturing at me with her bundle, she said, "Who's this?"

The owner of Friendly Fingers approached me with a scowl. "That's what I'd like to know. And what were you doing in the locker room?"

I cleared my throat. "I'm Frankie. The front door wasn't locked, but I didn't see anyone. So, I looked around."

About to explain how I found the late massage therapist, Bertie interrupted with a wail that made my skin crawl. She covered her mouth with her hand.

Norma squeezed her arm. "Is it just now sinking in, honey? Why don't you sit down?"

Bertie's expression didn't convey horror and grief, but fear. "I've just remembered. My test. It's this weekend. Charity was going to help me study. I know that sounds selfish but—oh, man."

Norma patted her arm, distracted.

Gutierrez and Bowers joined us. "Who yelled?" she asked.

Norma gave her young employee a sideways hug. "Bertie's just nervous about her test."

Fred jerked his head at the young woman. "The one she better pass now that we're short-handed."

The pale brunette had been flicking a lighter that also came from her carryall. Suddenly, the room filled with acrid smoke as she waved the flaming bundle over her head.

Gutierrez covered her mouth with her elbow. "Stop that!"

"I'm smudging the place with sage." Gazelle said this as if everyone in the room had voted for it. "We need to clear out the bad spirits."

"Not while I'm here." Ignoring the witch woman's protests, the detective snatched away the smoldering sage.

Outside, the patrol officer had his hands full keeping back the crowd gathered on the sidewalk in front of the spa. As Gutierrez opened the door, the woman with the bull neck tried to maneuver around his outstretched arm.

"I have an appointment."

Gutierrez called out and handed him the smoking bundle.

"Deal with this."

The eager customer stepped back when the officer tossed it at his feet and stomped on it, releasing more smoke.

Gutierrez didn't care about screaming women or an invasion of evil spirits. Fanning her jacket lapels to air them out, she walked up to Norma. "Ma'am, I noted a security camera above the door. Do you have access?"

"You need to talk to Allen. Allen Whitmore. He's the property manager. His office is the last one to the right."

The tall masseuse snickered, and when she spoke, her voice was low and scratchy. "You might want to let your partner go. Allen likes to touch, and you are definitely touchable."

Gutierrez gave her what I would call a Dirty Harry look. "I can handle him." I think she hoped Allen would grab her butt so she could smash his face into the wall.

"It would help if we knew in what order you all arrived," Bowers said.

His partner seconded the motion. Acting in synch, the two detectives pulled out their regulation notebooks and clicked their pens.

The employees squirmed, exchanging furtive glances but avoiding eye contact with either detective, so Gutierrez made it a direct question. She started with Fred. "Who arrived first?"

The male masseuse spread his arms wide. "How am I supposed to know? I didn't take inventory."

"What's your name?"

"Fred Saunders."

"What time did you get here?"

"Twenty minutes to nine. Fifteen minutes. I wasn't watching the clock."

The detective's eyelids lowered to half-mast. "Can you say whose cars were already in the lot?"

"You know, we're not the only ones who park back there." He waved a hand toward the tall masseuse. "I think I saw Dominique's blue Echo."

Dominique waggled her fingers. "That's me. My last name is Mendoza. I arrived at eight forty-seven. The radio program paused for a break."

"Okay. Ten to nine." Fred folded his arms across his chest and rocked on his feet. You might have thought he'd come up with the right answer to one of those tough quiz show questions.

Now it was Bowers' turn. At least, that's what I thought as I looked at him, expectant. He stood at casual attention wearing his neutral cop face. The one that took in every detail. When he caught my eye, his expression didn't change, and he made no move to speak. He seemed satisfied to allow Gutierrez to take control while he stood in the background, observing. He should be more assertive if he wanted to impress the committee in charge of promotions.

His competition turned to Bertie. "And you? What time did you arrive?"

"Right before I found her." She nodded in my direction. "About eight o'clock."

"You got here and went straight to the locker room? Why?"

"I heard noises."

"What kind of noises?"

"She was making noises."

They all knew who *she* was. Me. "I was?"

"You were whimpering. And talking out loud."

My face tingled. Did I say something to the iguana out loud? I didn't want to be the crazy lady who talked to animals. Not here. Not now.

Bowers avoided eye contact. Gutierrez did not. She eyed me and asked Bertie, "Did you catch what she said?"

"When I realized what was happening, I assumed she was counting out loud."

"I was," I said before Gutierrez could probe. She abandoned me and asked Bertie why she had come in so early.

"Almost an hour before everyone else."

Bertie gestured toward the hallway. "My test is Saturday. I keep my books in my room, so I don't have to haul them back and forth. I study every chance I get."

Gazelle volunteered her arrival time. "I was running late."

"As usual," Fred slipped in. "You like to run it close."

She jammed her hand onto her bony hip. "Are you the time police? I get here when I need to be here. Anyway, the *real* police wouldn't let me drive around back, so I had to do a U-turn down the block to park in the front lot. I came directly here."

After checking her watch, a slim, leather and gold number, Gutierrez added Gazelle's information to her notebook. "How do you spell Giselle?" The detective pronounced the name with a soft "G."

Fred snorted. "It's Gazelle. Like the antelope."

"Stuff it, Fred. It's Gazelle Carmody." The stick figure spelled both names.

"Why was Charity Samuels here so early?" Gutierrez now had Norma in her sights.

"As a courtesy, we offer early appointments for those who work night shifts and need to relax before going home. We don't open our doors every morning. Clients must call and schedule their appointments beforehand. The massage therapists take turns covering these additional appointments."

"So, it was Charity's turn?"

Norma tightened her lips. "I'm not in charge of scheduling."

"Who is?"

"Our receptionist. Tammy."

"Is that what she does?" Fred mumbled. "I wondered."

"What time did you get here this morning?"

"About a quarter to eight."

"So, you spoke to Charity? Who else was here?"

"I didn't take attendance. Everyone has their own key and is responsible for their own schedule. As a matter of fact, I didn't see Charity. I went directly to my office." Norma gestured toward a modular wall set ten feet behind the plexiglass. "After I took care of a few things, I headed to the kitchen to make coffee. I thought I heard voices coming from the locker room. When I investigated, I found this Frankie person giving Charity CPR in my Jacuzzi and Bertie watching. I ran to help. I worked for thirty years as a nurse and thought I might be able to aid Charity. I couldn't."

Gutierrez ran her gaze over those present. "Where is Tammy?"

"Not here yet, obviously," Norma said.

"She is too here." Gazelle pointed out the front window. Ten feet away from the police officer on duty, a young woman with the face of a teenager and the body of a Playboy Bunny sipped a large coffee drink.

"Invite her in," Gutierrez said.

Norma opened the door and called out to the young woman. The officer turned his head, acknowledged a nod from the detective, and let the receptionist pass. Upon entering, she walked through the gathered employees and cops and straight through the hall door, disappearing around a corner and reappearing behind the plexiglass. Not once did she question why we were hanging out in the waiting area.

As she set down her purse and coffee, she blinked at us and said, "Who's first in line?"

"What's your full name?" Gutierrez said.

"Tammy Kennedy."

"And you're the receptionist here?"

"Yeah."

"What time do you usually get to work?"

"Nine."

"It's nine-thirty."

She held up her cup of coffee. "I had time to take a walk before work, but I couldn't get back in."

"You schedule appointments for these people?" Gutierrez made a sweeping motion to include the massage therapists.

Tammy nodded.

"Did you know Charity Samuels would be here early this morning?"

"Sure."

"Who was her appointment?"

"Why don't you ask her?"

Bertie cringed. "Tammy doesn't know."

I swear Gutierrez held back an eye roll. "Charity Samuels is dead. So, who was her appointment with?"

"That's confidential."

"Oh, for heaven's sake." Norma slipped her hand around the plexiglass and pulled over the appointment book, spinning it around so she could read it. "Grant Williams. He's a regular of Charity's."

"Where is he?"

"I assume he didn't show. People do that sometimes. Though I would have thought Grant..." She made a hissing noise. "This is unreal. I don't understand it. What kind of depraved person would walk into my spa and kill Charity?"

"What about that guy that came in yesterday?" Gazelle demanded. "The one she was fighting with?"

I held my breath.

Gutierrez turned. "What guy?"

"Light brown hair. Great body. He knew Charity and asked to see her. She seemed happy enough when he walked into her room. She squealed and said hello. That's why it surprised me when things got loud."

"What did they argue about?"

Gazelle backtracked. "I wasn't listening to the words. The noise was upsetting my client, so I turned up the volume on my CD player."

Bowers finished the transition from fiancé to cop. He strode up to me and lowered his voice. His question bordered on unfriendly. "Frankie, where is Jeff?"

"Who's Jeff?" Gutierrez demanded.

So, Bowers hadn't told her everything. "I left him at U-Behave," I mumbled.

"He's at your place of business." From the way his jaw muscle pulsed, Bowers didn't approve.

Gutierrez snorted on the word *business*, but it was a feminine snort.

"It was kind of a joke—" I could see how Bowers wouldn't find it funny. "He came back after you left. He doesn't have money for a hotel. I wasn't about to let him spend the night at my place. What else was I supposed to do with him?"

Bowers' voice rose in pitch and volume, and the Friendly Fingers employees pretended not to listen. "Nothing. He's a grown man for Pete's sake. Just tell him to go away."

Behind Bowers, Gutierrez grinned at me, enjoying the show.

My fiancé took my hand and pulled me to my feet. "Let's go."

"Where?"

"Guess."

Still clenching the keys in my pocket, I followed him in my car to U-Behave.

TWELVE

We drove separately, which gave me time to think. Gazelle's surprising announcement about Jeff and Charity's argument had thrown a spanner in my plans to remain a neutral party. Jeff's involvement would somehow destroy my peace. I just hadn't figured out how.

By the time I parallel parked in front of my shop, I'd decided on the band-aid removal approach. Tearing it off would hurt less. If Jeff told Bowers everything he'd shared with me last night, my detective fiancé could look over the paltry facts and say, *"That's not so bad."* I didn't expect us to share a laugh, but Charity's murder could go back to being an impersonal investigation.

Bowers paced the sidewalk in front of the entrance to U-Behave. When I opened my car door, he met me wearing a grim expression.

"Stay here."

"I need to unlock the door for you."

He held out his hand. "Give me the keys."

Scooting around him, I unlocked the door and turned on the lights. No sign of Jeff. However, there were several bowls on my counter. From the odors lingering in the air, they had contained split-pea soup and chocolate ice cream.

"Where is he?" Bowers asked.

I maneuvered around the counter and found Jeff on the floor. He'd laid out several dog beds as a mattress and covered himself with the blanket I'd distinctly *not* given him and another he'd pulled from the shelf.

"Get up," I said, nudging the bed with my foot. "You need to tell Bowers everything you told me."

He sat up and rubbed his face, and as the blanket fell off, it revealed his nude torso. When I spotted his clothes folded in a neat pile on top of his gym bag, I backed into Bowers, who blocked my quick exit.

Flattening my hands on the counter, I hoisted myself up and scooted forward like a seal until I rolled off on the other side.

"What are you—" As Jeff stood, Bowers trailed off with, "Oh."

"You're paying for those dog beds," I said as I got to my feet. "And the blankets. They're used now."

My ex stretched. I whirled to face the front door because the glass counter didn't block the sights.

"For gosh sakes, put some clothes on."

Jeff's nakedness didn't faze Bowers, probably because guys spend a lot of time posing nude in locker rooms. At least that's what I think of when anyone mentions men's locker rooms.

"How long have you been here?" Bowers asked.

"All night, brother. Your girlfriend dumped me here last night. What time is it?"

"Almost ten," I said.

"That late? Man. It wasn't very comfortable here. I didn't get to sleep until early morning."

"You never left?" Bowers asked.

"Where would I go?"

"Friendly Fingers Spa."

During the pause, dishes and silverware clattered in the restaurant next door. Jeff said, "Frances?"

I turned around.

My ex had slipped on his jeans and had his hands on his hips. "Did you get them?"

Bowers stared at me. "Get what?"

I shoved my hands in my pockets and clenched Jeff's keys. They fit nicely into the impression left in my palm from gripping them at the spa. Ripping off the bandage and exposing Jeff did not include exposing me. "Them? I don't know what you mean."

"Frances, did you get them or not?"

"Get what?" Bowers repeated.

Resigned, I pulled out the keys and held them up.

"Awesome. I knew you'd do it."

Jeff held out a hand, but Bowers intercepted the keys.

"What are these?"

Jeff made a gimme motion. "They're my keys. The ones I use in Loon Lake."

"I'm asking Frankie." The detective held them up in front of my face so I couldn't miss them. "Where did you get these?"

"I picked them up."

"I'm only going to ask one more time. Where did you find them?"

After giving Jeff an extra harsh glare to let everybody know the source of my pain, I sighed. "Next to the iguana."

"Stripe." Jeff grinned. "Like the nasty character in the movie *Gremlins*." His smile didn't quite fade. "Why are you asking me about Friendly Fingers?"

I leaned in and placed my hands on the counter. "Did you set me up? Did you know what I would find?"

"Find?"

Bowers pulled me away from the counter and stepped sideways to block my view of Jeff. And vice versa. "When was the last time you saw Charity Samuels?"

I peered around Bowers' shoulder and noticed Jeff's smile had decided it didn't want to play with us anymore and had slipped off his face. "I don't like that question. It sounds official."

"It is."

"What's happened? Is she missing?"

Why didn't Bowers get to the point? Grabbing his arm for support, I leaned sideways. "I'll help your memory. Was it when you argued with her? Or are you going to deny the two of you fought?"

"Frankie, wait outside."

Jeff's eyebrows went up. "Why would I? I already told you about it."

"You told me she was surprised. Unhappy. You didn't mention you had a blow up."

"It wasn't a blow up. Charity did most of the talking."

Bowers swept his arm back to push me behind him. "I'm sorry to inform you your girlfriend is dead."

"Dead? From what? An accident?" From his tone of voice, Jeff seemed more puzzled than distraught.

"She was murdered."

"Ouch. That sucks." Bowers had his hands on his hips. I peeked through the gap. Jeff didn't appear emotionally connected to the event, especially when he asked, "Who did it?"

Bowers hesitated. He probably couldn't believe Jeff

didn't realize he was a suspect. "That's what we're trying to find out."

Just then, the bell over my door rang, and Gutierrez walked in. She took in the scene and approached the counter. "Are you Jeffrey Ross?"

He'd just heard that his recent girlfriend was dead, yet he found the strength to send an appreciative glance over the detective's fit form. To be fair, he didn't know Charity that well. "If you're asking, I am."

Gutierrez did something unexpected. She returned his appreciative smile with one of her own before she pulled out her badge. "Detective Juanita Gutierrez. I need you to come with me to the station to answer some questions about Charity Samuels."

And then I felt the *zing*. It ran through my chest and came out my fingertips. Gutierrez gave off an electric charge, and it only took a second to realize why. She wasn't flirting with my ex. She thought she had that promotion tied up with a bow, and she was going to get it by using my relationship with Jeff to make Bowers look bad.

While discovering a body could happen to anyone, hiding a suspect in your place of business had stickier implications. Especially when the one doing the hiding was the fiancée of the competition.

She nodded to Bowers. "Have you told him?"

"Yes. He seemed surprised. Or not. Hard to tell with him, as you'll see."

Gutierrez sized Jeff up, evaluating the challenge.

He responded with a charming smile. "I'll need a ride back here. Unless you want me to follow you in my rental car."

The detectives exchanged a glance. He'd just informed

them he had the means to get to Friendly Fingers in time to murder his girlfriend. Idiot.

Gutierrez practically purred as she motioned toward the exit. "I'll drive you and arrange for transportation when we're through."

"Wait." Bowers handed Gutierrez Jeff's keys.

I gasped. "Don't give her those." Key snatching from a crime scene would be another thing to hold against Bowers.

They both turned their heads and stared.

Giving the lamest excuse possible for my outburst, I mumbled, "How will Jeff unlock things?"

Bowers narrowed his eyes. "Since those *things* are in Loon Lake, Wisconsin, I suppose he'll survive. Unless there's something you're not telling me."

I shook my head. He turned back to his fellow detective and spoke to her in muted tones. He finished by saying, "It's your call."

She compressed her lips and took a small step toward me, almost involuntary. "I'll talk to you back at the station. Come on, lover boy."

Once again, I had egg on my face because of Jeff. But this time, I wouldn't be the only victim. My fiancé's career might suffer. My entire relationship might suffer. I was so angry, I wanted to scream.

"Aren't you going to cuff him?" I called out after her, but the closing door cut off my words.

I stared through the glass at the gathering storm clouds. The ones that came and went, came and went. Promising a long-awaited downpour, but never quite delivering. Just an occasional tease to leave me hoping for more. Like my life.

THIRTEEN

Bowers stood, his hands in his jean pockets. Was his watchful gaze coming from the eyeballs of a cop, or a fiancé?

"I'd let Juanita forget you existed. For a while, anyway." That shocked me into silence, and Bowers took advantage. He rested a hand on the counter and tapped at the glass.

"Walk me through how you found the body."

I explained how I searched the rooms, looking for someone who might help me. "I only went into Charity's room because of the terrarium. I wanted to see what was in it, but it was empty. Empty of animals, I mean."

"You didn't know what was in it. Then you weren't there on a business appointment."

"Um, no. I never said I was. Gutierrez assumed, and I didn't correct her."

"And then what did you do?"

Remembering how I'd been spooked, I explained about the door closing.

"The front door?"

"It seemed closer than that. Since I didn't find anyone

in the spa on my way back, it must have been someone leaving by the back door."

"If it came from that direction, it could have been someone walking into the locker room."

"Impossible. The showers are wide open. There's nowhere to hide. And the entrance from the hallway is the only way in or out." I furrowed my brow. "But when I looked out the back door, I didn't see anyone."

"You looked outside?" He restrained some strong emotion and moved on. "Okay. You're in the locker room. What do you see?"

"Nothing. Nothing lying around. Keys hanging out of the lockers. A basket for towels. Empty shower stalls. Toilets. If anything was missing, I wouldn't know."

"I understand the hot tub was behind plastic sheeting. What made you look?"

"I heard a noise. A splash. It must have been the iguana. He was there when I found her."

"How long before someone else entered the room?"

No matter how hard I thought, I couldn't answer. Once I'd found her, I lost track of time. It seemed like hours before help came.

"Who came in next?"

"It was right after I spotted Stripe. Someone asked who I was. Bertie. I asked her to help me, but she froze up. Norma came in and took over. While she worked on Charity, I called for an ambulance."

He hesitated. "When did Jeff ask you to get his keys?"

"Last night. After you left. He came back and gave me a sob story."

Bowers held up a hand to stop me. He didn't want to hear the sob story. "Did you find the keys before or after you found the body?"

"After."

He closed his eyes in a pained expression. "And then you removed evidence from Juanita's crime scene to protect your friend. Frankie—"

"Hold it." I held up a hand. "You're giving me too much credit. I didn't pick them up to protect anyone. The keys were the reason I was at Friendly Fingers."

"Explain."

So, I told him about my deal with Jeff and how getting the keys was the only way to guarantee he'd disappear. I backed up. "What do you mean? *Juanita's crime scene.*"

"It's her case. She gave me the okay to talk to you first."

The idea of being at Detective Gutierrez's mercy didn't appeal to me. Even worse, Bowers was, too. Since when did he need to ask her permission to talk to me?

"I know you and Jeff have a history, but he's a suspect in a murder investigation. Steer clear of him, Frankie."

While he talked about the necessity of keeping personal feelings out of the investigation, public perception, and conflicts of interest, his voice receded into the background. My breath caught in my throat as a sneering face came into view. Paul Simpson. Reporter for *The Wolf Creek Gazette*. An unethical creep who had it in for me ever since I silenced him with a mouthful of dog food at the pet expo.

Suddenly, headlines danced in front of my eyes. *WOLF CREEK DETECTIVE TIED TO MURDER SUSPECT.* Or worse, *WOLF CREEK DETECTIVE ANNOUNCES ENGAGEMENT TO CASTOFF OF MURDER SUSPECT."*

I knew what Bowers would consider worse than losing out on a promotion. Embarrassment. Humiliation. Because of me, both were headed his way at record speed.

"What are you so focused on?" he said with a mild grin. "You're making faces."

One of the habits left over from my fake pet psychic days. People were more impressed if they saw you struggle to make a connection with their animal.

My lower lip trembled. "It's not fair. I make *one* mistake. It's a horrendous, grotesque mistake, but it's safely buried in my past. Now everyone will know what a fool I was. And—" I couldn't even verbalize my fears for him.

Since Bowers didn't understand the depth and breadth of my worries, he set aside his detective persona and pulled me in for a hug. "Are you okay, sweetheart?"

"No," I mumbled into his chest.

He let me go and patted my arm. "Don't worry, Frankie. Everything will turn out okay."

How could he not see that things would *not* be okay? That they were already slipping down a slope that ended in a sheer drop? That his future with the Wolf Creek police department hung over that edge by its proverbial fingernails?

The bell jingled, and an elderly woman in a sky-blue nylon pantsuit walked in with her Pomeranian. I bit down on my lip. I had to hold it together.

"I'll see you at your place later," Bowers said. "You can expect me around six-thirty if all goes well."

As he stepped out my door, a stream of sunlight shone down on him, illuminating him like a sacrificial victim.

The woman, oblivious of the electric zing in the air, set her elderly dog on the counter. He smelled of pee.

"If all goes well," I muttered. "Are men optimists? Or are they oblivious?"

"Oblivious, naturally. Now, about my Whiffles."

FOURTEEN

The woman didn't need a pet psychic. She needed a vet. After complaining that the Pomeranian sitting on my counter was ignoring her, she asked me to find out if Whiffles was angry.

I snapped my fingers behind his head. He didn't even blink.

"He's deaf."

She sighed and nodded. "I suspected, but you were cheaper than the vet." As she gathered him in her arms, she asked if her sweet, deaf dog could have a treat. A free sample. I gave her two. It must be a bummer to lose your hearing. For the dog's sake, I hoped his sense of smell would follow.

I escorted her to the door, stopping short of pushing her outside. Then I slapped up my closed sign and fled through the back way and into the bistro.

The décor of Prickly Pear didn't match my mood. The booths, tables and chairs came in the pinks, yellows, greens, and purples of the namesake cactus. Not even the waitresses were safe from the happiness contagion. They wore rose dresses with white aprons. This month. Penny liked to change things up.

The morning rush had passed, but several diners milked their coffee, happy to stay out of the heat. The smells of breakfast already eaten lingered in the air like fond memories.

Penny's laugh rang out from the kitchen, and a man's voice responded. As soon as she returned to the restaurant proper, I waved to her and headed for our usual booth against the window. She arrived first and remained standing.

"I have so much to tell you," I said, moving to hug her.

She slapped me.

It wasn't much of a slap. My friend didn't have it in her to harm someone. Still, she wouldn't smack me without a reason, so I sunk into the booth and waited for an explanation.

"Are you getting back together with Jeff?" she demanded, refusing to join me. "Because if you are, I'm charging you rent."

I gasped. "Did he escape?" He had, and I'd seen the evidence myself. Split pea soup and chocolate ice cream. A word I never use in public came out, and the old geezer one table over glared at me. I held up my hands. "Sorry."

He mumbled something snide to his friends.

Since my horror was real, Penny condescended to sit down opposite me. "Vince and his service dog came in. I was out of treats and needed to borrow one."

Even though I'd seen Jeff leave with Gutierrez, my gaze drifted to the hallway that led to the bathrooms and the back entrance to my shop. I expected him to materialize, like an evil wraith.

"I demand an explanation," Penny said. "Please."

And so, I launched into the tale of the last twenty-four hours. When I finished, she hadn't stopped glaring.

"I overheard several customers talking about the death of a woman at Friendly Fingers. What happened?"

I gave her a detailed account of what I'd found in the spa.

"I can't believe you walked straight into a murder scene. Why does that keep happening to you? It's not normal." Her hand shot in the air, and she called on herself. "I know. Do you think it has something to do with your gift? Isn't there a dark side to every blessing?"

Penny will always think of my ability to be blindsided by complaints from wild and domesticated creatures as a present wrapped in glittery paper and shiny bows. But I couldn't dismiss her suggestion, as I knew little about how my ability worked.

"You might have something there, Pen."

"I don't think that means you shouldn't use it." She twiddled her thumbs and backtracked. "Maybe just have someone reliable around when you're talking to an animal."

My best friend longed to get an up-close peek at how my *gift* worked. She probably expected my appointments to involve tea and clever banter. She should have been there when the parakeet bit me before pooping in my hair.

"I'll have to look into it," I said. "Maybe talk to Father Damien at St. Mels." The priest had taken the news that animals talked to me surprisingly well. At least until I mentioned the dead dog.

Penny narrowed her eyes. She resembled a miffed kitten. "You went there because Jeff asked you to go."

"You think he knew she was dead? How is that possible? If she had been dead last night when he asked me to go, don't you think someone would have noticed before this morning? The locker room smelled like disinfectant. Don't businesses have cleaning crews that come in at night? And she hadn't been dead that long when I found her."

"No. I don't think he knew. But any time Jeff is around, things go wrong."

I kept my voice low. "Gutierrez took him to the station."

She pushed back from the table. "Get out. Does she really think he killed his girlfriend?"

"Maybe."

Her mouth snapped shut, and she blew air through her nose. "He didn't do it. Jeff is too spineless to kill." Her upper lip curled with disdain. "I bet he couldn't even wring a chicken's neck."

Having grown up on a farm, my perky friend is tougher than she looks. When she asked if the police hauled him away in cuffs, I detected satisfaction. "Maybe she'll give him the third degree. Serves him right."

"I just hope he doesn't drag me into it."

"You were an innocent bystander. I'm sure when you explained—"

"I didn't tell Gutierrez why I went there."

She gave me a wizened look, like a sage about to impart wisdom. "The truth always comes out. You should tell her. Once you do, she'll know you're the victim of a coincidence. But you better do it soon. She'll appreciate your cooperation."

"She already knows. Bowers took the keys from me and handed them over to The Python. Neither of them was pleased."

"Oh, my."

"There's another thing, Pen. Bowers and Gutierrez are competing for a promotion. You know how ruthless she can be. I'm afraid she'll use my association with one of the suspects to make things awkward for him. Especially as I lifted Jeff's keys from the crime scene. And there's the bit about harboring a suspect."

"You didn't know he was a suspect when you harbored him. Besides. She can't do that. It's not fair. Detective Bowers hasn't done anything wrong." My best friend still hadn't graduated to calling my fiancé by his first name.

"It doesn't matter. Gutierrez has Jeff. If it turns out he's involved, she'll rub Bowers' nose in it. Make jokes. Nothing overt, but enough to make people question his abilities. She'll *embarrass* him."

"You're overreacting. So, he'll be embarrassed. Kemper was embarrassed when he tripped on the stairs outside of Maxine's, but he got over it."

"But that wasn't job related. Men take their work very seriously. How would Kemper react if he presented a client with the wrong audit numbers through no fault of his own? And his fellow accountants kept riding him and making fun of him. And the people considering him for a promotion heard about it?"

"Jeepers. I see what you mean. He'd be devastated."

"And if Paul Simpson gets hold of the story...."

She stared at me with her cornflower blue eyes. I recognized that look and squirmed. It was the gaze of someone who believes in you. Trusts you. Thinks you're capable of working miracles. It's the same way Penny gazed at me when we were children. When she thought I was a real pet psychic just because I took a fifty-fifty shot at what sex a mare's foal would be and told her I had inside information when I was right.

"What?"

She sighed. "You're going to clean up this nasty business. You're going to clear Jeff's name. Not that he deserves it." She slid over the saltshaker. "First, we know he didn't do it, so clearing his name is the right thing to do, and you always do the right thing. Eventually."

"I hate that about myself."

Here came the pepper shaker. "Two. There won't be a story for Paul Simpson to run with, which will protect Detective Bowers' reputation."

Finally, the napkin holder joined them. "Three. Do you want to get calls from prison every week asking you to bring hamburgers and shaving stuff?"

"I could get a restraining order."

She put on a pout. "But then he'd call me."

"All right. Stop groaning."

Penny grinned and moved the table accessories back in place. My friend had enjoyed her past involvement in my murder troubles, and I had to admit she sometimes saw people more clearly than I did, since I always assumed they were morons.

Folding her hands on the table, she put on a serious expression. "What do we know so far?"

"Charity was Jeff's girlfriend. He met her in Milwaukee at a convention. He moved out here to be with her, but she didn't want him."

"She got sick of him that fast? Smart woman."

Meaning smarter than me. "It was a case of crossed wires. She didn't mean for him to move out here. When he showed up at Friendly Fingers, she was surprised. They argued. Her coworkers overheard the argument, so I'm sure the police know all about it."

Like I said. My best friend is my opposite. She always sees the best in every situation. "People argue. That's not a motive for murder." Penny's brow wrinkled. "So, they hadn't known each other long?"

"Less than an hour."

"That's too bad."

"Not for Charity."

"No, silly. I mean how much could Jeff have found out about her in that brief time? Like the names of her friends and family."

"I don't have a clue, but I wouldn't think he learned much."

"That makes it more difficult. You'll need to ask him to find out."

"If Gutierrez lets him go."

After thinking the situation over, Penny made her pronouncement. "The only thing we're certain of is Jeff didn't kill her. So, it should be easy to clear him."

"And why are we certain?"

"The bunny."

I frowned. "The bunny?"

"Don't you remember the poor baby bunny? The barn cats got at it, and you rescued it from their lair. But it was too far gone and suffering. You handed Jeff a shovel and begged him to put it out of its misery, but he couldn't bring himself to deliver the blow."

I'd forgotten Baby Bunny. "The little critter finally died of a heart attack while we were arguing, didn't he?"

"Which shows you Jeff couldn't kill anyone."

"Gutierrez will want to hear this story. I'm certain it will convince her of Jeff's innocence."

Penny clasped her hands, thrilled to contribute to justice. "Really?"

"No." I slapped the table. "I can't believe I need to save Jeff's butt so I can save Bowers' butt. That's the *only* reason I'm helping that rat. If he takes a fall and splatters, I don't want Bowers getting sullied by the mess."

I slumped back and groaned. "It's going to take time. Time I don't have. This is not fair. I should be planning my wedding. In fact, I wanted to talk to you about—"

"Gotta go."

I hadn't seen Penny move that fast since the bull in the pasture next door to her family farm got out and went for us.

Well, there was one person I could talk to who would neither flee nor talk back. If Bowers wanted to sit back and wait for a light bulb to pop on over Gutierrez' head, that was his choice. However, I, his fiancée, was not going to let his reputation—or his chances for promotion—suffer because of my ex. I grabbed my car keys and headed back to Friendly Fingers.

FIFTEEN

I drove past Friendly Fingers five separate times waiting for the last patrol car to leave the parking lot. In-between my passes, I checked my messages at my shop three times, stopped for a burger to replenish my energy levels, played seventeen games of solitaire on my phone, picked up a chocolate shake from Dairy Derby out of boredom, and called Bowers to find out if Gutierrez still had Jeff. He didn't return my call.

A few hours later, when the coast was clear, I made my move. Norma Hinkle drove up in a silver Honda hatchback right before I pulled in, so I parked in front of Drake Property Management and waited in my car until she'd been in the spa for ten minutes. After so much sitting, my leg muscles were stiff, as were the wrinkles in my air-dried jeans. I shook everything out and marched up to the entrance.

Ignoring the CLOSED sign, I rapped on the glass door until Norma finally jerked it open. "We've had a spot of trouble. We're closed today. Come back tomorrow."

A spot of trouble? I supposed she couldn't blurt out

details of a brutal murder on the premises and then expect customers to line up for appointments. However, trouble is why I'd come. As she pushed the door shut, I slipped through at the last minute. Surprised, she stepped back to let me pass.

On the reception counter, a stick of incense burned to mask the residual stench from the smudging. Now the place smelled like cinnamon and smoke.

"I know about what happened, and I'm so sorry for your loss." A little sympathy makes people more malleable.

She studied me, and her expression altered when recognition set in. All pretense of *a little trouble* left, and she embraced a new role. *Touched by tragedy*.

"Thank you." Her voice shook. "Maybe this is a test. A test of my will. Challenges make us stronger, you know."

"Yes," I said, thinking of Jeff. "Yes, they do."

I glanced around, noting the obvious out loud. "Are the police finished already?"

"They just released the place back to me fifteen minutes ago. Except the locker room." The door leading into the hallway stood open. "There's hardly anything in Charity's massage room. What there was, they took."

Dang it. "Including Stripe?"

She placed her hand over her mouth, and I steeled myself for tears. Norma didn't disappoint me.

"They took the hot stones from all the other massage therapists," she said, her voice low and trembly. A single tear rolled down her face. "I suppose they had to." She shook herself and gave me a brave smile. "Listen to me. Complaining about inconveniences when Charity's dead. I'm on my way to pick up replacement stones as soon as the insurance agent calls. Hopefully, they'll reimburse me. Even if they don't, I can't afford to stay closed."

"But what about Stripe?"

Wiping away the single tear, she said, "What do you know about Stripe?"

"Well, we've only had one conversation, but I hope to know more."

She let out a half-hearted laugh. "I told the police that Vali, that's Charity's boyfriend, would pick up the animal, but when I talked to him, he denied knowing anything about Stripe. Can you imagine? He *should* know all about the iguana. It was a gift after his last trip to Fiji."

The man in the picture must be Charity's boyfriend. Or was he the ex? Jeff said they'd gotten back together, so he was both the current boyfriend *and* the ex. Were Jeff and Charity together long enough for my ex to also count as Charity's ex? My brain hurt. People should have arranged marriages and supervised dating. It would make keeping track of relationships so much simpler.

"You're in luck. I'm here to take Stripe off your hands." I handed her my business card. She read it twice.

"That's very nice of you, but—I don't know if I'm comfortable—"

"The police often take the animals of victims into custody to make sure they're cared for. They've used my services in the past." Which was not a lie. One way or another I'd wound up with the animals of dead people. At least long enough to have a chat. "Of course, in a case involving a reptile, I'll have to call on my animal wrangler and a wildlife specialist."

That would be Seamus McGuire, owner of Canine Camp, and his girlfriend, Bethany. She and I weren't friends, but she'd helped me before. With a cockatoo. Who later died a suspicious death.

The mention of level-headed people with real jobs

decided it for Norma. She smiled. "If you wouldn't mind, it would be a relief. One less thing to think about."

She jumped when a phone rang from behind the plexiglass. "That must be the insurance company." After giving me quick instructions on where to find Stripe's things, she left me on my own.

Charity kept a bag of dried food in a cupboard in the facility's kitchen. It had a tear in the bottom, so I searched the room until I found a plastic bag in a cardboard box marked RECYCLE in bold, blue marker.

When I reached the late massage therapist's door, I gasped. Norma wasn't exaggerating. The police had taken everything, down to the massage table. Several gaps were missing from the carpet, revealing the dull stone tile underneath.

Stripe stared at me from his terrarium.

"I'm here to rescue you."

I hooked the bag of food around my wrist and hauled him out of the spa.

As I left Friendly Fingers, my mood lifted. All I had to do was ask Stripe a few questions and I could hand Bowers the killer. Gutierrez would gaze with wonder and befuddlement as my fiancé explained—well, he wouldn't explain. He'd just present the killer. But he would impress the committee that controlled his destiny.

Doubt niggled at me. What if Stripe had his back turned when Charity went into the water? What if the person had worn a mask, and the little guy couldn't name the killer?

Well, the iguana should at least be able to clear Jeff of suspicion. My feet slowed. But could he, really? He could show the massage therapist alive and well after Jeff walked out, but that was yesterday. Who could say if Jeff returned this morning? Did I want to see my ex holding someone's head under water?

Shaking off the image, I scolded myself for considering the possibility someone I had once dated would be capable of murder. The assassin had to be someone else. Another employee. Maybe a stranger.

I stopped walking and glanced over my shoulder. Any information Stripe gave me would need corroboration. Drake Property Management had a security tape with my name on it.

SIXTEEN

My feet took a detour to the manager's office—a glass door with Drake Property Management, Suite 12, stenciled on the glass in a crisp white font.

Gutierrez had already visited him, but I, using charm instead of fear tactics, might talk Allen Whitmore into sharing a tidbit or two. Something tangible I could wave in front of the detective's face at the appropriate time. A name Charity had dropped in conversation. Or perhaps she'd shared a photograph with Mr. Whitmore of someone who would make a nice suspect.

After nudging the door open with my backside, I turned into a narrow room. This had to be the smallest of the spaces available in this strip mall. Steel file cabinets sat in one corner behind an old oak desk with an overflowing IN basket and an empty OUT basket placed on either front corner.

A man in his early sixties with thick, silver hair and a handsome face stood on my entrance.

"What have you got there?"

He stepped around the desk and guided me to one of

the chairs along the wall. I'd expected someone his forties with stooped shoulders, oily hair, and long fingernails. Maybe a chunky pinky ring and a gold necklace. That was my idea of a nefarious lecher. This man resembled someone's grandpa in his plaid shirt, knit tie, and chinos. A man that age would respond well to charm, so I brought out Flirtatious Frankie for her world debut.

"Good morning to you." My tone implied *you big, handsome man*.

Once we got the terrarium settled, he put his hands on his hips. "That's Stripe, isn't it? How ya doing boy?" He met my gaze. "Can I help you?"

I put on my sympathetic face and held out my hand, careful to use an anemic grip. "I'm Frankie Chandler. You must be Allen Whitmore. I hope this *horrid* event hasn't been too painful for you. You seem to be holding up well, even if you're putting on a brave face. *Just* like a man. I, myself, am bowled over."

Gratified, he gave my hand a gentle squeeze. "It has been a shock. A terrible shock." He glanced at Stripe. "If you're looking to rehome the lizard, I'm afraid I'm not good with animals."

"No, no. I'm an important but reluctant witness from this morning's tragedy at Friendly Fingers."

"I'm sorry to hear that. No lady should have to witness violence."

"Naturally, I'm devastated. Almost incapacitated. However, the police asked me to look at the surveillance tape. They hoped some detail might bring up a terrible, tragic, frightening, um, scary memory. One must do her duty no matter how disagreeable."

He squeezed my hand again. "A Detective Gutierrez came here this morning. Pretty thing, but awfully serious."

"Heavens! Was she too, too terrible?"

Cocking his head, he asked me where I came from. "I can't quite place the accent."

My attempt to show a more feminine side had me talking like a Southern belle. Flirtatious Frankie retired from the stage.

"Sorry." I coughed lightly. "I had a frog in my throat. What did Detective Gutierrez say to you?"

"Not much. She wanted the security tapes." I deflated until he added, "So, I made her copies. I have the backup."

"Great. I'll just peek if you don't mind."

The office reeked of old coffee. When he offered me a cup, I felt obliged to accept. He disappeared around a corner to the left of the desk and returned with a chipped mug bearing the logo of a local gas station.

Since he took the chair next to me, I couldn't fake drinking it. The first bitter mouthful put me off taking a second sip, even if it hurt his feelings.

"What did you say your name was?"

"Frankie."

"I knew a Frankie once. He was a guy." He ran his gaze over me. "You're not a guy."

"Nope."

I'd disappointed him with my answer. After the tone set by Flirtatious Frankie, I think he expected a giggle. My giggles had abandoned me this morning.

"Anyway, my Frankie worked for the city. Landscaping. Gave his life for his job. Had an early morning call about a faulty sprinkler. A pack of coyotes ate him."

"Good golly!"

His features lit up on my reaction. "Pretty horrible, isn't it? Not the way I want to go. That's for sure." He rubbed his small tummy. "Of course, I've still got a lot of miles left. Do my exercises every morning. Eat right. I'm in great shape for my age."

"How old are you?" I asked, curiosity overcoming manners.

"Seventy-eight."

My eyebrows shot up. "Really? You *are* in excellent shape. Now, about that tape."

"Charity was such a lovely girl. Made time to talk with an old man."

He waited for me to object to the adjective, so I cooed something about people not being old until they hit their nineties. My nose twitched at an opportunity.

"What did the two of you talk about?"

"Just this and that. She was a smart gal. Curious. Took an interest in what I did here."

Managing tenants sounded like a direct path to brain atrophy. I suspected the massage therapist's motive behind her alleged fascination. "Did she want to know about anything in particular?"

"No. Just interested in the way I ran things. How I figured the rents. What was in the contract. What happened if tenants were late paying me. If I ever gave discounts. Just general questions."

"Gee whiz. Was she applying for a job?"

He laughed. "She was just one of those friendly people."

Super friendly, according to Jeff. "Did she ever share anything personal with you? Talk about her friends? Or enemies?"

Patting my hand, he told me I had nothing to fear. "I'm sure this was the work of a lunatic. Someone who didn't know how nice she was. I suppose that's why she worked at Friendly Fingers."

Since he chuckled at his own joke, I tittered along with him.

"About that tape."

"They certainly are a standoffish group, except for Charity. I'm still surprised she's the one who died."

"Really?" My nose twitched again. "Who at Friendly Fingers would you have chosen the play the victim?"

"You want me to pick one?" He raised his bushy eyebrows. "None of them. I just meant Charity was a nice girl, and nice girls aren't usually murdered at their workplace."

"True. Were *you* here early this morning?"

He nodded. "I was up and at 'em at four-thirty. Did my stretches. Went for a walk." He tapped the side of his nose. "Kept my eye out for coyotes. Didn't notice anything unusual, though."

"Friendly Fingers." I let the name roll off my tongue. "Sounds kind of...naughty."

"That's what I thought." Happy I shared his depraved outlook, he scooted closer and leaned in. "As a landlord, I have to be careful about who I rent to. I asked Norma about the name when she signed the lease. She got defensive. That may be why she insists on mailing her rent check. Usually, I make the rounds to collect from my tenants. Gives me a chance to get to know them. See how they're doing. Keeps it personal."

He patted my hand and squeezed. I pretended I had to scratch my neck and moved it without giving offense.

"You don't think there's anything going on at the spa that, well, *shouldn't*, do you?" Maybe Norma was a pimp, and Charity, one of her *girls*, held out on her.

Distracted by the possibility, Allen leaned back in his chair and rubbed his chin. "I wondered. Kept an eye on the comings and goings for the first month but came up with nothing. The girls, and Fred, that's the guy with the incredible mustache, they all seem respectable. So do their customers."

So, that was it. Charity didn't talk to him about friends or enemies, and he hadn't seen anything out of the ordinary.

"About that tape...."

He glanced at Stripe. "It will take me a while to pull it up and have it ready for viewing. You could come back without your little green friend. Around seven? We could have a light supper, a glass of wine, and make it an enjoyable experience." He rested a hand on my knee.

I removed it.

"That's past my bedtime. Besides. I'm engaged."

He leered, showing large teeth. "I don't see a ring on that finger."

I gritted my teeth. "Not yet. Anyway, I must get this fella home. I'll be back."

Hoisting the terrarium in my arms, I waited for him to get the door for me.

Did Allen behave in too friendly a fashion with Charity? She stopped by to feed Stripe that morning, and he caught her unawares. They struggled. Did he knock her unconscious before he carried her to the hot tub? Would he even know about the hot tub?

When I came back to view the security tape, I couldn't come alone. If Allen Whitmore was the killer, I saw no need to supply him with a second victim.

SEVENTEEN

On my way back to my car, I spotted Bertie Schweitzer walking through the parking lot. Her wail of dismay at Charity's death made me believe she could tell me about the late masseuse. I called out to her.

At first, she ignored me. In fact, her pace increased until I called out again. "It's Frankie Chandler. From this morning."

Her shoulders hunched, and she slowly turned, but when she saw me, she put the name with the face and headed over. I shifted the terrarium to my hip.

"That's Stripe," she said, staring at him. "What are you doing with Stripe?"

I made my expression solemn and lowered my voice. "Everyone forgot about him. Pitiful, huh? How are *you* doing?"

"How do you think?" She sighed. "I'm sorry. Not as well as I'd like."

"How about we grab some lunch?"

She studied me, wary. "That's okay. I grabbed something to eat on my way here."

Since she wasn't holding a takeout box or fast-food bag, I suspected Bertie wasn't comfortable with me.

"Why are you here?" I asked. "Didn't the police shoo you all away?"

"They made me leave my books inside. I still need to study for my test, even without Charity's help."

"That's this weekend, isn't it? Well, you need to eat to keep up your strength. I know I can't think straight if I don't have food in my tummy. What about dinner?"

She shifted her feet to add distance between us, evidently turned off by my persistence, so I slumped my shoulders and drooped the corners of my mouth in a mournful expression. "It's just, we both found her. It was such a shock. I thought it might help us *both* to talk about it."

"I'll let you know."

Raising a knee to balance the terrarium, I dug out a business card and handed it to her. "How about Prickly Pear Bistro at five? That way we'll beat the rush. If you decide to come, call me. Or just show up."

She agreed to consider my offer, and just in time. My arms tingled from the effort of holding Stripe.

My next stop was Canine Camp, a day care for pets and my go-to for information about animal care. According to my dashboard reading, the temperature outside had reached eighty-nine degrees. I assumed iguanas liked the heat, but I lowered all the windows and promised to make it quick.

Seamus McGuire and his girlfriend, Bethany, were in the play area with about fifteen dogs. When Penny had described him before our one blind date, I looked forward to meeting my twin. However, his auburn hair was dark enough to pass for mahogany brown, he had freckles, and he was a few inches taller than me.

I'd forgotten to close my mental doorway after connecting with Stripe this morning. The roar of a tornado hit me, pushing me back out the door.

Animals have different signatures, from high-pitched squeals to low rumbles. Unless I tuned into one, they all combined into white noise. In this case, deafening white noise.

Imagining a large wooden door, I swung it shut and sighed with relief when all I heard was the cacophony of barks, yips, and whines.

Seamus' bookkeeper and receptionist, a young goth woman with a purple stripe through her jet-black hair, popped her head out of the office. Charlie. The top accounting student at Scottsdale Community College. "Oh, it's just you." She grinned when she said it, so I didn't take her comment personally.

"I need to talk to the boss."

Seamus was already halfway to the gate of the pen, followed closely by the queen of all animals. When I'd first met Bethany, this remora-like tendency to cling to the dog trainer irked me. It still did.

"I have a favor to ask." In my self-centered excitement, I forgot to be polite, so I backed up the conversation. "Hello. How are you?"

"Congratulations. I hear you got engaged." Seamus grinned. Bethany did not. From her hooded glance to her smile—a flatlining stretch of her lips—she radiated envy. Her poor boyfriend was oblivious his woman wanted something more permanent than the shared joys of overexcited canines.

"Thank you. I have another emergency."

"Another bird?" Bethany once worked for an avian rescue and had helped me when a murder victim's cockatoo landed in my lap. Maybe I wouldn't mention Stripe's owner had also died a violent death.

"I have an iguana for a few days and I'm not sure what to feed it."

"What kind?" she asked.

"There are kinds?"

She exited the play area, using her foot to nudge back a dachshund determined to escape. As we walked outside, I got a whiff of ginger-peach perfume and covered my grin. Up until now, the usual scents surrounding the uber-expert on animals were the lingering odors of wet fur, dog slobber, and tinkle sprinkles from excited puppies.

The mating ritual had begun.

Once we got to my car, she took one look at Stripe and jammed her fists into her hips. "Where did you get this animal?"

"Um, from the owner. I didn't steal him if that's what you mean."

"This is a Fiji Crested Iguana."

"Okay. Good to know."

"They are *critically* endangered."

Sheesh. Talk about pressure. "Then I'll take very good care of him with your help."

Her skin flushed, and I got the impression I wasn't giving her the reaction she sought. She took a threatening step forward. Maybe she didn't mean to be threatening, but she towered over me by a good three inches. "It is illegal to own one. Now, where did you get him?"

Seamus must have been lurking and listening from the doorway of the daycare because he shot outside and stepped between us. "Hold on. I'm sure there's a good explanation."

I lowered my voice. "There is, but I'm not sure your girlfriend will want to hear it."

He cocked his head, puzzled, and then his green eyes popped open. "Oh. Right. Bethany, could you excuse us?"

That went over well. Not. She narrowed her eyes, trying to figure out what kind of secrets I shared with her boyfriend. When frenzied barking washed over us, she returned inside to deal with the doggies.

"A woman was killed this morning."

My bold statement didn't shock him as much as it should have, and I wondered if I was becoming predictable.

"Gosh. That's terrible. Did you know her well?"

"Never met her. But my ex-boyfriend knew her, and now the cops are looking at him like they want him for dinner. But I'm only interested because the investigation may blow up in Bowers' face. Anyway, this was her pet."

He skipped over any questions about my ex-boyfriend and got right to the point. "I take it it's the owner who is dead."

"Right. And I need you to stop Bethany from doing something I might regret."

"That's not possible."

Amazing that he didn't recognize his manly sway over her. The ginger-peach perfume should have alerted him to a change in her attitude toward him.

"Sure, it is. Seduce her."

He squawked.

"Or cajole her. Fire her. Whatever it takes."

He started to turn away, but I grabbed his arm. "I need some time, Seamus. I need time to talk to Stripe. That's his name. I need time to find out what happened. Then you and Miss Defender of the Animal Kingdom can do whatever you want with him."

His green eyes studied me, conflicted. He'd seen what I was capable of firsthand. In a unique situation, I had used him—without his permission—to help communicate an escape route to a dog in a burning building. Bowers had been there, too, and yes, I'd used him as well. Neither man spoke to me for months afterward. Probably because I'd accidentally read their minds.

I doubted that story made it to the list of life experiences he'd shared with Bethany. However, explaining the delay in calling the authorities was his problem.

"The animal is endangered. I'm required to contact—I'm not sure who to contact. But, I have to contact somebody."

"Could you dial slowly? Have trouble finding the right name?"

"I'm sure Bethany knows who to call. I bet she's doing so right now. She's proactive that way."

I sensed in him a lack of enthusiasm for her outstanding efficiency. Shoving him toward the front door, I told him to stop her. "Make something up. Tell her I was on my way to turn Stripe in. Anything. Just delay her for a day or two. Please?"

"I'll see what I can do.

"Wait! What do I feed him?"

"Fruit. They also eat leaves and flowers, but other than the hibiscus, I'm not sure which ones. Vegetables too, I suppose."

"Check." I took a deep breath. "Wish me luck."

As he stepped over the threshold of Canine Camp to confront his girlfriend, he muttered, "I'm the one who'll need it."

EIGHTEEN

About to set Stripe down while I unlocked my front door, said door swung open and Jeff grinned at me from inside my house. "You should lock your back entrance. Allow me." He took the tank from me and set it on my coffee table.

For once, I was happy to see my ex. On my way home, I'd thought over my talk with Penny. She was right. The only way to get Bowers out from under would be to clear Jeff's name. By the time he set the terrarium down and turned toward me, I had my pointer finger in his face.

"Listen up. Bowers is in an awkward position because of you. He might even miss out on a promotion. It is one hundred percent your fault. For once in your life, you're not going to walk away from your troubles. You *will* help me fix this."

"Shouldn't we leave it to the police? I wouldn't want Juanita to get mad at me."

I flinched at the thought of an angry Gutierrez. "No. The point is we need to work in the dark. The police can't know what we're up to."

He stepped closer. "Sounds exciting. Maybe dangerous."

"Not exciting or dangerous. Just something we need to do. You're going to help me. Refusal is not an option."

"Sure. If I can."

"Not can. Will. Now, did Gutierrez just let you waltz out?"

"Yeah. She told me not to leave town." He lowered his head and looked up through his lashes, a trick that used to make my heart jump. It did jump, but only because I caught the implications.

"You can't stay here."

"But Frances, what am I supposed to do? I used the last of my savings on the plane ticket and rental car." He folded his arms over his chest. "And I'm *not* staying at your doggie store again."

Recalling Bowers' words, I said, "You're a grown man. You'll figure it out. Get this straight. You are responsible for finding your own place to sleep, but that does not negate your obligation. Got it?"

"Do I have to leave right now? It's hot out there."

The iguana staring at us from my coffee table just might hold the key to solving Charity's murder. I refused to put off our conversation because Jeff might perspire. "I have something private I need to do."

"You won't even know I'm here. Promise." Here came the sob story. "Put yourself in my place. My girlfriend's dead. I'm stuck in a strange place with no money for a place to stay."

"She wasn't your girlfriend. At least not at the time of her murder."

"And Juanita told me I couldn't leave town."

"Stop calling Detective Gutierrez Juanita. It's creeping me out."

"Pretty name, isn't it? But the point is, I can't leave Wolf Creek."

"You don't have money for a return plane ticket anyway."

"I could hitchhike."

Impatient to start in on the iguana, I ordered him to my kitchen. Besides, I decided Jeff should remain handy in case Stripe gave me information my ex might need to clarify. "Sit at the kitchen table, and don't move."

After saluting, he followed orders, though he strolled instead of marched. I waited until I heard the chair legs scrape against the kitchen floor before I sat on the couch, eye-level with Stripe, trapped in his glass box. Pathetic.

As soon as I opened the door to the iguana, my stomach growled.

"Oh. Right."

I had taken the dried food from Friendly Fingers, but as a diet of pellets would depress me, I'd stopped by the grocery store on the way home. Since the iguana came from Fiji, I thought he might enjoy tropical fruits, like mango and papaya. I'd bought some already chopped along with six types of lettuce. Safeway didn't carry hibiscus plants.

After depositing a healthy feeding into the terrarium to make up for his missed meals, I filled a bowl with clean water and returned to the couch. I could sense his satisfaction as he ate.

First, I conjured up an image of Charity, cautious because of his last reaction. Stripe rolled his eyes at me, and his green stripes darkened a shade. I got a clear image of her cooing as she served him pellets, so I retrieved the wastebasket from my bathroom. When I had his attention, I opened the jar and shook until the last pellet plopped into the garbage. Then I tossed the empty jar after them with flourish. He stretched his front legs to make himself taller and nudged me, mentally, identifying me as his submissive servant.

Before I could poke him back, the clear, whistled refrain of *Sittin' on the Dock of the Bay* drifted out of my kitchen.

"I need to concentrate," I called out. The whistling stopped.

Now that Stripe no longer feared disgusting food, I brought up the image of Charity again with more confidence. No reaction. Norma said the police had taken all the hot massage stones. Was that how the killer disabled the masseuse? I created a shadow with a stone clutched in its hand, which the figure used to bash the massage therapist over the head.

Stripe continued to eat, uninterested. About to try again, a slightly sweet, woodsy smell with a hint of camphor overwhelmed me. I recognized that smell.

"I'll be right back."

Exiting out the sliding door, I approached the greenery growing in the planter that lined my patio. After breaking off the head of one flowering plant, I crumpled it between my fingers, rubbing to release the oils. Stripe had conjured up the scent of lavender.

But what did that mean? Snakes smelled with their tongues. Did iguanas? Even if he liked the taste of lavender, it hadn't been on the list of approved foods Seamus gave me. I wasn't taking a chance with his endangered body.

Returning to the living room, I held out my hand. He inhaled and gave a happy sigh. When I showed him another image of Charity, I felt a sharp tug. The connection broke.

My head jerked back. What in the—? I knew *I* could

break the connection, but did animals have that same ability?

I rebuilt the information highway and sent an image of Charity across. Something resembling a hurricane careened toward my masseuse mobile and smashed it head on, sending over the edge.

Stunned, I slipped a piece of papaya into his terrarium and stood. This had never happened before. My rescued mutt, Chauncey, had never let me inside his mind. I think it held dark secrets. But my dog had blocked me from entering, not sabotaged me as I connected. I rubbed my forehead, still feeling the tug.

If I wanted Stripe's attention, I had to find something to help jog his memory. Something other than images of Charity.

"Frances?" Jeff called out from the kitchen. "Are you finished? I need to use the bathroom."

"Be quick about it because we've got someplace to go."

NINETEEN

My watch said four o'clock by the time Jeff and I stood outside Drake Property Management. Already the sun had started its descent in the western sky. We had to get in and out so I could make my appointment with Bertie. If she showed.

I'd explained the plan on the drive over, but I didn't trust my ex to follow instructions. It was simple. Jeff would come in with me and keep his mouth shut. If Allen did anything untoward, Jeff would intimidate him. If a way to cock up these straightforward instructions existed, my ex would find it. Still, what choice did I have? Since I didn't want the property manager to make inappropriate advances—or kill me—none.

Allen sat behind his desk. He'd microwaved popcorn. The smell of salty butter made an improvement over the odor of burnt coffee. When I walked in, he sat up straighter.

"You're early."

His pleased smile faded when Jeff followed behind me.

"I'm back," I sung out.

"Yes. Yes, I see. I thought you'd—you brought someone with you."

Jeff puffed up his chest and looked intimidating. For about a second. If only he'd wipe the open interest off his face. He reminded me of a dog let loose to explore a new room. I'd have to trust he wouldn't mark anything.

I clapped my ex on the elbow. "This is my—" What word could I use for Jeff? Almost choking on it, I finished with, "My friend."

"A boyfriend?" With a glance, Allen reconsidered my moral fiber and surprisingly found me wanting. "I thought you said you were engaged."

"That's right." Improvising, Jeff threw his arm around my shoulders and pulled me tight against him. "She couldn't resist me any longer."

When wiggling and twisting didn't free me, I delivered a sharp jab to his ribs. He winced without removing his arm.

Leaning in, he whispered in my ear. "This is new. You like it rough?"

Aware of our audience, I turned my face into his chest. "I'll give you the rough, calloused skin of my hand upside your head if you don't behave."

Laughing, he kissed the top of my head and let me go.

Approaching the desk, I filled my smile with gooey sweetness. "Is the tape ready? You promised, and you look like a man who keeps his promises."

The building manager debated whether to show me the footage now that he'd lost his *quid pro quo*. He gave in and invited us to follow him.

What I thought was a nook with a coffee pot turned out to be a small hallway leading into a separate room. Living quarters by the look of it.

Allen must have been a soldier. Or a nurse. I could have

bounced a quarter off the quilt covering the twin bed. Two square pillows with homey, cross-stitched sayings on them rested against a light-wood headboard. He'd positioned the small television set so he could watch his favorite programs in bed.

There wasn't a dresser, but the sliding paneled door most likely hid a closet. Another door, standing open, led to a bathroom with a shower. The space had all the necessities for someone with few needs.

Photographs of a gray-haired woman with a pointed chin and crinkling eyes decorated the walls, with one framed in silver sitting on the nightstand next to the alarm clock.

The most startling thing about Allen's living quarters was the wood paneling that covered the walls. Without a window to open, the room seemed to close in on me. We'd have to hurry before claustrophobia kicked in. Not that I had claustrophobia, but I would if I spent more than ten minutes in here.

On the corner desk sat an old computer with a thirteen-inch monitor. The screen was split to show two images in black and white.

"It's not fancy, but it does the job," Allen said as he sat in an office chair set on casters. He wheeled up to the desk and typed on the keyboard.

Pleased to have an appreciative audience, the building manager waved his finger in front of the screen as Jeff looked on. "You're seeing the feed from both of the security cameras. Put 'em up myself."

"That must have been a tricky job." Jeff's voice held admiration.

"Almost fell off the ladder once."

"Get out."

Allen rolled up his sleeve and displayed a faded scar about two inches long on his forearm. "Got this when the screwdriver slipped going into solid wood."

"Did you drill a hole first to get it started?"

"I *thought* I had."

The lovefest could go on for hours, and already I had sweat on my upper lip from the cramped quarters. "I don't mean to be impatient, but I'm dying to see if I can help the police. Can you get to the right spot? Pretty please?"

"Frances," Jeff admonished, disapproving of my approach. "Let the man show us his equipment."

Allen, agreeing with Jeff's point of view, gestured at the left side of the monitor and continued to boast. "This one is over Friendly Fingers, since they're in the middle of the strip."

The camera's coverage didn't include the entrance to the spa. It started just beyond the walkway in front of the building and extended over two rows of parking spaces and beyond to the curb across the street. All of it was fuzzy, and both ends of the parking lot fell outside the camera's range.

In real time, a woman wearing a tight stretch outfit stepped into view, heading away from the building. Allen tapped a few keys. "I'm also able to zoom in." The woman approaching her car now filled the entire screen.

"You mean spy on people?"

He assumed I disapproved and added virtuously, "Just in case something suspicious captures my eye."

"You misunderstood. I like the idea. It could help me identify, um, whoever needs to be identified."

The woman had to be a client leaving Friendly Fingers. For one thing, her fitness level scored well below the employees I'd seen at the spa. Her bulbous bottom bounced with every step.

She wrestled her keys out of her purse, encumbered by the gigantic water bottle she refused to tuck under her arm to free her hand like a normal person. When she fumbled the keys, as we all knew she would, they landed on the ground. Bending at the waist to retrieve them, she gave us an unhealthy peek up her rear. I winced.

Allen and Jeff stared, which didn't surprise me. It was the same with sports. Put a man in front of the television, switch the channel to men in tights playing golf with helium balloons, and they'd still watch.

After Miss Stretchy Pants' performance, Allen tapped a few keys.

"*Very* cool." Jeff nodded. "I wonder if I could set up something like this at home."

Allen grinned. "It would cost you. Less if you're a do-it-yourself kind of guy like I am."

A circle whirled in the center of the screen, and suddenly, the feed caught up. The image, still the same view from Friendly Fingers, turned a darker hue. The lot was half full of cars and motorcycles.

"There wasn't anything from this morning before seven." He nodded at me. "Except you. The police wanted to see last night's tape, too. Here it is."

Since the film was in black-and-white, I knew it was night because the headlamps from passing street traffic glowed.

Allen hit fast forward, and a car zoomed into the spot in front of the spa. He let the speed return to normal.

A guy in jeans, tennis shoes, and a dark t-shirt got out of a sedan. With his black baseball cap on, I couldn't see his face.

"Freeze it."

Allen complied.

"Can you zoom in on him?"

"Sorry. That only works when it's live."

The hat's brim made it impossible to see his features, so I told Allen he could unfreeze the frame. The guy disappeared, beyond the camera's reach. The time stamp read 8:02.

"If he had an eight o'clock appointment, he was late. Did he come back out again?"

"I remember exactly when because the lady detective asked me the same thing."

"Juanita." Jeff gave the impression the detective and he shared confidences.

Allen punched in some numbers and took us to 8:54. The man strolled out the door, got into his car, and drove away. I still couldn't see more than a weak chin, but his relaxed movements didn't suggest he'd just murdered someone. Unless that was his thing.

Since the guy parked directly in front of the spa, the planter with the lantana blocked his license plate as he backed out. Vehicles now packed the lot. An SUV and another motorcycle hid the car's movements from my prying eyes as the driver straightened it out. Allen agreed to replay the man's exit.

Leaning forward, I squinted at the location I thought the license plate might make a brief appearance as the man straightened his car, but in violation of the law, he didn't have his plates lit.

"What time did Charity leave?"

Allen returned the monitor back to the original split screen in real time. "She didn't."

"What do you mean, she didn't?"

"She didn't leave. There's a back door that the

employees use to get to their cars, but I still didn't see anyone exit down the driveway in back. At least not her."

"You have a camera on the back door?" I almost squealed with joy. "Can we see that camera?" If the killer left that way while I was in Charity's room, we'd have him. Or her.

"I keep it focused on the dumpster. People are all the time bringing their trash and filling it up. People who don't rent here. I have a sign, but they ignore it."

He played around with the backup, and a dumpster popped onto the screen, partially blocked by a dark-colored pickup truck and several motorcycles. He ran his finger in the space in front of the dumpster.

"The corner of the building is on the left, so if anyone drove a car out of the parking lot, they would have to pass through this gap."

"What about this morning? Someone left while I was in Charity's room."

"Nobody drove in or out of the parking lot this morning except people who belong here. I checked, and so did the police."

The driver of the truck had backed in. He sat in the vehicle with his face in shadow. There was something familiar about that truck.

"What other businesses are in this strip?" I asked. "Could that guy be waiting for an employee?"

Allen angled his chair to face me. "The corner unit is a liquor store."

"So, they're open late?"

"Eleven o'clock at night.

And then I had it. That truck resembled the one I'd seen on my arrival this morning. The one parked in the back row of the front lot parallel to the liquor store. "What time do they open?"

"Ten o'clock. I don't know the individual employees, except Gerardo. He works the evening shift and has since they opened seventeen years ago. He's from Argentina. Interesting guy. His family raised cattle. He left after the economy collapsed. About twenty years ago."

Nothing against Gerardo but I wanted to move Allen along. "And next to them?"

"The Indian import store closes at seven. If they need to stock the shelves or do inventory, they might leave late, but it's a husband and wife. They would go home together. The education center tutors adults and closes at nine." He gestured at the night feed. "Maybe he's waiting for one of the students."

"Would they leave out the back door?" Jeff asked.

"Good point," I said, and he smiled. Why did his smiles always look like smirks?

Emboldened by my praise, Jeff took over the questioning. "What about the motorcycles?"

"That's customers from El Diablo across the street. It's a biker bar. They serve decent food, and they're usually packed. We wind up with their overflow, even though I've talked to the owner several times."

The guy in the truck was unusually tall. His head almost brushed the interior roof. I leaned forward and pressed my face close to make out his pixelated features. When he moved his head, security lights reflected off a pair of glasses.

He rested his arm on the open window frame and I caught sight of a dark mark on the back of his hand. A tattoo? Odd place for it. Not that I was an expert on tattoos.

Jeff suddenly stiffened at my side, and when Allen

raised his gaze to see over my shoulder, I turned. Bowers held Jeff's wrist in a vice-like hold. The hand attached to the wrist hovered suspiciously close to my bottom. I twisted and jumped out of range.

"Were you going to cop a feel?" I punched my ex's arm. "Jerk."

Mr. Whitmore looked confused. "What's the problem? A man should be able to pat his fiancée on the fanny."

"He's not my fiancé." I pointed at the angry cop. "He is."

Allen whistled. "Lady, you've got trouble on your hands."

"Wait for me at your house," Bowers said, his voice grim. "Both of you."

TWENTY

As soon as I unlocked my front door and stepped inside, I stashed Stripe and his terrarium in my bedroom. No need to get the detective more upset than necessary. I also told Jeff he would breathe his last breath if he mentioned a word to Bowers about what we were up to.

"I don't understand why you want to keep it a secret from him. I'd think he'd *want* you to help him."

Keeping secrets from Bowers sounded bad. "It's more of a surprise for him when we find the evidence to clear you. Like a present."

"If you say so."

I clenched my teeth, unwilling to debate. "It is uber important that we, um, *look into* things without telling him. He would object to our involvement. He would also object to me talking to you, let alone spending time with you. You would remain a suspect and spend the rest of your life a hunted man." Frustrated, I rubbed my forehead. "It's just better, okay?"

"It's not like we learned anything anyway."

"Charity didn't leave Friendly Fingers last night."

He blew out a laugh. "Seriously? The back camera features the dumpster. For all we know, she left and came back three times without anyone seeing. All she had to do was walk."

About to discuss this interesting observation, I zipped my lips just in time. Bowers walked in without knocking. He stood with his hands on his hips, studying us both as we sat on opposite ends of the couch like naughty children caught passing notes during class.

"What were the two of you doing at Drake Property Management?"

He directed his gaze at me because he thought I'd be the one to tell him the truth. It was a devilishly subtle move, but a powerful one. I couldn't lie to him.

"We went there—"

Jeff interrupted. "As you can guess, I'm bored stiff. Finding things to do without money stinks. Charity told me Allen had a nifty setup with his security cameras."

"Your late girlfriend discussed security cameras with you." Bowers tone questioned the sanity of anyone who'd believe such a ludicrous statement.

Jeff didn't even blink. "And I wanted to see them. Even though I don't work for Chris anymore, he's a good guy. I knew he'd love the idea. Unfortunately, her idea of a cool setup was...what can I say? It was pretty lame."

"And you took Frankie with you because?"

Jeff didn't look at me, which was a smart move. If I coughed out the breath I was holding, it would ruin his lie.

He gave Bowers a sheepish grin. "It's well-known that Allen is susceptible to pretty women. I thought her presence might loosen him up." He turned to me. "I used you, which is pretty rotten. Forgive me?"

The coughing fit came. How did he know I struggled

with forgiving him for Buffy? He didn't. It was a heinous coincidence that he'd used that phrase.

"Yeah. Sure."

Bowers continued to watch us until he made up his mind.

"Mr. Ross, you are becoming a problem."

I snorted, but the look Bowers gave me silenced my follow-up comment.

"You and I can talk later in private," he said to me. Oh, poop. He'd figured out what we were up to. Here came the lecture, and even worse, the disappointment.

"For now, you, Mr. Ross, need to find a place to stay, and eat, and sleep. A place that isn't here. In fact, I want you to stay away from Frankie."

That would hamper our investigation, but what could I say?

My ex nodded. "Okay."

My innocent fiancé had just handed Jeff a way to avoid helping me to help him. I couldn't let that happen. Tapping my fingers on my lap, I said, "Now that Charity is dead, Jeff doesn't know anyone in town. Gutierrez won't let him leave. He might need my help. Not that I *want* to help him." I gave my ex a pointed stare, and he got the hint.

"Right. Yes. Like where the restaurants are, and—and—stuff like that."

Bowers jabbed a finger at Jeff. "Stay." He took my arm and walked me all the way to my sliding back door. Once outside, he let go and leaned against the stone wall a few feet away from me.

"You need to make up your mind."

Here it comes, I thought. He was going to ask if I meant it when I'd said I never lie to him. The one thing he wouldn't tolerate. Did omissions count as lies? And if Jeff lied and I didn't clarify, was that my lie, too?

"You're either going to let me handle Jeff, or you're not. Decide."

Jeff? We were talking about Jeff? But if Bowers handled Jeff, my ex wouldn't help me make Bowers look good. Or at least not look bad.

"It's not that simple." I hated the whiny note in my voice.

"But it is. Your ex-boyfriend could be a killer."

I blinked. "Do you really think so? I have trouble seeing him as dangerous. Blame Penny. And the bunny."

"Please. Enlighten me."

And so, I told him about the baby bunny, attacked by cats and left for dead. "If he can't even kill a bunny, how could he kill a human being?"

Bowers' expression didn't change. "Was he emotionally attached to the bunny?"

"I—what?"

"Did they have a relationship? Killing an innocent animal and striking out in the heat of an argument with someone you are emotionally involved with are two different things. I repeat. The man could be a killer. You haven't seen him in years. People change."

I shook my head. "Change means evolve. Jeff will never evolve, not even into a killer."

Evidently, Bowers wasn't angry with me. He closed the distance between us and rubbed my arms. "Frankie, I love that you think the best of people."

"Huh?"

"You think you're tough and jaded, but you're not."

"I'm not?"

In fact, you're pretty innocent compared to most people

I run into. I love that about you." He tucked my hair behind my ears. "Spending time with you after a day dealing with addicts and pimps...it refreshes me."

How could I argue with a man who'd just compared me to a cool, sparkling stream?

"Wait. We have pimps and addicts in Wolf Creek?"

He laughed. "Innocent. I don't want to see you lose that. And I don't want you hurt. I'm asking you to trust me on this."

I puffed up my cheeks and blew out air. It would go smoother if he thought I agreed. "Okay." Meaning okay, I would avoid getting hurt.

When we returned to the living room, Bowers had his arm around my shoulder. "Listen up. I appreciate you're in an uncomfortable spot, Mr. Ross, but you need to man up and deal with it. No more coming to Frankie for help. Understood?"

The reason nobody has yet killed Jeff is because he's a great schmoozer. He stood to better display his deference to Bowers as a cop and yet keep things friendly, as in *between the guys*. It was Bowers' own fault for using buddy language like *man up*.

"Sure." He held out a hand and Bowers shook it. "I want to thank you for all your help. It's been a weird trip." Before he strolled out the door, he nodded at me and said, "Frances."

My fiancé kissed me and told me he'd come back after he reviewed the day with Gutierrez. And then he left me on my own, which was not a good decision.

TWENTY-ONE

Once they left, I returned Stripe to his spot on the coffee table. Opening the Internet on my phone, I looked up Fiji Crested Iguanas and found they were indeed endangered. One reason was a loss of habitat due to grazing goats and farmers setting fires to clear away last year's crop leftovers. The other reason was feral cats.

My gaze darted to the top of the bookcase where Emily, my black-and-white cat, stared down at us, her tail twitching. She wasn't exactly feral, but I couldn't risk coming home to one less Fiji Crested Iguana. His terrarium had a mesh lid, but her ability to swipe the pantry door open to nibble on my water bottles negated any confidence I had in the lid as a safety feature.

Since my cat hadn't yet figured out how to open locked doors, I wrangled her into the bedroom and closed the door. After further reflection, I dragged her litter box into the bedroom along with her food and water. No reason to let her suffer because of my house guest. Not that she would suffer. She'd probably wipe her fanny on my pillow to show her displeasure and fall asleep on the same pillow.

I opened the mental door and prodded Stripe. No iguana was going to get the best of me. Since he'd spent his time in Charity's room, I opened with a long shot of the table, chair, and folded sheets. Instead of using a highway, I sent the images on a jet plane.

When that met with dead air, I showed him the other Friendly Finger employees walking in to chat with his keeper. He did give me a spray of lavender, but when I ran the faces by him again, *everything* smelled like lavender, and I couldn't tell if it applied to one person.

I let someone faceless enter the room and waited for him to fill in the blank. Slowly, an image appeared dressed in jeans and a sloppy t-shirt. It was difficult to judge height because he saw everything from his perch on the tabletop. With her back to me, she bent down and grabbed the waste basket. It must have been the cleaning woman. I got a good shot of her reaching up her bum to pull her panties loose. A gurgle filled my chest, and I gaped at Stripe.

"Did you just laugh?"

Remembering the guy who showed up Monday night, I had him walk in with his baseball cap on. No reaction. Since my visions are G-rated, I fast-forwarded to him on the massage table, covered with the sheet, as Charity rubbed his shoulders.

Nothing.

"You're not being very cooperative. Don't you want to know who killed Charity?"

Suddenly, Stripe entered the scene, though he'd grown to the size of a Komodo Dragon, a lizard that can take down a deer. He grabbed hold of Charity, and in a violent move that made me jump back, rolled and twisted across the room with the massage therapist in his jaws. I'd seen alligators do the same thing, but not this fast and frenzied. When he stopped, Charity lay in a broken heap.

I broke the connection. Once the urge to be sick passed, I returned him to my bedroom and made sure Emily wasn't in the vicinity, though my worry was now for my cat.

When my cell phone rang and showed Jeff on the screen, I snatched it up. "Where are you?"

"I thought I should make myself scarce."

"You aren't trying to get out of your obligation to help Bowers?"

"Not an obligation. A favor."

"Whatever you want to call it." It took me a few seconds to choke out some gratitude. "Um, thanks for rescuing me and answering Bowers' question."

"You were about to crack. Obvious. I don't understand why you don't just share the information with your detective, but it's important to you, so we'll play it your way. And if it gets me out from under, I'm all for your plan."

"I appreciate that. We need to know more about Charity. We have to talk to her friends. Or her coworkers."

"Good luck with that. You'll scare them stiff if you start lurking around the entrance to Friendly Fingers. They might think you're the killer, lying in wait for your next victim."

We both chuckled over that scenario.

"You're right, though. I saw Bertie and asked her to lunch, but she seemed wary of me. Is that suspicious? I mean, who turns down lunch?"

He laughed. "Same old Frances. You are classic." His voice turned serious. "But you've changed. It's hard to explain, but you're more focused. More driven. Confident, even. It's kind of sexy."

Unsure how to respond, I ignored the compliment. "I

did get her to agree to dinner. Or at least not reject the idea. She'll meet me at Prickly Pear Bistro at five-thirty. It makes sense to talk to people in the order they appeared that morning, don't you think?"

"Excellent idea. Score one for Team B."

"Team B?"

"The police are Team A."

"I need a plan. It stinks that I don't know more about her relationship with Charity. If she liked her. Or how observant Bertie was about her. Or if she knows anything about Charity's clients."

"All questions you can work in while talking to her." He sighed. "Frances, you're anticipating problems again. Just talk to her and see where it takes you."

Jeff being helpful. What a surprise. Unless he had an objective.

"I need to ask. Did you kill Charity?"

"No."

He didn't pause to think up a good response. No elaborate lie. A simple no.

"Okay. Good to know."

Hopefully, my conversation with Bertie would lead me to a suspect that would deflect attention away from my ex. And more importantly, Bowers.

Because, right now, I had nothing.

TWENTY-TWO

Penny, my best friend in the entire world, agreed to reserve our usual table for me and put the waitress on high-speed so I could make it back in time for dinner with Bowers.

The closest available parking space was a block past Prickly Pear Bistro in front of Wolf Creek Drugs, a family-owned gift store, pharmacy, and post office branch. I backtracked and then maneuvered my way past seven or eight people waiting outside the restaurant.

As I stepped inside, I congratulated myself on the foresight to reserve a booth. Fannies occupied every available seat.

From behind the counter, Penny gave me a thumbs up. Bertie had accepted my offer and waited for me in my usual spot. On my approach, I studied the esthetician for clues to her current mood. Tonight, she wore jeans and a yellow, long-sleeved t-shirt with an embroidered collar. Her casual dress and unrestrained afro matched her relaxed expression.

As I slid into the booth, Bertie smiled at me. "I've never heard of this place. It's so cute."

Prickly Pear Bistro *was* cute. And cheerful. My best

friend's generosity permeated the atmosphere. Works by local artists, available for purchase, were displayed above every table. A coyote bitch and her pups, painted by part-time artist and full-time exterminator Carlos Rodriguez had replaced my Gambel's quail painting on the wall. The glass dog cannister next to the register invited diners to donate to a local pet rescue. Signs behind the counter announced specials for seniors and veterans, though I knew almost anyone in uniform got a discount. I was probably the only customer who paid full price.

For the dinner hour, Penny added a single red rose in a skinny glass vase to each table. She had a kind, romantic heart. It still amazed me we were friends.

"Are you really a pet psychic?" Bertie stated her question boldly, as if I had dared her not to.

That wasn't what I'd come here to discuss. "Sure. That's me. Let's order."

Laminated menus were another benefit of the evening service. The specials for the day included a sirloin steak with fries, which I would normally jump at, and a fruit bowl that came with cottage cheese and a side salad. The slim wannabe masseuse ordered the latter, which is why she was slim. In less than an hour, I'd be eating again, so I got the same.

Once the waitress took our orders, I asked Bertie how she was holding up.

"Fine, I guess. It feels so strange, knowing someone who's been murdered."

I'd known several people who had wound up the victims of violent crimes, but they weren't my friends. I didn't *know* know them.

"Where you and Charity close?"

Bertie wrinkled her nose. "We didn't go out to dinner

together or hang out outside of work. When she heard I wanted to get my massage license, she offered to help me study. I didn't even have to ask. No way was I going to turn down her offer."

"Why?"

Her smile faltered. "Because I needed a study partner."

"I mean, she used up her spare time on you, but you weren't even friends."

"She was generous, I guess."

"How's that going? Do you think you'll pass?"

She held her fists up to her face and made a groaning sound. "I'm praying. I've been studying every waking moment."

"What made you want to be a masseuse? Er, massage therapist? Doesn't being an esthetician pay as well?"

"It's not that. I could make a good living if I had a steady client base, but massage therapists have regulars. I do too, but once I wax a bikini line or clean up someone's eyebrows, they don't need to come back for a while. People get regular massages. Sometimes weekly."

Trying to keep my smile from dissolving into a disgusted sneer, I said, "You spend your days waxing and removing hair?"

"I do scrubs and wraps and other treatments too, but those are considered a luxury, whereas people tend to look at massages as a health necessity." She perked up. "Are you interested in a seaweed wrap? Seaweed is rich in vitamins and minerals." She waved a finger, indicating my face. "And it can help with those fine lines by stimulating collagen production."

My hand went to the outside corner of my eye, covering my fine lines. "I'm on a non-luxury budget. Sorry."

The waitress brought dinner, and just in time, too. I

needed a pause so I could make a smooth transition to the next topic. But I got distracted.

In the center of my plate, resting on a crisp piece of lettuce, sat a perfect ball of cottage cheese. Though I had no intention of eating it, I gave into the childish desire to obliterate perfection and smashed the middle with my fork.

"I wonder how cottage cheese was invented. I mean, who looked at this and said *Yum. I'd like to try me some of that.*" Bertie didn't share my snicker, so I left off shaping it into a disc and ate a piece of melon.

"It's hard to believe anyone would want to kill a simple massage therapist," I said, musing out loud.

Bertie only nodded. I bet she didn't have the strength to do anything else. Cottage cheese, fruit, and salad. Brrr.

"From what you've told me, Charity seemed like a nice person. Helpful. Not the typical target of a murderer unless the killer was a random stranger. Or maybe it was an accident."

It wasn't an accident, but I wanted to see her response. She went with hopeful.

"You think so? I suppose she could have slipped and fallen into the hot tub and hit her head on the stairs. When she rolled into the water, she drowned."

Wow. She'd given this some thought. She had almost convinced me. Almost.

"You arrived right after I did. Was there anyone else in the parking lot? Anyone walking away?"

"No one. The other businesses in the strip mall don't open until nine or ten, so I would have noticed."

"Did you see a black pickup truck parked in the front lot?"

"I think so. Yes. On the side by the liquor store. But no one else. I was there early to study, but we only need to get to work around ten minutes before we open. Usually, we set up the night before. Most of the time, Norma's the first one in, but she doesn't need to be. So, it's not a surprise no one was there."

"Gazelle was late."

"That's her M.O."

"Did she get along with Charity?"

She rolled her eyes. "The massage therapists think they're above the rest of us. Except Dominique. They don't socialize much with the minions." She pointed at me with her spoon. "The two of them must have been friendly. Recently, they started waiting for each other so they could walk out to their cars together."

"How recently?"

"Maybe two weeks ago? Or maybe that's when I noticed."

Thinking back to Charity's massage room, I remembered the wrinkled sheet. "Charity didn't."

Bertie scraped the last of her cottage cheese from her plate. "Didn't what?"

"Set up for her appointment the night before. There was a wrinkled sheet on her massage table."

She chewed on that for a few seconds. "That's odd."

"Was she nervous Monday afternoon? Or distracted?"

"She was in a grouchy mood because of the early appointment. Charity always griped when it was her turn."

"And her room was in order when she left?"

"I can't remember," Bertie said slowly. "It's not like I went in there for anything."

"Not even to talk about studying for your test?"

"We had plans for Wednesday night. She said she'd stay after work and go over the questions with me and let me practice a few techniques on her."

"Do you know where she went after she left Monday afternoon?"

"Sorry. We weren't that close. She has a boyfriend. I assume she went to see him."

"Was there anyone she noticeably *didn't* get along with?"

Bertie wiped her lips on her napkin and pushed her plate away. "You can't listen to gossip. Charity and Norma were both strong women. Sometimes personalities clash. But Charity brought in so many clients that Norma had to put up with any differences they may have had."

"Differences like what?"

"Business differences. Nothing personal. I shouldn't have said anything. I don't want you to get the wrong impression. I'm sure there are people who rub you the wrong way sometimes."

"More like always," I said, thinking of Jeff.

"You wouldn't kill them."

No. Then again, I wasn't a murderer.

"Did she have any close friends? Other than her boyfriend."

She searched through her fruit with her fork, spearing a grape. "Obviously, we didn't move in the same circles."

It wasn't obvious to me, but she seemed to think I would know what she meant. I'd save that question for Jeff.

"She never talked about an incident? *So-and-so makes me so angry.*"

She frowned. "There *was* this one woman who came in and practically attacked Charity."

"When was this?"

"Last week."

"Who was it?"

"It wasn't a client. I think it was a client's girlfriend."

She waved her hand in the air. "I don't know what it was about, and I don't want to know. I like to stay positive."

A disappointing attitude, and one that wouldn't get me far in learning the dirty secrets hidden under the fluffy towels and scented oils at Friendly Fingers. So, I welcomed the diversion when Jeff walked in and pretended to spot us. He raised his brows in surprise, waved, and strolled over, dropping into the booth next to me.

"Imagine seeing you here. What a lucky surprise." He gave Bertie his special grin, guaranteed to make hearts flutter. "I recognize you. You're Bertie." He snapped his fingers. "From Friendly Fingers."

She sent her gaze downward and blushed. At first, I thought she'd fallen under his spell, but she disabused me of that notion as soon as she spoke. "I don't judge."

His smile froze. "Judge?"

"I heard you and Charity arguing. I want you to know I wasn't the one who brought it to the attention of the police."

No, Gazelle had done that. Was it intentional? Meant to divert our attention away from her?

Jeff relaxed into a smile. "The cops talked to me and saw it had nothing to do with her death, poor kid."

"I'm glad."

He leaned his head back, evaluating her. "You're going to be a massage therapist."

"If I pass the exam. I don't suppose one of you could quiz me on Friday night. The test is Saturday morning."

"Sure. Frances, give her your address."

On the spot, I fumbled my response. "I'm kind of in the middle of something right now." I glared at him. "Something important."

"That's okay," she said. "I understand."

Jeff rubbed his chin with his knuckles. "Did Charity let you practice on her clients?"

That question seemed to come from the ether, so I asked Jeff what he meant. He kept his gaze on Bertie.

"When you're in training, before you get your license, you can give a supervised massage as long as you don't take money."

She finished the last of her fruit and pointed her fork at him. "None of the massage therapists at Friendly Fingers are willing to let me work on their clients." She set the fork down and wiped her fingertips on the napkin, which was cloth for the dinner hour. "I understand. Someone pays for a massage; they want a professional."

Jeff grimaced in a friendly way. "Give yourself some credit. When you get that piece of paper, will that change how you give a massage? You're already a professional, just without the paper."

My ex had already proved he had little respect for official papers. Like marriage licenses.

Lifting her chin, Bertie said, "You're right. I could give you the best massage you've ever had right here on this table." She tapped the table to make her point.

"After you're licensed, I'll take you up on that." He winked. "If Penny agrees."

Before she left, I asked Bertie what her plans were.

"They gave me the next few days off to study for my test."

We all stood, and I wished her good luck. As she walked away, I checked my watch. I'd just have time to pick up dinner.

TWENTY-THREE

That night, I dropped the case. Or I should say I took a respite.

As a peace offering, I'd picked up dinner from Bowers' favorite Chinese restaurant. Emily and Stripe had changed places, with the iguana safely tucked away in my bedroom.

Stripe seemed indifferent to the move, especially when I treated him to some extra mango. Emily, however, bore a grudge. She spat at me from her perch on the bookcase, daring me to lock her away again.

Fortunately, my fiancé was running late. The food waited in the oven on warm. Already ginger and garlic permeated the room. I found some mismatched candles and set them out on the coffee table. The soft glow, soothing with a touch of romance, set the mood. I approved until I tripped over a cat toy. For safety's sake, I turned on the kitchen range light for backup.

When I finally opened the door to Bowers, I held myself tight to ward off a wince.

He'd changed into a dark grey suit and neutral tie. The lines around his eyes were noticeable, and his expression was set on neutral. He'd forgotten to put down his defenses.

It hurt my heart to see him this way.

"Oh, honey." I opened my arms for a hug, but he needed more.

In a sudden movement, he wrapped one arm around me and pulled me to him for a kiss that made me forget where I was. With the other hand behind my head to keep my lips firmly on his, he lifted me off my feet, and carried me inside. A backward kick took care of closing the door.

I clung to him, ready to forget all about Jeff, and murder, and propriety. Even dinner.

His fingers were working the second button of my blouse when he took my shoulders in his hands and stepped back, his breath shaky. "This time next year...." It sounded like a warning.

One of Grandma Chandler's sayings popped into my head. "Many is the slip between the cup and the lip."

He exhaled a burst of air that sounded like a laugh, and as he regained his composure, an amused smile played at the corners of his mouth.

"I didn't stop to check. Are we alone?" His question had a sharp edge.

Emily rubbed against his trousers and purred like a harlot. "Well, not quite alone."

"The cat I can handle."

How would he feel about the iguana? I giggled, and his face muscles relaxed. After he slipped his jacket off, removed his tie, and hung both neatly over the arm of the couch, I took his hand and led him to the middle cushion.

"Sit."

His gaze landed on the plates I'd set out, and he noticed the candles for the first time. He dropped down with a sigh, leaned back, and closed his eyes, while I took the spot next to him.

"How are you doing?"

"Not good. Charity's parents just got back in town. They were on vacation. We had to give them the details of their daughter's murder."

"I'm so sorry." My lame words couldn't help, but I offered them anyway.

"Nothing new has turned up yet." He sighed. "So, your friend isn't off the hook, but we don't have the handcuffs out yet. I thought you'd like to know there's no reason for you to poke around. We're on top of it." His lips tried to give me a weary smile.

Obviously, he needed a break from the investigation.

"Let's not talk about Jeff or the murder." But I twisted my fingers as I remembered the massage therapist's slack features when I turned her over. "How long had Charity been dead when I found her?"

He opened his eyes and gave me one of those looks that tells me nothing about what he's thinking. "She died this morning. Drowned, as you'd expect. Before that, someone hit her on the back of the head with something smooth and hard. We think one of her massage stones. Two are missing from her set."

Shifting to face me, his irises seemed to darken in the candlelight. "You could have walked in on the killer. You could have been hurt. Even killed."

Swallowing hard, I said, "Jeepers."

"You have to promise me you'll leave Jeff to fend for himself. This isn't a request. Not only am I concerned for your safety, but you could inadvertently do something that would negatively impact our investigation."

"Our? As in no longer Juanita's?"

"She's the lead detective, but it's all hands on deck for this one. Charity Samuels is the daughter of City Councilman Mark Samuels. Everyone's watching."

"That sounds like a lot of pressure."

"It is. I don't want to have to worry about you as well."

He searched my face. Reflected in his eyes, I saw worry, frustration, and a small amount of fear.

In that moment, I decided to give up my ineffectual dabs at investigating this murder. I didn't want to be the cause of even a smidgen of Bowers' anxieties. If standing by, docile, while he worked the case brought him peace, so be it.

Though I still planned to get whatever information I could from the crabby iguana, but that was a matter of professional pride.

"You won't. I promise."

He waited to see if I added any weasel wording that would leave me room to ignore this conversation. When I didn't, he asked what we were having for dinner.

"Chinese. It's a new recipe I'm testing."

Irritated by the flash of panic that passed across his features, I said, "Relax. It was a joke. I picked up dinner from Yang's Palace."

We decided to eat on the couch. Once I plated the food and sat back down, he started in on his chicken chow mein. I had the chow fun with rice noodles and a beefy sauce.

As he ate, his mood improved. Note to self. Once we were married, call Bowers daily to make sure he'd eaten lunch.

When we finished, he leaned back and thanked me for dinner. A full tummy lowered his guard. "Jeff's not the only suspect if that makes you feel better."

"He's not?" I stopped myself from asking who else Gutierrez had on her list, reminding Nosy Frankie I was no longer interested. "It does make me feel better. Is that weird? To know I'm grateful there were more people out there who wanted Charity dead?"

Including Stripe.

When he responded, "Yes, you are weird," his voice carried a hint of sleep in it.

He put his arm around my shoulder and pulled me close. "We should set a date for the wedding. We need to enroll in Pre-Cana."

Bowers was a devout Catholic. My parents had raised me Catholic, but I'd drifted away. Pre-Cana was the marriage preparation class required by the Church meant to weed out the weaklings. If you could tough out an interrogation by a priest, you were strong enough to stay married to the same person for the rest of your life.

"What if the priest says you're too good for me?"

He pursed his lips. "I suppose I'll have to dump you."

I grinned. "What if he says I'm too good for you?"

Turning his head, he frowned. "I would have to ravish you and force his hand."

The laugh I was holding back escaped through my nose.

"Is the idea of me ravishing you funny?"

I kept a straight face, and he pounced.

"No fair tickling," I shrieked. Bowers was so serious most of the time. It made the moments when his playful side broke through even more special.

The tickling subsided, leaving me panting for breath. I threw open my arms, acting helpless. "Ravish away."

A dangerous light entered his eyes, so it was just as well the doorbell rang.

"If that's Jeff, I'm going to shoot him," Bowers said as he answered the door.

It was Jeff. I sat up.

"Hey guys. Watcha doing?" He glanced at Bowers' disheveled hair. "Am I interrupting?"

"Can I help you, Mr. Ross?"

Jeff peered over Bowers' shoulder and waved hello. I made a face and motioned for him to leave. First opportunity tomorrow, I'd release him from his obligation to help me.

"Just killing time."

"Kill it somewhere else." Bowers shut the door firmly in his face. Turning back to me, he ran a hand over his hair. "I'm sorry, Frankie. It's your house, and I really had no right to do that, but I'm reaching my limit."

I'd been so selfish and preoccupied with my own complications with my ex, I hadn't considered how Bowers might feel about him showing up after all these years and hanging around. "You're not jealous, are you?"

He dropped onto the couch and let out a breath. "No. Not jealous. He's just so damn irritating."

Relieved, I giggled and scooted closer, resting my head on his chest. "Why, Mr. Bowers. I believe you've finally met the real Jeffrey Ross."

When the doorbell rang again, Bowers' expression made me worry he might be serious about shooting Jeff. That wouldn't look good on his resume. But it wasn't Jeff, it was Detective Juanita Gutierrez.

TWENTY-FOUR

All playfulness left my fiancé as he invited his colleague into my home. They spoke in low voices until she replaced him on the couch next to me, while he stood before us with his hands on his hips. Cornered, I fought the urge to disappear into the couch cushion and sat up straight, crossing my legs to imply this was a casual conversation. Then I remembered crossed legs indicated defensiveness, so I uncrossed them, which made me appear fidgety.

"Miss Chandler, will you come to the station and give us a set of your fingerprints?"

"What? Why?"

"We need to identify a set of prints on the deceased's cell phone."

With a sheepish cringe, I directed my answer to Bowers. "I forgot to tell you. It was on the floor in Charity's room. I picked it up and set it on the counter."

She nodded. It was a triumphant nod. "You admit you handled it."

"That sounds ominous. I'm telling you I picked it up. The screen showed an unfinished email."

"Did you read that email?

"I glanced at it. Like I said. It wasn't finished."

Something crashed on my patio. Bowers moved to the sliding door and flicked on the outside light. "Did you leave the umbrella up?"

I followed him out and helped him right the table. The umbrella, anchored through a hole in the center, buckled and jerked in the warm wind as we raised it. While Bowers held on, I turned the crank until the fabric folded neatly into place.

"Hold the base."

I did so. He loosened the screw and pulled the umbrella out, setting it flat next to the wall.

Gutierrez watched from the doorway. "What a homey scene," she said. Bowers grinned. I did not.

Even though she was being a stinker, I answered the rest of her questions, which didn't elicit any new information from me. Finally, she stood, not bothering to hide her disappointment.

"Thank you for your cooperation."

"No problem."

Bowers walked her to her car, and when he returned, he sank onto the cushion next to me.

"Before you say it, I know. She could have dropped the phone when she was attacked, which means I just missed the killer."

He answered with a grunt and closed his eyes. Soon, his breathing settled into a steady rhythm. Just as I was drifting off myself, I heard a sneeze and held my breath.

"God bless you," Bowers mumbled.

Kissing his cheek, I excused myself to get a tissue but passed the bathroom door and slipped into my bedroom.

Softly, I closed the door behind me and flipped the light switch.

Splatters of white snot covered the glass walls of the terrarium.

"Are you sick, fella?" I whispered. "Please don't be sick."

Stripe lifted his head and sneezed again. White snot shot out of his nose in a fountain.

"Oh, crap."

Hadn't Bethany warned me that the iguana was hanging onto the endangered list by the tips of his toes? How would I explain that, by disregarding her advice to turn the iguana in, I'd lowered the species' number by one? One mattered a lot when you were endangered.

It took me a few minutes to sneak my cell phone into the bedroom and call Seamus. I still had his home number on my phone from our blind date. Fortunately, he answered.

"I think the iguana is sick. He's sneezing snot all over the room."

"He's sneezing snot?"

Muffled noises and mumbling filled my ears until Bethany took control of the phone call. "Is it white?"

I confirmed it was.

"Iguanas sneeze salt out of their noses. Look. You really need to get that animal to a safe place."

"Right now, he's comfy cozy in my bedroom in his terrarium." Someone had murdered Petey the Cockatoo in this same bedroom. Suddenly, I didn't feel so confident.

"Have you cleaned his terrarium yet?"

I sniffed the air. "Is that what smells?"

"Make sure you wear gloves. Their droppings can carry salmonella."

Killer poop. One more worry.

"What are you feeding him?" she asked in a super snooty tone.

"French fries and chocolate."

"What?"

"Papaya. Mango. A variety of lettuces."

"Well, that should be okay. I don't understand what's between you and Seamus, but my concern is for the animal."

That's what her mouth said, but her tone said the secret was edging out the iguana for first place on her list of concerns.

"He understands there is something I need to do. Something private. Nothing that will harm Stripe."

She made a scoffing noise.

"Hey. I didn't name him."

"He shouldn't have a name at all. He should be in the wild, making other little iguanas."

I heard a noise from my living room. Bowers was awake. "I have to go. Bye." She was still talking when I hung up.

Before I opened my bedroom door, I turned off the light so Bowers wouldn't see Stripe. Good thing because my fiancé had come looking for me.

"I fell asleep. Sorry about that." He stretched and yawned. "I should go."

Just as I stepped into the hallway to join him, the iguana sneezed again. Bowers froze with his arms in the air, staring, so I covered my mouth and faked another sneeze.

He lowered his arms. "Who's in there?"

"In where?"

"Your bedroom." His expression darkened. "I'm a patient man, Frankie, but if you stashed Jeff in your bedroom while I was asleep—"

"Don't even."

Striped sneezed again, and my cheeks burned.

"Frankie?"

My fiancé yelling about an iguana seemed the lesser of the evils facing me. I pushed the bedroom door open and flipped the light switch.

Bowers didn't spot him at first. He sent a puzzled gaze around the room. About to come back to me, spotted the terrarium.

"There was an iguana in the victims' massage room."

I joined him and gazed at Stripe in his snotty, glass home. "And he would have stayed there if I hadn't rescued him. He was starving to death. They'd forgotten all about him. And just so you know, he's expelling salt. Not blowing his nose. In case that makes it less gross."

"Is that what that smell is?"

"No. That's iguana poop, but I need a hazmat suit before I deal with that problem."

He rested his hands on my shoulders. "It's very sweet of you to be concerned about the animal, but is there any other reason you brought him home and hid him in your bedroom?"

"To protect him from Emily."

His eyebrows went up. "Really? Would she—I suppose she might find him interesting."

Before he could press for my real reason for having Stripe, my phone rang. I picked it up from my nightstand, and when I saw it was Jeff, I answered with the speaker on.

"I'm standing here with Bowers. What do you want now?"

"Frances, some guy with arm muscles the size of my thigh is trying to kill me." Loud pounding and the shouts of a male voice in the background supported his statement. "I don't want to sound like a weenie, but could you send your boyfriend over?"

"Fiancé," I snapped. "Where are you?"

"The Overnight Motel."

"Stay in the room," Bowers said, wide awake. "I'll be right there."

I closed the bedroom door to keep Emily away from my guest. "I'm coming with you."

Forgetting my decision to stay out of the investigation, I thought, *"Hurrah. Someone wants Jeff dead. We're finally getting somewhere."*

Which I admit was not a nice thought.

TWENTY-FIVE

Local rumor had it the optimistically named Overnight Motel rented rooms by the hour. It was a flat structure made of beige stone with bright orange trim. The management office was located on one end, and the rooms stretched out to the right. The neon blue-and-orange sign reflected in the windows of the gas station across the street. The one next to an abandoned lot.

Each guest had direct access to his or her room. No lobby for these folks. An ice machine, pop machine, and snack machine provided all the amenities the guests could expect for the low-priced accommodations.

Outside the second door from the end, a dark-skinned man with short-cropped hair and lots of muscles pounded on the door. His deep voice called out.

"I know you're in there!"

Bowers took his time approaching the man, keeping his open hands in view. I stayed behind my fiancé, though I walked close enough to him that I stepped on his heel.

"Frankie, please get back in the car."

Too late. Jeff's angry visitor spotted us.

"Good evening." Bowers came to a stop about four feet short of the guy and flipped open his identification. "I'm Detective Martin Bowers of the Wolf Creek police force. What seems to be the problem?"

Now that I could see him better, the man had a trim beard and wore a short-sleeved shirt across his muscled torso. The t-shirt was black with an intricate design throughout that turned light blue at his shoulders. FIJI Airways was written across the chest in bold, white letters.

I recognized him and tugged on Bowers' jacket. "He was in a picture with Charity in her massage room."

The guy heard me.

"That's right." His lips tightened. "My girlfriend is dead, man. I just found out the bozo in this room may have had something to do with it."

Bowers sighed. "Are you Vali Prasad?"

"I am."

Even as the man clenched his hands and hunched his shoulders forward, Vali Prasad's eyebrows raised at the center, and the middle of his full lips pushed up, while the edges pointed down. His dark eyes glistened with unshed tears. The man's anger was a cover for a deep well of sadness.

When I rushed past Bowers, he made a grab for me, too late. I placed my hands on Vali's bicep. "I am so sorry for your loss."

"Thank you." As a tear escaped, he wiped his cheek with the back of his hand and cleared his throat. "It's been a shock. You can see why I feel the need to—to talk to this man."

Being a cop, Bowers excelled at playing dense to get an explanation from the other party. "I'm afraid I don't."

"I need to find out what he knows. If he had anything to

do with her death." He unclenched his fists to show he came in peace. "I just want to talk to him."

"How did you find out about Mr. Ross?"

Vali's eyes opened in surprise. "You know about him? Why isn't he under arrest?"

"I know him," I offered. "And Jeff can be a bozo, but he's not a killer."

Our voices must have carried inside because the door cracked open. "Is it safe?"

And then I got a demonstration of two wild elk fighting for dominance. All they needed were the antlers.

Vali rushed the door. Jeff pushed back. Two extremely fit men shoving a piece of wood between them, each trying to gain ground, should have impressed me. Possibly titillated me. Instead, I got annoyed.

"Aren't you going to stop them?"

Bowers grinned. "I love your confidence in me." He assessed the situation. With Vali the more compact of the two, but Jeff the larger, they seemed evenly matched. "I'd get between them, but there's a door in the way. If it moves past this phase...maybe."

I thought he would enjoy seeing Jeff get his butt kicked. I would, too, but patience isn't my virtue. If this was Charity's boyfriend, I had questions. Scratch that. I wasn't involved. Bowers had questions, and I wanted to hear the answers. Just for my own edification.

Raising my thumb and pointer finger to my lips, I let off a shrill whistle that hurt my ears. The two men grunted to a stop, panting.

Resigned, Bowers approached them. "Did you get it out of your systems? Because I have questions for both of you. If not, I'll have to take you to the station, and if I do, I'll call in a colleague who won't be as understanding as me."

My fiancé raised an eyebrow at Vali, and Charity's boyfriend nodded. When he gave the same look to Jeff, my ex complained.

"He started it."

At Bowers' responding glare, Jeff shut up and opened the door wide. He had nothing on except a pair of boxer shorts and an undershirt.

As Vali crossed the threshold, Jeff nodded at his t-shirt.

"The Flying Fijians? Are you on the team?"

If Jeff loved anything, it was sports, so I wasn't surprised he recognized a team shirt from the other side of the world.

"Just a fan like the rest of my countrymen. Now what did you do to my girlfriend?"

I swear the Fijian expanded in front of us, his muscles bulging. Even his neck.

Now that backup had arrived, the display didn't impress my ex. He had the confidence to turn his back on Vali and walk farther into the room.

"I don't know what you're complaining about. She told me the two of you broke up. I flew all the way here to see her to find she'd gone back to you. Meanwhile, I'm stuck here—completely alone—in a cheesy motel until the cops figure out what happened."

Without asking, Vali sat down on the edge of the bed. Dark circles propped up intense brown eyes, and the rest of his features were tight with pain. I looked away.

The rumors about The Overnight weren't true. As I glanced around the room in search of stains and grime, all I saw was old. A bed cover with a sixties psychedelic design in oranges and yellow that matched the curtains, an old television, the kind that came without a remote, and pictures of naked women in poses that suggested they *might* be art.

"We broke up before she went to Milwaukee," Vali

began. "It was my fault." He rubbed his eyes. "We argued, so I went to The Moon with my buddies." He named a popular sports bar in Glendale.

Vali's voice was soft. Almost hypnotic, which was a shame. The television next door blasted a crime drama. Gunshots and screams punctuated his words. Then the couple in the room on the opposite side launched into a lover's spat, and following the conversation became a challenge.

"When did you last see her?" Bowers asked.

You promised twenty years ago you'd leave her. Twenty years of my life down the toilet.

"We had dinner together last night," Vali said, raising his voice. "We made it an early night because she had an appointment first thing the next day."

Blam! Blam!

"When did she leave you?" Bowers asked.

"We ate at six. Hung out for a while."

(Sound of car tires screeching.)

"She left before eight."

I told you. When the kids grow up—

They're in their thirties!

When the woman—the live woman, not the one on television—shrieked, Bowers strode to the wall and pounded with his fist. The voices went silent. "What time did she usually show up for work?"

Vali lowered his voice. "She got there half an hour before her shift. She needed to take care of—" He glanced at the cop in the room. "To take care of setting up."

That terrarium was heavy. Too heavy to cart back and forth from work. I suspected she left Stripe in her room at Friendly Fingers and took care of his needs in the morning. Did the killer find her there tending to her pet and render her helpless with a hot massage stone? Is that why she'd dropped her phone? But how did Stripe get free of his terrarium? Did the killer let him go? Maybe the killer was an animal activist, and Stripe's confinement was the reason the massage therapist had to die. Maybe.

Someone banged on the door, and Bowers answered with his badge in his hand. While he took care of the irritated lovers, Jeff sat down next to Vali. "About me and Charity. There's not much to tell. I assume you're Vali."

With narrowed eyes and a hard edge in his voice, the boyfriend said, "Why?"

"Charity talked about you a lot." He thumped Vali's back. "She really cared about you."

Bowers returned in time to catch the last part, and we exchanged a glance. Who was this compassionate person doing and saying the right thing?

"Did Charity like lavender?" It just came out. What was wrong with me? Questioning a man in the throes of mourning made me a bottom-feeding carp. Or a catfish. Catfish were cuter. And tastier.

"She did." Vali sniffed. "She wore lavender scent all the time, except at work."

Stripe might be sending out the scent as a sign he missed his guardian. I frowned. If he always stayed at Friendly Fingers, and Charity never wore it at work, how would he associate her with the scent?

Since Gutierrez had already interviewed Vali, Bowers didn't put much effort into his next question. It seemed more like habit. "Mr. Prasad, did your girlfriend mention anything to you about being afraid of someone?"

The boyfriend jerked his head up. "If she had, I would have taken care of them."

Bowers showed no surprise at the answer, and I remembered how tired he was when he turned his head to stifle a yawn. "And she had no enemies?"

"Enemies? No." His lips curved into a slight smile. "The other massage therapists were jealous of her success. But I can't see any of them killing her over it."

After Vali talked himself out, he shook Jeff's hand before leaving. "Sorry, bro. My brain is messed up and had me thinking all sorts of things. That and the lady cop made some suggestions." He made a face.

"That's her job," I said with an airy wave of my hand. "To trick you into getting emotional and letting something slip. If there is anything to slip, that is."

As soon as Vali was gone, Jeff dropped the friendly act. "That guy wants to kill me. I'm not staying here."

I turned to Bowers. "More important, did you believe him? His body language said he was stricken with grief."

He took my hand, ready to break unwelcome news. "That doesn't mean he didn't kill her. If he acted on impulse, he might regret his actions and still miss her."

"Which is why I'm leaving," Jeff said.

His clothes from today sat in a folded stack on the room's only chair. As he slipped on his t-shirt and jeans, my ex asked if he qualified for police protection. "You saw that guy. With all that anger fueling those muscles, he could break me in half."

From his irritated frown, I guessed Bowers was about to tell him *tough toenails*. Instead, he told Jeff to pack his stuff.

"You're staying with me. At least then I can keep an eye on you."

"Cool." When Jeff grabbed his backpack, something fell out and bounced on the carpet. My mouth hung open as I stared at a black, smooth stone.

Bowers dropped my hand, and his voice came low and steady. "Frankie, honey, get behind me."

Though I took several steps back, I couldn't stop staring at that rock. What did it mean? Was I wrong about Jeff? I looked into his eyes and saw panic.

"Jeffrey Ross, put your hands on your head and turn around," Bowers ordered in an official voice that made me forget the rock. He'd pulled his weapon. Stifling a yelp, I flattened myself against the wall.

"It's not what you think." Jeff lifted his shirt, revealing a bruise on his chest. "She threw it at me."

"Why would you keep it?" I said, exasperated.

He lowered his shirt. "As a token of what we had."

Bowers didn't care about Jeff's reasons. He ordered him to comply and cuffed him. When he dropped me off on the way to the station, I lurched into the house, forcing my feet to move forward.

What a horrid mess I'd made. Trying to do the job of a professional with all the arrogance of an amateur. And how helpful of me to invite the killer along to help me dig up clues. If Jeff were the killer and not a sentimental boob.

From the moment Gazelle the Antelope had brought up Charity's fight with my ex, my only thought was to disassociate Jeff from the murder for Bowers' sake. But now, my fiancé would walk into the police station with my ex-boyfriend under arrest. Gutierrez would do a celebratory dance—a professional tango which she would execute perfectly, without mussing her hair.

Bowers' reputation was mud. The promotion a hazy memory. My fiancé would marry me, but only so he could divorce me.

TWENTY-SIX

There were plenty of available parking spaces outside the Wolf Creek police station at a quarter to seven the next morning. Mine was one of three cars that weren't patrol cruisers. Criminal activity must experience a lull in the early hours. Good to know.

Pulling open the glass front door, I caught the sergeant at the front desk as she spotted me before she stifled a laugh. Pulling her mouth into a straight line, she asked, "How can I help you?"

I looked around the small lobby and the waiting area off to my right. Both were empty. "Is it possible for me to see Jeffrey Ross? I believe he's being held here."

When she bit her upper lip to keep from grinning, my cheeks burned warm. Did I have sleepers in my eyes? I wiped my mouth in case I had missed a trail of toothpaste. Hardly comedy club material.

I'd dressed in black slacks, a black blouse, black flats, and a necklace with a gold cross my parents had given me for Confirmation, but the sergeant wasn't impressed. She picked up the phone and jabbed at some buttons, and when she spoke, she raised her voice unnecessarily.

"There is a Miss Frankie Chandler here to see the prisoner."

Before she set the phone in its cradle, several heads popped out of the offices lining the hallway behind her. Offices of other detectives. Gutierrez appeared in her doorway, crossed her arms over her chest, and leaned against the door frame, a smirk on her full lips. The other detectives looked over when Bowers stepped out of his office. One of them called out. "Hey, Bowers. Your imaginary fiancée is here." The rest burst out in unrestrained laughter.

Did they know about my relationship with Jeff? Were they pointing out that Bowers had chosen poorly? Spots appeared in front of my eyes.

He nodded. "Very funny, fellas." When he got to the front desk, he glanced at the sergeant. "Could you give us a moment?"

She skittered down the hallway to let out the giggle she'd been holding back.

"Frankie, what are you doing here?" He sounded concerned.

The skin above my upper lip spasmed. "What did he mean, imaginary fiancée?"

"A bad joke."

"Because I'm right here." I let loose a hollow laugh. "You can see me, right?"

"Sweetheart. Ignore him."

I struggled to stay on point. "Is Jeff under arrest?"

"He's being held. Forensics isn't in yet to perform tests."

"Do you think he did it?"

He hesitated. I held my breath. Bowers never lied. "I can't say."

"Can I talk to him?"

He shook his head. "I'm sorry, Frankie."

"I'm the one who is sorry. Jeff should be my problem, not yours. If only I hadn't agreed to pick up his keys."

"Charity Samuels would still be dead."

"But you and I wouldn't be involved. Okay. You'd be involved, but only as a detective. Instead—"

Another voice called out. "I got a mouse in here that needs talking to."

That could only be a reference to my pet psychic business aimed, indirectly, at Bowers. Something happened in my guts. The same thing that happens to mother bears any time the male tries to eat her babies. A protective instinct kicked in, one that discarded caution and common sense.

I leaned forward. "I can hear you, you ape!"

Raucous laughter followed, and Bowers stared as Non-confrontational Frankie took a long-needed vacation.

Gutierrez raised her perfectly plucked eyebrows, the amused smirk still in place.

"And what's wrong with you, Python," I said. She jerked, startled. "I thought cops watched each other's back."

Fresh faces joined us from the remaining doorways.

"Take a deep breath," Bowers muttered, stretching forward to take my hand. I stood on my toes to see over his shoulder and addressed them all.

"Instead, when one of you, through no fault of his own, is thrown into an awkward position, you surround him like a pack of jackals."

Something passed over Gutierrez' expression, and she left her vantage point to return to her office. I noticed the rest of the crew didn't find that observation giggle-worthy.

"Honey, they're just letting off steam," Bowers said.

I snorted. "I don't care what they're doing. As long as they *stop screwing with my fiancé!*"

Ignoring Bowers' frozen expression, I took several deep breaths through my nose. In a more pleasant voice, I said, "Right. Will I see you later?"

"I can't say," he said. "Things are pretty busy. I'll call you."

He didn't need my worries on top of his own. I gave him a bright smile so the gaping zoo animals could see things were fine between Bowers and his invisible fiancée. "Okay." I slapped the counter. "I'll talk to you then."

As I walked back to my car, my phone rang. I fumbled with it because my hands shook from the high of unrestrained emotion. Maybe Bowers was calling me from the privacy of his office. I answered without checking the caller ID.

"Frankie?"

I stopped walking.

"Good morning, June."

June Baxter, the woman who had raised Martin Bowers after the death of his mother, her sister. The oldest of seven sisters who kept him wrapped in a steel cocoon, ready to repel threats. I'd met her last month on her farm in Northern Arizona and found her a kind, motherly soul, probably because she'd raised all her siblings.

"What's going on?" she asked. "Is Marty all right?"

"What do you mean?"

"It's all over the Internet."

"What is? The murder?"

She made a noise. "Maybe you should read the *Wolf Creek Gazette* and call me back."

"Oh, crud."

"Who is Jeffrey Ross?"

How to explain.

"He's someone I used to know a long time ago."

"And what's he doing in Wolf Creek?"

"It's a really long story."

"Save it for tonight."

"Tonight?" Was June going to drive all the way from her farm to handle things?

"On the Zoom call. We'll all be there."

All? All could only mean the pack of sisters who guarded their baby brother like she-wolves. I'd only met four of them. "*All* of the Bowers girls will be there?"

"Well, not all. Cissy is traveling, but she promised to try. And Edith, she's hard to predict. It's better if she doesn't come. I'll send you the email link for five o'clock tonight. Now, tell me what's going on."

It felt good to unburden myself to this stable, strong, maternal woman, so I told her everything and waited for her pronouncement.

"This is worse than that breeched calf we delivered last week. Maybe not. At least no one's life is in danger. Do you still have feelings for Jeffrey?"

"I thought I hated him. Now I just hate what he's doing to Bowers."

That answer satisfied her. "You show up and we'll get it straightened out. Life is full of unhappy twists, and we survive them all. Don't let it get you down."

"Okay, June. Thanks."

After I hung up, I exercised my women's prerogative and changed my mind. Those buffoons in the police station were picking at Bowers' confidence, taking potshots at him while Miss Python looked on and enjoyed the spectacle. I was not going to sit by and watch that happen.

I would not only clear Jeff, but I would find the son-of-a-gun who started this avalanche and give her—or him—a piece of my mind. And a swift kick, too. Bowers would know that he'd made an excellent choice picking me as a helpmate. I wouldn't let him down.

Playing out my revenge scene, a tiny part of me acknowledged that giving in to my emotions, though exhilarating, had frightening aspects. I should dial it back and let reason and self-control take the lead again. But the scene at the station repeated in my head, and emotion won the day.

Even though my appetite had abandoned me, I headed for the Prickly Pear. Making a real effort to find the killer would take energy. And I needed to keep up my strength for my morning appointment. An angry gerbil.

TWENTY-SEVEN

Penny couldn't join me until after I'd already started on my corned beef hash. When she slid the morning paper across the table without a word, I forced myself to read the article marked by her pink, painted fingernail.

WOLF CREEK'S *OWN CHARLATAN IS AT IT AGAIN.*

FRANKIE CHANDLER, *the woman who takes money from gullible pet owners in exchange for her "psychic" services, has, once again, butted in on a murder. Readers may remember when Ms. Chandler literally fell over the corpse of Elvira Jenkins, the short-lived Blue-Ribbon Queen. This reporter thought discovering one corpse would satisfy anyone's lust for bizarre thrills.*

Ms. Chandler upped the count to two yesterday when she discovered the body of Charity Samuels at the Friendly

Finger spa. Ms. Samuels is the daughter of esteemed Wolf Creek city councilman, Mark Samuels.

This time, Ms. Chandler is personally involved. In a bizarre love triangle, Charity Samuels was in a relationship with Jeffrey Ross of Loon Lake, Wisconsin. At one time, Ms. Chandler shared a residence with Mr. Ross, though records show the two were never married. Does that give her a motive for murder? Was Charity Samuel's death the result of a jealous rage? It gets better. Or worse.

Rumor has it that Wolf Creek's own Detective Martin Bowers is engaged to Ms. Chandler, though at the time of this report, she is not wearing an engagement ring. Could this romance be another flight of Ms. Chandler's overactive imagination? Much like her belief that she can converse with animals like a female Dr. Dolittle? Rumor has it she is attempting to get into the head of the victim's iguana. Sounds like animal abuse to me.

The police have taken Mr. Ross in for questioning, but we were unable to confirm the circumstances before this edition went to print. The citizens of Wolf Creek might be better off if Ms. Chandler was the person behind bars.

"SON-OF-A—" Except I said the entire word.

"Disgusting. For the love of—waitress."

The same group of geezers from yesterday morning were at the table across from my booth. The leader jabbed his finger at me. "Could you move us somewhere we don't have to hear this person?"

"It's not that bad," Penny said, patting my hand.

I shoved the newspaper back at her. "Tell me the good part, Pen."

"Well...." She scrunched her face. "It doesn't mention you attacked Jeff."

"I feel much better. No wonder that female sergeant was laughing at me. And now the invisible fiancée comment makes sense."

"Invisible what?"

Rubbing my forehead didn't help with my headache, so I dropped my hands on the table and blew out a huff of air. As I replayed my visit to the police station, her mouth opened a bit at a time until she gaped.

"You had an altercation with a police officer?"

"About seven of them. They had it coming."

She lowered her voice to a whisper. "Did you actually use the word *screwing*?"

When she said it out loud, it came across as unbelievably crass. "Do you think I overreacted?"

"I couldn't have done it." She tapped her chin. "But if someone made fun of Kemper...I don't know. I hope I never find out."

"We need to figure this out and fast."

"Have you learned anything new?"

On my request, she retrieved an order pad and pen so I could make a list on the back.

"Number one. Charity was killed in the morning." I wrote it down.

"Are you sure?"

"That's what the ME said. The killer struck her on the head and drowned her in the hot tub."

"Efficient," she said with approval.

I scribbled another note. "Jeff's five-minute girlfriend spent part of the evening before with her *real* boyfriend." Thinking back to what the angry Fijian told us last night, I held up a finger. "Although, she left Vali in time to get back to Friendly Fingers for an eight pm appointment. One that nobody knew about."

"Does that matter?"

I frowned at my list, unhappy at the thought of abandoning one of my points. It was a short list.

"I guess not. But it's strange. No one saw her leave, including the security cameras." A thought flickered at the edge of my mind but refused to make itself known.

She waved her hand. "Oh! Oh! Unless she was held there overnight and killed in the morning."

"True." Tapping the pen on the table, I voiced a concern. As a closet pragmatist, I was happiest when every detail made sense. "I wonder why she would schedule an appointment after hours. Maybe it wasn't business." But that wouldn't explain the wrinkled sheet on Charity's massage table. "Nix that. Someone definitely got a rubdown that night, and they had it in Charity's room."

"So, she had a secret assignation that went wrong." Penny's eyes glowed with excitement as she developed her story. "She met someone at Friendly Fingers." She gasped. "A lover? Maybe the sheet was on the massage table because she and this person, um, enjoyed each other."

Jeff had messed around with Charity during a massage. Did he stop by for a repeat? No. Not after the rock-throwing incident.

"All night? And unless he was a praying mantis, why would he kill her afterward? Anyway, it's the female mantis that kills her mate."

"Because they had a tiff." Penny spread her hands like a magician revealing a spectacular illusion. "Hear me out. Charity was tired of, um, having relations in uncomfortable places. She wanted more. He refused. She threatened to tell the guy's girlfriend, or even better, *his wife.* In a huff, he tied her up and kept her there while he thought about what to do with her. But he realized he was stuck in a mess of his own making. One that didn't have a way out. By morning, he killed her."

"Except she hadn't been tied up. Bowers would have mentioned it last night when he was telling me about her murder. At least, I *think* he would have."

She deflated. "Maybe they just talked all night."

"And then he killed her before the sun came up so he could escape under the cover of darkness? That makes him a vampire."

She took offense at my crack and pointed out that I wasn't even sure the person who opened the door to the late-night guest was Charity. I refused to let minor details discourage me.

"Fine. That means Monday night has nothing to do with her death. I like that. We won't allow ourselves to get sidetracked by Monday night."

The optimist thought she'd found the silver lining. "That lets Jeff out for sure. He was sound asleep at U-Behave Tuesday morning. I saw him, remember?"

"You did. However, he could have been faking sleep. He has a rental car and could have driven to meet her at Friendly Fingers. And there's something else."

She was less impressed by the massage stone clue. "I can see him keeping a trophy."

I stood. "If Jeff killed Charity, I think I'll be sick. Then I'll join a convent. I really don't think he's capable of violence, but either way, I need to know. But first, business."

TWENTY-EIGHT

"It sounds silly, but this isn't the Wilbur I know and love. He's attacked me twice."

We stood in the living room of a small apartment that expressed the tenant's desire to bring about world peace with ambient music, patchouli incense, and framed, inspirational posters calling for everyone to lay down their arms and hug each other.

Missy Tonks, resident of the apartment, wore a short skirt and t-shirt and nothing on her feet. Evidently, she loved her golden gerbil, Wilbur. He had a spacious cage. She'd covered his exercise wheel in leather to keep his feet and tail from falling through the bars. The ceramic dish, a healthy choice as it kept tempting plastic away from his teeth, contained gerbil nuggets as well as a few bits of cereal treats. She'd given him blocks of wood to gnaw on, supplied plenty of fresh water to drink, and used strips of toilet paper to make the floor covering three inches deep so he could burrow. He even had a nesting box filled with hay. This gerbil had it good, but he wasn't in the mood to appreciate his comfortable quarters.

He sat up in the middle of his living quarters, his little paws pressed together in prayer. I noted the red stains by his eyes. Red tears were a sign of stress. So were attacks and the high-pitched squeaks he gave me now. And he stomped his back feet like he was auditioning for River Dance.

Always reluctant to open my mental doorway, I asked if she'd considered getting him a playmate.

"I was just about to do so when he started attacking me. I'm afraid he would hurt another animal right now."

She gave her pet a weepy look with her doe-like brown eyes. Fine, fine. I opened the mental doorway.

"Aah!" Doubling over, I covered my ears with my hands and squeezed my eyes shut. "What is that noise?"

As she frowned and sent a glance around her apartment, I grabbed her arm.

"What. Is. That. Noise."

She shook her arm free. "Stop shouting. There *is* no noise."

Wilber looked at me, his eyes wide, and I swear he nodded.

Keeping my fingers in my ears, I fired some questions. "What's changed recently?"

"Nothing."

"How long ago did this start?"

"It started Monday night."

"What happened two days ago?"

She walked to the kitchen and returned with a date book. As she casually flipped through it, I wanted to shake her until her teeth rattled to impress upon her the urgency. Glancing over her shoulder at the book, the numbers blurred as the searing pain in my head increased.

"Nope. No appointments."

Desperate, I snatched up Wilbur in my cupped hands,

careful to avoid his tail, and fled into the hallway. As soon as we'd escaped the apartment, the noise subsided. It didn't stop, but it was bearable now. Wilbur collapsed and panted with relief. My client, however, was furious.

"Are you trying to steal my pet?"

"Stay here with Wilbur," I ordered.

I had a suspicion, and as I rummaged through her closets, giving extra attention to the corners on the upper shelves, I grumbled about people's stupidity. Did they never read directions? Did they bother to think before acting?

My search ended under the kitchen sink. Yanking out a small white gadget, I carried it to the hallway, dropped it on the floor, and smashed it to smithereens under my shoe, several times for good measure.

"Hey! That cost money."

Jabbing my finger at the mess on the floor, I mustered up self-righteous indignation, which wasn't difficult with my ears still ringing. "*That* is a sonic mouse repeller."

"I know. I got them because I heard noises in the wall." She shuddered. "This was the humane way of getting rid of rodents."

"You almost got rid of Wilbur."

She gaped. "You mean?"

"Read the box next time, lady. You said *them*. I'll wait with Wilbur while you clear out the rest. And make sure you get all of them."

While she rushed into the apartment, I let out a long exhale and scratched Wilbur behind the ears.

"Nasty noisy repeller."

A simple thing like a noise, one that humans couldn't even hear, could cause so much pain and frustration to animals. I paused my scratching. Just like delicate scents, something we ignored every day, could be potent to the sensitive nose of a pet. Was I thinking about the lavender the wrong way? Maybe it wasn't a fond memory of Charity. Did it instead represent something terrible? Did Stripe associate the smell with an event too horrible to name? Like murder. Missy stepped into the hallway just as I whispered, "Lavender."

"You have to be careful with essential oils. They can be harmful to some animals." She seemed pleased to impart this information, probably to make up for almost killing her pet through ignorance.

It could be that simple. Stripe sent me the scent of lavender hoping it would kill me.

When I noticed she was holding two of the sonic traps, I backed up.

"It's okay. I removed the batteries."

Handing Wilbur to her in exchange for the noisy nightmares, I dropped them on the floor and disabled them permanently. "Better to be safe."

Once Wilbur was back in his cage, he leapt in the air with happy squeaks. He paused and sent me an image of another gerbil.

"He'd like that playmate now."

She paid me my fifty bucks, but not until after I swept the hallway.

TWENTY-NINE

My anger over the *Gazette* article had pushed news of tonight's Zoom pow-wow out of my head. I'd left Prickly Pear Bistro without telling Penny about the dreaded event, so I returned to my unofficial headquarters.

There were only a few diners left from the morning rush, and our usual booth was free. I slid into the bench and waited.

For the second time in two days, the happiness fairy had abandoned my best friend. Her frown muscles didn't get much exercise, so when she plopped onto the bench across from me, folded her arms on the table, and dropped her face into the waiting nest, my instinct was to put her out of her misery before she pulled something important in her face.

"What now?"

On cue, a man's voice sliced through the air. "Get out!"

Jeff stepped out of the kitchen holding a piece of breakfast sausage between his fingers and a newspaper tucked under his arm.

I slapped the table. "How in the name of everything that barks—"

Penny lifted her head, her lower lip trembling. "He showed up a half hour ago. What could I do? You have to get rid of him."

I should explain to Penny how I'd coerced Jeff into helping me. She would never speak to me again.

"Javier is the best." Jeff dropped down next to me and held out his prize. When I declined to take a bite, he popped the entire sausage in his mouth. After reaching across me for a napkin and using it, he spread open the paper to the sports section and propped it against the table's edge.

"Who's Javier?" I asked my friend.

"My new cook. The one who is getting a *very* bad impression of my restaurant."

Jeff glanced up. "I was watching him. He must have worked at a truck stop before this because he's like a machine. Knows what he's doing and he's fast. It was amazing to watch."

I grabbed his chin and yanked his face toward me. "I ask you again. Did you kill Charity Samuels? Because a lot depends on your innocence."

His jaw muscles flexed as he grinned. "No, Sherlock. My self-preservation instincts are finely tuned. I'd never risk life in prison. And why resort to violence? There are plenty more fish in the sea."

With a huff of disgust, I released his face. "How did you get out of jail?"

He refolded the paper and set it aside. "I showed the doctor my bruise, and it matched the shape and size of the stone I had in my backpack. There wasn't any blood or hair or skin or whatever on the stone they took from me. And it was the wrong size for Charity's wound."

"You mean she wasn't killed with a massage stone?"

"They were discussing that possibility when I left. My feelings were hurt because Juanita looked disappointed. Your boyfriend didn't smile, but I could tell he was happy."

"Fiancé." At least Bowers was pleased.

Monica, the younger of Penny's full-time waitresses, approached the table with a coffee pot. She had her chestnut hair pulled into a ponytail and her usual smile ready for us. Her interested gaze landed on Jeff, and she blushed prettily.

"Back away from the bad man," I growled. "He has diseases."

Monica shuffled sideways, toward Penny.

Jeff bumped me—not gently—with his shoulder. "She's joking."

"Oh, look." Monica held up the coffee pot and jiggled it. Some brown liquid sloshed out the spout. "Empty. I'll come back." Turning on her heel, she skittered away.

"Sorry, Penny. I hope she doesn't quit, but I need Jeff to focus."

Okay. Time to tell her about Jeff's involvement in the case. That's what best friends are for, right? To listen to your worst and love you anyway.

"I don't have a disease," Jeff repeated.

"No one cares." I cleared my throat. "Penny, Jeff is going to help us fix the problem he caused. Aren't you Jeff?"

He nodded, solemn. "Jail wasn't any fun."

"I don't care what motivates you, as long as you do your part."

Penny eyed him warily. "Okay, Frances. You know what's best. Though I don't see how he can help you."

"He can, and more than he knows. We haven't tapped into our closest source about Charity yet."

"Who's that?" She stared at my ex. "You mean *him*?"

"That's right." I turned to face him. "Spill. And don't leave anything out."

"I already told my story."

"Tell it again and start at the beginning."

"Fine. Buffy and I broke up."

"She dumped you. You should stop cheating on your girlfriends."

"I didn't." He said it so softly, I almost missed it. Pity showed up, but I chased her away. Jeff was a first-class liar.

"So, the two of you split. You lost your job."

"I loved that job."

"And went to an employment fair and slept with Charity."

"Wait." Penny held up a hand. "You slept with Charity with potential employers around?"

Jeff laughed. "No."

She sighed, relieved.

"The massage convention was next to the job fair. That's where I met her, and we hit it off."

"Ew!"

"Focus, Pen. Charity said it would be fun if you moved out here. You took that as an invitation and came."

"I had nothing to lose."

"Did you see her again?"

"We went to dinner. I spent the night in her hotel room."

"The two of you couldn't—I mean, all night—" Jeff's lips spread in a slow grin. Penny guffawed, and my face burned with embarrassment. "I'm saying some of that time must have been spent talking."

"Sure."

"By the time she went home, what did you know about her?"

"She was good at her job. Ambitious."

"Ambitious how? She wanted to be the best masseuse in the world? Own her own business? Be the massage therapist to the stars?"

"She had plans. She called it a career map. You don't have a career map unless you're ambitious."

"Was one of the pit stops a job as a building manager?" I snapped, remembering how closely she questioned Allen Whitmore about his business.

"Don't be jealous. Do you have a career map?"

I narrowed my eyes. "No, you donkey, I don't. Do you?"

"Gee, Frances. Lighten up."

"Did she talk about family? Best friends? Somebody we could speak with. Anybody."

"I don't think you could get an appointment to see her father. I don't know what he does, but she said he was a Wolf Creek mucky-muck."

"A city councilman."

He raised his brows. "Sweet. She didn't mention siblings or friends. I got the impression she didn't have time for friends."

"What exactly did she say when you showed up at Friendly Fingers?"

He leaned his head back and squinted. "First, she seemed happy to see me. *Jeff? Is it really you?* Lots of squealing. I said I just got off the plane and would love to take a shower if she could give me the keys to her place. That's when she lost it. She asked if I was out of my mind. Then she started talking about Vali, her boyfriend. How they had gotten back together, and I was going to ruin it, which was harsh."

"That's it?"

"Pretty much."

"Not very helpful. We need to figure out how to reach her boyfriend. I think he might be more open without Bowers there."

"Don't look at me." He spotted a sympathetic audience in Penny. "Did Frances tell you the guy tried to kill me last night? Unbelievable."

I snorted. "Just before you dropped what was possibly the murder weapon on the floor of the Overnight Motel. Which reminds me. Why did she throw the stone at you?"

"I asked if I could stay with her anyway until I got a job."

Penny giggled. "You dork."

"Does that mean I can crash at your place until this is over?"

My best friend paled to the color of her white-blond hair.

"He's kidding, Pen. Did you see Charity after she threw the stone at you?"

Jeff rubbed his chest. "Heck, no. That's why I asked you to get my keys."

"Wait. How did you manage to drop your personal keys? Why would you have them out? You had separate keys for your rental car."

"Optimism. I thought she'd give me her apartment key so I could get settled."

"That's not optimistic. That's arrogant." He had a protest ready, but I talked to Penny over him. "There's a conference tonight. I got a call from June. *All* the sisters will be there."

Missing my ominous tone, Penny clapped her hands together, delighted. "You'll get to meet the other three. How wonderful."

"Do I get to come?" Jeff asked.

If Bowers dropped by and found my ex there, he might have a meltdown, forget his oath to protect and serve, and shoot Jeff. Also, the thought of *the pack* meeting my mistake didn't appeal to me. "That doesn't sound smart. They'll be emotional. You know. Strained nerves. Concern for their brother. They probably blame me for Bowers' troubles."

"What troubles?"

After counting to ten, I said, "Listen up. It is more important than ever we work fast and in the dark. His coworkers are already mocking him because of my former relationship with you. And because I found the body. When I saw him earlier, he blew it off, but I don't know how much more he can stand."

Jeff laughed. "You're overreacting. From what I saw, the other cops all liked him. They were joking a lot."

My left eye twitched. Now that we'd scared Monica away, it didn't look like I'd get a coffee refill. And I wasn't about to talk about other important topics, like engagement rings, while Jeff made snide comments. I elbowed his ribs and told him to move. He obliged.

"I have to prepare for an appointment."

"You mean like a doctor's appointment?" He touched my forehead with the back of his hand. "If you're not feeling good, it would explain why you're so cranky."

I slapped his hand away. "A *business* appointment."

"Business? You mean that store you made me sleep in?"

Penny said, "Ha, ha. As if you didn't know."

My shoulders hunched. "Leave it, Pen."

But my advocate strolled up to Jeff. "She's a pet psychic, and she's good."

"Penny, please." I rubbed my forehead, willing her to drop it.

Jeff smirked. "You're still doing that? I thought after Buffy—"

"Humiliated me?" I clenched my hands into fists. I might have shrieked because several diners looked over, including the old cuss who had it out for me. Why was he still here? Did he have something against homecooked meals?

"No. No." I shook my head until I felt dizzy. "You are not coming with me."

His brow wrinkled. "Gee. If you feel that strongly about it, of course I will. I mean leave you alone. I can hang out with Penny."

Penny's expression, desperation mixed with horror, decided it.

"All right. You can come with, but you're staying in the car."

"It's hot."

"I'll leave the windows cracked."

THIRTY

Jeff and Buffy had been right about one thing. Back in Loon Lake, I made my living as a fake pet psychic. Using the same tricks that mediums and mind-readers have been using for centuries, I simply watched the pet owner's body language as I talked and mixed in common sense and animal behavior knowledge. And I really did help my clients. Just not the way they expected.

Then a golden retriever named Sandy knocked me on my keister when he showed me a murder he'd witnessed. When Sandy opened that door, he let in every other furry, feathered, or scaled creature who wanted to chat.

I'd eventually learned how to control the messages. Sort of. I'd created a monstrous, mental wooden door intended to keep out the whining, nagging complaints from animals. Without it, I'd go insane. By closing that door, I could keep their voices out. Usually. Unless they really, *really* wanted to talk. The truth? Whether they got in was a fifty-fifty proposition, but the door still helped.

As I parked in front of a house on N. Lamont Drive in

Fountain Hills, the one with the rooster weathervane on the front lawn next to the lemon tree, I prepared to converse with a Chihuahua.

Small dogs tended to be the chatterboxes of the animal kingdom. Trying to follow the rush of information gave me a headache. The aspirin were waiting in my glove compartment.

I took a deep breath and closed my eyes.

Jeff poked me. "What are you doing?"

"Be quiet."

Bringing up my mental barrier, I unhooked the lock I'd installed to guard against the more persistent creatures. Once open, I only widened the door a crack. My client didn't require much room, and I didn't want to let anything larger, and scarier, inside my head.

When I finished, Jeff smirked at me.

"Are you preparing for your performance?"

"It's not a performance."

"Don't tell me you've bought into your own shtick."

"It's none of your business. Stay here. I'll be back in about twenty minutes."

I grabbed my purse and exited the car. After ringing the front bell, a car door opened and banged shut behind me. Before I could tell Jeff to turn back, he was standing at my side, and we were looking into the face of a small man with whiskers. If it was supposed to be a beard, Maynard Sewell should surrender hope.

"Ms. Chandler?" He glanced at Jeff and his nose wrinkled.

"I'm her assistant. Mr. Ross."

Since I couldn't punch my assistant with the client watching, I ignored him and stepped inside. My stomach muscles tightened as soon as I entered the living room. Something terrifying lurked behind the paisley print couch. Or past the swinging door on the other side of the room. It floated behind the collection of adorable, tiny teaspoons, and in between the worn leather books on the single shelf. Something big. Something that wanted to play with me before tearing me to pieces. I started to tremble.

Stepping back, I bumped into Jeff. Still feeling the fear, I leaned into him. He was big and muscled and capable of dealing with a fanged monster. When he rested a warm hand on my shoulder, I relaxed. I wasn't alone.

"Ms. Chandler? Hubie is over here."

"Hubie?" I squeaked. Was Hubie the monster? I didn't want to meet the monster. No. Hubie must be the tiny brown dog seated on the couch. He shook so hard his teeth rattled.

"He's been acting strange all week."

Removing Jeff's hand, I adjusted to my professional persona and bent to stare into Hubie's bulging eyes.

"What is it, boy?" I murmured as I created the information highway between me and the animal. In my experience, Chihuahuas fell into one of two groups. Those who wanted to peel the skin off your ankles, and those who jumped if a fly sneezed. Hubie obviously belonged to the latter.

The room turned black as pitch. Fear squeezed my chest muscles so tight I longed to tug the band of my bra loose to allow me to breathe. When I heard guttural panting, I froze, but only for a moment.

My ex was having a laugh at my expense. He must have turned off the lights, and now he wanted to scare me with spook house noises.

"Knock it off, Jeff."

"Knock what off?"

His voice came from far away. Even worse, the panting continued while he talked. It wasn't Jeff.

Suddenly, a gaping maw opened in front of me in 3D. Drool dripped from razor-sharp fangs. A blast of hot, moist breath blew my hair back, and my nostrils filled with the stench of rotting meat. I yelled.

"What's happening? What have you done to him?"

As Hubie's owner swept him into his arms, the connection broke.

"Mr. Wells," I said, resting my bottom on a delicate, embroidered footstool while I recovered my poise. "Do you have a cat?"

The client gaped at me. "Are you serious? Why would I have a cat? I already have a dog."

"Hubie is afraid. *Incredibly* afraid."

"Of what?"

"A cat."

The little man stared.

Jeff let loose a haw-haw. "That's a switch."

I rose, took Maynard Wells by the arm, and led him into the foyer for a private consultation. Sensing I might say something unpleasant, my client left Hubie on the couch.

"Does your neighbor have a cat? Have any cat's been hanging out in the windows?"

He chewed on the inside of his cheek. "They have a big tomcat next door that comes in my yard. I've sprinkled hot pepper over the grass. They say that keeps cats away. I don't know what you mean by hanging around. He strolls through my garden like he owns it, but I've never seen him looking in my window."

Maynard Sewell's gaze darted over my shoulder. "What's he doing?"

I turned my head. Jeff knelt in front of Hubie. He had the index and middle finger of each hand on the dog's temples while he stared into the dog's eyes.

"Leave that pup alone," I demanded.

My ex shushed me.

When I moved forward, Maynard restrained me with a hand on my arm. "Wait. He's performing a Vulcan mind meld."

"Like Spock," Jeff whispered back.

"Doctor Spock?" I frowned. "He worked with children."

"Mister Spock." My client said the name with such reverence, it clicked. Grown men and women dressed in colorful knit outfits and pretending to talk in strange tongues. Nerds. "You mean from *Star Trek*?" There went my credibility.

Jeff stood and dusted his hands together. "That should fix it."

Hubie directed his bulging eyes at his owner.

"Interesting," Maynard said, completely taken in. "What was wrong?"

"Privileged communication." Jeff swept his hand toward the dog. "I'd need his permission before I shared it with you."

"His permission? But he's *my* dog. If he was a child, and I was his parent, you'd tell me."

"How old is he?"

"Seven."

"Seven times seven is forty-nine. He's an adult."

"What in Hades are you talking about?" I demanded.

The client tsked. "There's no need for foul language."

"That's not how you work out a dog's age," I said, my voice trembling. "And that Mister Spock nonsense isn't going to help Hubie."

"Look at him. He's fine."

Maynard and I looked. Unlike when we arrived, the dog sat perfectly still.

Jeff grinned down at his patient. "Our work here is done."

While Maynard headed toward a small antique desk, he sang Jeff's praises. "And to think. It only took you a few minutes to cure him."

I connected to the dog to find out why he'd stop shaking. He envisioned Jeff as a big, dopey canine who had committed to protecting him from the cat.

"Who do I make the check out to?"

"U-Behave," I answered without thinking. "No. Wait. The dog isn't okay. He's still afraid of the cat. We must find out which cat or else as soon as we walk out of here, the fear will hit him again."

Maynard tore the check from the register and handed it to Jeff with heartfelt thanks. All I got was a scolding finger wag. "You could learn a thing or two from this young man."

With his hands in a prayerful pose, my ex bowed to the client. "And the student becomes the master."

"What's that from?" I snorted. "Some stupid kung fu movie?"

Both men gasped.

Taking a deep breath, I tried to reason with Maynard. "Don't you understand? Your dog is still afraid. Maybe it's the tomcat roaming your yard, but if that's not a new situation, it means there's something else out there. Have you been around a cat lately? Pet one? Even been near one? A dog's sense of smell is incredibly fine-tuned."

Maynard glared at me. "You are creating a problem where none exists. I think you want to keep treating Hubie so I have to keep paying you. That's unethical. I should report you. I *will* report you. Who's your boss?"

I grit my teeth. "The Bureau of Psychic Phenomenon." Let him try to find *that* in a directory.

As we exited the house, Jeff suddenly turned back and held up his hand, making a V with the pinky and ring finger on one side and the index and middle finger on the other. Maynard, holding his dog, smiled to acknowledge the gesture. As the door closed, he gazed fondly at Hubie. The dog was still trying to work out what just happened.

Jeff snickered all the way to the car. Once there, he leaned back against the door and pulled me to him. "I felt that."

Pushing against his chest only made him wrap his arms around me.

"The way you leaned into me."

"I was momentarily nonplussed by the gigantic cat. Now let me go and give me my check."

Instead of doing as I asked, Jeff placed one hand at the base of my neck, lowered his head, and kissed me. I froze. For about two seconds. Then I wrenched my mouth away from his. He let go, laughing.

"Wasn't it good for you?"

"Compared to Bowers? You don't even rate."

"Touché." He held out the check in his fingers and grinned. "You're welcome."

I snatched my fee from his fingers and moved around the car to the driver's side. Wiping my mouth on the back of my hand, I made gagging noises. "Ptooey. I probably have Buffy cooties. Ack!"

"This pet psychic stuff is kind of fun. I can see why you do it."

"Argh!"

Once he'd arranged the seatbelt and settled back, he asked, "Where to next? Are we going to find the cat?"

"Shut up."

For some reason, he found that hysterical.

THIRTY-ONE

"We've talked to Bertie. She was first in after Charity. Norma was next. We also need to talk to Charity's other co-workers. Among other things, we need to confirm what Bertie told us. We can take care of everyone with a trip to Friendly Fingers. We'll split up so we can cover more ground, but you're paying for your own massage."

As I stepped through the doors of Wolf Creek's only spa ten minutes later, my concerns over needing an appointment snickered and strolled away. A murder on the premises had cleared the room of customers.

Tammy stood behind the plexiglass in front of the reception counter. She had on a yellow racerback sports bra that bared her middle. She didn't acknowledge us, even when we stood directly in front of her.

"Hi. We'd both like a massage."

She picked up a reusable water bottle and sucked on the straw. "We don't have anything available right now."

After a pointed glance at the empty chairs, I said, "We'll wait."

The expert on women moved me aside. "What's your name?"

He knew her name. I'd told him.

She gazed up at Jeff with limpid brown eyes and arched her back in case he missed her bust. "Tammy."

"Nice name. Is it short for Tamara?"

"Why would it be?"

"Ah. Just Tammy." He leaned forward with his hands splayed on the counter. In his sleeveless black t-shirt, she got an eyeful of his flexed arm muscles. "I really need to relax, and you're just the person to help me."

"But I don't give massages. At least, not at work." She sucked on her drink again until she'd emptied the contents and air rattled through the straw.

Norma stepped out from behind the modular wall. "What's going on, Tammy?" She gave me a wary look and frowned at Jeff, trying to place him. However, as soon as she discovered we were there as paying clients, a smile lit up her features and she pulled over the appointment book.

"Let me see who's available."

Tammy set down her cup. "That's my job."

"And you do it so well, dear."

As Norma scanned the pages, her receptionist leaned against the wall. Her stretchy pants had a bluish bar running up the side, and as she played with her phone, she resembled a model for a magazine article on bored millennials. *How to waste time in style.*

"You were on the front page of *The Gazette*," Norma said, too casual.

Tammy jabbed her thumbs across the screen and settle back to study her phone. She flickered a glance my way, so I knew she was catching up on the news.

"Don't believe everything you read. Paul Simpson

doesn't like me." Determined to avoid getting sidetracked, I added a cheerful lilt to my voice. "Your massage therapists must be extra busy now that Charity's, um, not taking clients."

The spa owner glanced up and ran her gaze over the empty waiting room. "We're adjusting." Perhaps realizing this response lacked compassion, she added a few token sentiments. "Charity was a valued employee. She was a big part of our family here, but we will survive. Technically, for tax purposes, she was an independent contractor, not an employee."

"I would think customers would flock here to see the place where *it* happened."

"Unfortunately, not everyone is as morbid as you suggest. We've had a few cancellations from regulars."

"There's always the hot tub. Once it's done, the new attraction should help you rebound. You know. Lure back customers. Once they forget." My words trailed off, but there was no need to worry about my insensitivity. If she even noticed my *faux pas*, Norma skipped right over it.

She beamed. "Don't you think so? It's a Jacuzzi. Beautifully made with Italian tiles. Jets of hot water are just the thing for sore muscles." She laughed, embarrassed. "Listen to me. Now, is there a massage therapist you'd like to request?"

I moved closer and peered down at the book. "Who do you recommend?"

She picked up a pen and let it hover over the page. "Will this be a couple's massage?"

Jeff said yes the same time I said no. "It will not. Two separate rooms, please."

"Do you prefer a man or a woman?"

"Fred's available," Tammy said just to spite Norma.

"Definitely a woman." Apparently, Jeff didn't want to waste his physique on hairy fingers.

Defeated, Tammy gave her attention to her cell phone.

Ever since I'd heard the name of the business, I'd wondered. Friendly Fingers had the ring of a service that might cross certain lines. Not that I thought Bertie would take part in something unethical, but maybe she didn't know. Only the masseuses were privy to the *specials*.

Folding my arms on the counter and lowering my voice, I said, "Depends on what you mean by *prefer*."

Norma slapped the pen on the counter and gritted her teeth. Tammy giggled. "You don't need to rub my face in it."

I stepped away. "I didn't mean—"

"Gee, Frances." Jeff put his hands on his hips. "Get your mind out of the gutter."

"Friendly Fingers was a *cute* name! It sounded upbeat. It sounded *nice*. You people have dirty minds. I wish I'd called the place Nothing But a Massage, but that would have excluded our other services, like the manicures, wraps and facials."

Before she could throw me out, I interrupted her tirade. "To answer your question, I'll take a girl masseuse." There was no way I was letting a strange guy put his hands on me.

"Dominique is in a session, so there's only Gazelle and Fred. Your friend spoke up first, so he gets Gazelle."

"What about Bertie?" Jeff asked.

Tammy looked up with interest. "She's not here."

He knew darn well Bertie was studying at home, so I wondered what he was up to.

Norma barked out a laugh. "Let's not push it. She has to pass her test this weekend first." She held up crossed fingers. After making a note in her book, she pressed two buttons on an old intercom system. In the distance, I heard a mellow bell chime twice.

The antelope trotted out and, once Norma pointed to Jeff, motioned for my ex to follow her into the hallway. Standing on tiptoe, I whispered in his ear. "Get her talking about Charity's relationships, and not just the people here. Find out why she and Charity were so friendly lately. And don't get distracted by the pretty girl." Not that I thought she was that pretty.

He tweaked my ear. "Back at ya."

That left me with the guy with the handlebar mustache. To my surprise, he led me to the room with the dentist's chair. It also had a massage table.

"It's a little cramped in here because the esthetician uses both the table and the chair," he said.

"This is Bertie's room?" I asked with interest.

"You know Bertie?"

"We had dinner last night." My response didn't answer the question, but it might help if he thought Bertie and I were pals.

"Normally I don't use her room," he said with a note of apology, "but she's not here today, and the other massage room is undergoing changes."

That was one way to describe how the police had stripped Charity's room clean.

"You don't have your own room?"

"I'm a floater. At least I was. Now they need me full time."

"But won't Bertie be full time once she passes her test?"

"*If* she passes it, she'll only be part time. She's still the spa's esthetician."

I thought he should have more confidence in Bertie. However, in a way, she was his competition. I wondered if his full-time status would be in jeopardy if Bertie became a full-time massage therapist.

He gestured to the chair in the corner and told me to take off my clothes.

"Take them off?" I said, stunned.

He smiled. "Is this your first massage? Here's how it works. I close the door so you're all alone. You take off your clothes and get on the table, face down, with the sheet over you. That's all there is to it."

I didn't like being vulnerable, and lying naked in a room with a strange man gave me the willies. "Are you sure it won't work with my clothes on?"

"You can keep your underwear on, but I think you'll be more comfortable nude. I promise not to peek." With a wink, he left the room.

Since I was paying big bucks for this massage, I followed Fred's advice. Once I stripped, I folded my clothes and left them on the chair in the corner, making sure my underwear was on the bottom of the pile. If I'd known someone might see my delicates, I would have worn a pair without frayed elastic. If I owned one.

Once Charity's killer was behind bars, I hoped Bowers would appreciate my sacrifice.

Just as I'd climbed onto the table, adjusted the sheet to cover everything important, and planted my face on a headrest with a gap in it for my nose, someone knocked gently on the door.

"Are you ready?" It was Fred.

"As I'll ever be," I responded.

The massage therapist came in, closed the door behind him, and straightened the sheet. Before starting the massage, he rummaged through the available CDs and chose one. A minute later, sounds of flutes and gentle breezes filled the air.

"You didn't specify what kind of massage you wanted."

I mumbled into the headrest. "There are kinds?"

"The Pretzel is a deep tissue massage to get out the knots." He pressed a spot under my shoulder blade. I yelped. "Or did you want something lighter for relaxation."

I lifted my head. "Relaxation."

"We have the Friendly Fingers. That's the house special. Have you considered the Molten Lava? That uses the hot stones."

At the mention of massage stones, every muscle clenched.

"I'm telling you," Fred continued. "You'll be so relaxed; you'll pour off the table. It's only twenty dollars extra."

"Let's stick to the Friendly Fingers." Casually, I asked, "Do you use scented oils?"

"Chamomile. It will help you relax."

"What about Lavender?"

"Unfortunately, someone had a strong allergic reaction, so we stopped using it."

"Who?"

He uncapped a bottle from the holster hanging from his belt and poured some oil into his hand. "I don't know. It was before my time. A client, I assume. Norma's afraid of lawsuits. Can't say I blame her."

I spent the first few minutes adjusting to a stranger getting personal with my body. Soon, Fred's expert technique and the calming music floating from the CD took effect. My muscles unclenched. I almost hated to talk, but I was here with a purpose.

"It sounds as if Charity's death is a lucky thing for you."

Fred must have lost his balance, because his hands

slipped off my back and into my hair. "Sorry about that." He quickly regained his rhythm.

"Your schedule will be packed now that Charity's not here gobbling up all the business."

"We'll have to see how it goes. It's too soon to guess."

"I would think *someone* would benefit. Not that they wanted her to die."

"Of course not. That's—that's too terrible to contemplate."

"You said you got here at ten to nine that morning."

"How did you—that's right. You were here. I thought I heard—" He stepped away from the table. "Didn't you find her body?"

I turned my head sideways to get him in view. "Sort of. Bertie was there, too."

He rubbed his mustache, grimaced at his hand, and wiped the oil off his face with the back of his wrist. "Was she alive when you found her? Did she say anything?"

"Not that I heard. I think she was gone before I reached her."

He resumed massaging distance and rubbed my shoulders, though the movement wasn't as focused as before.

"Charity was already dead by the time you got here, so if the killer snuck out the back door right after killing her, you wouldn't have seen. But sometimes killers like to see the results of their demanding work. Was anyone sitting in their car out back? Like they were waiting for something to happen?"

"No."

His tone seemed a little curt. Time for flattery.

"You're observant. Like you noticed how late Gazelle gets in every morning. I suppose if she's usually late, that means her coming in after the rest of you arrived on that particular morning isn't, well, suspicious. It wasn't as if she killed Charity, slipped out, and then took her time coming back. Is it?"

He performed a motion on my shoulder muscles that reminded me of Chauncey's forepaws as he dug up my marigolds, but he didn't answer.

"Who do you think killed her?"

He moved my arm behind my back. "Just keep that there." Then he cupped one hand under my shoulder joint and lifted.

"Criminy!"

"Breathe into it," he said, and I swear I heard a smile in his voice.

After several deep breaths, I reminded him that he hadn't answered my question.

"I have no idea." When he jammed his thumb into a spot under my shoulder blade, I saw stars.

"Why don't you relax your muscles? Talking tightens up your neck and keeps you from giving in to the massage."

For the sake of my low pain threshold, the next few minutes went by in silence, but when my shoulders were out of range from Fred's hands, I forged ahead.

"Funny thing. I heard Charity and Norma didn't get along, but just before I came in here, Norma was singing Charity's praises."

"You'd better talk to Norma about that."

He lifted the sheet to expose my hip. My hand shot out and yanked it back down.

"I can't massage what I can't see."

"Oh. Right." I gritted my teeth and let him readjust the sheet. If I focused on the questions, I wouldn't feel so naked. Something off-topic so he wouldn't suspect my motive in asking about the late masseuse.

"Is Tammy related to Norma?"

"I don't think so. Why?"

"She seems like a charity hire."

"What was that?" His tone turned unfriendly, and it dawned on me how close his strong hands were to my neck. I cleared my throat.

"A charity hire. You know. Norma has a niece who's not *all there* and gives her a job to make her mom happy. Tammy seems, um, deficient upstairs."

Fred let loose a deep belly laugh. "I thought you meant Charity hired her. That girl is smarter than she looks."

"Which girl? Tammy? So, she's faking it. What a good actress."

"The boredom? The disinterest in her job and anyone other than Tammy? Not faking it. Her inability to chew gum and talk at the same time? Faking it. Now, enough chatter. Just relax. Do you like what's playing?"

The ambient music had moved on to a mix of flutes and synthesizer noises.

"Sure."

He worked his way around to my other leg, adjusting the sheet as necessary, but by now I trusted him not to yank it off and laugh hysterically. I let him work on a particularly tight muscle for a few minutes before pretending a question had just occurred to me.

"Was Charity a nice person?"

His rhythm slowed as he thought out his answer. "She was all right."

"Which means no. But she must have ticked someone off enough to make them want her dead. In fact, I heard about an incident that happened last week."

"You mean Grant's girlfriend."

"Grant?"

"One of Charity's regulars."

"You mean Grant *Williams*?" Grant Williams was Charity's eight am appointment the morning she died.

"They argued in Charity's room. I couldn't help but overhear some very naughty words, especially as the girlfriend had a volume control problem. She told Charity to back off, which was ridiculous. Charity already has a boyfriend."

"Gosh. What was her response?"

"She could have handled it better." Fred decided to change the topic. "I heard you're taking care of Stripe. It's kind of you. That unfortunate critter would have sat there until kingdom come before anyone remembered him. I mean, a reptile can't bark like a dog to get your attention."

"True."

I took a break from asking questions. "Mmm." My eyelids got heavy, and I was about to drift off when Fred told me to roll over. He held up the sheet as a shield and turned his head to give me privacy, covering me once I'd made the move.

He walked to the head of the table and looked down at me. "Your neck muscles are incredibly tight. Do you clench your jaw a lot?"

"Recently, yes."

"A regular massage would help with that. I can put you on my client list and call you with reminders."

"I'll let you know." From my vantage point on the table, I could see his lips compress and felt bad for him. "It's not you. I might be moving out of state."

"But if you don't move, you'll give me a call, right?"

Unfortunately, now that I'd rolled over, he could see my expression. "You're right. I shouldn't talk," I said. And then I closed my eyes.

THIRTY-TWO

Once Fred finished the massage, he left me to dress. As I was leaving the room, I heard noises. Naughty noises.

"Oh, baby."

That was Jeff's voice. That jerk! Without thinking, I whipped open the next door over and stood, staring. Jeff sat on the edge of the massage table, fully dressed. Gazelle leaned over the table, resting on her elbows. Both broke into fits of laughter.

"I didn't believe him when he said you'd come barging in."

Ignoring my throbbing headache, I shifted my purse and raised my chin. "Apparently, you *like* being used by your clients. My mistake." And I turned on my heels and escaped down the hallway, followed by more laughter.

Back in the car, Jeff asked how I liked my first massage.

"You're a goat, you know that?"

"We were having fun with you."

"Yeah. Fun. Like that awful massage." I rolled my sore shoulder to loosen the muscles.

"Did you get a deep tissue?"

"The Friendly Fingers."

"Huh. That shouldn't hurt. You must be extra sensitive."

I held up my hand and crinkled my nose. "What is that smell?"

"Wasn't me."

"It's nutty." I sniffed my arm. "Chamomile isn't nutty." I leaned across the console and sniffed my ex.

"It *is* you."

"Oh. That. I got the Island Vacation. Coconut oil and a light pressure."

"Did Gazelle use the entire bottle?"

"Sort of. She spilled it on my back. Maybe she's naturally high strung, but she seemed nervous to me. Twitchy."

"The murder probably has her spooked. Did you learn *anything*?"

"Gazelle wasn't much of a talker."

"I can't believe it. You *did* make out with her."

"She's way too skinny for me. Anytime I tried to bring up Charity, she changed the subject."

"Did you ask her if they were friends?"

"Yes."

"Or how other people got along with her?"

"Yes."

"And she said nothing?"

"Not a thing."

I had my own news. "I found out who confronted Charity last week. Fred mentioned a customer named Grant Williams. The same Grant Williams who was Charity's early morning appointment the day she died. His girlfriend came in and argued with your favorite masseuse about the attention she was giving her boyfriend. I didn't get the girlfriend's name."

"Nina." He grinned. "Gazelle didn't have a problem dissing the clients. Oh, yeah. I found out how Charity wound up with so many customers."

Thinking it was nicer not to say anything, I said nothing. He told me anyway, and it wasn't what I expected.

"She bribed Tammy. Gazelle had a lot to say about that. Charity would give the receptionist a kickback for every new client she sent her. It was done on the sly.'

"Then how would Gazelle know?"

"Tammy approached her after Charity died and asked if she wanted the same arrangement."

"And?"

"She told her to get lost." He tapped a beat on the glove compartment. "I've been thinking about those cameras. Anyone who knew how they were set up could have avoided the ones in back."

"That means the killer must be familiar with Friendly Fingers. It could be any one of the employees. Sorry. Independent contractors. Especially if they knew about Charity's arrangement with Tammy. I'd be furious."

"I'm glad to hear there are other suspects," Jeff said. "I think that hot detective thinks I killed Charity. Or might have."

"Her name is Gutierrez. You must admit, you followed the victim here from Wisconsin, fought with her, and your breakup left you in dire straits. You had a reason to be angry with her."

"Disappointed. Not angry."

Surprised, I tried to remember a time when I'd seen Jeff angry, and I couldn't come up with one. I guess you have to care before anger kicks in, and Jeff never got too attached to anyone. Including me.

"I'm aware it doesn't look good," he continued. "You know, I have an interest in solving this case, too."

It wouldn't hurt to be gracious. Much. "I appreciate your helping me and Bowers."

"I want to help me, and I can do that by helping you."

I slipped him a glance. "Are you being honest with me?"

"I didn't think you'd believe me if I came over all concerned about you or your boyfriend."

"Fiancé."

"Not that I'm not concerned. I am, but you wouldn't believe it."

"Probably not." I stopped for a red light. "We need to speak to Grant Williams' girlfriend and find out how angry she was with Charity."

THIRTY-THREE

Jeff found an address for Grant P. Williams in Mesa on East 14th Place next to Hohokam Stadium, home to the Oakland A's. At least for Spring training.

We parked in front of a small ranch house with a lone saguaro cactus standing tall in the middle of dirt. However, under the front windows, flower beds displayed a vibrant mix of color and form. I recognized marigolds and rose bushes. The rest were beyond my horticultural knowledge.

After turning off the ignition, I faced Jeff. "I do the talking. You're here in case the girlfriend thinks I'm interested in her man. I don't want to get attacked." I thought he needed clarification. "You're a body. That's it. Got it?"

He smirked. "I always knew you wanted me for my body."

"Get out."

He unlocked his door. "I think you're wrong about not using my talents."

"And what talents are those?"

"Not to brag, but I know how to connect with people."

He lowered his chin and raised his eyebrows. "Not just chatter at them."

"We don't have enough time for you to suss out Nina's cup size."

"Ouch." We both got out of the car. He leaned against his side with his arms folded over the top. "You're right as usual. You have such a pleasant way with words. You'll win him over in no time. What do you plan to ask him?"

"For his girlfriend's address."

"What if she lives with him? As you know from experience, it's not unheard of."

I slammed my door shut and adjusted my purse. "If she's here, I'll ask her about the fight."

"And she's going to tell you all about it why?"

As I came around the car to join him, I said, "It's *my* boyfriend who's in trouble, so I get to—"

He burst out laughing.

"What's so funny?"

"Did you hear what you said?"

My eyes opened wide. "I meant fiancé. It's your fault. You keep calling him my boyfriend, and I slipped."

He grinned. "You said boyfriend."

My hands balled into fists. "I meant fiancé. Fiancé, fiancé, fiancé!"

He lowered his baritone to a whisper. "But you *said* boyfriend."

"You're an ape, you know that? I think I hate you."

"Hate and love are so similar. Am I the only one getting turned on?"

"Ugh. Yes, you are. Ape."

Leading the way, I noted the only vehicle in the driveway. An older model white Honda Accord. Corroded metal vases sat on either side of the front door, overflowing with dried flowers. No one answered when I knocked. When I didn't get results by my third try, I peered through the crack in the front curtains. A large stereo system placed near the window blocked my view of the front room.

"Back here," Jeff said from the side of the house. I followed him over a strip of gravel to a backyard of cement and rocks bordered by more flowers and shrubs. A man with dark hair sat at a round table under a tan umbrella. If he stood, he'd be about four inches taller than my ex, though Jeff had a bigger build. His glasses had slipped to the end of his nose, and he fiddled with the back of a radio with a small screwdriver that looked miniscule in his large fingers.

He looked up at the crunch of our footsteps.

I gave him a bright smile. "Hi. Grant Williams?"

"If you're selling something, I'm not interested."

I chuckled as if he'd made a joke. "I'm not a salesperson. I promise. I need to ask you a few questions about Charity Samuels."

He fumbled the screwdriver and set it down, closing his eyes and compressing his lips in a pained expression. "Who are you? I already spoke to the police."

"We're Team B," Jeff responded gruffly.

Grant's eyes snapped open. We had his interest.

Glaring, I mouthed *Be quiet* at Jeff, which only piqued our subject's interest.

"What's Team B? You mean FBI?"

Before Jeff could have us both up on charges for impersonating law enforcement officers, I said, "Private."

"PIs? I've never met a PI." He unfolded his long legs and moved to stand.

"No need to get up. We just have a few questions."

"I want to see your badges."

Another glare went to my ex. "We're only required to show them before we arrest you."

"Is that true? I don't think that's true."

"It is for us. Special forces, you know." This lie was sprouting wings. Before it could take off, I said, "You were one of Charity's clients."

That made him sit still. It's well known that people get uncomfortable and chatty when you make statements, so I waited for the flow of conversation.

"Yeah."

Ten seconds passed without another word.

Okay. New tactic. Intimidation.

"Where were you Tuesday morning? You missed your appointment with Charity."

He sighed, bored with that question. "It's like I told the police. I was running late and had to cancel. I tried calling, but no one answered. When I heard what happened, I wished I'd been there to save Charity."

His said this last bit with a dreamy quality. Almost certainly he'd replayed the scenario, this time, with him as the hero. It might have endeared me to him if I hadn't thought he was lying.

A black pickup truck sat in the back of the parking lot when I arrived Tuesday morning, but there hadn't been anyone in it. There had also been a pickup truck behind Friendly Fingers on Monday night.

The guy inside the truck on Monday had been exceptionally tall. Grant must be at least six-foot-six. Quite a coincidence. However, since the pixilated video footage made it look as if a swarm of locusts had invaded Wolfe Creek, I couldn't be sure it was the same truck.

"What kind of vehicle do you drive?"

"What kind of vehicle did you see when you drove in?"

He had me there, so I moved on to point two. "I heard your girlfriend didn't like your relationship with Charity."

He went back to operating on the radio. "Relationship? I didn't have a relationship with her. I was a client. I liked the way she gave massages. I have a lot of tension. After spending so much time on the phone, I need work on my neck muscles."

Call it arrogance, or pigheadedness, but I couldn't let go of my suspicion that Grant Williams was the guy in the truck. "Did you have an appointment with Charity two nights ago? After hours?"

He looked up, surprised. "She took appointments after hours?"

"It didn't have to be a massage appointment."

"Why else would I see her?"

Either he was stalling, or his brain didn't fire on all pistons. "A date."

A tall brunette stormed out the back screen door, her mules clumping as she descended the cement step. Apparently, she'd heard everything. "You've got five seconds to tell me who you are and what you mean by *appointment*."

Smiling, I held out my hand. "I'm Frankie Chandler. And you must be Nina."

She crossed her arms over her large chest, pushing the fabric of her neon pink dress down and giving Jeff a good look at her cleavage. "You didn't answer my question, Missy."

Missy? *Missy?* She did *not* just call me Missy. We were around the same age, give or take. Early to middle thirties.

"Or are you another tramp after my boyfriend?"

"For your information, I'm engaged."

Her eyes flickered over Jeff. She sneered. "You must be dreaming. I don't see a ring on your finger."

If I'd been wearing long sleeves, I would have rolled them up as I moved toward her. Jeff cut me off.

"Hi. I'm Jeff." He grinned and took her hand in his, getting an eyeful of boobs as he stood over her. She responded with a demur smile and made a show of adjusting her neckline, leaving enough chest exposed to keep him looking.

"I'm Nina, Grant's girlfriend." She sent a sorry glance at Grant, who wasn't half as handsome as my ex.

"One of the massage therapists at Friendly Fingers explained how you told Charity off. My girlfriend," he gestured to me, "wanted to hear all about it."

"She's your girlfriend?" Grant pointed the screwdriver my way. "Then you aren't PIs?"

Jeff skirted the question by ignoring it. In fact, he ignored everyone except Nina. That was his talent. Making a woman feel as if no one existed for him but her. Until he wanted an upgrade.

"She thought Charity was hitting on me. Maybe she was and I didn't notice."

I snorted. Jeff noticed. He had radar that gave him a heads up if any woman in the vicinity glanced his way twice.

"But Frances didn't have the nerve to say anything. You're kind of her hero."

Only my extraordinary will power kept me from gagging as Nina ran her critical gaze over me.

"A woman who can stand up for herself is my hero too." Jeff gave her his trademark sexy grin that questioned why the two of you were still wearing clothes.

Grant jumped to his feet, bumping his head on the umbrella. "I don't want my girlfriend to be any guy's hero."

She smirked. "Sit down, Grant. It's nice that someone

appreciates me. *You* told me not to be mean to your little massage woman. I wasn't mean. I was honest." Her tone turned sugary sweet for Jeff. "Won't you sit down?"

Nina thought Jeff needed her help finding the table. She hooked her arm through his and led him to a seat next to her, which left me sitting next to Grant. When she grabbed Jeff's arm, I noticed a tattoo on the back of her hand. A quick glance at Grant showed he had the same tattoo. It wasn't a good tattoo. Purple and shaped like a clown.

The person in the truck parked behind Friendly Fingers Monday night had a tattoo. Or at least a dark spot. Really, it could have been an unsightly mole. But since Charity died the next morning, and Grant seemed taken with the massage therapist, and Grant had a dark spot on the back of his hand...it had to mean *something*.

My ex put his elbows on the table, his chin on his knuckles, and smiled down at Nina. Did I ever think that pose was cute? Nina enjoyed it. She mimicked his position and smiled back, though she had to look up.

"First thing I said was she had no business putting her hands on another woman's man."

"Wasn't that her job?" Common sense spoke up before I remembered I was supposed to be on her side. "I mean, was that Charity's answer?"

"Something like that. I wasn't listening. I told her I was on to her. I told her I was going to file a complaint with the board for unethical behavior."

"The board?" I said. "You mean the Arizona State Board of Massage Therapy?"

She snorted. "Seducing Grant so he'd keep coming back to her."

"She didn't seduce me," Grant said, struggling not to

sound pleased at the prospect. "I have a form of gigantism. I need my tendons stripped."

"Golly." Stripped tendons sounded painful.

"You don't have a disease," Nina scolded. "You're just tall."

He raised his chin with dignity. "Even if that were the case, which it isn't, massage works best if you're regular."

Nina sent him a look that silenced him. "Is that what she told you? And you didn't help. *Charity's so good. Charity knows what she's doing.* When I tried to massage your neck, you pushed me away."

He yanked down his collar, exposing a long red mark. "You scratched me."

She held up her hands, fingers splayed, and displayed two-inch talons. "Some men like that."

"Getting stabbed in the neck?" Grant frowned. "It doesn't feel good."

As they bickered about the various pleasure/pain points, my attention wandered. I could smell something. Something familiar. Standing, I turned to survey the yard, and when I spotted my quarry, I almost cheered.

"Is that lavender?"

Pausing mid-rant, Nina blinked as she gathered her thoughts. "Yeah. It is."

"Do you wear lavender scent?"

"I use it in my bath. Why? Oh. You've heard of my business." She jumped up and scurried into the house.

"Now you're in for it," Grant said with an evil grin.

Nina returned with a large wicker basket that she carried by the handle. She swung it onto the table and pulled out a sachet. After holding it up to her nose, inhaling deeply, and letting out a rapturous sigh, she handed it to me.

A hexagon label, bordered in the same hot pink as her

dress, had the name *Nina's Nummies* written in script, and under that, in purple, *Lavender Dreams*.

The beautiful scenery in Wolf Creek attracted artsy-craftsy people. Apparently, Mesa had the same problem. I took a delicate sniff. "Is it edible?"

Grant threw back his head and laughed. "She's got you there."

"No," Nina said, hammering her words. "They are *nummy* as in *scrumptious*."

Still sounded edible to me. She watched me with a vulture's gaze, so I handed over five bucks. As I tucked the sachet into my purse, I glanced at my watch. One hour before the online conference. With limited time, I took the bold approach.

"Which one of you was sitting outside Friendly Fingers on Monday night? Around nine o'clock in a dark pickup."

If I ever have a chance to tell ghost stories around the campfire, I'll include a description of the way Nina slowly turned her head toward Grant, her expression frozen.

"Grant? What did you do?"

Standing behind my seated ex, I gripped his shoulder with one hand. Nina knew her boyfriend was a killer. He was about to confess to murder. Once he did, the two of them would decide to eliminate the witnesses.

Jeff patted my hand. Fool. His instincts weren't as refined as mine. He wouldn't see it coming. That meant I could get a head start on him when I ran. Good thing I drove.

"I didn't do anything," Grant said. "I just, well, I was driving by Friendly Fingers on my way home from work." He looked at us. "I'm a telemarketer for Bizbo's Insurance. Second shift. We're international."

A telemarketer. I hid my revulsion.

"It's not on your way home," Nina said, her voice trembling.

"It was. I, uh, stopped at a drive-through. Someone let a guy into the spa, and I knew it was after hours, so I wanted to ask if they had extended their hours. That's all." He lifted his chin. "It would be convenient to go later in the day instead of early morning. I just pulled in to ask. And I don't know what you're talking about, hanging around in the back parking lot. I pulled up to the front of the building."

"Who opened the door?" I asked.

"For me? No one. No one answered when I knocked. I thought that was strange."

"Who opened the door for the guy who went in before you?"

He blinked at me. "Charity, of course."

"Are you positive?"

"I...I didn't get a good look. I assumed."

Nina slapped the back of his head, sending his glasses flying. "That's because you've got Charity on the brain."

She berated and he defended as they dove into the argument. My hand still on Jeff's shoulder, I gave it a squeeze. "We have to meet mother in ten minutes, dear heart."

Nina stopped glaring at Grant long enough to roll her eyes. "That's one of the reasons I won't marry Grant. At least not until his mother is dead."

And on that note, we left.

As Jeff buckled up his seatbelt, he said, "Admit it. I was pretty good back there, wasn't I?"

Reluctant to give him praise, I said, "The situation called for your skill set. You're a flirt and a liar."

He clutched his chest. "Fatally wounded."

"All right. I'll give you credit for getting her talking, but only this much." I held my thumb and pointer finger about a centimeter apart. He grabbed my hand and tapped it in a gentle slap before letting go.

"So, Sherlock." He grinned. "Did you learn anything?"

Pleased to be the more observant of us, I said, "Didn't you notice the mark on the back of their wrists? The driver of the black truck had a mark in the same place."

"I was more interested in the truck."

Disappointed that my big reveal hadn't brought me applause, I dared him to deny that Nina was a nut.

"Sure, she is. But a killer nut?"

I thought about it. "Probably not. Although now we know for certain that Nina threatened to report Charity to the massage board. That must have been what the masseuse was emailing about the morning she died. She was trying to get in her side before the complaint came in. We also know that Grant stopped by Friendly Fingers the night before Charity's murder, which makes him the guy I saw parked in the lot Tuesday morning. I think. If only we could see his truck. Because I don't believe that little white Honda is their only vehicle. You'll notice he didn't give me a direct answer when I asked what vehicle he owned."

"So, are they on the suspect list or not?"

Turning my head, I raised my eyebrows and pulled my face muscles down, going for a superior expression. "First rule of investigation, my dear boy, is no one gets crossed off until we're certain."

I started the car. "And that includes you."

THIRTY-FOUR

I wanted Jeff gone before Bowers came by, as he usually did after work. Just to be sure when that would be, I dialed my fiancé's cell phone.

"Detective Bowers."

"Hi. It's me."

"How are you feeling?"

The way he said it lacked enthusiasm, and I wondered how much trouble I was in.

"Are you still going to swing by tonight?"

"If I can. I have to meet with Councilman Samuels at his home to give him a progress report."

"Can't Gutierrez go?"

"She'll be there, too."

A voice called out. "Hey, Bowers. Any leads from the iguana yet?"

His words turned muffled. "*Getting old.*"

When he came back to me, his voice had an edge. "I have to go. I'll stop by if I can."

He hung up.

As I got my laptop ready on the kitchen table, Jeff

wandered the room, bored. He held up one of last night's dinner dishes. I'd left them in my sink.

"If you rinse them right away, they're easier to clean."

"I was busy saving a guy at the Overnight Motel."

"Touché."

While he got my dish rag wet, added soap, and scrubbed, I hopped online.

"I don't care what you do, just stay out of view. Understand?"

He rinsed the first dish. "Am I your dirty little secret?"

"Yes."

Now for the online call. Facing Bowers' sisters and explaining this mess had as much appeal as…it had no appeal. Still, they would give me different perspectives, or make known something I'd missed. At this point, I would have accepted help from Jack the Ripper. I clicked on the meeting link and reminded Jeff to stay out of sight, which was a good thing. They were waiting for me.

I recognized June, looking every bit like a mom with her curly gray hair and her plump pleasant face. The wooden doorframe behind her meant she was in the kitchen with her back to the living room.

Agnes, her dark hair bobbed into a page boy, reminded me of a corporate head. She sat at a table in what looked like a home office. Bookshelves and a printer on a credenza stood out in the background. She folded her hands in front of her, her expression daring attendees to wander from the point of the meeting.

Dymphna, half woman, half ghost, wore a multi-colored outfit in flowing fabric. In her lap sat a small white dog, Windy. The curly tufts on the top of the pooch's head cut into my view of Dymphna's face. That's when the two of them weren't disappearing into the virtual garden background she had chosen.

The other two women were new to me. Both were in their fifties, but that's where the resemblance ended. One was a plump woman with short dark-brown hair whose expression defied all those who assumed jocularity increased with poundage. She wore a faded yellow t-shirt that said *Ask me if I care?* The other wore a serene smile, a modest blouse in light blue with a Peter Pan collar, and she kept her long, greying, light-brown hair loose, except for a sparkling butterfly barrette that held her bangs to one side.

June acted as liaison. "Frankie, you know Aggie and Dym." I waved. Dym returned it. Aggie did not. She was the closest in age to her baby brother and a wee bit protective.

"The woman on my right—"

Dymphna interrupted in her whispery voice; her face framed in flowers. "Agnes is on your right. At least on my screen."

Bowers' middle sister liked to give the impression she flitted between planet earth and the spirit world and filled her hours smelling flowers and petting fawns. Most people bought the act, but I'd seen how well she handled a gun when a bad guy threatened her dog.

"Mary," June said. "Raise your hand."

The woman in yellow flipped her hand in my direction. More of a spasm than a greeting.

"Now you, Martha."

Martha wiggled her fingers at me.

And that was my introduction to two more of the clan.

Martha said, "I'm so pleased to finally meet Marty's fiancée."

"Thank you."

"There's time for chit-chat later," June said. "Give us an update, Frankie."

"Well, Bowers—Marty—is meeting with the victim's father tonight. He's an important Wolf Creek politician."

"That'll be a good career contact," Mary said.

June, ever practical, shook her head. "Only if he solves the case."

They all started chattering about how, of course, little Marty would find the killer because his instincts, reflexes, and general mental abilities made Batman look like a sissy. When June quieted them down, she asked what else I knew.

About to answer, my breath caught in my throat. Two golden eyes on a ginger face appeared on the screen. The dog had his front paws on June's lap so he could investigate what had her attention.

"Chauncey," I whispered.

His broad mouth opened in a grin. When he licked her screen, he left behind a smudge.

"You stinker." June pushed him off her lap. I heard a woof off-screen from Hero, June's German shepherd, and the scramble of nails on linoleum. June turned her head. "It's just Carl coming in." She called out. "I'm on the computer with Frankie and the girls."

He answered with a greeting.

Something in my expression made her take the time to assure me my sweet boy was having a fun time. "They're getting dinner, so don't ask me to bring him back in here." She rubbed at the slobber, leaving a smear on the screen. "Later, they'll go out for a patrol run and settle down with the horses in the barn."

After nodding dumbly, I pulled myself together to

answer her question. "I don't *know* anything, but I've been trying to get information."

"Who's that?" Agnes asked.

I looked over my shoulder. Jeff stood behind me, drying a dish. "Do you have something to snack on?"

"Who is that, Frankie?" Agnes repeated, her tone sharp.

Sighing, I accepted defeat. "He's helping."

"Well," June said, "what's your name, son?"

Jeff slipped into his good-boy routine. "Jeffrey Ross, ma'am."

"Jeffrey Ross?" Agnes squinted. "According to the news reports, you're Frankie's ex-boyfriend. In fact, the story said you two *lived* together. What are you doing with my brother's fiancée? And why are you drying her dishes?"

They all looked to me for an answer, and considering their expressions, it needed to be good. At least it seemed they were staring at me. It's hard to tell on a laptop screen.

My tongue stuck to the roof of my mouth. My moment of humiliation had arrived, and I had frozen like a bowl of ice cream. To my surprise, Jeff saved me.

"Excuse me, ma'am."

Agnes, who was in her early forties, bristled at the moniker. "It's Agnes."

He grinned. "Do they call you Aggie? That's a great nickname. Strong, yet fun. As I was saying, Frances and I dated a long time ago."

"And lived together."

The kitchen knives were two steps away. If only I kept them sharpened, I could commit Seppuku and die an honorable death.

"For a day. After a flood in her apartment building." He gave them a shy smile, expressing deep embarrassment. "I let her have the bed and slept on the couch."

As I stared at him, murmurs of *how sweet* and *what a gentleman* followed. But Agatha wasn't letting him off that easy. "It said in the news story—"

"It might just be me, but I never believe what the papers say. With good reason. I've known personal situations where…let's just say they did a lot of damage."

"Well—"

"He's got you there, Aggie." June gurgled with delight.

"But it said—"

Mary stepped in. "Make up your mind. Either you believe the papers, or you don't."

Agnes frowned. "Of course, I don't. I have a brain and think for myself."

And then Jeff, who considered winning over a group of hostile women child's play, set down the dish, slung the towel over one shoulder, and wove the tale of his deep love for Buffy. How he thought it was forever, how she tore out his guts when she left him, and how, in his pain, he made a grievous error. By the time he got to Charity winging a rock at him, he almost had *my* sympathy.

"You poor thing," Dymphna said, her voice extra wispy. "Did she hit you?"

Like a war veteran reluctantly displaying his battle wounds, Jeff lifted his shirt. A chorus of "Oohs" and "Aahs" followed. Some of them expressed admiration along with pity.

Windy stared into the screen, unblinking. The pooch had Jeff's number down.

"Well, gang?" From the way June's head moved, she was scanning their faces on her screen. "What are we going to do about this? We can't let Marty suffer because of some awkward circumstances."

"It's worse than you think." I explained Gutierrez' role and the promotion at stake. They had conflicting responses.

"A woman needs to do what she can to get ahead," Mary said.

"But at Marty's expense?" Agnes snapped.

"I'm just saying we shouldn't judge her."

Dymphna's gaze hadn't strayed from Jeff. Her lover died last month, and she appeared to be sizing him up for rebound material.

"Let me tell you what I've done so far," I said to move things along.

"What *we've* done." Jeff softened his admonishment with a playful pinch on my arm. If only he'd seen Agatha's grim frown when he touched little brother's fiancé, he would have wiped the smile off his face.

"Fine. *We've*. So far, the solid suspects are a stalker named Grant, his jealous girlfriend, Nina, and the building manager, who they say is kind of a lech. There's also Norma, the owner of Friendly Fingers, Charity's boyfriend, Vali—"

Agatha, shoulders shaking, came up for air. "Friendly Fingers?" She hooted with laughter.

"It's the name of the massage parlor she worked at."

"Spa," Jeff said.

"Massage parlor?" Mary snorted. "A typical job that glorifies in the objectification of women."

Jeff objected. "It's a skill. You have to be licensed and do continuing education." This coming from the man who'd slept with Charity during his first massage.

"She was a grown woman. Nobody forced her to work in the field," Agnes said.

June, who'd been taking down the names on a pad of

paper, asked, "Any other suspects?" And that's when Bowers walked in.

THIRTY-FIVE

Every face froze on the screen, except Windy. Windy yipped. I leapt to my feet, almost toppling my chair.

"You're here."

He took in their expressions. "I am."

"You can't be here," said June, the first to recover. "We're discussing the wedding."

"We're inviting suspects to the wedding?"

She gurgled out a laugh. "That's what we were calling the bridesmaids and groomsmen. Our list of suspects."

He wasn't buying it. "Don't *I* get to choose the groomsmen?"

"That's why they're suspects. We suspect who and how many you'll ask. Frankie needs to know, since she has to have the right number of women to pair up with them. You know, Marty, you're spoiled. You have seven of us, but poor Frankie doesn't have a sister to help her."

Giving my fiancé a mournful expression, I made a note to never spar with June.

Bowers' gaze went to Jeff. "And Mr. Ross is helping with the details?"

"He's been very insightful," Dymphna gushed. "Just wonderful."

"That's surprising."

I'd forgotten to close my mental door and felt a tickle in my temple as something wiggled its way inside my head. Windy growled, and a sudden vision of my ex after the attack leaped in front of my eyes. I clutched the back of the chair to keep from dropping to the floor and gnawing on Jeff's ankles. Quickly nudging her furry butt out of my skull, I slammed the mental door shut.

"What's wrong with Frankie?" Agatha said. "She's making faces."

Grabbing the dish towel, I fanned myself. "It's humid in here."

Bowers, recognizing the signs, looked from Windy to me and frowned.

"Now Marty," June began, "I know you don't like to talk business, but I read on the Internet that a tough case landed in your lap. Is that true?"

"There is? It has?" Martha exclaimed, feigning ignorance. "Why didn't I hear about it?"

Agnes folded her arms. "Do you need our support, dufus?"

He laughed. "It's under control, but thanks."

The sisters jumped in with questions about baby brother's eating and sleeping habits—was he getting enough of both—as well as questions about the wedding. Thank goodness he didn't mention the lasagna. I sat down and wiped the sweat off my upper lip.

"Next time you talk about the wedding, I want an invitation."

"We didn't think you'd be interested," June said. "I forget how different things are these days. Couples' showers. Men at baby showers. In my day, a man showed up at the church and we all prayed he wasn't hungover. We haven't got the next call scheduled, but when we do, I'll send you the link."

After saying his goodbyes, he told them he needed to borrow me for a minute, took my hand, and led me to the living room.

"What happened back there? It's not that humid."

"Windy doesn't trust Jeff."

He snorted. Looked interested. Even opened his mouth to say something but decided against hearing about my *gift*. "I'm glad you get along with my sisters."

"They're great. And I got to meet Mary and Martha. Only one left to go."

His grip tightened. He let go when I gasped, and I shook my hand to get the circulation going again.

"We need to talk about what happened at the station this morning."

My stomach dropped. "Sure. Later. I don't want to leave your sisters alone with Jeff. Dymphna's looking at him with dreamy eyes." I changed the subject. "Do you have much information for Councilman Samuels?"

"Unfortunately, no. Just the usual. It's early days. We've got every resource working on it. That won't be much comfort."

I couldn't let him know what I was up to, but I longed to help him. "Funny thing. When I was running errands today, I ran into a few people."

He pulled his head back and looked down at me. "What kind of people?"

About to make up a story involving a search for the iguana's allegedly missing toy, my promise to never lie to Bowers tugged at my conscience. Making things up was another bad habit from my days as a fake pet psychic. "Well, I went to Friendly Fingers for a massage. Jeff and I did. Separately. I mean separate massages in separate rooms."

"You did."

"While there, I got the impression there was tension between Charity and Norma. Norma *said* Charity was the best thing since sliced bread, but I've heard different."

"Not everyone gets along, and I wouldn't expect Ms. Hinkle to criticize her recently deceased employee."

"True. But there was this one customer's girlfriend. The woman caused a scene last week, accusing Jeff's fling of hitting on her boyfriend."

His lips tensed. "This is the first I've heard."

"Maybe Gutierrez knows and hasn't shared it with you."

Moving his hands to his hips, he said, "That's not how it works, Frankie. We pool our information. Help each other out. More likely, the good citizens working at Friendly Fingers didn't bother to tell us." His tight tone expressed exactly how he felt about good citizens who didn't spill their guts to the police. "So, Charity Samuels argued with a customer. Is that it?"

"A customer who threatened her."

"To hurt her?"

"No. To report her to the board for unethical behavior."

His expression cleared. "The email on her phone was addressed to the Arizona State Board of Massage Therapy. Now it makes sense. She was probably trying to get her side in or even find out if a complaint had been filed." He looked at me, resigned. "I don't suppose you have this client's name."

Squinting my eyes, I pretended to search my memory banks. "It might be Grant Williams."

His eyebrows shot up. "The same Grant Williams who didn't show for his eight o'clock appointment?"

Since I wasn't sure about the truck, I didn't mention Grant might have made it as far as the parking lot that morning. "And his girlfriend *might* be Nina. I can get you their address."

"Frankie, I know you think you're helping," he laughed, "and you are, but I don't want you asking people questions. This is my job. I'm trained for it, and I can protect myself if necessary. Okay?"

I smiled the smile of the innocent. "Good luck with your meeting. Let me know how it goes. And to be fair, I'll tell you all about my appointment with the gerbil. I'll throw in the Chihuahua because I like you."

That made him grin. "I can't wait. But it probably won't be tonight." Embarrassed, he cleared his throat. "Do you have that address?"

I jotted it down and tucked it into his shirt pocket. In return, he gave me a long kiss and added a hug. "I'm glad I stopped by. I love you."

Squeezing him extra tight, I said, "I love you, too."

When I walked back into the kitchen, I must have had a goofy smile on my face, because the sisters stopped talking to Jeff and beamed at me. All except Mary. She seemed indifferent. And Dymphna. Jeff had pulled a chair next to mine and joined the conference call. She stared at him with a worshipful gaze that worried me.

As I sat down, I moved to detach the bond growing between the two of them. "I forgot to mention. Jeff is a Protestant-Episcopalian-Methodist-Baptist. PEMB for short."

Mission accomplished. Their smiles dimmed, and all

thoughts of matching him up with a Catholic friend, or, in Dymphna's case, coveting him for herself, disappeared.

"She's joking," he said in his defense, but the damage was done, especially when he added, "I'm not religious at all."

"We need an action list," June said, briskly moving attention away from the heathen. "I've written down the names of the suspects. The boyfriend seems the most likely. Let's start with him."

"Vali said he last saw Charity the night before she died. She left him at half past seven because of her early appointment." I explained about the late-night visitor to Friendly Fingers and how it might have something to do with her death. Or might not. Charity didn't die until the next morning.

"You can't say for sure Charity opened the door to the client Monday night," June said to clarify.

"No. And if she had an early appointment, I don't see why she would agree to a late-night appointment. It doesn't make sense."

"If she didn't die until morning, why are we wasting time on the night before?" Mary lifted her shoulders in an exaggerated shrug.

"Be nice," June warned.

"She has a point," I said. "We found out about the after-hours massage and the truck parked behind the building before we knew what time she died. Both circumstances seemed odd, so we thought they might be important."

"My vote is for the owner," Agnes said.

A little yellow hand—the *raise hand* feature—appeared next to Martha's face. "Have we finished with Vali?"

Agnes brushed the boyfriend away with a dismissive gesture. "Talk about the boyfriend all you want. I think the owner killed her. Employees can be a royal pain. It was—what did you say her name was?"

"Norma," I said.

"Norma owns the place. She must know everything that goes on inside those walls. She's responsible for it, anyway. Charity gave her lip one time too many, and that was the end of her. Another thing, an owner would be the first one there in the morning, right? She could have killed her and gone back to her office."

I clapped my hand over my mouth, then lowered it. "No matter who killed Charity, that person could have been hiding behind the modular wall in the reception area when I came in. I called out, but I never checked."

Agnes nodded. "Thank your lucky stars you weren't killed, too."

"Don't be silly," Mary put in. "The person drowned her. Did this Norma person carry around a bucket of water just in case she needed it?"

"You weren't listening," Agatha said. "The killer hit her on the head with a massage stone first."

"They aren't sure about that," I said, but Mary forged ahead.

"You think he or she hung onto the stone in case someone else walked in? If it was the owner, she expected her employees to show up any minute. I assume she didn't intend to attack them all."

"That's a great point." I searched their faces. "What did she, I mean the killer, do with the rock?"

Dymphna raised her hand. "She could have returned it to nature."

We all stared.

She massaged Windy's ears. The pooch leaned her head back in ecstasy. "Maybe she put the massage stone outside with a bunch of other rocks so it wouldn't be noticed."

"If it were me," Jeff said, with an apologetic glance for Dymphna, "I would have put it in with one of the other massage therapists' hot stones. If anyone found it, the other massage therapist would get the blame."

The ladies looked at him with respect, including me.

"I'm sure the police went through everyone's kit," June pointed out.

"Darn." Martha covered her mouth and apologized for swearing. "We should have asked Marty."

"Except he's not supposed to know we're talking about the murder, honey." June tapped her finger on her notebook. "Who else?

"The client, Grant Williams, has a girlfriend who didn't like his relationship with Charity."

Agatha raised an eyebrow. "Did he have one?"

"I thought he seemed a little, um, attached to her. What did you think?" I looked at Jeff.

"Grant was obsessed. Obvious."

Mary snorted. "If I was his girlfriend, I would have killed *him*, not the massage therapist."

"But she reported Charity to the licensing board instead," I murmured. "That would have taken away her motive to kill because she'd already delivered a blow. If I reported someone, I'd want them alive so I could see the fallout." I looked up. "Don't you think? She got it out of her system. Why would Nina bother to report Charity if she wanted to kill her?"

Mary squinted. "Or maybe she reported her to throw the police off her trail. Women are clever that way."

June checked her watch. "I know we haven't covered

them all, but I've got to get dinner on the table, so let's move on. What are we going to do about these suspects?"

As we went down the list, I made notes, though I crossed off Martha's suggestion to simply ask them all if they did it. "Confession is very freeing," she insisted. "I'm sure the killer would feel better after he got it off his chest."

Mary objected. To the use of the word *he*, not the idea. "A woman is just as capable of murder as a man."

"Make it *he or she* and get on with it," Agnes said.

By the time we signed off, I had a list of eight action items, most of them unfeasible. I put a line through *follow them all*.

"Don't be a downer," Jeff said, putting away my washed dishes. "I thought that was a promising idea."

"Can you bi-locate? Because I can only be in one place at a time. And how long do we follow each one? You'll never get out of Wolf Creek."

"Okay, smarty. What about confronting each suspect and telling them we know they did it?"

My pen hovered above that line, ready to strike it through. "That's an effective way to get killed."

"Not if we're both there."

"I'll give you that one," I looked over the list, "but I'm not prank calling each one pretending to be Charity contacting them from the grave." That suggestion came from Dymphna.

Toying with my pen, I struggled to find the words to thank him for preserving my dignity with my future in-laws. "That was, um, I appreciate—"

"It wasn't their business."

"And I hope I didn't hurt your feelings when I called you a PEMB. Dymphna's emotionally vulnerable right now. It looked like she was interested in you, and I thought you might need help extracting yourself from—from the attraction."

"No problem. I should thank you. Her dog was creeping me out."

In the end, we had three options. "We confront each suspect saying we know they did it. June vetoed that, but Agnes thought it was a great idea, seconded by Mary. Two. We talk to them all again and see if we missed a clue." I tapped my teeth with the pen. "I don't see what excuse we could use to see them again."

"What about another massage?"

"And invite Vali and Grant and Allen Whitmore?"

"There aren't enough masseuses, even if Bertie jumped in to help out, which she can't until after this weekend."

"Three. We let the police handle it. Also, from June. But that defeats our purpose of helping Bowers without him knowing."

I tossed down the pen. "This is pointless."

"Don't be a Don't Be, Frances. Be a Do Bee."

"That is so lame." Still, I laughed.

"You and I can start talking to people tomorrow. I say we decide our approach when we get to each person."

"Deal."

He stood. "I've got to find someplace to stay. Somewhere Vali won't find me." He held up a hand. "Not here. Your boyfriend made that clear."

"Fiancé," I said as he walked out the door.

THIRTY-SIX

The rest of my evening went as expected. Horribly.

My gardening gloves were in the utility closet. I donned them before I did toilet duty on Stripe's terrarium. Uncertain if iguanas were sensitive to soap, I simply cleaned his droppings, put them in a paper sack, and promptly tossed them and the gloves in the garbage. The outside garbage. I was taking no chances with salmonella.

Even with the improvements to his home, the iguana refused to send me a helpful hint as to who killed his pet parent. Not even a silhouette of the doer of the deed.

Frustrated, I took a shower—in case salmonella spread through air molecules—and turned in for the night. Between the warm winds drying everything in their path and the occasional batches of clouds disbursing humidity, my night's sleep promised to be uncomfortable. I opted to give up my blanket to save on expenses rather than turn the air conditioner down. After once waking to the coyotes making a kill, I *never* slept with the windows open.

Stretched out under my sheet, I delved into the recesses of my memory, searching for questions I'd left unasked.

Why hit Charity *and* drown her? Why not one or the other? I imagined what it would take to repeatedly hit someone on the head. Maybe the killer hit her once to stun her and then decided the stone was too messy. And personal.

Did Grant Williams' visit the night before have anything to do with the murder? It could be nothing more than a coincidence.

"Oh. Hello."

Emily jumped onto the bed and snuggled under my armpit. I nudged her away.

"You're too warm."

She plowed into me with her head. After ten minutes spent playing that game, my eyelids drooped, and I gave up for the night.

My lights were already off, so I rolled onto my side, punched my pillow into shape, and moved Emily's tail off my face. And that's when I heard a tinkle of breaking glass.

Jerking to an upright position, I held my breath. Had I imagined it? Maybe passing teens had tossed a bottle in the street. I clung to that hope until broken glass crunched under a footstep.

Grabbing my phone from the nightstand, I powered it up under my sheet to hide the light. I had Bowers on speed dial.

His voice mail kicked on. Short and stoic. *Leave a message.* I muttered, "Pick up, pick up, pick up," but when I heard another crunch, I stifled a cry and disconnected. At least the burglar walked slowly, perhaps scared of waking me. That gave me time.

Somebody swore. It sounded closer than the crunch. Were they headed this way? What did they want? One look at my furnishings and any self-respecting burglar would abandon hope for a decent score.

I slipped out of bed as silently as possible and searched for a weapon. All I could come up with was a cat toy, a bird that swung from a stick.

Creeping into the hallway, I clung to the wall until I reached the door that went into my living room. With my back against the wall, I leaned my head sideways and peeked into my living room.

The sliding door stood open. Shards of glass sparkled in the moonlight, eliminating that escape route. Once my bare feet had suffered the inevitable cuts, I'd never make it over my wall, especially if my invader pursued me. The chilly desert night air sweeping in sent a cool wave over me. I wrapped my arms around my middle and shivered.

Shadows made my own living room unfamiliar. Threatening. My uninvited guest could be lurking anywhere. Suddenly, one of the shadows moved, and I screamed. It wasn't a classic scream, like the heroine in a movie. More of a shriek and yell combination. But it did the trick.

My intruder streaked toward the patio and disappeared over the wall. I ran after him, her, it, and as I paused to navigate the glass, I heard scuffling and the solid thump of someone large landing on the cement.

I took off in the opposite direction. If I hadn't been screaming, I might have heard the keys in my front door. I grabbed for the chain just as it burst open. It caught my left shoulder and hip, and the impact sent me spinning like a top before I landed on my face.

Bowers crouched at my side. "Oh, honey, I'm sorry. I'm so sorry."

On hearing him, relief turned into tears, and I sobbed

into my carpet. When he grabbed my left shoulder with one hand and pulled to turn me over, I cried out.

"Okay. Okay," he said as he released me. "Which way did they go?"

"The back door."

"I have to leave you for a minute. I'll be right back."

At the crunch of glass, I raised my head in time to see Jeff stroll in. Bad timing.

Bowers holstered his gun. "That's it! I am going to kick your a—"

"Bowers! It wasn't him." Using my right arm, I pushed off the floor and got to my knees. Both men rushed to my side when I whimpered. "Not the left side. Don't touch the left side."

Bowers swung my right arm over his shoulder, lifted me, and carried me to the couch. He set me down gently, but I still winced.

He ran his hand over his mouth. "Tell me what happened before I lose it."

There was a five-minute delay because I sucked in a breath and hissed, "Emily." The search ended under my bed, where my cat had curled into a tight ball. I closed the bedroom door to keep her from getting out the broken patio door. Or the broken front door. When I returned to the couch, Bowers sat next to me.

"Talk to me."

"I heard glass breaking. I called you, but I got your answering machine."

He ran a hand over his hair. "When I listened to the message, I heard you cry out. Then the call disconnected."

Turning my head to look at him, remembered fear washed over me, and I started to tremble. "I couldn't find you," I wailed and burst into tears.

He swore and pulled me close, careful of my left side. "Shh. It's all right." He stroked my hair while I choked and slobbered on him.

Jeff picked up the story. "She called me and said someone was in the house. When I got here and she didn't answer the door, I might have overreacted."

"How?"

My crying jag had reduced to sniveling, so I detached myself from Bowers, though he kept his arms around me.

"The shadow heard Jeff and left by the back way. I ran for the front door, and when Jeff kicked it in, it knocked into me."

"You screamed," Jeff said in his defense. "I didn't know what was happening in here."

I furrowed my brow. "How did you get here so fast?"

"Since I couldn't afford a hotel, I thought—I preferred the dead end on your street to the desert."

Bowers raised my chin with his finger. "Did you get a look at the person?"

"I was more focused on getting to safety."

"Good decision."

While I talked out my terror, Bowers evaluated my arm. I could lift it and move my fingers. It just ached. He got up and positioned his body to block Jeff's view before he pulled back the elastic waist on my bed shorts, making me lean into him so he could see the hip joint. It figured that the first time my fiancé touched me intimately, it wasn't any fun. When he finished, he patted me gently and adjusted the shoulder of my nightshirt.

"I'll take you to the ER so a doctor can have a look, but I think you're just bruised." He set his jaw. "You're coming home with me."

"I can't leave Emily and Stripe alone. What if the person comes back?"

"I'll spend the night on your couch and keep watch," Jeff offered.

It seemed like a promising idea, but the thought of getting dressed and traveling somewhere made me ill. "Can't I just sleep in my own bed tonight and see how I feel tomorrow? I can't face getting dressed and answering questions."

Bowers gave it some thought and turned to Jeff. "I'm taking the couch. You can have the floor."

Jeff stooped and picked something up. When he tossed it in the air, I saw it was one of the bricks that lined my patio.

"The person must have thrown this through the window."

Bowers groaned. "Well, if there were prints, they're gone now."

"You can get prints from a brick?" Jeff asked with interest.

"Probably not, but we could have tried."

After walking me back to my room, Bowers left and returned with two kitchen towels filled with ice. He made me turn onto my right side, and he applied the homemade ice packs. Once he arranged them, he removed his shoes and stretched out on the bed facing me so he could hold the one on my shoulder in place. I wiggled closer so I could lean my forehead against his chest.

"What do you think the intruder was after?"

I lifted my head to gaze at the terrarium on my dresser. I'd placed a heavy book on top of the mesh lid to keep the curious cat from flipping it open.

"Could be. Who knows he was here?"

"Norma gave him to me. And Bertie saw me with him. And Fred knows."

"Fred?"

"My masseuse. Everyone at the spa probably knows. I brought him with me to Allen Whitmore's office. And I assume Vali knows where he is. Maybe."

"But why would anyone want an iguana?" Occasionally, Bowers slipped back into feigning ignorance of my abilities. It made him feel better, close to normal, so I didn't mind.

"I understand he's rare."

"So, he's worth money."

Emily came out of hiding and joined us, snuggling into the small space between Bowers and me. Her fondest desire was to push me over the edge so she could have my fiancé to herself. Like me, she adored him.

He shifted the ice pack on my shoulder and Emily swatted his arm, demanding playtime. She had to settle for ear scratches from me.

"How did your meeting with Councilman Samuels go?"

He blew out a long stream of air that tickled my face. "It's difficult talking to a victim's family. It's worse when it's a parent."

Resting my hand over his, I squeezed. "I'm sorry."

"It's part of the job. The worst part."

"Did any of what I said help?"

"It all did. I was able to give him some concrete examples of how we're working to find his daughter's killer. No one at Friendly Fingers mentioned anything about Norma and Charity not getting along. We'll see if they are more forthcoming tomorrow. And now we have Grant Williams and his girlfriend on our list." He moved his hand down to my waist. "However, none of what you found out was worth it if this was the cost."

"It's my own fault. I heard Jeff kick the door once and should have guessed he'd keep kicking. I panicked."

We lay there in silence until it was time to remove the ice packs. As he was leaving my room, I called out to him.

"What do you need, Frankie?"

"Could you stay with me until I fall asleep?"

He gave me a gentle smile. "Sure thing. Let me put the ice away."

I nodded off before he returned.

THIRTY-SEVEN

When I woke the next morning, I wondered if a car had entered my bedroom and run me over during the night. Slowly, my memory of the previous evening's events came into focus.

Once I inched out of bed, I hung my bathrobe over my shoulders. Moving stiffly, I peered into the living room. Someone had cleaned up the glass. I'd slept so soundly I hadn't heard the vacuum. Tape held cardboard over the hole in patio door. As for the front door, a kitchen chair wedged under the doorknob kept it closed.

The form curled on the couch had light-brown hair. Lured to the kitchen by the aroma of coffee, I found Bowers sitting in his chair with a mug and a plate covered in toast crumbs. He was in his slightly wrinkled dress shirt which, knowing how bad I was with an iron, added a homey feel to the scene. When he saw me, he pushed his chair away from the table, but I told him to stay put, poured a cup for myself, and joined him.

"How do you feel? Do you want me to take you to the doctor?"

"I feel...bruised." Raising my arm, I moved it around to show him my range of motion hadn't been impaired. My hip protested more, but it moved. He could see the bruise on my arm. He winced when I showed him my hip.

"You were lucky." He sipped his coffee, peering at me over the edge of the cup. "I'm sorry I wasn't there for you."

"Don't be. You were working. Last night I babbled because of the shock."

"If Jeff hadn't been available...."

"But he was. And this isn't something I can see happening again, can you?"

He grimaced. "Once is too much."

After a final swallow that drained the remains, he stood. "I called in a favor. The man's name is Hector Mendoza. He'll be here around noon to replace your doors. He'll show you identification."

He slipped on his jacket. The same jacket he wore yesterday. Was I getting proprietary? Wanting my fiancé to look his best when he collared the bad guys?

"I spoke with Jeff. He'll stay with you today. Don't try to ditch him. I'll feel better if I know you're not alone."

I stood and wrapped my arms around his neck, wincing slightly as I stretched out my sore shoulder. "I could come to work with you."

He blanched at that suggestion, and everything I'd said to his coworkers came rushing back.

I lowered my arms. "Or not."

He placed them back around his neck and held me by the waist. "You need to understand something. Bad jokes and ribbing are how we let off steam. It doesn't mean anything." He grinned. "They enjoyed replaying the scene. Over, and over, and over again."

"Who played my part?"

His smile tightened at the corners.

"Don't tell me Gutierrez."

"She's the only female detective we had. She had to fight Jennifer for the honor."

"The desk sergeant?"

"We gave her a consolation prize. She gets to be jackal of the week."

Groaning, I leaned my forehead against his chest. "I'm so embarrassed."

"Get over it. Because they are never going to let you forget. Ever."

"You'll have to go to office parties alone."

Using a Bogart voice, he said, "Toughen up, sweetheart."

I laughed. "Okay."

"So, you understand it's not personal?"

"If you say so."

"I don't like seeing you get that angry over something silly. Save it until we're married. I'll give you plenty to get mad about."

He gave me a warm kiss. With his lips still against mine, Bowers said, "Though it was nice having someone go to bat for me." He lifted his head and looked thoughtful. "After I got over the fear. But now I know if I'm unconscious in an alley at the mercy of a psychopath, I can count on you to come to my aid." He kissed me again, rubbed noses, and left.

In the living room, Jeff snored lightly. I gathered an outfit from my bedroom and carried it with me to the bathroom. With my ex-boyfriend wandering around, I didn't want to get caught between rooms in a towel.

I was still in the hallway when my front door opened.

"It's just me," Bowers called out, and I went to greet

him. He looked at me, still in my bathrobe and holding my clothes, and gave Jeff a poke.

"Wha—?" My ex rolled over and sat up.

"I need a ride to the automotive shop. My battery is dead."

Jeff stood, stretched, and scratched his chest. "I'll take a look."

Bowers glanced at his watch. "I don't need you to look. I need to pick up a new battery."

My ex ignored him and shuffled toward the door in his boxers.

"Pants," Bowers said.

"Right."

While I threw on my sweats and a t-shirt, I heard someone moving around my kitchen, but by the time I finished, both men were outside.

Jeff had popped the hood on Bowers dark-gray Ford Explorer and both men leaned over the engine. I hung over the side to observe, at least until I saw what was in Jeff's hand. I moved around the car to get a closer look.

"Is that my turkey baster?"

My ex had also taken my kitchen towel, my baking soda, and my toothbrush. Using the latter, he scrubbed the place where the wires met the battery.

"How am I supposed to brush my teeth?"

"I wasn't going to ruin mine," Jeff mumbled, concentrating.

Once he'd made a mess, he rinsed with water from the baster, dried it off, and reconnected everything.

"Try her now."

Bowers slid into the driver seat and turned the key. The engine started right up.

Jeff gathered his equipment and let the hood slam shut.

Leaning his elbow on the edge of Bowers window, he grinned. "Just some corrosion. That'll be fifty bucks."

"Very funny. How about I give you a place to stay tonight instead?"

"Even better."

After Bowers drove off, I skipped the shower and tackled dressing. Throwing on sweats didn't count. It took me longer than usual, but when I stepped out of my bedroom, I had on a white blouse with three-quarter length sleeves to hide the bruise, navy slacks, also to hide the bruise, and had managed to apply makeup. My hair I left loose. If I controlled my expression, no one who looked at me would guess how miserable I felt.

Jeff was in the kitchen in jeans and a sky-blue t-shirt, rummaging through the refrigerator for breakfast.

"You need new carpet. My neck hurts. So does my face. And I need to do laundry."

Cutting in front of him, I leaned into the fridge. Orange juice. Half a loaf of bread. An apple. "Tell you what. You take a shower, and I'll make toast and pour juice. Or we could go to Penny's. My treat for fixing Bowers' car."

At the mention of Prickly Pear, he brightened. "Give me five minutes."

THIRTY-EIGHT

I lied. We didn't go directly to Prickly Pear. First, we hauled Stripe, Emily, and Emily's bed, litter box, food, and dishes to Bowers' place. With Hector focused on fixing my doors, my cat might pull off an escape. Plus, I wanted Stripe in a witness protection program of sorts, which meant only I knew where he was. And Jeff.

My ex had to do most of the heavy lifting, but he didn't complain. He also had to drive his rental car because my arm hurt too much to operate the steering wheel without grunting.

His rental was a bright-yellow Hyundai. Not really his style, but when I asked if they were out of pickup trucks, he called me shallow.

"It's got everything I need. Good mileage *and* it's a top safety pick."

"How adult of you not to care about your image."

"My own car is different. When I'm driving someone else's car, I stick with the essentials."

It was a ride, and that's all that mattered to me. Soon we were at Desert Villas. Bowers' townhouse backed up against a golf course. The walkway from the parking lot to his front door cut a trail through pink stones and native plants tastefully arranged, like the entrance to a charming hotel.

The buildings were light peach stucco with white window frames and doors. Bowers had an electronic lock. He had given me the backup key so I wouldn't have to remember the code.

I'd told Bowers I felt like a visitor in his home. Really, it was fear. Fear that I would break something. I opened the door, and we entered my fiancé's domain.

He had drawn the beige speckled drapes closed to keep the sunlight out and the rooms cool. I switched on a lamp with a chocolate brown shade and looked around for a place to set Stripe. And the litter box.

A large brown leather couch rested against one wall with a dark wood coffee table holding a few books on the lower shelf. From the pristine top, the television remote ruled the room. The coffee table, along with all his furniture, came without dust.

A few paintings, one of Peruvian dancers and another of a modern art piece featuring guitars, decorated the walls. Above the fireplace, a reproduction of *September Morn* hung in an antique gilded frame. Not a bare spot available for my quail painting.

In pride of place sat the soft leather recliner placed on an angle in front of a wide screen television set. Jeff let out a low whistle and moved to set Stripe on the coffee table so he could investigate the television.

"Wait. I haven't thought this through."

A counter separated the kitchen from the living room. No door to keep Emily and the iguana apart. I scratched her ears.

"Looks like it's the bathroom for you, little lady." Then I

changed my mind. My cat needed room to roam. The iguana couldn't leave his terrarium anyway, so I set Emily down and slid the litter box from the top of the terrarium.

"Put Stripe in the downstairs bathroom."

While Jeff did as I asked, I put the litter box in Bowers' kitchen because marble patterned tile would be easier to clean than the thick, off-white carpet. I pulled her food and water dishes out of my bag. After filling them both, I placed them on the floor against the silver-and-black refrigerator.

Back in the living room, Emily sprawled on her back soaking up Bowers' scent. When Jeff returned from his errand, I nodded. "I feel better. Let's go."

Ten minutes later found us back in our usual booth at Prickly Pear, flagging down Monica. Jeff joined me after buying the morning paper from the machine outside. He insisted the ritual made him calmer. Masochist.

Monica kept her distance from Jeff, who had ignored the unoccupied bench across the table and settled in next to me. She raised her voice and took our orders from about seven feet away.

"The usual," I said, and when Jeff raised his brows, I told him corned beef hash.

"That's right. You're a hash addict." He said he'd have the same thing, and once the waitress filled our coffee cups, we were alone.

"Who's our top suspect?" he asked. "The break-in changes things."

"Right now, I think we should talk to Grant. Without Nina. He was the guy in the truck both times. I just know it. And he seems creepy when it comes to Charity. And both he and his girlfriend have a tattoo on the backs of their wrists. Maybe it's a gang symbol."

He snorted. "That's not a tattoo. It's a stamp. Like from a concert. It's probably washed off by now."

"What concert?"

"I don't know, but you get a stamp so you can get back in if you go to the parking lot. I guess it could be for an amusement park, but you don't have one out here, do you?"

"Not in Wolf Creek." I toyed with my spoon. "Speaking of concerts, Penny said that night we got separated at the Kenny Chesney concert, you connected with someone who wasn't me."

He blew on his coffee. "Honestly, Frances, I don't remember."

"You have sex with someone and it's not even important enough to remember?"

Suddenly, he grinned. "You're not my girlfriend anymore, so I don't have to argue with you about it."

"I'm not arguing," I snapped. "I'm trying to understand. At the time, I thought our relationship meant something."

"It did. I'd never lived with anyone before. You were special."

"But not special enough to stay faithful to. How many other women were there?"

He leveled his gaze at me. "Let it go."

I had to because Penny took a seat across from us. "I wish I could do something to help."

"Talking with you helps, Pen. A lot. I count on you to keep me sane."

"Speaking of losing your mind," she said with a giggle, "how did the Zoom call go?"

"We got a lot of ideas."

"That's great."

"Lots of useless, useless ideas. We're going to meet with

our list of suspects again and—how did you put it, Jeff? Decide on our approach when we get there."

Penny gave my ex a quick glance. "I'm glad you're going with her. You keep her safe or else."

Stretching his arms to show off his muscles, he grinned. "I did a pretty good job last night."

"What's that supposed to mean?" My best friend's nostrils flared, and I swear her ears flattened against her head. If she'd been a horse, I would have backed away, slowly.

"Someone broke into my house. Jeff got there right before Bowers and saved the day."

Her eyes opened wide. "Did you catch the person?"

"No, he didn't, but he did destroy my front door breaking in. And he ruined possible evidence."

"Details," Jeff murmured.

When Monica brought our orders, she had help. Penny's senior waitress, Ann, a stout middle-aged woman, accompanied her. Ann had a daughter of her own at home to defend from hormonal males, so she had bodyguard experience. She kept her watchful gaze on Jeff as the younger waitress set down our plates.

"Do you need anything else?" Ann asked, daring my ex to suggest something.

"Frances? Penny? No? We're good, thank you, ma'am." Jeff gave her a winning smile. She chuckled as she left us, recognizing a schmoozer when she saw one.

My ex let me get one mouthful of hash down before he ruined my appetite. "Have you seen the *Gazette* this morning?"

I swallowed. "No. And I don't want to."

"That's the right attitude," Penny said. "It wouldn't help

you to know that Paul Simpson announced..." She caught Jeff's eye. "Stuff.

"Well, it was kinda funny."

"Funny how?" I asked. Jeff fidgeted and played with his coffee spoon, dying to tell me. I sighed. "Okay. Tell me the worst."

"He has *no* news. Do you Jeffrey?" Penny attempted to make his head explode with her fiery gaze. "None."

When the muscle in the corner of my friend's mouth spasmed, an uncomfortable sensation wormed its way into my belly. "Maybe you better tell me."

Jeff stretched one arm over the back of the booth. "He said you and I were a crime solving team."

My fork slipped from my hand and clattered on my plate. Choking on my breakfast, I covered my mouth with a napkin until I recovered sufficiently to ask, "Us? You and me? He announced it to the world?"

The wedding was off. As soon as Bowers learned I'd ignored him, he'd dump me. His sisters would start writing poisoned pen letters. I was a marked woman.

"He was being sarcastic," Penny snapped. "Didn't you read the part about hurdling over commonsense? And speeding past the Wolf Creek police force with complete disregard for their authority? He also said Stripe was the brains of your outfit. Sarcasm, Jeffrey."

"You're not giving him credit," my ex protested. "He was concerned for Stripe's welfare. I call that considerate."

"That was later. In the part where he described the vagaries of a demented woman who thought she could communicate with animals. Sorry, Frances. That's what he said. He worried about Stripe's welfare and warned that anything was possible with a delusional woman. Except solving the crime."

I came out of my horror-induced trance. As I pushed my way out of the bench, my feet tangled with Jeff's, and I only avoided a face plant when he lunged and grabbed the waistband of my pants. My hands, which I'd thrown out to catch my fall, dangled in the air, and my feet weren't touching the ground. If only he had let me fall, I might be in a lovely, peaceful coma by now. But I wasn't, which meant I had to face the problem.

"Move, move, move," I shouted at the floor like a drill sergeant as the blood rushed to my head.

He set me down and righted me. "Where to?"

"We're running out of time. The only way Bowers will ever forgive me is if we serve him the murderer on a gold platter. We need to talk to the rest of our suspects before they read the newspaper. No. Wait. I need to talk to Stripe again before they get to him. Shoot. I need to do both."

He took my face in his hands. "Frances. Calm down. They would need a search warrant to enter your house, right?"

I took a deep breath. "Right. Unless...Bowers has a key. He could just go in there and get the iguana. If the police are looking for the iguana, he'd have to."

Jeff grinned. "But Stripe's not there, is he."

"Right. You're right."

"Frances," Penny said. "Just because it's in the paper doesn't mean the police are going to care. At least, not right away. Their first concern is the murder. Besides. They might talk to Norma and find out she *gave* the iguana to you. *Somebody* needed to care for him. And those people don't want to talk to you anyway." She smiled. "Maybe Paul Simpson's article will scare them into cooperating."

Blowing out a stream of air, I said, "You're both right." I glanced up at Jeff. "You can let go of my face now."

He did so and pinched my cheek. "You're cute when you freak out."

Though I wanted to believe their comforting words, deep down I thought Penny and Jeff resided in fantasyland. Of course, Bowers would hear about it. If he didn't read the paper, his chums wouldn't be able to resist rubbing his nose in Paul's article. I put on a brave face.

"We should get moving so we can get back to my house in time for Hector the door guy."

THIRTY-NINE

Jeff said I should let him handle Grant, and as I was physically sore and mentally frustrated, I acquiesced. When Nina responded to his knock, I had to fight to keep the smile on my face. Didn't these people work?

She had on pink stretch pants and a matching tank top, and from the heavy, floral scent washing over me, she had indulged in one of her Nummies. Naturally, I jumped right in without waiting for Jeff.

"Where were you and Grant last night?"

She stepped outside in her bare feet and closed the door behind her. "You two are starting to creep me out, especially after what I read about you in the *Gazette*. What's your deal?"

"Someone broke into my home. Was it you?"

"Does this have anything to do with Charity?" She clenched her hands into fists. "Even dead I can't get rid of that—"

The door swung open, and Grant stood there. "Who is it? Oh. It's you."

"Where were you last night?" I asked.

He took a step back with a worried glance in Nina's direction.

"Frances is confused," Jeff said. "But that's to be expected. She took a knock last night when someone broke into her home. We're here because I wanted to talk to you about your truck."

We all stared at Jeff.

"It's a 2009 Ford F150, right?" He made a skimming motion with his hand. "Sleek."

Grant's lips twitched. He was bursting to smile like a child with a supersized lollipop, but he kept his features set on cool dude casual. "Thanks."

Jeff put his hands on his hips and looked thoughtful. "I wasn't a fan of the platinum trim, but it grew on me. The 248 horsepower is what makes me happy. Can I take a closer look?"

Nina perked up, too, but for a different reason. "Do you want to buy it?"

Folding his arms, Grant gave his girlfriend a dirty look. "I told you, Nina. I'm not selling. Ever."

"Fine. Men and their toys." She went back inside and closed the door, leaving me outside to play with the men and their toys. Grant told us to wait a minute and retrieved the keys. While he did, Jeff grinned down at me.

"Once I noticed the model and good condition, I knew that truck was the way to open him up."

"You were able to identify the make and model on that fuzzy security tape?"

"Easy as pie."

Grant led us to a gate in the back fence. We crossed an amazingly clean alley to a garage that resembled a large shed. Grant opened the door the old-fashioned way, by pulling it up by the handle. He invited us inside while he popped the hood on his F150.

As soon as the two men leaned over the engine, I looked for someplace to sit down. This was going to take a while. Resting my bottom on an old paint can, I set my elbows on my knees and my chin in my hands and left Jeff to it.

"You keep her clean," my ex said. "Nice."

Grant rubbed a hand over the bumper. "She's my hobby."

Ten minutes later, my eyelids drooped, and my fanny was asleep. I stood. "Speaking of hobbies, I forgot to ask you something about Charity."

Standing so fast he hit his head on the propped-up hood, Grant spun around. "That topic is off limits. It's none of your business."

Defensive sputtering. I ignored it. "We noticed this beautiful truck parked outside of Friendly Fingers on Monday night around nine o'clock. Parked out *back*. That doesn't sound like you just stopped by."

He slammed the hood shut and beelined toward the gate until I called out, "I also saw you there Tuesday morning."

Executing a reverse spin, he came at me and only stopped when Jeff blocked his access.

"I went for my appointment, okay? While I was waiting, you showed up. The door was open, obviously, so I followed you in. You weren't in the lobby."

"And you followed me inside? Wait. Did *you* go out the back door while I was in Charity's room?"

He recoiled, scandalized. "No! I got there early once and walked back to the massage room on my own. Charity got *very* angry. So, I waited a few minutes. When she didn't come get me by five after eight, I got uncomfortable and went outside to call. Then I heard sirens and saw the ambulance come. When the first police cruiser pulled up, I got out of there."

"Weren't you curious? What did you think happened?"

"I thought Norma had a heart attack or something. She is older."

"Sheesh. She's only fifty or so."

Crossing his arms over his chest, he squinted his eyes and gazed at something down the alleyway. Both tells of someone who's uncomfortable. "The thing is, I told Nina I was going to the gym. She would have been furious if she found out I'd gone for a massage."

I stepped around Jeff. We stood side-by-side, and I gave my partner a nod.

"This makes Monday night even more interesting."

Jeff, eager to reinforce our identity as a team of PIs leaned in and lowered his voice, but not enough that Grant couldn't hear him. "You think? Could be." He shook his head at Grant. "Dude."

It worked. The telemarketer tried to read what lurked behind our deadpan expressions. "What? What?"

I sighed. "I know why you *said* you went there Monday night, but what's the truth? You were in the back parking lot. We know you were. Did you kidnap Charity, hold her hostage until morning, and kill her?" Penny's suggestion sounded just as silly when I said it. Jeff coughed to cover a laugh.

"I—what? You're crazy."

"Yeah. My mind works that way when I don't have the truth. So, maybe the truth is better?"

Glancing at Jeff with the resentment of one betrayed by a fellow car lover, he gave in. "I parked my car in back because I was worried. When no one answered my knock, I realized she was alone in there. The guy might have been a maniac. After all, he had California plates."

"You noticed his plates?"

He repeated the number by heart, and I took it down on the back of a receipt, which was not very professional for a PI.

"Did you talk to Charity that night?"

"No. She must have left out the front."

Jeff and I exchanged a glance. "Try again," he said. "No one left out the front door except the client."

"Look. I waited until ten o'clock and she never came out the back door. I swear."

When I asked what he and Nina had been up to last night, they were both at her place of work. She waitressed the evening shift at Cowboy Tom's Bar & Grill. Grant sat at the bar and chatted with the staff, who knew him and could verify he was there.

Back at the car, I said, "Do you believe him?" My left side had stiffened up, and I struggled with my seatbelt. Jeff snapped it in place for me and started the car.

"I do, but I don't know what it means."

"Maybe the guy who stopped by was there for something other than a massage. To work on the hot tub or something. I never got a look at the office behind the reception area. Did you?"

He said he hadn't.

"Maybe there's a cot or couch in there and Norma stayed to let him in and spent the night."

"Why would anyone sleep at a spa?"

I looked at him. "Why would anyone spend the night in an animal behavior store?" I suffered a stab of guilt and added, "By the way, you did a decent job back there."

"We make a good team."

My phone rang. I didn't recognize the number, but I thought it might be Hector, so I answered.

"Is this Frances Chandler? Also known by the nickname Frankie? Originally from Loon Lake, Wisconsin?"

It was a woman with a penetrating voice that made me think I might not want to be Frankie Chandler.

"That's me?"

"You don't know?"

I cleared my throat. "This is she."

"This is Edith. Edith Bowers."

Bowers' sister? June must have given her my number. "Um, it's nice to meet you."

"Why?"

Why indeed. "Because you're related to Bowers?"

"Is that what you call him?"

"Um, yes."

"I just found out about Marty's problem. Take care of it, or I will."

"What's that mean?" I said, but I was talking to dead air. She must have meant the *problem* we discussed on the Internet call, right? Or could she be talking about this morning's online edition of *The Gazette*? Was I the problem? I sure hoped not.

"Bad news?"

The phone rang again. If it was Edith calling back, I had to answer. She'd know I was ignoring her, and I didn't want Edith Bowers to dislike me. If she didn't already. I pressed answer and waited.

"This is Armando Cozzani. I'm one of the reptile curators at the Sonora Desert Reptile Rescue. Is this Ms. Frances Chandler?"

"Um, *nein spreche los, la,* um, *el inglés.*" And I hung up.

"You do realize you were speaking both German and Spanish, and neither of them well."

"That was a reptile rescue."

Jeff's eyes left the road and we both said, "Stripe."

"What's the guy doing reading a crummy paper like *The Wolf Creek Gazette*?" I demanded.

"Maybe Paul Simpson called him."

I checked the time. "Thank goodness we left him at Bowers' place. Right now, we need to get back to meet Hector. Just in case, avoid the driveway. We'll park down the street, go around the house, and climb the wall."

Jeff grinned. "An action scene for Team B. It's about time."

FORTY

We were still on Main Street, headed for my house, when I remembered the California license plate number Grant gave me. We were about to pass the Wolf Creek police station. I grabbed Jeff's arm and said, "Pull in here."

The tires on the rental car screeched as Jeff broke hard and turned into the parking lot. He swung into the closest space and left the car idling.

Bowers' coworkers would think I couldn't take a joke, especially after my last visit. If they'd read today's newspaper, they'd have plenty of fodder for their comedy routines. Someday, there would be an office function, like Randy's retirement party. Bowers would want me to go, and it seemed unlikely he'd allow me to make a furtive entrance and hide out in the women's restroom all night. I didn't have the energy to dread something that long.

Taking my fiancé's advice to *toughen up*, I decided to walk right into the jackal's den and pretend nothing had happened. Even if they had a new routine.

Jeff insisted on waiting in the car. "Not a chance I'm going back in there. They might not let me out again."

And so, I pushed through the glass front door alone. To the right, the small waiting area had benches and chairs arranged so people wouldn't have to stare into the faces of their fellow guests. All the seats were empty, so there wouldn't be witnesses if the encounter went south.

Dead ahead, behind the front counter, the same desk sergeant waited to greet me. When she recognized my face, her body gave a little jerk, but she held her expression in check.

Reaching the counter, I mumbled, "I'd like to see Detective Martin Bowers."

She pointed behind me. "Is that him?"

When I turned to look, I didn't see a soul.

"I have—"

She'd distracted me so she could slip on a fur hat with pointy dog ears and stuff wax fangs in her mouth. Though she was the only person present, I could sense the rest of the crew listening from their offices.

My face got warm. "Yep. I get it. Jackal of the month."

She arched her fingers into claws, made a few swipes, and growled.

Stay positive, Frankie. "You do that well." Thinking it might sound more friendly, I added, "Jennifer."

Laughing, she spit the fangs into her hands. "Bowers isn't here."

About to walk away, I fought back pettiness. The license plate number should be in police hands, and Juanita Gutierrez qualified as police. "How about Detective Gutierrez?"

"Not here either."

Resting my arm on the counter, I appealed to her, citizen to police officer. "I need your help. I'm not sure who else to ask for. I have information on the Charity Samuels murder that might be important."

She still had on the hat, and she toyed with one of the ears. "Who's your source? The iguana?"

A wheezy giggle rang out from one of the offices, confirming we had an audience.

I sighed and dug the grocery receipt out of my purse. "It's the California license plate number of the car that pulled up to Friendly Fingers on Monday night a few minutes after eight. The guy that went inside."

She slid off the hat, and the humor left her expression. At the same time, Randy, a tall man in his early sixties, stepped out of his office and joined us. Other detectives leaned out their doorways to watch. All of them had a hungry look in their eyes.

"Good day, Miss Chandler. May I see that?"

I handed Randy the receipt. He read the plate number back so I could confirm my lousy handwriting.

"That's right."

"If you don't mind my asking, where did this come from?"

"His name is Grant Williams."

One of the detectives standing in a doorway turned back into his room. Once they were through with Grant, I'd be hearing from Nina.

"Do you know how he managed to get it?"

"He said he pulled into the parking lot at the same time as the California guy, and, well, he liked Charity. A lot. Since it was after hours and nobody answered at Friendly Fingers when he knocked on the door, he got concerned and took the number down. That's what he said."

Randy held up the paper. "What was he going to do with it?"

"Search me."

He nodded. "We might have more questions for you later."

"Sure."

He smiled, meaning it. "And thank you."

"No problem."

This time, I walked out of the Wolf Creek police station with my head held high. They weren't so bad. They might even be glad to see me next time I came in.

FORTY-ONE

Getting over my back wall was harder than I anticipated. Unable to put pressure on my sore arm, Jeff had to lift me by the waist and set me on top of the wall. I didn't appreciate his grunt as he raised me. Once I swung my legs over, I dropped to the ground, careful to land with more weight on my right leg.

Jeff easily vaulted the wall and dusted his hands together as we both turned toward the perfectly good glass patio door leading into my house. I grabbed the handle and tugged, and when it didn't budge, I swore.

Cupping my hands to block out the glare, I pressed my forehead against the window and searched the room, jumping back when a shadow moved from my kitchen to the front door.

"There's someone in there."

Before I could stop him, Jeff rapped on the window. The shadow turned around. When I gave a tiny wave, it moved across the room, morphing into a medium-sized bearded man in jeans and a brown shirt. He unlocked the door and slid it open a few inches.

"Can I help you?"

"Hi. I live here."

He glanced at the wall over our shoulders, noting it lacked a gate. "Why didn't you use the front door?"

"Um, we didn't want to disturb you."

Pulling the door open to let us in, he welcomed me into my home with a grin. "That was considerate. So, what do you think?"

I stared blankly until I realized he was gazing at the sliding door. "Oh. It's perfect. I appreciate how you made time for me."

"I owe Detective Bowers." That's all he said, so I didn't know whether Bowers had loaned him his car or kept him out of jail. "Let me show you the front door." He paused to stare at Jeff, so I introduced them before we continued.

The fiberglass door resembled wood painted moss green. Six inlaid rectangle panels decorated the front under the peephole. An attractive glass accent of opaque oranges, blues, and white gave my entrance a touch of class, but the most impressive feature was the lock. The handle had a spot in the center for my key, but directly above sat a digital keypad.

"Wow."

"I have an instruction booklet on how to set up the code. I'll leave it with you so you can take your time and pick a number. Don't be one of those people who use 1234, or your birthday. Too easy to crack."

Jeff, being a man, wanted to see how it worked and discuss electrical components, remote access, and automation. Finally, I asked my ex if he would pick up Stripe and Emily from Bowers' place. I wanted them out of there before my fiancé returned.

"I'm supposed to be your bodyguard. At least that's what I heard your boyfriend say. I was still half-asleep."

"Fiancé. And I'll be fine with Mr. Mendoza."

Jeff looked him over, shrugged, and left.

"Do you have your cell phone on you?" Hector asked. When I pulled it out of my purse, he held out his hand and grinned. "Detective Bowers asked me to take care of this part for you."

Since I have a hard enough time finding the answer button on the screen, I happily handed it over. After downloading and opening an app, he walked me through my ability to check the locks from any location and, if I'd forgotten to lock it, to do so remotely through the press of a button.

"What if I forget the code?"

"You can reset it, but you'll need your password."

"Me and passwords don't get along."

"Is there's someone you trust enough to share it with?"

"Bowers. Definitely Bowers."

"You can also have a separate code for each person."

"As long as I only have to remember one."

Hector, under the impression I was kidding, laughed. He removed two tarps from the floor, and after asking for my vacuum, cleaned up his own mess. I retrieved my wallet. "How much do I owe you?"

"Your fiancé took care of it."

Blinking back my surprise, I said, "Oh. Thank you."

As he was leaving, Detective Gutierrez and a wiry bald man in tan slacks and a black t-shirt took advantage of the open door and stepped inside.

"Don't I have to invite you in?" I asked. "Or is that vampires?"

She gestured to the man. "We're here for the iguana."

The detective slipped him a dirty look, one that said he was wasting her talents.

I blinked back alleged surprise. "You're looking for an iguana?"

The man, impatient with our clever banter, let loose. "A Fiji Crested Iguana. I'm here to rescue him."

"Norma Hinkle said she gave him to you to take care of," Gutierrez added.

"That doesn't call for a rescue. Besides. There's no iguana here. You can search the place if you like."

The man wasn't comfortable going through my underwear drawer, but Gutierrez had no problem taking me up on my offer. I wouldn't give her the satisfaction of accompanying her.

The reptile guy made eye contact, so, I smiled. "It must be nice to work with animals all day."

"You have to love them. Fortunately, I do."

After Gutierrez checked out the kitchen, she approached me until she stood uncomfortably close. I could smell her breath. Surprisingly sweet. Rose water, I thought.

"Where is he?"

"Not here, obviously."

"Do you deny you took Stripe from Friendly Fingers?"

"The way you put it, I organized a clandestine operation and stole him. It wasn't a secret. Norma gave me full permission to take care of him." I turned to the expert in all things reptile. "And good thing, too. They'd forgotten about him. No one had fed him for twenty-four hours. The pitiful guy was prostrate with hunger."

Armando wasn't impressed. "Iguanas can go two weeks without eating."

"That doesn't mean they like it," I snapped.

"We're going to find that iguana," Gutierrez said,

spurred on by the challenge. "It will go easier on you if you tell me where he is."

I could have told her, but I wanted another shot at talking to Stripe. I thought I could break him.

"Easier? I haven't done anything wrong."

Her upper lip raised in a snarl, and I felt a zing in my chest. I must have winced because she looked at me funny. She looked at the entire room funny.

"Where's your cat?"

"My cat?"

"I don't see him."

"Emily. She's a girl. She's probably hiding."

A slow smile spread across her face. "*She's* not *here*. But I know where you might keep her." She motioned to Armando. "Come on. I think I know where to find your iguana."

Poop, poop, poop. If she got to Bowers' place before Jeff left, how much trouble would my fiancé be in? Not to mention me and Jeff. It was as if she read my thoughts. A slow smile spread across her lips.

"I definitely know where it is."

FORTY-TWO

Jeff didn't answer my first call. Or the second. I sweat it out until he appeared at my door ten minutes later, the terrarium in his arms. I pulled him inside. "Gutierrez is on her way over to Bowers' place."

As he set Stripe down, he snickered. "I know. I saw her pull up. She didn't go in, though."

I clutched his arm. "Did she see you?"

"Relax, Frances. She didn't. Let me get Emily and I'll tell you all about it."

While he retrieved my cat, Bowers called.

"I'm meeting Juanita at my place. Is there anything I should know before I open the door? Any surprises I'm not going to like?"

"Nope. Not a thing."

"You're sure."

"Let me think about it."

"Frankie?"

"I'm kidding. Nothing should be out of place. Although I did drop Emily off there for a while so Hector wouldn't spook her. There might be a little litter on the floor in your kitchen."

"Litter. That's it?"

"Yep."

"Did Hector make it?"

"The doors are installed. He was a very nice man. I'll have to pick a code for the lock. Maybe we could do that together later?"

"Sure," he said, sounding pleased. "Why don't you drop by tonight. I'm bushed, so I'm turning in early. How's five-thirty?"

"Perfect. I'll bring dinner."

No response.

"Pizza."

"Perfect. See you then."

"Wait. I heard from Edith today."

"Is she there?" His voice, edged with panic, rose an octave.

"No. Should I expect her?"

"I hope not. What did she say?"

"She didn't make a lot of sense. She said I should fix things or else she would."

He swore. "I've got to go."

And then he hung up, leaving an unpleasant cloud hanging over me.

I told Jeff about my plans for the night, meaning he should find something else to do tonight. He took it with good grace.

"What do we do until then?"

"I think we should talk to Norma again about the tensions between her and Charity. I wonder if it's true?"

"Well, duh."

Staring, I unconsciously mimicked Bowers by saying, "Explain."

"Charity brought in a lot of business. Well, we've discovered that Tammy *gave* her a lot of business. She told Norma it was time to make her a partner or else."

"Or else? Sounds like a threat to me. Maybe Norma killed her in self-defense."

"Or else she'd leave, knucklehead. Charity wasn't a hoodlum."

Having zero tolerance for threats, I said, "Let her leave. She couldn't have been worth that much."

Jeff grinned. "Tammy gave her the clients initially, but Charity kept them. Forty percent of the spa's business. She liked working longer hours, and her clients liked her."

"If she gave them the same service she gave you, I can see why."

"She was good at her job. I was an exception. She'd split with Vali, and I'd just broken up with Buffy. We were both at a low point, and it just happened."

"Amazing how that kind of thing *just happens* to you."

We drove in silence until we reached the strip mall. When we got there, Jeff continued past, while I leaned out the passenger window and gaped.

Vehicles occupied every available space. Jeff turned right at the next corner, and we discovered the overflow parking. Not only did cars line both sides of the street, but a news truck, double-parked, blocked our way.

"You find parking. I'll see what's happening."

I jumped out and trotted to join the group, who had their attention fixed on a couple in their late fifties. Both the man and the woman wore black suits.

Allen Whitmore stood on the periphery with his hands clasped respectfully in front of him. I sidled up next to him.

"Is someone having a sale?"

"Those are Charity's parents. Her father is making a plea to the public."

Councilman Samuels had distinguished silver hair, a thick build, and a double chin. The woman, slightly padded in her knee-length skirt, buttoned jacket, and pearls, would have looked good for her age had she not compressed her lips and stared ahead like a zombie.

"And the reward for information leading to our beloved daughter's murder stands at one hundred thousand dollars. And if you kill the son-of-a—"

Mrs. Samuels clutched his arm. "Mark." Her clear alto shook with emotion.

He patted her hand. "My wife is reminding me that Charity would have wanted us to remain positive." He scanned the people standing in front of the spa's entrance. The Friendly Fingers massage team. When his gaze landed on Norma, he nodded and she stepped forward, uncertain.

"I wasn't going to say anything, not now, but in keeping with Charity's wishes for good news, well, we're honoring my daughter's memory with a plaque over the new Jacuzzi at Friendly Fingers." His voice caught. "Charity would have loved that Jacuzzi."

Allen approved. "Isn't that nice?"

Embarrassed, the owner of Friendly Fingers Spa gave the cameraman a quick smile and a nod before retreating into the background.

"Again," Councilman Samuels continued. "If anyone has any information, please contact the Wolf Creek police department at—" And he gave their number.

"It's probably not the right time to approach him and tell him I'm sorry about his daughter," Jeff said into my ear.

"And when he asks who you are, what are you going to tell him?"

"Good point."

The reporter with the microphone finished her spiel, and it was over. The crew packed up their equipment. Those still left in the crowd returned to their cars and drove away, though one group jaywalked to El Diablo.

By the time we walked into Friendly Fingers, Tammy had assumed her position behind the plexiglass, with her face buried in her phone, as usual.

"Hello, Tammy."

Her eyes raised just long enough to identify us as homo sapiens.

"Whatcha looking at," Jeff asked.

"Stuff," she mumbled.

Her clothing choices for today were black stretch pants and either a workout top or a bra, I couldn't tell which. Both were covered in white and gold triangles as if confetti had exploded and stuck to the receptionist.

"I'm a curious gal."

She didn't care.

"And my curiosity makes me ask why you didn't park in the parking lot Tuesday morning, the day I found Charity in the hot tub."

Tap, tap, tap. Her thumbs flew over the screen. I longed to reach behind the plexiglass and snatch her toy away. To shock her out of her hypnotic state like a television PI. *Listen up, dirtbag. We got you and your scum bucket accomplice dead to rights, and we'll go easy on you if you spill it all now.* Except there was no accomplice. Just dopey Tammy and her mesmeric cellphone.

Jeff scooted me aside and went to work repairing his

success ratio. I'm sure his *Tammy/Tamara* failure still smarted.

"Are you wearing Tiffany Jordon's?"

Her thumbs paused. "Yes."

"I knew it. You can't mistake her brand, and if I may say so, she targets her designs for people with your figure."

After deliberating, she slipped the cell phone into a side pocket, leaving a rectangular bulge on her thigh. "Do you think so?" Angling her arms out to her sides to unconsciously mimic the triangles on her outfit, she slowly turned, swaying her bottom at the appropriate moment to make the design dance. When she concluded her rotation, Jeff's praise was sincere.

"Definitely."

She answered my question, the one I wasn't sure had penetrated her brain. "I parked at the coffee kiosk and walked back. I do that lots of times." Her gaze ran over and discarded me. "You have to exercise when you can. Unless you *like* your body that way."

I want the extra pounds behind my punch when I knock you flat. Okay. I didn't say it out loud. Besides. She'd given me what I wanted. An explanation for her late arrival. But then I thought of another question.

"Was the Monday evening appointment, the one that took place after hours, in your appointment book?"

She pulled out her phone. "That's confidential."

"No, it's not."

Her lips parted, showing confusion.

"Confidentiality only covers what happens during a business's posted hours. Anything after hours is public knowledge."

"Oh. Then no." For the first time, the receptionist

displayed emotion. Anger. "No one is supposed to schedule their own appointment. It's my job."

"Do you know who booked it?"

"No. If I did, they would be in big trouble."

"I can see that. Now, may we speak with Norma?"

She wrinkled her brow. "Norma doesn't give massages."

"That's good because we don't want a massage. We'd like to talk to her."

"About what?"

Jeff leaned forward. "My friend and I need to talk to Norma about," he lowered his voice, "*what happened* earlier this week."

She blinked. "What?"

"To Charity."

"Oh, that. Charity's dead. I hope you didn't have an appointment with her. I can't reschedule you today. We're booked."

Jeff turned to me, once more out of his depth. I leaned back my head and called Norma's name. She scurried out from behind the modular wall.

"Good heavens. What's happening?"

"Sorry about that," I said. "Tammy was having difficulty understanding us."

Norma's glare bounced off the young woman, who, once again, clutched her security blanket cell phone. "Tammy understood just fine, didn't you dear."

The young woman didn't answer except for a slight smile.

"Could we step into your office?" I asked.

"My—oh. Of course. Is it about Stripe? A policewoman came by with someone from an animal rescue. I told them you were caring for him. Funny they didn't already know."

While she talked, she let us come through. We passed

Tammy and went behind the modular wall, which was the backdrop to a small cubicle. A desktop covered with paperwork and a computer extended from the wall, and there was only one chair. No cot.

"The police are so busy they sometimes forget details," I said.

"How is that going?" She laughed, uncomfortable with the subject. "Are the two of you, uh, getting along?

"We're fine. Anyway, we aren't here to talk about Stripe."

Norma sat down and spun her chair to face us. "Okay. What's so important that you disrupted my business? Heavens. Our customers probably heard you yell."

She didn't have customers right now. Not unless every massage therapist had abandoned his or her client to listen to Councilman Samuel's statement. I apologized anyway.

"We wanted some clarity about Charity."

"A poet and didn't know it," Jeff murmured, and I elbowed him.

"What about her?"

We could be about to unveil the killer. Or embarrass ourselves. Either way, I kept my muscles tense, ready to move. "We know she threatened you."

"I don't know what you mean."

"You don't?" Was Jeff's information bad? Maybe Charity indulged in some fantasy bragging to impress my ex.

Jeff smiled. "She wanted to become your partner. Charity told me all about it."

The pen in Norma's hand snapped in two, and she grabbed some tissues to sop up the ink. Once she tossed it all in the wastebasket, she smiled.

"I was a nurse for twenty years." She looked to us for a response.

"Thank you for your service," I said.

She nodded. "I gave a lot of service. Helped deliver babies. Held people's hands while they died. It was rewarding, but it was tough. When I got an opportunity to start my own business, I was so excited. Finally, I could help people in a way that didn't involve needles, and blood, and...other fluids. I opened Friendly Fingers, brought on some massage therapists, and went from there." She tapped her desk a few times with her index finger. "I built this place. I'm extremely fair to my contractors. I pay them more than the usual rate and don't whine when they need time off. I'm a great boss."

Again, she waited for agreement.

"Sounds like a good deal," I said, eager for her to get to the good part.

"I think so. Two weeks ago, Charity asked for a private meeting. I stayed after work to meet with her, thinking she was unhappy with her room or wanted to change her hours. But no. She explained how this business, *my* business, was dependent on her good graces, and how she would condescend to stay if I made her a partner so she could share in the profits."

At this point in her recitation, Norma's hands trembled. She clenched them into fists.

"What did you say?"

"I told her I'd think about it. Fat chance. I started calling massage therapists and offering them a higher percentage. I was not about to give in to that," she unclenched her fists, "to that opportunist."

Nodding to show my agreement, I said, "And so, when you found yourself alone with her Tuesday morning—"

"Are you saying...I didn't *kill* her. Oh, no. Don't be silly. I couldn't kill anyone. I spent my life *saving* people." She beamed at both of us. "It's awkward, I know, that I can't think of anyone else who would kill Charity. But I can't. Killing is so unnatural. It must be a monster."

Monster, indeed.

"You said you called Vali, Charity's boyfriend about the iguana."

"I did. He said he didn't know what I was talking about. A lie. Isn't that suspicious?"

"Did he ever visit her here?"

"He picked her up several times. That's how I met him."

"Did they get along?"

"I wouldn't know. We didn't talk about our personal lives."

Scrunching up my face, I said, "Hmm. That makes it doubly odd."

She eyed me warily. "What's odd?"

"That you would allow a plaque of Charity to mark your new hot tub. Sorry. Jacuzzi."

With effort, she put on a smile, but anger simmered in her eyes. "Councilman Samuels is a very important man. I didn't like to say no." Her eyelids fluttered. "Because he's grieving. It would have been insensitive to deny him this opportunity to memorialize his beloved daughter."

I kept pushing. "But it's *your* Jacuzzi. Made in Italy with beautiful tiles you chose after a lot of thought. Not Charity's. But now everyone who sees it will associate your lovely project with the woman who planned to blackmail you out of half your business. Doesn't that make you angry?"

Instead of forcing a reaction, my goading brought her

peace. She relaxed into her chair. "Life's not fair. It goes much smoother if you know how to compromise." She smiled. "When you're stepping into a hot tub to relax after a soothing Friendly Fingers massage, would you bother to walk to the opposite wall to read a plaque?"

If I were honest, no.

She saw my answer in my face and craned her neck to ask Jeff. "How about you?"

"Not a chance."

"See? I made a compromise that will make him feel he's accomplished something but won't matter one bit. No one will read the plaque. No one will remember Charity."

We spent the next ten minutes telling Norma how strong she was for starting a second career, how she'd created such a relaxing environment, blah-blah-blah. By the time we left, we had Vali's phone number.

"I wouldn't blame Norma if she did it," I said with a noise of disgust.

"That's harsh."

"Think about it. If you built a business from the ground up with your sweat and money, would you be okay with someone demanding to take half ownership?"

"Charity brought in a lot of business."

"She was *given* a lot of business by the pretty little idiot behind the counter in exchange for a payoff."

"Still, it's fair."

I snorted. "So like a guy."

"What's that mean?"

"I don't know, but I suspect it means you wouldn't think that way if it were an ugly ogre who demanded half of Jeff's Autobody Shop."

"Jeff's Autobody Shop. I like the sound of that." He pulled a face. "But I see what you mean. It stinks, but so does business in general. I mean, life's not fair. Look at me. I lost my job because I broke up with my girlfriend. Tell me that makes sense."

"It doesn't. I already told you I thought Chris shouldn't have fired you."

"At least you're consistent."

"So, what's to say Norma didn't kill her?"

"She spent her life caring for and saving people." At least he snickered when he said it.

"Until she killed Charity."

FORTY-THREE

"As long as we're here," I said, glancing toward Drake Property Management, "I want to see the back parking lot video from Tuesday morning. I can't believe the cameras didn't record anyone leaving. Someone left out the back door while I was there, and I want to know who."

"You did get my hint, right? About the Tiffany Jordon's?"

"I'm tired, Jeff. Spell it out for me."

"It's not a cheap brand. And that was an iPhone 13 she had her nose in. Not cheap."

"She has expensive tastes," I said. "That's why she was taking bribes. How much would a pair of Tiffany Jordon's cost?"

"Around ninety bucks."

"Sheesh. What a waste. I wonder how much she got from Charity for each appointment. Did Gazelle tell you?"

He held the management company's door open for me. "I don't think that was the point. It was the idea of a shakedown that had Gazelle angry."

Allen Whitmore looked up on our entrance, surprised, and shoved something into his middle desk drawer.

"Back again," he said, sounding too hearty for the circumstances.

"Could you show us the video feed from Tuesday morning? The one that shows the dumpster. And the camera that shows the front parking lot from the same time."

Because of the lack of windows in his living quarters, Allen had to turn on the lights. Once again, I noted the many pictures of the woman with the crinkly eyes.

It took a few minutes, but Allen found the right spot, which meant, unlike his original assertion, he never needed time to get the backup ready. There was no reason for me to return except the manager's desire to have dinner with me.

The back lot showed a lonely dumpster starting at seven o'clock. As he fast forwarded, no vehicles entered or left. Not until seven-thirty, when Roberta's hatchback entered the lot. Ten minutes later, Charity came around the corner in a car so small it didn't have a back seat. I knew the drivers of the car because Allen told us.

"I know everybody's car."

At eight-thirty, a procession of vehicles passed. Some of them belonged to employees of the other businesses in the strip.

A zippy hatchback drove in.

"That's Dominique's."

Next came an older model sedan. A boat. I held my breath as it took the corner. The proud owner turned out to be Fred.

"I didn't see Bertie."

"I've never seen Bertie park back there. In fact, I've no idea what kind of car she drives." The building manager sounded surprised.

As the parade of cars passed, I continually scanned the footage for a shadow. Something that would indicate a person off-screen scootching along the building to avoid the security cameras. Nothing.

The front parking lot showed my car, gradually joined by police vehicles. Anyone else in the lot had parked outside of the camera's range.

"Thanks. I thought it was worth looking again."

About to walk away, I turned back. "Can you show us the front and back parking lot from Monday night?" In answer to Jeff's questioning look, I explained. "I just realized something. No one saw Charity leave Monday night, but did they see her arrive?"

When Allen replayed the feed from both cameras, all three of us leaned in with interest. Her car left the back lot around four-thirty, but the vehicle never showed up again in either lot.

"Strange," Allen said, leading the way out of his back room.

"You said it, brother," Jeff said, offering me a high-five. "Smart thinking, partner."

After I accepted the praise and the hand slap, I bent down to pick up an overturned photograph from the floor. "You dropped this." Before I handed it off, I flipped it over.

Jeff, leaning over my shoulder, made a noise of surprise. "What are you doing with Charity?"

The manager's face puckered as he blustered. "Doing with her? Nothing. It's a picture. That's all."

Jeff folded his arms. "A picture you tried to get rid of quick when we came in." His eyes angled down at the drawer. "What else is in there?"

Before Allen had time to react, Jeff yanked the drawer

and grabbed a small handful of photographs. He brushed away the older man's hands as he snatched at them.

"Give those back."

Jeff tossed them onto the desktop one at a time. "Charity. Charity. Charity. Were you stalking Charity? Although it looks like she posed for these, and they're all tame."

Drawing himself up, Allen said, "I've never stalked anyone in my life. Or harassed them. We were friends."

"Friends?"

"Well, friendly."

As I looked Allen over, his pleading eyes, trembling bottom lip, and shifting feet, an idea formed. He had plastered his private living space with pictures of the same woman. A woman I had yet to meet.

"Why is this place called Drake Management? Your last name is Whitmore."

"It was my wife's maiden name."

And that explained everything. "How long has she been gone?"

He shuffled to one of the guest chairs and dropped down. "Two years now."

Jeff and I exchanged a glance, and I took a seat next to him. "I'm so sorry."

He gave me a trembly smile. "Dana was the best. What you would call a soul mate. She started the business long before we met and ran it until the week before she died. I quit my job as a contractor and took over. It seemed a shame to let her business die with her." He took in the dinged-up metal filing cabinets, the scuffed desk, and the paneled walls with a touch of nostalgia mixed with grief. "I think I've done okay. It's all I have left of her."

"You live here?"

He wiped the tip of his nose. "This is where I feel

closest to Dana." Glancing around the room with watery eyes, he said, "She spent a lot of time in this office."

Jeff held up a photo. "What's that got to do with Charity?" Stepping back, he gave the living quarters a deliberate stare. "Did you meet up with her here?"

"Oh, no. Nothing like that. You're young and handsome. You wouldn't understand. She had time for me. Didn't mind listening to me rattle on about Dana, or anything else. We never had children. She's the one who suggested I take the photos. Said I needed family pictures to brighten the place up and I could start with her and add some of my friends."

I smiled and chided him. "You mean like your friend, Frankie, who was eaten by coyotes?"

He laughed. "Frank lives about two miles from here. I was pulling your leg."

"Just to be clear," Jeff said, "you weren't stalking Charity."

"Jeff! He's not a stalker. He's lonely."

Allen turned his head. His eyes were still watery, but maybe it was just age. I gave in to an impulse and leaned in and hugged him. His hand moved down by back and patted my bottom. I gently pushed him away.

"I'll give you that one, but that's your limit."

FORTY-FOUR

As I stepped out the front door to Drake Property Management, a silver Honda passed. Norma Hinkle sat behind the wheel.

"Quick." I grabbed Jeff's arm and pulled him toward Friendly Fingers. "The guard has left the premises."

As we approached the entrance, I clarified my motive.

"You said Gazelle was nervous, right?"

"Nervy. Yes."

"She wouldn't talk about Charity."

"Not a word."

"And yet she and Charity started leaving at the same time. At least, that's what Bertie said."

"Maybe they were friends without much to say."

I opened the entrance door. "Did she sound like Charity's friend when she ripped into her about the setup with Tammy?"

Surprise, surprise. With the boss gone, the receptionist had abandoned her post. However, that suited my purpose. Once in the hallway, I signaled Jeff to halt. Strains of music drifted down the corridor from behind the last door on the right. Dominque's room. I motioned that we could proceed.

In the large room to my right, two middle-aged women looked up from painting the nails of their respective clients.

"Can I help you?" asked the one applying sienna polish to a woman's thumb.

I took a step forward and lowered my voice to a respectful whisper. "We're friends of Gazelle's. She asked us to meet her here, but she forgot to tell us which room was hers." I smacked my forehead. "And stupid me forgot to ask."

The woman who was adding what looked like a flower to an elderly woman's big toe paused to point down the hallway. "The one across the hall."

"Thank you so much."

As soon as we left the room, Jeff took my arm and whispered in my ear, a note of glee in his voice. "You are such a liar. I'm so proud of you."

Pleased with myself, I accepted the compliment. As an afterthought, I pointed a finger at him. "But I don't lie to Bowers. He's off limits from my lies. Just so you know."

He patted my shoulder and steered me into Gazelle's room. Which was empty.

"Maybe she's on break," Jeff said.

I wandered to her table and pressed my knuckles against the side of the container that held the hot stones. "She's still here. It's warm."

Bottles of essential oils and lotions stood like little soldiers, waiting for orders. She had her own CD player, and a selection of music stacked next to it. A long, flat incense burner with moons and stars carved into the wood held a single stick of incense. I leaned in and sniffed. Patchouli.

"Who invited you in?"

I spun around. Gazelle posed in the doorway like a gunslinger, with her hand resting on the bottle of lotion in her holster.

"Nice room," I said, "especially the flowers." I nodded at the hideous glass arrangement. My gaze moved to the poster encouraging me to love my...girl stuff. "That, not so much."

"I like it," Jeff said. "Women should be proud of their...package."

The fact that he couldn't say the word spelled out in the poster meant there was hope for my ex.

The massage therapist's posture, shoulders leaning forward, feet spread shoulder width...she looked like she wanted to tackle me. So, I went on offense.

"We were wondering why you and Charity had become so chatty. Especially as you didn't care for her."

She walked into the room like a panther on the hunt, one foot in front of the other, moving slowly. When she got to the side table, she suddenly turned to face me. "Who says I didn't care for her?"

"We can't reveal our sources." Raising one eyebrow, I cocked my head. "Or is our source wrong?"

Her voice rose in pitch. "No. We weren't friends. But I won't let any woman walk to her car alone if she feels afraid."

Her direct eye contact didn't mean anything. Lots of people stared straight at you while they lied, including me. But the change in pitch was a tell.

"Charity was afraid? Of whom?"

She picked up a stick of incense and tapped it against the tabletop. "Grant Williams, I assumed."

Fidgeting. Another sign of a liar. Jeff excelled at fibbing because he didn't fidget.

Was Grant stalker material? From the way he let Nina push him around, I didn't believe he could induce any woman to be afraid of him. Running my finger along the edge of a burgundy flower, I said, adding disbelief to my tone, "She didn't tell you who?"

"She didn't need to. And that's all I have to say about it. You can leave now." She glared at my hand. "I don't like people touching my stuff."

"You like things just so, huh?"

"Yes. I do."

Removing my hand from her glass monstrosity, I took another long, slow look around the room just to annoy her. Large bottles of lotion refills sat under the table. Tucked behind one of the bottles rested a used water bottle with water still in it, along with a used napkin stuff inside. I grinned. Gazelle was a slob, just like me.

"What?"

She followed my gaze. "That's not mine."

"Right. It crawled in all by itself."

Jeff backed me up. "It was there during my massage yesterday afternoon."

After huffing a few times, she picked it up. "Gross. Is that a used napkin?"

Turning the bottle over for a better look, we all froze as the contents inside began to bubble. The plastic bottle itself expanded in front of our wide-eyed gazes.

"Drop it!"

She looked from me to the growing bottle and tossed it toward the wall behind me. I don't think she was aiming for me. Jeff grabbed my shoulders and twisted to put his body between me and the device. I heard the explosion and felt him flinch.

When it was over, the room reeked of Italian dressing.

"A vinegar bomb," Jeff said. "We used to set them off when I was a kid. But not in close quarters."

"Turn around." I lifted his shirt. A red welt was forming in the middle of his shoulder. About the height of my head. Stooping down, I snatched up the bottle cap and held it up.

"I think someone is trying to tell you something, Gazelle."

When I turned to see her response, the massage therapist wasn't there.

FORTY-FIVE

"Are you sure we shouldn't report it to the police?" I asked as we scurried to Jeff's car like criminals leaving a crime scene. Gazelle wasn't on the premises, and it seemed best to leave Friendly Fingers, especially after the manicurists followed us through the building while we searched for the masseuse.

"Where's the harm? A wet and smelly carpet. It was a joke. Probably put there by...."

I opened the passenger door. "That's the question, isn't it? A bored passing teenager? Hey, look. There's a massage parlor. I bet they'd love seeing my new trick. And isn't the point to watch the thing explode?"

"You have a point."

"So do you," I said, fastening my seatbelt. "No one got hurt. I can tell Bowers about it later. It's not important enough to interrupt his day."

The explosion had sprayed Jeff with vinegar. He turned the air conditioning on high, directed the air vents to face him, and cracked open his window.

"Where to next, boss?"

"We have Vali's phone number. You drive, and I'll call." While Jeff pulled into traffic, I put my phone on speaker and dialed the boyfriend's number. Vali answered on the third ring. When I told him who we were, he remembered us right away.

"Can we stop by and ask you a few questions? We just want to clarify something."

"Why don't you ask me over the phone?"

I couldn't tell him I wanted to look for signs he was lying while he answered us, so I said I couldn't talk on the phone and drive.

"Don't do that. It's dangerous. Come by Revving Motors on Scottsdale Boulevard. It's near the Whataburger."

Since Whataburger made the best hamburgers in the world, I knew exactly how to find him, and twenty minutes later we pulled into a parking space in front of the motorcycle shop. We were the only four-wheel vehicle in the area.

Inside, pristine parts and accessories lined the shelves. I stopped in front of a display of helmets in assorted colors and styles. One looked like Darth Vader's headgear, and the one next to it was Spiderman. Vali approached us and pointed to a flat black helmet.

"This one has a microphone and Bluetooth." He took a step back. "What's that smell?"

"Italian dressing. Jeff's a salad fiend. And thanks for the advice, but I'm not motorcycle material. I'd fall off within seconds of mounting. If I did get one, it would have to be a three-wheeler."

"If you go that route, make sure the two wheels are in front. It's more stable on the turns."

I started to say something but heard a muffled voice.

"Frances. I am your father." My ex stood behind me, wearing the Darth Vader helmet.

"Take that off."

He did so, complimenting Vali on the store's fine selection of products.

Charity's boyfriend glanced at the man behind the front counter. "You're not here to buy anything, so stop playing with the inventory and make it quick."

I took him seriously and talked fast. "First, did you give Stripe to Charity?"

He grabbed my elbow and pulled me away from the nearest customer. "Keep your voice down. I did, but if the cops ask, I didn't."

"Because it's illegal to own a Fiji Crested iguana."

"No kidding."

"Second. Did Charity ever talk about Gazelle?"

"The Masked Booby."

I blinked. "Pardon me?"

"It's a bird. When I was telling her about life in Fiji, I mentioned it. She thought the name fit Gazelle. Not that she called her that to her face."

"So, I can assume they couldn't stand each other."

"Well, I wouldn't put it so strongly. She thought Gazelle had certain useful talents."

"Useful talents?" I repeated, and he flushed.

"Charity could be analytical about people sometimes. But that was only when she was in business mode. Personally, she was a warm, loving person."

My next question took him by surprise. "I need to know why you and Charity broke up."

Jeff raised his brows along with Vali.

"I told you. We argued."

"But about what?"

He glared at Jeff for some reason. Since the masseuse didn't meet my ex until after the couple split, it didn't seem warranted. "Is it important?"

"It might be. I don't know. I'm having trouble understanding your late girlfriend. She sounds part saint with a side of ruthlessness thrown in. And people don't break up because their other half stands them up one night. Women will put up with a lot before they call it quits. I want to know what would move her to leave you."

He stepped toward me and lowered his voice. "This is the truth. I'm only telling you so you won't think worse and damage her reputation. A customer of ours, a regular, came in. He bought a hands-free voice command."

"And?"

Glancing around to make sure we were alone, he said, "I noticed the kid didn't have on a helmet. He's under eighteen. I made the mistake of mentioning it to Charity."

"Once again...and?"

"Arizona law makes it illegal for anyone under eighteen to ride a bike without a helmet. She thought I should have reported his license plate to the police."

"She broke up with you over that?" I didn't believe him.

"No. *I* broke up with *her*. Man, she reported the kid to the police. They couldn't do anything about it because they hadn't seen him driving without a helmet, but still. It was too much. Charity was a stickler for the rules. He was breaking the law. He should get a ticket. That's the way she looked at things."

"She kicked me out of my massage at thirty minutes to the second," Jeff said. "She said the sign said thirty minutes and that's all I'd get." He didn't even blush.

Vali narrowed his eyes. "She told me all about you."

"Dude. Sorry about that. I'd just been dumped myself.

We were in the same head space." He shook his head. "A bad head space."

I interrupted because I didn't care about head spaces. "That doesn't make sense. No one who thinks right and wrong are black and white would blackmail a woman into giving up half her business. Or set up a scheme to steal customers from the other masseuses. That's what I'm talking about." I held out one palm. "Half saint." And then the other palm. "Half ruthless."

Vali chewed on the corner of his lower lip. "Look. Sometimes Charity would get so focused on the prize, the line between right and wrong would get gray."

"You mean she had different standards for herself when it was convenient."

"She always snapped out of it. Now, are we done here?"

"Thank you for your time. Again, I'm sorry for your loss."

On our way back to Jeff's car, I expressed my frustration with a naughty word. "If it weren't for Bowers, I'd say good riddance to Charity Samuels."

"That's harsh. Whether you agree with it or not, she wasn't doing anything against the law."

In his self-centered way, my ex had helped me understand the victim. She was a female Jeff. Skating perilously close to the line without crossing over. Able to justify her actions with an acumen that both impressed and disgusted me. But there was one difference. Whereas Charity behaved like a hall monitor if someone violated her standards, Jeff would have let it slide. And then he'd walk away. Just like he walked away from me.

A horrible thought grabbed hold of me and twisted my insides. "What did I do to make you cheat on me?"

He did a double take. "Nothing, kiddo. It was all me."

"I must have done something."

"Would you feel better if I said you were a nag?"

"I was *not* a nag."

"I didn't say you were. I asked if it would make you feel better if I said so."

When I spoke next, my throat constricted. I had to choke out the words. "I need to know so I don't make the same mistake with Bowers."

He stopped walking and turned to look at me. "Aw, man. You're crying."

Looking away, I mumbled, "Allergies."

"Frances. Listen carefully. You didn't do anything wrong. You don't have to fix yourself. From what I've seen, you're better than ever. You've found your place in life, and you and Martin Bowers were made for each other. You and I weren't. That's all."

I nodded, wiping my eyes and wanting to believe him. But those soothing words had come from the king of lies.

FORTY-SIX

After Jeff dropped me off, I took the time to make myself look nice, even changing into a swishy skirt made of a light, peachy fabric with a floral print. It came above my knees and made me feel feminine, especially with the matching peach knit shirt that showed the tiniest hint of cleavage.

I picked up a large Cowboy style pizza from Papa Murphy's, one we would have to bake, and drove to Bowers' with my windows up and the air conditioning on so as not to mess up the braid I'd managed to pull off after several attempts.

As I unlocked Bowers' front door, I heard yelling. My heart jumped into my throat, and I stumbled in with my arms full of pizza. Bowers and Jeff were on the couch and leaning forward on the edge of their seats. Beer bottles, most of them empty, cluttered the coffee table. The object of their ire was the guy running the bases on Bowers' gigantic flat screen television.

Jeff groaned. "Man, he stinks."

When Bowers, subdued by my presence, only nodded,

Jeff held up a hand. My fiancé gave him a hi-five, albeit a half-hearted one.

"I'm glad to see you two boys are bonding."

Jeff threw an arm around Bowers' shoulder and shook him. "This guy defends the Cardinals like an animal." He made a fist. "Respect."

Bowers glanced my way and ignored the offer of a fist bump. Instead, he stood, gave me a quick kiss, and took the box from me. As I set my purse on the floor next to the coffee table, I asked Jeff if the police department had billeted him with Bowers.

"It's my reward for fixing his car. Remember?"

After slipping the pizza in the oven, Bowers led me to his throne and insisted I take it. The recliner he allowed no one to sit in but him. I settled back and grinned at the envious glance from Jeff. All I needed was control of the remote and I would rule.

Bowers returned to the couch. "We might be out of beer."

"That's okay. How was your day?" I asked.

"Slow but sure," Bowers said.

Jeff finished the last of his beer, and as he set the empty bottle on the coffee table, he gave a small laugh. "I thought detectives worked twenty-four hours a day until they solved the case."

"They don't need sleep on television," I said. "This is real life. As for you, Mr. Detective, I have information. *We* have information."

Don't ask me why, but my fiancé looked wary. "What kind of information?"

Jeff beat me to it. "Frankie had lunch with Bertie Schweitzer yesterday. Did you know that? We'll start there. She's the esthetician at Friendly Fingers. She has a test this weekend. Charity was going to help her study for it. From what Charity told me, Bertie might be overestimating her abilities. She's too technical. She doesn't respond to the person on the table, but I put that down to nerves. Charity thought she could help her with that after she passed her test. I guess that's a bummer for you because that means Bertie would have wanted Charity alive."

"And you know all that how?" Bowers was being polite.

"Charity liked to talk when she gave a massage."

I held up a hand. "Too much information."

"Get your mind out of the gutter. I'm talking about in Wisconsin. At the convention."

"So am I." When I sent an eye-roll to Bowers, it surprised me to find him studying Jeff with interest.

"What else did she talk about?" he asked.

"Vali, of course. How he would take off with the guys one minute and shower her with gifts the next. Was she wearing that leather and turquoise bracelet when she died?"

The thought of her corpse made me shudder. "Um, I didn't notice."

"A gift from Vali. So was Stripe."

Bowers pulled his gaze away from Jeff for a moment and settled it on me. "We'll talk about the iguana later." He turned back to my ex. "What else?"

Jeff, happy to be the center of attention, leaned back and crossed his arms over his chest. "She talked about the people at Friendly Fingers. Dominique kept to herself. Gazelle was a fair masseuse. Didn't sound like she cared for her, so it's funny she's the one Charity picked to walk her to her car. *If* she was afraid of someone like Gazelle suggested before the bomb went off."

Bowers didn't move. Not even a blink. "Bomb?"

I forced out a weak laugh. "I was going to tell you, but it didn't seem important enough to interrupt your day."

"The bomb wasn't important," Bowers repeated.

Jeff laughed. "Vinegar bomb. You take—"

"I know what a vinegar bomb is."

"Anyway, it didn't do much damage. Obviously, a bad joke."

"When and where did this bomb go off? Around Frankie?" Since Bowers' voice had turned super polite, I knew he was furious. He didn't even look at me.

"Jeff took the brunt of it," I explained, leaning forward and raising my voice in case he'd told his ears to ignore me, too. "He got between me and the bottle after Gazelle threw it. In fact," I pushed out another feeble laugh, "he now has matching marks. One on his chest from the hot stone, and one on his back from the bottle cap."

I'd hoped to calm him down. It didn't work. Not going by his tight expression when he looked at me.

"Jeff shouldn't have been in harms' way." He shifted his body to remove me from his sight. "Could you show me this mark?"

My ex obliged, twisting and lifting his shirt. The angry, red welt could have been a bee sting if I hadn't known better.

Bowers jaw pulsed. "Thank you for looking out for Frankie."

"No problem, bro."

"What happened to Gazelle?"

Jeff scratched his ear. "We *think* she ran off. We couldn't find her, and we searched Friendly Fingers. But she was already skittish when she gave me my massage yesterday." He shrugged and said, "Girls. You know how they are."

Once his shirt was back in place, he continued sharing Charity's observations, unaware that his recital had moved into a statement.

"The guy at Friendly Fingers, Fred, was full of himself because the female clients swooned over him. Charity couldn't understand it. She said his mustache came right out of the seventies, and he'd have to shave it off, especially if he moved to full time. Let's see. Did I already mention Charity thought of Bertie as her protege?"

Charity's helpfulness was getting on my nerves. "She only helped Bertie to help herself."

"Naturally. Once she was half-owner of Friendly Fingers, she'd want everyone to perform well."

"Half owner?" Bowers brow wrinkled. "She said that?"

"Absolutely. She pulled in a lot of regulars."

"Not really." I shook my head at Bowers. "She bribed the receptionist to send new clients to her. It's not the same thing."

"But she said she was going to own half the business," Bowers said, clarifying.

"Charity thought it would make sense for Norma to make her a partner. Which Norma confirmed when we talked to her. Although, she said it would never happen. She was planning to replace Charity."

"Norma told you this? Was Charity aware she was about to be replaced?"

"I doubt it." Jeff perked up. "Although maybe she wasn't mad at me after all. Maybe Norma told her to clear out and I just got in the way."

"No." I shook my head. "I'm pretty sure throwing a rock at someone is personal."

Bowers got up to grab his phone. "Juanita needs to know this. All of this."

Oh, goody. Another conversation with Wolf Creeks' most beautiful and unfriendly cop. Lucky me.

When Bowers moved to the kitchen to make his call, Jeff didn't return to watching the game. Instead, he became unusually silent and still.

"What's wrong?" I asked. "Snitches remorse?"

He looked at me with his honey-brown eyes. "I miss Buffy."

The way he said it, so simply and without excuses, surprised me. I moved to the couch and sat next to him. "Tell Frankie all about it."

He took me up on my offer and let out a long sigh. "I don't understand it. I thought we were doing fine. Out of nowhere, she said I needed to leave."

Fairness is my middle name, so I asked, "Were you living in your place?"

"She didn't like my apartment. She has very specific opinions about decorating."

Probably chains and spiked collars on the wall marking her past victims.

"Okay. If you were living at her place, I guess she had that right, though it's still mean to leave someone without a place to stay."

"I crashed that night at my brother's house. When I showed up for work the next morning, Chris told me I didn't have a job."

"Could he do that?"

"It's not like we had a contract or anything. Besides. I didn't want to put him in an awkward spot. Buffy's family is tight. They would have called and harassed him into letting me go eventually. I put him out of his misery before that happened."

"Sounds like you had a near escape."

When he didn't answer, I bent my head to see his face. Holy smokes. His eyes teared up.

"Frances, I think I love her. And now she's gone."

Gadzooks.

"Come here," I said, pulling him in and patting his back. "She's not gone. She kicked you out. You deserve someone who treats you right. Someone who loves you for who you are. Don't you dare go crawling back to her." Was I really giving this pep talk to my ex? It wasn't my fault. He gave off the vibe of a mistreated puppy.

It's not like he sniveled and sobbed, but my neck was damp by the time I heard Bowers walk in. With my chin on Jeff's shoulder, I held a finger to my lips. My fiancé looked around for a quick escape that wouldn't bring him past the couch. About to return to the kitchen, he stopped when Jeff stood and mumbled something about needing to use the john.

"What was that all about?" Bowers asked.

I stood and met him halfway across the room. "I think Romeo finally met his match."

"Buffy?"

I wrapped my arms around his middle and leaned back, looking up. "Why Bowers. You're so clever. You could almost be a detective."

He sighed. "Well, what do you want to do about it?"

My smile broadened into a grin. "I'm glad you asked."

Naturally, since my plan involved messing with people's lives under the guise of helping them, Bowers didn't approve. I finally convinced him I'd think about it. Which I already had while I was talking to him. And I'd made up my mind.

FORTY-SEVEN

Gutierrez came directly to Bowers' place, changing course from her drive home. When she arrived, Jeff sent an appreciative glance over her fitted black suit. I don't think she owned a suit in any other color.

Before my fiancé could ask, I relinquished the recliner. As the lead detective on the case, she outranked us all. By the time Bowers related our information, Gutierrez had pulled out her regulation notebook, crossed her legs to get comfortable, and prepared her attack.

"You went for a massage together?"

"We were both pretty stressed out," Jeff said. "It seemed silly to drive separately."

"It seems even sillier to get a massage at the one spa where there had been a murder."

Ah, Gutierrez. So confident. So proud. She didn't know who she was dealing with. King Liar. He gave her his most innocent smile. The one that grandmothers loved. I sat straighter, interested in the duel.

"Since I'm from out of town, that's the only spa I know. Frances doesn't get massages."

"Frances?" She looked at me and laughed through her nose. I let it slide because I felt sorry for her.

"Pretty name, isn't it? Anyway, she wasn't any help finding a place. So, I convinced her there were other massage therapists and other rooms at Friendly Fingers and said we might as well go there." He leaned back and put his hands behind his head, relaxing into the game. "Frances was nervous at first, but I convinced her we wouldn't even be near the locker room. Besides. People die all the time. It's only recently we've looked at death as an unnatural thing. Someone might have taken their last breath in this house."

We all gave in to the urge and followed his gaze around the room. Gutierrez was the first to break the silence.

"And once you were at Friendly Fingers, you thought you might as well speak with Norma Hinkle." She thought our talk with Norma happened during the same visit, and far be it from Jeff to clarify.

"We wanted to express our condolences." He raised his brows, surprised she'd asked. "And see if she was all right. It seemed the polite thing to do. She must have wanted to get it off her chest because she invited us back to her office space." He shook his head at the wonder of it. "We tried to leave several times, but the lady kept talking. Telling us how she used to be a nurse. How she got started."

"And she just blurted out Charity Samuels wanted half of her business. To you. A stranger."

He grinned. "I'm afraid that was my fault. Charity mentioned it to me back in Wisconsin, and I thought the decision was mutual. That they both wanted it. So, I brought it up."

"Why?"

It's my belief Gutierrez thought keeping her question short and direct would give her control. Fat chance.

"Just making small talk. You know. What are you going to do with the other half of your business now that Charity is gone?" His brow wrinkled, expressing deep regret. "How was I to know it was a sensitive topic?"

"And then, when you had your massage, this Gazelle person told you all about Charity's stalker."

"Well, I don't know that I'd call him a stalker. Just an enthusiastic client. It came up naturally. You know how it is," he said. "In *your* job, you get to know human nature. The murder is still big news there. I know it's in bad taste, but that's all she wanted to talk about. The story grows. Suddenly Grant's a stalker."

"And how did you wind up back in Gazelle's room in time for the bomb?"

Working in our third visit would take finesse. Jeff had it covered.

"I forgot to leave a tip."

When Gutierrez cut to me, I shrugged. "What he said. I hope you appreciate that Charity was a complex woman. She had the morals of an alley cat, sorry Jeff, and yet she had a high opinion of right and wrong. At least as it applied to other people." As long as they were listening, I dove in headfirst. "One thing I haven't mentioned. Lavender. It somehow plays into the murder. I think." I clenched my teeth and muttered, "Unless the little stinker is playing with me."

"Little stinker?" Gutierrez smirked. "Let me guess. The iguana. The one you don't have."

Sending an apologetic glance to Bowers, I explained. "Charity loved wearing lavender. No one could use lavender oil at Friendly Fingers because a client had an allergic reaction. Nina, Grant Williams girlfriend, makes

Lavender sachets. Every time I try to communicate with Stripe, he sends me a whiff of lavender."

"You have lavender in your backyard," Bowers said. "Maybe he's reacting to that."

Gutierrez shot my fiancé a suspicious glance. She didn't want to believe I could talk to animals. However, if Bowers was taking me seriously, she had to consider the possibility.

Jeff snorted. "Frances." He shook his head. "There isn't a paying client around, so I can say it. You really need to give that up. You have other talents. You don't have to make a living being a fraud. There's no dignity in it."

I thanked him for his opinion.

"That's right," Gutierrez said, as if she'd just thought of it. "You helped expose her activities to her victims in Loon Lake."

He fought to keep his pleasure at the pretty lady's compliment from overtaking the shame he felt from betraying me.

"It wasn't supposed to go that way. I didn't mean to hurt her." He looked me in the eye, completely serious. "I wish I could take it back. I'm sorry, Frances."

I frowned. This was my big moment. The one I'd dreamed of since the sky fell on my head in Wolf Creek two-and-a-half years ago. Except for the part where I imagined him on his knees, kissing my feet and begging me to take him back. I'd refuse to forgive him, and he'd spend the rest of his life pining after me, knowing how he'd lost the best thing that ever happened to him. That part hadn't happened yet. Not that I wanted it to. Not anymore.

Sitting back, I stared at my hands, willing an emotional reaction. Since I wasn't paying attention, Gutierrez couldn't get any play out of me, and she moved on to asking Jeff about the vinegar bomb.

"Frankie."

I came out of my study and looked up at Bowers. He gave me a gentle smile. "Help me in the kitchen?"

"Oh. Sure."

He held out a hand and pulled me to my feet. We left Jeff to Gutierrez. My fiancé led me to a corner out of view and pulled me in for a hug. Then he held me at arm's length.

"Are you okay?"

"What do you mean?"

"You got quiet. I imagine hearing Jeff apologize for all he did to you must have, I don't know, been an emotional moment. I made an excuse to get you in here because I thought you might not want an audience."

Looking up into his deep-blue eyes, seeing the concern there, my face crumpled, and the tears came.

"Aw, sweetheart." He took me in his arms again and rubbed my back.

It felt so good to rest my head on his chest that I talked into his shirt. "I'm not crying over Jeff. I'm crying over you."

I felt him stiffen. "What did I do? Should I not have mentioned it?"

After sniffing a few times, I stepped back and wiped my eyes. "When Jeff apologized, I thought it would be a relief. But when he did...." I shook my head because shrugging hurt my shoulder. "Nothing. I didn't feel a thing."

"I suppose that's a good thing. It means you've moved on. But why are you crying?" He took my face in his hands and wiped away my tears with his thumbs.

"Because of you. Because you care about me." Sniff. "And worry about me." Hiccup. "You're the most wonderful man I've ever met, and I love you so much."

Once he got over his surprise, he smiled. "I love you, too."

"And I could tell you were mad at me before." Should I mention today's article in *The Gazette*? Since he hadn't brought it up, I kept it vague. "I'm afraid I'll push you too far and you'll leave me."

He cocked his head. "Leave you?"

"Get tired of me. I know sometimes I'm a pain...."

Bending his head so he looked directly into my eyes, he said, "I love you and want to be with you for keeps. It's a decision I gave a lot of thought to before I asked you to marry me. Sometimes you drive me crazy, and I'm sure I do the same to you, but I want the full package. Don't you?"

I nodded.

"And there are things about you I don't understand, but I get to spend the rest of my life figuring them out. And vice-versa. I look forward to it. Understand?"

He gave me the tenderest kiss I've ever received. Time stood still, and my surroundings disappeared. If I'd slipped into a warm pool of water at night and floated, it might have the same affect. Too soon, he pulled away.

"Do you need to stay here for a minute?"

I nodded. I wanted to savor that kiss.

"I'll make your excuses."

I don't know what he told them, but Gutierrez left about ten minutes later, and when I stepped out of the kitchen, Jeff had left the room.

FORTY-EIGHT

We made it an early night. Jeff took Bowers' downstairs guest bedroom, and I returned home. On the way, I made a quick stop at the garden center and snagged two hibiscus plants, the last two they had left. What can I say? I felt sorry for the little bugger, trapped in his terrarium without his favorite yum-yums. I know I need my infusion of chocolate chip cookies to remain sane.

Before I went to bed, I tripled-checked the locks.

The next morning, I set the plants outside next to my table. After grabbing my coffee, I secured Stripe in Emily's harness, stuffed paper towels around his body to make it fit, and secured the harness to her leash. According to the Internet, iguanas could run twenty-one miles per hour, and I didn't want to take a chance on him escaping and becoming the most expensive meal ever eaten by a local hawk.

His little head popped up as soon as we were outside. Slowly, he approached his dream plant, climbing into the pot and hugging the branches. He plucked a flower with his teeth and chewed. With the bright pink petals hanging out of his mouth, he looked comical. Sweet.

About to settle back with my coffee while he enjoyed breakfast, a wave of longing passed through me, and I clutched my chest. Briny ocean breezes filled my nostrils as fluttering wings and chirps rose in a cacophony of cries. My skin tingled in the sizzling heat, and I longed to close my eyes and nap even though I'd just dressed for the day. Right after I had a good cry.

He watched me as he chewed, and I knew this hollow ache came from Stripe. He missed his home. Was that why he hated Charity? Because she'd dumped him into a terrarium where she could look at him or ignore him, depending on her mood? Somewhere he could spend his nights alone dreaming of other iguanas. It made me dislike her, too.

So, I made a deal. I conjured up an image of a tropical island. He stopped chewing. I held up a separate image of a shadow whacking Charity on the head with a stone and dumping her into the hot tub. He turned his head away and snorted. Derisively, I thought. I put myself and him in the picture and had us exchange the images.

While he mulled over my offer, he continued to chew on his Hibiscus flower. I got the wary feeling in my stomach that came any time a website asked for my email. Why did they need my information to browse their wares? Was it a trap? Would I suddenly receive a thousand credit card offers in my in box? The iguana didn't quite trust me.

How could I offer him a guarantee? I didn't have a plan to get him home. Vali might have a suggestion.

Stripe sensed me waiver and transmitted his disappointment.

"I understand." Pressing my lips together, I nodded and sighed.

After tugging on the leash to make sure the knot was

tight, I took my coffee and leaned against my wall. It was hard to believe I'd done the same thing only three days ago while waiting for Bowers to show up for dinner. So much had happened since Monday.

Charity had died. I'd lost interest in murdering my ex. I'd hooked up with Jeff in a weird, crime-solving capacity and interviewed possible killers, all while dodging the authorities who were searching for the small lizard in my care. I'd say that made for a full week.

The Gambel's quail darted between the bushes in front of me. A row of chicks alternately lagged and shot forward to catch up.

To the right of them, a shadow moved. A roadrunner stalked the group from behind a shrub. Glancing back at the family of birds, I saw one chick separated from his siblings. The roadrunner lowered his head, and my mouth filled with the tickle of feathers.

Without thinking, I shot an image of Wile E. Coyote to the roadrunner, saliva dripping from his fangs. The roadrunner skid to a halt, and the family of quails disappeared into the brush.

He stared after them, uncertain, then turned and loped away. A cloud of sadness and hunger enveloped me. I jerked away from the wall, spilling my coffee on my pant leg.

As I brushed at the spot, nature mocked me for my arrogance. I thought by saving the chick I'd be a hero, but something else had suffered from my interference. It was like Grandma Chandler used to say. *You're damned if you do and damned if you don't.*

I looked up to find the iguana watching me.

"I hope you're full. It's time to go back inside."

I removed the leash from under the chair leg, and as I

straightened up, an image of the Friendly Fingers building entered my head along with the ominous feeling I get watching horror movies, right before the crazed killer leaps out of the closet.

The only time Stripe had seen Friendly Fingers was as I carried him away on Tuesday morning. Did he understand what that building meant?

A slide show of Charity's room, the hallway, snippets of the other rooms as seen from the hallway, and the waiting area of the spa played before me. Finally, the locker room and the hot tub behind the plastic sheet. The angle on the images came from the ground.

Okay. He understood. But what did it mean? "Is that it? Someone at Friendly Fingers killed Charity?"

The iguana's color changed to a darker green.

"Why not tell me who?"

An image of Bertie floated by. I gasped. "Bertie did it?"

But soon Norma made an appearance.

"Norma did it?" I asked with less enthusiasm.

Tammy's head floated by. He was parading the entire staff of Friendly Fingers past me in a weird lineup. Before he could send the next person, my phone rang. His color returned to normal.

Since my cell was inside the house, and it would be too dangerous to leave him out here alone, I gathered him up and returned him to his terrarium.

I'd missed a call from Armando Cozzani.

Stripe didn't trust me enough to give me the answer, but he was willing to give me a hint. I'd have to work with that.

FORTY-NINE

"All we need to do is figure out who at Friendly Fingers killed Charity."

I'd called an emergency meeting. We'd taken our assembly into U-Behave after Penny informed me her cranky old geezer customer had petitioned her to have me banned. My friend donated three chairs, and we three sat facing each other, our knees almost touching, in the front corner next to the collars and harnesses. It was the only spot with solid wall instead of window, so curious passers-by wouldn't spot us.

Penny's response to my revelation was to let her eager smile slip a few degrees. "At least that narrows it down."

Jeff crossed his arms over his chest and leaned his head back. Bowers must have let him use the laundry machine because he had on his original white t-shirt. And he didn't smell. "Let's see. Dominique, Gazelle, Frank, Bertie, and the manicurists work there. Norma owns it. Grant and Nina have both been inside. Allen Whitmore might have dropped by. He liked to talk to Charity, but we don't know for sure she always went to his place. And Vali came by at least twice to give his girlfriend a ride home. Did we eliminate anyone?"

"Random serial killers," I snapped. Jeff was right. Stripe's clue wasn't worth the price I paid for it. Nothing.

"Couldn't you ask the iguana to be more specific?" Penny again, looking for the upside.

"Frances." Jeff cocked his head at me. "Don't tell me this clue came from Stripe. It's useless."

Penny raised her hand. "Let's focus on making the clue valuable. If Stripe meant someone he associated with that building, it would probably be someone who went into Charity's room."

"Again." Jeff sighed. "Grant was a client. The other masseuses could have stopped by to borrow things or talk to Charity. Norma was her boss. Bertie, her protege. And Nina went in there to tell her off."

She smiled. "We've eliminated the manicurists."

"Did we ever suspect them?" I didn't even know their names. "Let's look at motives. We decided Nina wouldn't have had a reason to kill Charity if she reported her. Grant was in love, or at least in lust with her."

"I have it," Penny said, excited. "Maybe Charity refused his advances."

Jeff snorted. "Did he strike you as someone who would press his unwanted attentions on a woman?" Since he looked to me for an answer, I had to say no.

"There has to be something we missed. A question we didn't think of asking. We need to talk to everyone again."

"Nina's right," Jeff said. "I'm starting to feel creepy."

"You've always been creepy. Pen, can we use the bistro? It's a neutral spot, so they might put their guards down. The spa doesn't close in the middle of the day, so they must stagger their lunch hours. You, Jeff, can stand guard in case one of them is the murderer and goes ballistic. Penny, you can help me issue the invitations."

And so, I made the calls, intending to space the meetings an hour apart with a guarantee from Penny of fast service.

Gazelle hadn't shown up for work. Since it wasn't possible that someone could have snatched her in front of Jeff and me, and she left of her own free will, I wasn't worried. I left a message on her extension.

I had Bertie's cell phone number, but she didn't answer her phone. I left another message.

When I called back for Norma, Tammy recognized my voice.

"You just called."

"I did."

"For Gazelle."

"And now I'd like to speak to Norma."

"Norma doesn't give massages."

I'd had enough of her games. Since she was smart enough to count her take from Charity, I pegged her as one of those people who play dumb to avoid responsibility, which is not dumb. And didn't Norma say that Tammy understood perfectly?

"Listen, you half-whit. Transfer me to Norma or I'll tell her about your bribery scheme with Charity."

"Charity's dead."

Her victorious smirk made it through the phone line.

"Gazelle isn't."

She transferred the call. Norma refused to leave Friendly Fingers while they were shorthanded. She took a rain check.

Before I readied myself for my only lunch date so far,

Dominique, I tried Bertie one last time. She answered on the first ring.

"Why are you whispering?"

Her whisper turned into a squeak. "I'm in the police station."

"Oh, my gosh. Did someone attack you with a vinegar bomb?"

"Vinegar...no. Frankie...it's crazy. They think I killed Charity. What am I going to do?"

"Did you do it?"

"No!"

After advising her to call an attorney, I disconnected and gave Penny and Jeff the news. Penny covered her mouth with both hands.

Jeff said, "I wondered."

"What do you mean *you wondered*?"

"Charity was emailing the massage board when she was killed."

"Right," I said. "To head off Nina's complaint."

"There are other reasons to call."

He waited for me to figure it out. My exasperation showed when I demanded, "Like what?"

"I practically told you when we were sitting there with Bertie. If an unlicensed person gives a massage and accepts payment, it means big trouble. That's why I asked for Bertie at Friendly Fingers. I wanted to see if Norma was willing to bend the rules."

"The way I heard it, Bertie offered to massage you on the table *after* she got her license."

Penny curled her upper lip. "On one of *my* tables? Are you trying to get me fined by the health department?"

I held up a finger. "Unless you—you didn't, say, drop by her house for a massage."

"No. But I wondered. Did she say the same thing to California guy?"

It took a moment to absorb his point. "*Bertie* opened the door Monday night and gave the guy a massage?"

"Here's the thing. Charity wouldn't have left a dirty sheet on her massage table. The woman cleaned as she went. For pity's sake. She was pulling the sheet off the table before I got up."

Penny giggle and bit her lip. "I just assumed you didn't get an actual massage. You know. Because of...you know."

It made sense. "And we've thought all along it was strange for Charity to take a late appointment if she had an early massage the next morning. So, Bertie gives the guy a massage. Takes money. Leaves the sheet, which was not smart. When she gets there the next morning to clear away the evidence, Charity is waiting. She figures out what happened and calls the board to snitch. And Bertie loses it."

Jeff looked over my shoulder. "Your appointment is here."

In the doorway stood a man in a fitted yellow t-shirt, jeans, and leather sandals. He wore his curly dark hair in a bushy ponytail. The door, caught by the wind, flew open. He had to tug it closed.

When he saw me and waved, I gaped. It was the tall, Hispanic masseuse with the raspy voice.

"Dominique's a guy." Jeff snickered at my ignorance. "Couldn't you tell?"

"How could I tell? He makes a better-looking woman that I do. Or is it she?"

"He. Dominique is a cross-dresser." He frowned. "Or is he a transvestite? Charity didn't specify. Anyway, he's cool."

"He's way more than cool," Penny murmured.

"Dominique?" I said, grasping the hand he held out to me.

He grinned, showing a nice set of teeth. "Dominic. I'm only Dominique at work."

"No offense. I mean you look great dressed as a woman, but you're an incredibly handsome man."

When his smile grew, it emphasized his fabulous cheekbones. "Thanks. I'm lucky that way."

I motioned toward the reserved booth, and we took our seats. To speed my appointments along, back when we thought there would be several, Ann had set the table and left menus.

"Dressing as a woman when I do massages puts me in touch with my feminine side. It makes me feel nurturing and gentle." He opened his menu and glanced at the selections. "My girlfriend suggested I wear looser clothes to stay comfortable when I had a long day scheduled, and it just evolved. She had a wonderful time dressing me up as Dominique until I got it down."

"There's been a change since I asked you here. Did you know Bertie has been arrested?"

He set down the menu. "Arrested? Whatever for?"

"She said the police thought she killed Charity."

He raised one brow while lowering the other. "No. Seriously."

"I'm just repeating what she said. By the way. Did Gazelle ever show up for work?"

"No idea. It's my day off. I forwarded my calls because I can't trust Tammy to take a decent message." He let his shoulders drop. "Aw, man. Norma better not ask me to cover for her."

"Has Gazelle disappeared before?"

"Not that I know. Blue Cheese Bacon Burger and fries."

He said the last bit to Ann. I told her to make it two, and he ran an approving gaze over me.

"Good for you. Here's a secret. Most men don't like stick figures."

I couldn't help but smirk. "You mean like The Antelope? Do she and Charity know about Dominic?"

"I pride myself on never going out of character until I'm back home. But if they do? Who cares?"

With my chin on my balled-up fist, I asked, "Are you surprised Bertie is the killer?"

"I don't think she is. The police have it wrong."

"Why do you think so?"

"Before you can kill a person, I assume you must believe what you want is more important than their right to live. Bertie is the most unselfish person I know."

"But Charity was going to report her for giving someone a massage before getting her license."

"The guy who dropped by Monday night?"

We waited until our waitress set down our plates before continuing the conversation.

"How do you know about him?"

"Are you kidding?" He took a healthy bite of his burger. "The police asked us about it. Over and over and over."

"Who would you pick to murder Charity?"

I saw a hint of Dominique when he rolled his eyes. "How about all of us? Charity could be—let's say she wouldn't have won employee of the month. Ever. Honey, Charity didn't do anything that didn't benefit Charity."

"True. If she was going to be a partner with Norma—"

He gaped. "She what? Was Norma considering it?" Pulling his cell phone from his pocket, he said, "I've got to tell Gazelle about—" He set the phone down. "For a minute there, I forgot Charity was dead."

"Would it have been that bad to have her as a boss?"

"That depends. My gut tells me she would have cut our percentage. If that happened, goodbye Friendly Fingers. I have to admit clients seemed to prefer her." His hand spasmed into a fist. "It's so not fair the way people choose blonds over brunettes. It's discrimination."

"You didn't know Tammy was accepting bribes to send new customers to Charity?"

He slumped back. "That witch Charity and her little dog, Tammy, too. I suspected Tammy couldn't be as dumb as she acted. A bus would have gotten her before now."

"What about Gazelle? Did she and Charity get along?"

He turned thoughtful. "I wouldn't have said so, but lately they've been very chatty. Walking out to their cars together."

"Because Charity was afraid of someone?"

"Afraid?" He laughed. "I suppose it's possible, but I would have described their behavior as furtive. Not scared. If fact, I wondered what they were up to."

"Are you and Gazelle friends? I mean, you were going to call her just now." I raised one eyebrow.

"Not friends. It's a case of sticking together against the evil one. Discontented Charity. Always changing things."

I waited.

"Okay. Take the lunchroom. Obviously, it's a place to grab lunch in-between massages. Charity said we should only allow vegan food. If someone walked by and saw us eating a burger..." He held up the remainder of his lunch as an example. "She actually said vegans were forced to inhale meat that floated through the air every time I took a bite. I told her she could have a whiff of my ham sandwich if she liked. Little Nazi. Trying to control what I ate."

And with that, he took that last bite of burger. As a dedicated meat eater myself, he had my sympathy.

"You were going to call Gazelle. Were you going to tell Fred, too?"

Guilt infused his handsome face. "Fred's a floater. He's not there all the time, so it's easy to forget about him. Although now he'll be full time. At least, I assume so."

"Can you think of anyone else at Friendly Fingers who especially hated her?" To be fair, I included the manicurists.

"We didn't actually hate Charity. We just didn't like her. There's a difference."

He had plans with his girlfriend, so he thanked me for lunch and left.

I strolled to the front counter and slumped against it. "He doesn't think Bertie is a killer."

"It's up to the police now," Penny said.

"Did you reach anyone else? We'll have to cancel. With Bertie at the police station, there doesn't seem to be a point."

"I got hold of Nina and Grant."

"Are they coming?"

"Only if you want to die like a dog. Those were Nina's words if we didn't leave them alone. What does that mean? Die like a dog. I imagine they die just like the rest of us."

I rubbed my forehead to clear my thoughts.

Jeff nudged me. "Here's someone you might want to talk to."

Bowers stood just inside the entrance and looked around until he spotted me. Instead of coming inside, he waved me over.

As I followed him outside, the wind blew his sport coat open. Dark clouds blocked the sun, but I wasn't impressed. I'd caught this show before. The weather fairy would tease us along, and the moment the first sprinkles cooled our skin, a few gusts would rearrange the sky, pushing the clouds out of range before they released their payload.

He skipped the hug and got right to it. "Armando Cozzani from the Sonora Desert Reptile Rescue will be at your house at four o'clock to pick up Stripe. You need to be there, Frankie. And you need to hand over Stripe."

I lifted my shoulders and dropped them, letting out a big sigh.

"So, if you want to—to talk to him…I mean say goodbye to him, you better hurry."

Bowers was hedging. Holding back what he really wanted to say. Which meant it had something to do with my animal communication skills, or, as he usually called it, my *thing*.

"What about Bertie? I heard the police had pegged her for the murder. She's the one who gave California guy a massage, isn't she?"

He stared. "How did you…no. I don't want to know. Riley Reynolds from San Diego, California, identified her as his masseuse. He was one of Charity's regulars when he lived in the area and dropped by on the off chance she could give him a last-minute appointment. Bertie obliged."

"And Charity was going to report her to the board the minute she found out."

He hedged again. "Frankie. If you want to say your goodbye's, you need to hurry."

So. Detective Martin Bowers didn't think Bertie was the murderer. Good to know.

FIFTY

On our way back to my house, Maynard Sewell called my cell phone.

"You need to get over here right away."

"I'm in the middle of an important meeting. Can we schedule for tomorrow?"

"Right now." And then he hung up.

Jeff remembered the route, and at my encouragement, he drove at breakneck speed. We screeched up to the curb behind a cube truck with the name Phoenix Wildlife Control written in bold green lettering over a picture of a family of raccoons.

The front door opened as we approach, and Maynard folded his arms over his chest and directed a frown at Jeff.

"You were wrong."

My ex spread his hands. "Did you need me to talk to the dog again? Maybe he left out a detail during our last meeting."

"You were wrong," Maynard repeated, and then he grabbed my hand in both of his. "And you were right. I'm so sorry, my dear woman. It's all my fault. I cast aside your experience and embraced your assistant's dramatic solution. What a fool I am."

"The important thing is that Hubie is okay. We saw the truck."

After a full body shudder, the client led us inside to the couch, where the brown Chihuahua curled into a ball under one of the decorative pillows. "My poor boy. When I think about what could have happened if you had not hinted at cats. That made me more aware, and just as I was about to let Hubie out for his morning relief, I spotted the devil."

We followed him to the back door off the kitchen. Maynard had a decent size yard covered in environmentally friendly fake grass. Flowering shrubs lined the border. A man in a brown uniform, on his hands and knees, reached under one shrub, his arms covered in leather gloves that reached over his elbow. I opened the door and stepped outside.

"Got it." The man stood and showed his partner a baby bobcat before adding his catch to a crate with three other kittens. In a second crate, mom crouched, growling and spitting at the man handling her babies.

"I think that's the last of them."

The two men performed one final meticulous check along the border and came up with a fifth kitten.

"That's it for sure."

Maynard balked when I ordered him to get Hubie, but he complied and returned with the dog clutched tightly to his chest.

"Hold him up so he can see what's happening."

When Maynard raised his pet, Hubie trembled so hard I thought he'd have a stroke. I motioned for my client to join me in the yard.

Connecting to the dog, I showed him the backyard, empty of visitors, with his tiny, furry body standing proudly in the middle, surveying his kingdom. He trembled again when I showed him the bobcat, but I made her pathetic, trailed by her babies. His head cocked.

Maynard entered the scene in a knight's outfit. I had trouble envisioning the details, but I gave him a red cape. The knight-errant swept the cape over one shoulder, revealing a dangerous-looking sword. Raising his hand in summons, the men in brown appeared, along with the bobcats, which they gathered into the crates. With all the majesty of a king, Maynard pointed, banishing the bobcats. The rescue team bowed and did his bidding.

Then I returned to the current scene. Hubie craned his neck around to look at his savior, who puckered his lips and made kissy noises. The dog sent me a searching glance to make sure I wasn't mistaken.

Just then, the workers lifted momma's crate and carted her around the side of the house. In a few minutes, they returned for the kittens.

Once the truck engine started, I created a cartoon of the vehicle driving a winding road, over and through several mountain ranges, until they released their catch in a forest far from here. Little hearts surrounded the family reunion, and the bobcat led her kittens into the surrounding trees. Hubie enjoyed the show.

My confirmation of success came when his skinny tail gave a tentative wag and the dog wriggled to get down. He approached the shrubs with caution, released a quick tinkle to mark his territory, and scurried back to his owner's arms.

"I can't thank you enough." Maynard gushed about my abilities until a surreptitious peek at my watch showed me I had less than an hour before Stripe's removal from my home.

I handed him a business card, just in case he'd torn up the last one, and hurried back to the car.

As Jeff drove away, he slipped me a quick glance. "Lucky guess."

It wouldn't be kind to rub his nose in his failure, especially with the satisfactory outcome. So, I agreed. "Right. Lucky."

FIFTY-ONE

Jeff opted to stay in my bedroom with Emily, saying he'd had enough trouble with Gutierrez to last a lifetime. He didn't want anything to do with a stolen iguana.

"Norma *gave* him to me."

He snorted. "That's not what it said in *The Gazette*. Seriously though, that woman looks at me funny as it is. I don't want to give her ideas."

"Fine. Go hide in the bedroom with my cat."

"Could you bring me some chips or something? I saw pretzels in your cupboard."

So, I retrieved the pretzels. When I returned to the bedroom, Jeff had closed the door. Behind it, my ex's voice rumbled in conversation. My guilt lasted half a second. He couldn't accuse me of eavesdropping in my own house. Everything in here belonged to me, including the air. And the sound waves.

I don't know if she's under arrest. I just know she's at the station. You better not say your source said the police are holding her because that's not what I'm telling you.

My stomach lurched. The police had *sources*. So did

reporters. My original fury returned in a rush, and I swung open the door.

He turned with a guilty start and disconnected the call.

"You forgot to give your sweetums a kiss goodbye." I threw the open bag of pretzels at his head, missing by a mile. They showered the room, adding drama, but making a mess I'd have to clean later.

"It's not what you think. That wasn't Buffy."

"Right. Who else would you—" Placing the back of my hand against my mouth just like a useless heroine from a black-and-white monster movie, I bit my knuckle. "Paul Simpson." I spat the name out.

He passed a hand over his mouth. "Look. He came to me for inside information. I thought if I told him what was going on, he would tell it straight. Make you look good."

"You *can't* be that gullible. And after you read the first article, you should have known you weren't helping." An eerie calm descended on me. Temporary, but effective. Just like the eye of a tropical storm, which everybody knows is the most dangerous part. It allowed me to speak without choking.

"You made fun of me. Again. I can't believe I fell for it. You know, for a few minutes, I actually thought you weren't repulsive."

Having said my piece, I walked away. The eye of the storm is brief, and I didn't want to lose it in front of him. He followed, raising his voice.

"He twisted my words."

Raindrops drummed against my roof in a slow, discernable rhythm. I yanked the sliding door open and stepped outside, raising my face to allow the droplets to wash away all memory of the past few days.

Jeff joined me. "Frances, listen to me. I didn't *want* to talk to Paul."

I forced out a hollow laugh. "Someone forced you?"

"I owed him." He let out a roar and clutched at his hair with both hands, knocking the phone against his skull. "Ow! How do you think I paid for my motel room? I was in a spot, and I found a way out. So, sue me."

I nodded. "Fine. I understand. In fact, I'll help. You can stay out here and chat away with your rotten ratfink friend."

"Frances." He'd added a layer of cajoling to his tone, but when he saw it left me unaffected, he switched to a desperate whine. "Can't we talk about this?"

Ignoring him, I stepped inside, slammed the glass door closed, and locked it, closing the curtains for good measure.

"Frances," came his muffled voice. "My keys are in there. Can I at least wait in my car?"

"Stupid, stupid, stupid," I muttered, walking aimlessly around my living room. "How could I be so stupid. Frankie, you are too dumb to live."

I dropped onto the couch and faced the irritating iguana.

"You're out of time. People are coming for you, so anything you want to tell me you'd better tell me now."

Ignoring the light rap on my back door, my imagination stepped inside Friendly Fingers, passing Tammy behind the plexiglass, and pausing to look at Norma. No response. Opening the pretend hallway door, I stepped onto the ice-blue carpet and got a surprise.

Suddenly, my hips and shoulders wiggled with pleasure, and I stretched my fingers and toes. Even my belly got into the act, and a giggle escaped.

Stripe's tongue flicked out.

"Did Charity let you run loose after hours? No wonder you know the layout of the spa."

I felt the wiggles come on again but controlled them this time.

"That's one point in her favor."

The manicurists' stations held no interest for him, nor did Bertie's esthetician equipment. Dominique got a favorable response, and I learned the cross-dressing massage therapist snuck him pieces of seedless watermelon and bananas on days when Charity left early.

Gazelle got the equivalent of a raspberry, and when I showed him Bertie, he yawned. Throughout it all, the scent of lavender wafted around me.

"I give up. Thanks a lot."

It was over. Stripe wasn't interested in helping me. As I stared into his button eyes, shame crept over me. How could I be angry with an innocent animal? It wasn't his fault.

Jeff had also given up. I imagined him huddled in his car, wishing he could turn on the heat. Who was I kidding? If he could get into the vehicle without the keys, he could hotwire it.

I still had half an hour to go before Armando Cozzani arrived. Would the iguana's future hold something larger than a terrarium?

Going with an impulse, I removed the mesh lid and gently picked up Stripe with my fingers wrapped around his belly. My carpet wasn't as good as the one in the Friendly Fingers hallway, but he might get a little tickle out of it.

To make the experience more pleasurable, I retrieved the last of my chopped mango and hand fed him as he stretched out. I didn't know whether iguanas enjoyed a scratch on the head or belly rubs like Emily, so I rested my back against the couch and let him be.

The rhythm of rain on my roof picked up speed. Turning my head toward the patio, I felt a twinge of conscience about leaving Jeff outside. I even got up and moved in that direction. Before I could do something stupid, like let him back inside, someone knocked on my front door.

Stripe scurried off to investigate his surroundings, but he couldn't get far. Besides, Armando would know how to wrangle him back into his temporary home.

"Oh. Hello."

Bertie stood on my stoop, soaking wet and holding her textbooks under her light jacket. She stepped past me to get out of the rain and stomped her ballet flats on my inside mat.

"What are you doing here?"

I wasn't *exactly* afraid of her. Bowers knew something I didn't that took her off his list of suspects. Or she might not be off his list, but they didn't have enough evidence to charge her.

Bertie's eyes opened wide in surprise. "I got a message to come here. That you would quiz me."

I glared at my back door. Jeff had volunteered my services so he could get an exclusive interview with the accused. Maybe lightening would strike him.

After she struggled out of her jacket and I hung it over a kitchen chair to dry, I asked her to tell me what happened at the police station. "You sounded pretty scared."

She grimaced. "They found out I was the one who gave Riley a massage Monday night."

"But Charity was killed on Tuesday morning. Why would they care about Monday night?" Gesturing to the couch, I invited her to sit down.

"They thought it gave me a motive. The police said someone attacked her while she was writing an email to the massage board. They also went through her phone records and saw she called me early Tuesday morning." She puffed up her cheeks and blew out the air. "She figured it out."

"You didn't put much effort into covering your tracks. You left the sheet."

"By the time the massage was over, I was so tired. How was I to know Tammy had given her an early appointment?"

"Did you accept money from Riley?"

Bertie covered her face with her hands. "I know, I know. I shouldn't have, but it was awkward. If I explained I didn't have my license yet, he might get mad and make things worse for me. I thought I could get away with it. Not a chance. Charity was furious. Said she couldn't trust me. But I would have given her the money. She could have kept it, or donated it, or whatever. That wasn't why I did it. I needed the practice. I tried to explain, but she hung up."

"And that made you mad."

She looked up. "More like scared. She could have ruined my chances. But it was my own fault. What could I do?"

"And the police accepted that explanation?"

"They had to. I had fifteen witnesses."

My eyebrows went up. "That's overdoing it."

She stared, then giggled and relaxed. "I decided to stay away from Friendly Fingers but changed my mind. If I talked to Charity in person...." She held up her hands. "I thought she might understand. So, I caught a later bus. It's the one time I was glad I take public transportation."

And that's why Allen didn't know what kind of car she drove. She didn't drive.

As she opened her textbook, ready for our session, I scratched her off the suspect list. "No offense, but now is not convenient." At her disappointed expression, I told her if she stuck around for a while, I'd make time.

Her gaze landed on the empty terrarium. "Where's Stripe?"

"He's around here somewhere."

"Reptiles creep me out." Bertie covered her mouth with her elbow and sneezed. "Maybe I'm allergic to him."

"Can you be allergic to reptiles?"

She sniffed. "I'd prefer that to a cold."

Since I didn't want Mister Cozzani to accuse me of neglecting the iguana, I reached for his food and water dishes, intending to clean them out. One plant rested on its side, so I righted it, exposing the rocks hidden under the leaves.

"Is that–" I reached for a smooth, black stone but left it when my doorbell rang. Once again it wasn't the posse in search of Stripe. Norma Hinkle stepped in out of the rain. What happened to waiting for an invitation to enter?

She looked over my shoulder. "You have company."

Bertie waved at her.

"The police and that little man from the zoo have been bugging me about Stripe. I want him back so I can hand him over." She noticed the empty terrarium. "Where is he?"

"Around. Come on in. His wrangler will be here any minute."

"I don't have much time." She gestured at the terrarium. "If you could just put his things together, I'll be on my way."

I laughed. "Sorry. I shouldn't have said wrangler." My purse was next to the couch. I set it on the coffee table and dug through it for Armando Cozzani's business card. "Just a minute. It's here somewhere." I pulled out a few dog treats and set them aside. The used tissues I stuck in my pocket. My wallet, plastic business card holder, a flyer from the community theater advertising a production of *Mama Mia!*, Nina's lavender nummy.

"Here it is. What's wrong?"

Norma's face contorted into a massive sneeze. "Excuse me."

"Are you getting a cold, too?" Bertie said, sympathetic.

"That must be it."

"Jeepers." Still holding the sachet, I waved my hand in front of her face. "Your eyes are running."

She flinched and held up her hands. "Could you put that thing away? I'm sensitive to scents. All sorts of scents. Perfumes, room fresheners, fresh flowers. Too many to name."

"What about the essential oils the massage therapists use?"

"It's not a big deal. I forgot to take my medicine this morning."

Frowning, I stared at Nina's Nummy. My gaze darted to Bertie and my hand shot out in her direction.

"How about you?"

She leaned over and inhaled. "Lavender. One of my favorites." Covering her mouth, she sneezed. "Darn it. I *am* getting a cold."

"Do you mind?" Norma shrieked.

"Sorry." I took the sachet into the bathroom and tossed it in with the rest of the potpourri in the basket behind the toilet.

Both women sneezed, but only Norma reacted to the sachet. The *lavender* sachet. Had Stripe given me a solid clue right at the beginning? Only I'd been too dense to see it. I cut myself some slack. *Lavender* was a mighty broad clue.

Norma owned Friendly Fingers. Had Stripe sent me an image of the entire business not to suggest someone *in* the spa had murdered Charity, but to suggest ownership? An iguana wouldn't understand rental agreements.

As the person who rented the space, Norma would know about the security cameras. And we had no one's word but Norma's about anything that happened before I walked in those doors.

A noise like a soft cry came from my living room. When I stepped out of the hallway, something wasn't right. Bertie slumped sideways on the couch, and Norma crawled on her hands and knees, peering under the coffee table.

Right then, a fist pounded on my front door. "Miss Chandler, open up." Gutierrez.

Norma sprang to her feet. She clutched one of my kitchen knives in her hand.

"That's probably not sharp," I warned. Everyone knows dull knives are more dangerous because the blade tears.

"I'm sure it will puncture." She stabbed one of my decorative pillows to make her point, though she had to stab twice to make the tip go through. Since she would stab me as many times as necessary to get what she wanted, I took her threat seriously.

"Now, where is that reptile? Not that I *really* believe you can talk to it, but I've worked much too hard to take chances."

Gutierrez's voice followed. "Frances Chandler, this is the police. We're here for the iguana."

"She has a knife," I called out.

Jeff's muffled voice came from my patio. "Who has a

knife? Frances? Unlock the door." He pounded a few times to clarify which door.

"But you weren't in the locker room until *after* I found Charity." Replaying the scene in my mind, something interesting popped out at me. "You were carrying your shoes, but I didn't see you kick them off." I squinted at her. "Why were you carrying your shoes?"

She rolled her eyes. "So inefficient. You didn't look in the bathroom stalls."

I made a face. The thought of standing on a toilet in my bare feet grossed me out. "And how did you manage to kill her? Charity, please lay down in this unfinished hot tub. And why kill her? You were going to fire her."

"I couldn't fire her, you twit. She *owned* me."

"Owned?"

"An exaggeration, but she told me if I didn't make her a partner, she'd call in daddy's loan."

"Loan?"

"For the Jacuzzi!" She sniffed. "My beautiful Italian tiles."

Norma stood with her back to the open kitchen door, so I saw Stripe first. As soon as he spotted her, the skin under his chin puffed up and his tail whipped back and forth. He raised himself up and opened his mouth. And then his skin turned completely black.

His impressive display startled me into making a noise. When Norma turned her head to look, he lunged. She screamed. To Norma, the black, puffed-up pet must have been Nemesis herself, come to enact retribution. Except Stripe was a he.

Jeff pounded and yelled. Gutierrez pounded and yelled.

Norma pulled back the knife, ready to strike the defenseless iguana. I threw myself on her, grabbing the arm holding the knife with both hands. After years of hauling patients in and out of bed, the older woman showed surprising strength.

As we fell back onto the couch, I struggled to hang on, but my arm muscles tired easily and wanted a break. Summoning up my puny energy reserves, I tightened my grip and jerked her arm back and forth. Finally, I dived forward and bit her arm. When she dropped her weapon, she ran for my patio, flung open my curtains, unlocked the door, and pushed outside.

Heaving a sigh, I pulled myself up. Jeff could take care of Norma. Still, I hurried to the front door. Gutierrez could make the killer's capture official.

When I swung open the door, the detective's leg was already in motion. At the sight of me, she checked herself, but her bare foot hit my stomach hard enough to knock me off balance and on my butt.

Jeff rushed past her, soaking wet and dripping. He offered me a hand.

"Why aren't you in back catching Norma?" I demanded.

"Sheesh, Frances. I was looking for another way in."

Armando Cozzani pushed his way through. "Where's the iguana?" Then he spotted Stripe.

The pleased reptile, back to his normal coloring, rubbed his toes on my carpet, an expression of ecstasy on his face. The handler hurried to him, picked him up in gloved hands, and cuddled him. "Are you okay, boy?"

Jeff and I raced to the patio and found Gutierrez leaning over the wall with an incredibly bright flashlight. The spotlight roamed over the riverbed behind me, illuminating the falling rain. No sign of Norma.

A low rumble vibrated in my ears. "Oh, crap."

Wiping my face, I leaned over the wall and strained to see up the creek, but it was too dark.

"What's that?" Jeff asked. "Thunder?"

I pointed, and the three of us followed the glow of Gutierrez' flashlight as branches, dirt, and anything not anchored to the creek bed rumbled past in a foamy, thick ooze.

"It's not moving very fast."

Poor Jeff. The ignorant out-of-towner. Gutierrez knew better, and when an engine turned over in front of my house, we looked at each other.

"There's a dip in the road two miles from here."

While she pulled out her cell phone, I grabbed Jeff and dragged him through the house. "Where's your car? Do you have your keys? We have to go after Norma."

I'd forgotten poor Bertie. She sat up with her head hanging forward. Stripe was back in the terrarium, and Armando Cozzani pressed a washcloth bulging with something I assumed was ice against her jaw. The hand not busy with his ministrations was holding one of hers as he murmured encouragement.

I ordered the reptile wrangler to stay in the house and guard the animals and the esthetician.

My ex had his keys out of his pocket by the time we got to the car. Since I was near the dead end, there was only one direction Norma could have gone. We followed as fast as we dared in the blinding torrent. The windshield wipers were useless, even on high.

As we crested a hill, taillights came into view. Lightening flashed, illuminating her silver hatchback.

"That's her."

Once we rounded the bend, the car moved parallel to

the creek. The rumble of water and mud was louder here. I rolled down my window and tried to catch a glimpse of the moving death.

"Start honking at her."

"I think she knows it's us, Frances."

"We have to warn her. There's a dip up ahead." I looked at him. "One she shouldn't try to cross."

"Oh." His eyes widened. "Oh."

He pounded on the horn. She reflexively braked, and her back tires swayed on the slick road. Instead of stopping, she hit the gas.

"That idiot is going to get herself killed."

Just as she reached the dip, her headlamps illuminated a sign. *To cross in the rain means pain.* She skidded to a stop, opened her car door, and got out to take a better look. We pulled up behind her, and at the sound of my car door slamming shut, she gave us a quick look and got back in her car.

The churning, foaming wall caught up with us and rumbled across the road. Waving my hands, I ran forward. "Norma, stop! You'll never make it!"

But the owner of Friendly Fingers had faith in her little, silver hatchback. The car gave it a shot. When she blasted into the crossing and made it three-quarters of the way, I thought she might succeed. But her economy-sized vehicle was no match for the raw power of nature. We watched, horrified, as the roiling avalanche lifted her car and carried it downstream.

Gutierrez pulled up and joined us, still on the phone. "I've got the fire department on the line. Where is—oh." She spoke into the phone. "Yeah. We're going to need you." She gave them our location.

When dry, the creek bed revealed large, round stones

the size of soccer balls. Shrubs encroached on either side. Norma's car bounced from rock to rock like a pinball until her vehicle turned into the arms of a hopseed bush. Forward momentum halted for the moment. Encouraged, she swung open her car door.

We all three shouted for her to stop.

With cautious steps, I picked my way along the bank, pushing past shrubs and skirting cacti.

"Get back here," Gutierrez yelled.

Stumbling, I grabbed the branch of a young Mesquite and held on as my feet slipped on slick stones. Now parallel to the silver hatchback, I swore as Norma, standing half out of her car, hovered a foot above the admittedly shallow water. Her uncertainty turned to confidence as she assessed her chances. I understood. It seemed a simple proposition to wade through a little water and mud to the shore, if you ignored the force behind it, capable of uprooting small trees and moving loose boulders.

I called out over the rumble. "Don't move. The fire department is on its way."

She lowered her foot and immediately lost her balance in the strong current. Still clutching the car door, she jerked back. The motion wrenched her car loose. As she hung on with both arms, her feet swung out over the dangerous foam. She screamed.

I crouched and patted the ground, looking for a fallen branch or something that might reach her. But in a flash, I forgot all about Norma and her car.

At first, I thought it was more flotsam floating by, but then it squeaked. Without thought, I lunged forward, scooping up the quail chick in my cupped hands. Unfortunately, I overbalanced and fell into the unrelenting wave of nasty water. Twisting so my shoulder would take the brunt,

I landed hard on the boulders. One for my shoulder, and one for my head.

Even as stars flashed before my eyeballs, I managed to hold my hands high, but my moment of victory ended when the wave rolled me to my stomach. Sputtering, I tried to get to my knees using only one hand while the other clutched the chick, but I flipped onto my backside again.

The force pulled my legs downstream. I jammed my feet against a boulder and pushed back, straining my leg muscles until they screamed from the burn.

Suddenly, two hands wrapped around my upper arm in a vice-like grip. "Push!"

Using my remaining strength, I shoved away from the rock. Jutting stones scraped my arms and back as my rescuer dragged me onto the bank, where I lay, gasping for air. Without moving my head, I raised my hand over my face and opened my fingers. The soggy chick blinked at me, his tiny chest heaving, and I started to cry.

Bowers helped me to my feet and wiped the rain from his brow.

"I swear you're going to kill me," he yelled. "I'm going to have a heart attack one of these days, and it will be your fault."

"Am I that heavy?"

He choked out a laugh and pulled me tight against him. "I'm not letting you out of my sight." And he didn't. With his arm around my shoulder, pinning me to his side, we joined the others. In a few minutes, we heard the sirens.

The fire department, following Gutierrez' instructions, approach from the other side of the creek. The woman who had easily scaled my back wall, twice, had used her superpowers to climb on top of her hatchback. The car, stuck on another shrub, stood still long enough to allow two irritated but heroic firemen to pluck her to safety.

To mock us, the rain petered out right after and left us surrounded by the frisky, clean smell of fresh rain coming from the creosote bushes.

I smiled up at Bowers. "I love that smell."

FIFTY-TWO

Turns out, Norma only scaled my wall once in her attempt to flee justice. Back at my house, I dried myself off, dropped my soggy clothes into the hamper, and dressed in sweatpants, a denim big shirt, and fuzzy blue slippers before I brewed coffee and plated a package of chocolate sandwich cookies buried in the back of my pantry.

Bowers arrived first. He came inside, his hands in the pockets of his police windbreaker, and stared at me. He had something to say, but he didn't get a chance, as Jeff and Gutierrez arrived next.

Even though we had company, he sat so close to me on the couch I was almost in his lap. His arm crossed over my collar bone, holding me to him. Gutierrez settled on the remaining cushion, while Jeff retrieved a chair from the kitchen. As soon as I'd done hostess duty, offering everyone coffee, which they accepted, and the cookies, which no one took except Jeff, I demanded to know the details. Bowers deferred to Gutierrez. I cut her off before she began.

"Who hit Charity?"

"Tammy, naturally."

"Why naturally?"

"She had an arrangement with Charity. Her spending habits left her desperate for extra cash."

Making a circling motion with my hand to speed her up, I said, "I know that part."

"Okay. Then you probably know she's the one who tried to steal your iguana."

"Get out!"

"She heard you discussing the iguana with Norma and looked him up. Once she found out how rare he was, she thought she had a way to big cash. More than she made through her bribes."

"Why did she hit Charity?" Jeff asked. "Tammy had it good."

"The receptionist got there early in answer to a summons from Charity. Confident that Norma would accept her offer, the new half-owner decided she didn't want Tammy making deals with the other employees. She fired her. So, in a fit of pique, little Miss Tammy picked up one of Charity's massage stones and threw it at her, knocking the massage therapist senseless."

"Tammy left out the back door," I said. "That's who I heard."

"And she walked to the closest coffee kiosk and had a latte. She might be a psychopath."

"But she didn't kill Charity?"

"No. She only explained her part because she didn't want to take credit for the murder. And she took it back right after she confessed. Said we tricked her and let us prove it if we could. We can't."

Raising one finger, I told Gutierrez to hold that thought. Mister Cozzani had taken Stripe away in a burlap sack, leaving the terrarium behind. It was now home to the Gambel's quail baby. I carefully moved one of the plants aside and revealed the black massage stone. "Will this do?"

Faster than I could say her name three times, Juanita yanked a pair of stretchy blue gloves from her pocket and took command of the rock. Bowers went to his car and returned with a paper sack into which she dropped the stone before labelling it.

While she did so, I congratulated Jeff on his perceptions about Bertie. He shrugged, attempting modesty.

"I just figured there were other reasons to call the board. Giving someone an unsupervised massage and charging for it before getting licensed?" Jeff shook his head. "Big no-no. And Charity didn't seem the type to worry about a complaint before it was filed."

"I should have guessed. Bertie kept her test books at work. It makes sense that she would stay after to study, especially now that I know she would have had to lug them home on the bus."

Bowers nodded. "Bertie found a quiet place to study at Friendly Fingers. She just happened to be there when Riley Reynolds, former resident of Wolf Creek, stopped by to see if Charity would make time for an old client. That license plate number helped." He nodded, expressing approval. "I understand you delivered it in person."

"I did. And you can thank Grant Williams and his stalker tendencies for the plate number. Is that why Gazelle started walking Charity out to her car? She was afraid of Grant?" I gasped. "What happened to Gazelle? Shouldn't you look for her body?"

"Gazelle came to us the day after the vinegar bomb," Gutierrez said. "As the two of you should have done. But sooner."

Bowers jumped in to deflect her criticism. "Charity approached her about a management role once Norma made her a partner. When Charity died, she suspected who was behind it, and when the bomb went off in her massage room, she thought Norma had heard about Charity's offer and planned to get rid of her, too."

"That doesn't sound like Norma," I said.

His eyes lit up. "Very good. The credit goes to Tammy."

"Gazelle should have found a nicer way to turn down Tammy's offer." Jeff looked from Bowers to Gutierrez. "Does anyone know what that offer was?"

"Fifty percent of the first massage," Bowers said. "After that, it was up to Charity to keep the customer coming back. Some of those massages are expensive. Tammy's cut could have been up to seventy dollars."

"This all sounds fine as far as Tammy is concerned, but what about the murder? Do you have any evidence Norma killed Charity?" I asked.

"It's all circumstantial," Gutierrez admitted. "She was there at the right time. She had a motive. However, she did confess her role to you. Most of which I heard."

"Me too," Jeff said. "Except when I was jumping the wall and running to the front of the house."

"With several witnesses, including Armando Cozzani, we'll see how long she holds out."

I picked up a cookie and tossed it Jeff, who was distracted by Gutierrez. It bounced off his chest. "Did you tell Bertie I would quiz her tonight?"

"Me? When did I have time to call her?"

Bowers pulled me closer. "Norma couldn't be sure you'd give up Stripe. I suspect she got Bertie there to take the blame if she had to—" he cleared his throat, "use force."

My fiancé stood, and Gutierrez took it as a sign to leave.

She smiled brightly at him. "Are you sure you don't want to help me with the paperwork?"

"That's the price you pay for being in charge." He told Jeff he would meet him back at his place. "Frankie and I need to have a long talk."

FIFTY-THREE

Once we were alone, I asked Bowers if he'd like more coffee.

"No, thank you."

"How about some pretzels? Scratch that. They're scattered on the floor."

"Not even tempted."

"Wine? Tea? Scotch? It will only take me a minute to put together."

He led me back to the couch.

Once seated, I twisted my fingers together and avoided eye contact until he rested a hand over mine to halt my fidgeting.

"I know this case was difficult for you. I mean on a personal level."

I let out a breath, relieved he understood. "It was."

"Since it was an odd situation, I'm making an exception. But I want your promise you'll stay out of my investigations in the future."

"Technically, it was Gutierrez' investigation. Okay. Bad joke. But I don't think a comparable situation will come up again, do you?"

"I certainly hope not."

"I mean, the Wolf Creek police department is small, so climbing the promotional ladder must be a short trip, right?"

He held up a hand. "I think we're talking about two different things. I'm talking about how you tried to save your ex-boyfriend from a murder conviction. I can see why you would want to help Jeff. He's personable. Reminds me of some of the gang leaders I've spoken to."

I gaped at him. "You think I approached murder suspects and let some strange guy touch me—I'm talking about the massage—and suffered through a break in and bruises and a kick to the stomach—"

"Someone kicked you in the stomach?"

"Gutierrez, when she tried to break in my door. Understandable. People were screaming. Still, next time I let someone in, I'll get an *all clear* first." I had wandered from the point. "What I'm asking is, you think I went through all that for Jeffrey Ross?"

"Didn't you?"

I snorted a laugh, but then my voice choked up and I shoved his hand away. "No." When my face crumpled, I turned away so he wouldn't see if my nose ran. Before my silent crying could turn blubbery, I got to my feet and took a deep breath with my hands on my hips, willing the tears to stop.

He pulled me back down, pushing my hair behind my ears so he could see my face. I rubbed my nose, just in case.

"Is getting involved in murder something you can't control?" he said, chiding me. "There are doctors. Expensive doctors, but we can give up takeout and watch our pennies." When I didn't laugh, he sighed and leaned forward, his elbows on his knees.

"I'm not a good guesser, so why don't you tell me."

"I did it for you," I mumbled.

His eyebrows went up. "For me? I think you'd better explain."

"You had this promotion coming up, but the murder happened. And when it looked like Jeff was involved—and Paul Simpson wrote those articles—and your fellow cops were making fun of you—and Gutierrez would cut off her mother's arm to get ahead let alone make you look bad to the committee—"

"I didn't get the promotion."

When I gasped out Gutierrez' name, he shook his head. "Smitty got it."

"Was it because of me?"

"Because of *you?*"

He got quiet. Too quiet. My stomach knotted up. He was lying. The committee passed him by because of me and my involvement with a murder suspect. Because of my interference. It didn't matter which of my actions caused his loss. Just that he was stuck in the same job forever, and it was my fault. Would his resentment grow over the years? Because he must resent me. Would he learn to hate me? Choose to sleep on the couch until we were too old to care? I couldn't bear it.

Finally, he tapped the center of my chest. "You feel things deeply. That's one of the reasons I love you. And you're drawn to helping people, which is admirable. However, you're not responsible for clearing obstacles out of my path. Even my sisters know better than to try that. If you're worried about something, talk to me."

He held up a finger. "Another point. If you share your thoughts with me instead of keeping me in the dark, I won't get blindsided. Like when you freed the squirrel mascot in the biker bar without giving me a warning."

"I did warn you. I asked if you had your gun on you."

"After you took the squirrel."

"Okay. You have a point."

Leaning back against the cushion, he pursed his lips. "I remember the first time I saw you."

"After Margarita Morales was murdered."

"I thought you were a flake."

"Hey!"

"Even so, I wanted to know more about you. The more I knew...the first few times I thought about asking you to marry me, I dismissed the idea. The hours I work make it difficult to live a normal life. And so many cops I've known have wound up divorced. The lifestyle is hard on a marriage. But I saw how much love you had to give. How much you care for the animals you help. And for Penny. Even your nutty Aunt Gertrude." He cleared his throat. "And I wondered what it would be like to be a recipient of all that love until, finally, I couldn't not take a chance." He grinned. "If you blew me off, I could ask my sisters to deal with you."

"Gosh." His confession had left me speechless. For about a minute. "But I'm impulsive. I don't take directions well. I can't cook, and I stink at decorating. And I have a job that your colleagues seem to enjoy mocking. By most standards, I'm not a prize."

"Frankie, you agreed to spend the rest of your life with me. To love me. To laugh with me. To grow old with me. Everything else is gravy. In fact, there's only one thing that would make it perfect."

"What's that?"

He picked at a snag in the couch cushion, refusing to meet my eyes. I steeled myself for bad news.

"It was my turn to wear the jackal hat, but someone stole it."

I gawked. "Seriously? You expect me to compete with a jackal hat? It's too much. As Jeff would say, we're over."

"Maybe you could investigate its disappearance."

"You're on your own, mister."

He cocked his head. "Oh yeah?"

"If I start to think about you during the day, I'll snap a rubber band against my wrist to stop myself."

He scooted closer. "You better be thinking about me. Maybe you need motivation." He pulled me to him and planted his lips on mine in a demanding kiss. I pulled away, breathless, and laughed.

"Or maybe I should get a hamster, and I'll lavish all my love and attention on him."

He threw his hands up in mock surrender. "I can't compete with a furry face."

I placed my palms on his cheeks. "So, grow a beard."

And then I kissed him back.

FIFTY-FOUR

The next morning, all signs of heavy weather had evaporated. Literally. The sun shone hot and nary a puddle survived. I scanned the creek bed, littered with debris, and didn't leave for my appointment until I heard the call of my Gambel's quail and spotted one of the chicks darting around a muddy plastic bag. The chick in my hands responded, and mother quail made a U-turn around a shrub and headed my way.

Leaning over the wall, I lowered the chick until I could drop it gently on the ground. It took off running toward the others. Mom greeted it with cries of joy and it fell in line with its siblings.

Later that morning, Bowers, Jeff, and I hung out in my fiancé's living room, preparing for a trip to the Sonora Desert Reptile Rescue to visit Stripe in his new home. I kept checking my watch and coming up with last minute tasks. I'd already visited the downstairs bathroom three times with various excuses, the final involving a reference to *feminine issues* which Bowers didn't believe but was afraid to question. Right as Bowers insisted we get going, the doorbell rang.

My fiancé moved to answer, but I held him back. "Could you get that Jeff?" I rested my hand on Bowers arm. "Just watch."

Jeff opened the door and stared. Buffy Beaumont stood on the threshold in stretch jeans, flip-flops, and a miniscule red tank top. My former nemesis. She had the physical build of Betty Boop, including the big head. Except she was blond.

My ex's shoulders stiffened. "Buffy."

She gave him a quick onceover, ignoring those of us in the background, and spoke her piece in a rush. "Jeffrey, get your things and come home. You don't belong here."

"Home?" He crossed his arms over his chest. "You threw me out." Tossing a glance back at us, he added, "I kind of like it here. I've made some new friends."

I squeezed Bowers' arm to keep him from responding and whispered, "Let it play out."

She clenched her hands. "You're coming home with me and we're getting married, and *not* by a justice of the peace."

"It takes two to get married. I'm not sure I want a wife who throws me out when she gets angry. I deserve better."

Her false eyelashes opened wide. I don't think she expected pushback, and I enjoyed her shock more than I should have. Her eyes darted in my direction. Jeff noticed and turned sideways to include me in the conversation.

"Frances is pretty spectacular. Amazing I never noticed. We've spent a lot of time together these past few days. You know, while I wandered after losing my home because you kicked me out."

"This is ridiculous," Bowers muttered. About to move forward, he stopped when I dug my nails into his bicep.

"Do *not* introduce yourself," I hissed. "You'll ruin his advantage."

Bowers' eyes narrowed as he caught on. "What if it backfires? He'll never leave."

"Trust me on this."

"You shouldn't have run off," Buffy pouted. "We didn't have a chance to talk."

"Without a job, I didn't have much choice. In fact, I went to a job fair and met—"

"My cousin!" Everyone looked at me when I yelled. "And she said the job market out here was fabulous and Jeff came here to check it out."

"Yeah," my ex said, and I could tell he realized he'd just avoided disaster. "Your cousin."

"Close call," Bowered mumbled.

I whispered back. "He overstepped his bargaining position and was moving into spite."

"Bear, your fluffy bunny is so sorry she was mean to you." The wheedling tone Buffy used made the nicknames even more disgusting. She reached out for him, but Jeff had the wisdom to step out of her reach. If she touched him, the negotiations would end.

"I'll think about it. Did you already buy a return ticket?"

Her fingers twisting together, she said, "I got two. I hoped you would come back with me."

"Well," he sighed, "we can talk about it on the plane."

While he collected his stuff from the guest room, I strolled to the front door and invited her in. She eyed me, suspicious, but when she saw Bowers had joined me, she slipped through the door and skirted past me to the couch. I think she suspected I would kick her rear end.

He put his mouth close to my ear. "You called her?"

"I did."

"You couldn't leave it alone."

"I couldn't."

"Thank the Lord." He raised his voice. "Did you have a nice flight. I assume you flew here."

"It was all right."

Jeff came out of the downstairs bathroom with his gym bag. He dug through it in a hurry, doublechecking he had everything. At one point, he fumbled his keys.

"Make sure you have your rental keys *and* your house keys," I said.

He looked up, and since his back was toward his girlfriend, he grinned at me and gave me a thumbs up. He wiped the expression away before he turned to her. With great nonchalance, he threw his gym bag over his shoulder and sauntered to the couch. Buffy sprang up, eager to leave.

"Wait." I stepped in front of the happy couple as they headed for the door. Placing one hand on each of their shoulders, I said, "I forgive you both."

Buffy opened her mouth with a retort, but then her brow wrinkled. Finally, her features relaxed, and she almost smiled. At least until Jeff pulled me into a hug and whispered, "Thanks," in my ear.

After he let me go, the brand-new fiancé grinned. "Maybe you guys want to come to the wedding."

Bowers, Buffy, and I all shouted an emphatic *No!*

"HE LOOKS GOOD."

Stripe hung on a branch—a real live branch—of a small tree. His legs and tail dangled, showing a state of complete relaxation. The surrounding foliage represented the dry tropical forest that he belonged in as well as a pond. I had no idea if Fiji Crested Iguanas swam.

Bowers squeezed my hand. "He looks happy."

The vines under the tree moved, revealing a second iguana. A mate? Now Stripe could have a family all his own. The thought pleased me.

As we walked away from the enclosure, a moment's sadness passed over me. "It's not fair. They should take him in at the sanctuary in Fiji."

"But they can't risk bringing him back. Not now that he's been exposed to who knows what."

"Stupid Vali," I mumbled. The boyfriend had admitted sneaking him off one of the islands as a present for his late girlfriend. He didn't ask the iguana if he wanted to be a present.

"At least he's no longer in a little glass house," Bowers said, trying to cheer me up.

"You're right."

As we walked to the car, I linked my arm through his. A single white cloud occupied the blue sky, offering an apology for the havoc wrought by his older siblings. After the burst of rain, the landscape appeared to have bloomed overnight. Flowers topping the Saguaro cacti, blankets of desert marigolds, and blooms on creosote bushes. Survivors, grabbing their chance to shine. It made me proud to be an Arizonian.

An Arizonian. I was an Arizonian woman engaged to an Arizonian man who would spend the rest of his life with me. We'd make a home together. Raise kids. I felt like a pioneer, forging a new life. The thought made me giddy.

Bowers looked at me. "What are you grinning about?"

Wiping the dopey smile off my face, I said, "Are you going to help me decide on a combination for the lock on my front door? I have a desire to keep people out for a while."

"I have a number I don't think you'll forget."

He said it too casually.

"What? Please don't tell me it's the date you proposed to me. I'm lousy with dates."

"You won't forget this one."

I stopped walking, intrigued. "And what happens on this special date?"

He glanced around the nearly empty parking lot. "This isn't exactly how I planned it."

"Come on." I nudged him. "You started it."

"That I did."

He got down on one knee, and two passing female volunteers giggled.

"That's so sweet," one woman said.

I tugged on his arm, trying to make him stand. "What are you doing? You already proposed. I said yes. Remember?"

He reached into the back pocket of his jeans. "But I didn't have a ring." He opened a small box, the red fabric outside worn and faded. Inside sat a simple gold band with a solitaire diamond.

"Frankie, will you marry me six months from now, on November twenty-eighth?"

I gasped. "You saved me from having to pick out a ring." Throwing my arms around his neck, I peppered his face with kisses. "Yes. Absolutely."

He scooted me over to sit on his lap and slipped the ring on my finger. It was a tad loose. "We might have to have it resized." When his eyes met mine, his were misty. "It was my mother's. June gave it to me. Said she was saving it for me because my sisters would only fight over it."

Now *my* eyes were wet. "Oh my gosh. I'm—" I stared at the ring and all it represented. Bowers' past. Our future. "I don't know what to say."

"I think my mom would have been proud to call you daughter. I'm sure of it. You're kind, and funny, and brave. A bit impulsive, but your heart is in the right place."

He swung an arm under my legs and stood, taking me with him.

"Don't do that. You'll get a hernia."

He laughed, dropped me to my feet, and put his arm over my shoulder. As we continued our walk to his car, I chided him.

"I'm darn near perfect, huh?"

"Well, maybe after a few cooking lessons with June."

"I like June. I like all your sisters."

He grinned. "I'm glad."

"So, tell me. What's the deal with Edith?"

He lost the grin.

TO FIND out what's up with Edith, keep reading for a preview of *A Scape Goat for Murder*. You'll also find Book Club Questions and more.

IF YOU ENJOYED THIS BOOK, please consider leaving a review. Reviews help readers discover new books, and the author, who socializes mostly with dogs, appreciates the human feedback.

A NOTE FROM THE AUTHOR

When I first decided to incorporate a reptile into the story, it was a toss-up between a bearded dragon and an iguana. My research showed bearded dragons have friendly personalities, and that would never do. Iguanas for the win! But I wanted my iguana to be special. I knew I'd found Stripe when I discovered the Fiji crested iguana. The island of Yadua Taba is now a sanctuary for these endangered and exceptionally beautiful creatures. Sadly, once an iguana has left the island, he can't be reintroduced because of the danger of importing diseases to the mess of iguanas already living there.

(I'm not being mean. A group of iguanas is called a "mess".)

A PREVIEW OF A SCAPE GOAT FOR MURDER

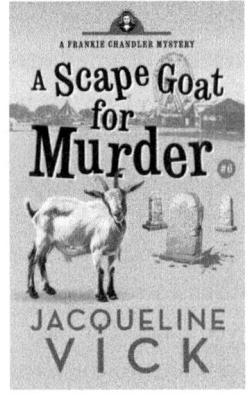

Sometimes Life with a capital L steps in and kicks you in the teeth, making your priorities excruciatingly clear. A speed lesson. I got mine the third week of September, about six weeks shy of my wedding.

"AND IF HE doesn't stop piddling on the floor, I'll have to get rid of him."

Bart Waller's droning diatribe over his new morning ritual of mopping tinkle from the kitchen floor was getting on my nerves. I couldn't see why it bothered him so much. It wasn't a great floor. The beige tile was the cheap stuff that comes on a roll. It went with the white Formica countertop and wood cabinets in need of a coat of varnish to cover years of wear.

The room smelled of scrambled eggs and stale coffee. The former still clung to the dishes in the sink. Not my idea of the Ritz.

As the man continued to complain, I slipped a quick glance out the kitchen window over the sink. Not a single cloud dotted the September Arizona sky. Our flight from Phoenix's Sky Harbor airport tomorrow morning should take off without a hitch. However, as I feel it's my responsibility to clutch the armrests and hold up any aircraft I'm in, I kept the weather under close watch.

"And then I stepped in it," he continued.

Biting my lip to hold back my opinion that any man who ran into piddle two weeks running should learn to watch his step, I put an end to his comments. I still had to get my cat, Emily, to her sitter and pack last minute odds and ends. After that, I would sit on my couch and sweat nervous perspiration until my fiancé, Detective Martin Bowers, and I arrived in Loon Lake, Wisconsin, for his first in-person meeting with his future in-laws.

"Be quiet," I snapped. "Please." Holding up one hand, I switched to the airy-yet-somber tone most people expected from a pet psychic. "I need silence to connect with Sparkles."

He was a beautiful roan—the dog, not the guy—with

his liver-colored base coat lightened by strands of white and speckles of liver throughout. His snout was mostly gray, but that wasn't a surprise in a ten-year-old dog. Neither was his inability to hold it all night. Heck. I sometimes woke up with a need to tinkle, and I was only in my mid-thirties.

After slipping a glance at my watch and confirming I had wasted too much time on this appointment, I opened the imaginary yet intimidating wooden door I used as a mental gateway to stop random messages sent by animals from sneaking into my head.

Every creature has its own signature vibration. Sparkles gave off a sweet flutter. Once I created a path of light between the dog's mind and mine, I sent him an image of this same kitchen at night. Then I focused on the doggie door and raised my eyebrows.

Sparkles lowered his head. His long ears covered his eyes in shame.

My head drooped in sync with Sparkles', and my limbs trembled along with the dog's. With extreme clarity, the animal showed me the fastened lock on the doggie door. I exclaimed with disgust.

"What's the matter?" Bart whispered the question.

"If you block off his access to his toilet, where do you expect him to go potty?"

A vibration from my back pocket warned me the persistent caller who'd already tried to reach me three times during this appointment hadn't given up. I ignored it.

Bart barked out a laugh. "You think I lock him in?" He strode to the door. "I unlock this door every night before—"

He paused, fingering the fastened lock. "I don't understand. I—oh." In an act of feigned confidence, he puffed out his chest and cracked a grin. It wasn't difficult to read his genuine emotions in the micro-expression that escaped before the grin. Guilt. Embarrassment.

"We had a raccoon get in a few weeks ago. He was after Sparkle's food. Or she. I'm not sure. How do you tell the difference between a male and female raccoon?"

His babbling confirmed it. This man was up to his neck in a puddle of his own making. I ignored his attempts to divert my attention.

"And how long ago did Sparkles start relieving himself on your floor?"

He coughed. "About the same time."

To his credit, especially after the comment about getting rid of the dog, he cried out, fell to his knees, and pulled the cocker spaniel into a hug.

"Sparkles, Daddy is an idiot. I'm so sorry. And I was just venting. I'd never let anyone take you from me."

The spaniel's short tail thumped a beat on the floor. He gazed at me over his "daddy's" shoulder, eyes bright. Dogs were so willing to forgive. I, however, cared little for my fellow human beings and resisted the urge to express my disappointment with a slap to the back of Bart's head. People. Ugh. Other than my best friend, Penny, and my fiancé, and my parents, of course, I could do without most of them.

As I tapped my foot, waiting impatiently for the love fest to finish, I ran down a list of what I had left to do before my plane took off tomorrow morning. Before I drove my cat to the sitter's house, I had to clean the litter box. Last minute toiletries were on my bathroom sink, left out so I wouldn't forget to put them in my carry-on. I needed to shower tonight, since it was an early flight.

When my client stood, I cleared my thoughts and gave him a professional smile. "Do you have questions?"

"None." He took his wallet off the counter and pulled out a fifty-dollar bill. "Thank you so much."

"My pleasure," I said, accepting my payment.

I'd made it to my car but hadn't opened the door when my cell phone rang again. "Mother," I said through gritted teeth. I'd already suffered a flurry of phone calls with reminders to pack a dress for dinner with the Douds, Penny's family. And earrings. And makeup. My mother planned to traipse me, her engaged daughter, past her friends like a calf in a 4-H competition. More like a mature cow. Most of their daughters had wed in their twenties. It had taken me a decade longer to find my mate.

I snatched my phone from my back pocket and cleared most of my irritation from my tone. "I can either finish packing or spend my entire vacation on the phone with you."

It wasn't Mom. The clear alto belonged to Detective Juanita Gutierrez.

"Get to Holy Cross Hospital. Now."

And then she hung up.

BOOK CLUB QUESTIONS

A Scaly Tail of Murder

• Jeff had to have some good points, or we would wonder why Frankie liked him in the first place. What do you think his good points were?

• Did you at any point hope that Frankie and Jeff would get back together? (Be honest!)

• Frankie combines forces with Jeff to investigate the murder. Would you ever join up with an ex to accomplish something important?

• Bowers' coworkers razz him about Frankie. He tells Frankie this is a tension release, and it doesn't bother him. Does that sound reasonable? Or do you think she was right to be concerned?

• Frankie worries that Gutierrez will use the awkward situation with Jeff being a suspect against Bowers so she will look better to the committee deciding on the promotion. Did she have every right to do this? Or would it have been a breach of trust between coworkers?

• Stripe is a Fiji crested iguana, an endangered species. Is it all right to have an endangered species as long as you take care of it?

• Charity used her popularity at Friendly Fingers Spa as leverage to get Roberta to make her a business partner. Was this fair?

• Dominic/Dominique dressed as a woman when he gave massages. He said it put him in touch with his gentler nature. Should he have told his clients he was a man? Or doesn't it matter as long as he does a good job?

• Did you find Tammy the receptionist clever or dumb?

• In the end, Frankie helps Jeff get back together with Buffy. Would you have facilitated a meeting? Or held a grudge and let them both suffer?

ABOUT THE AUTHOR

Jacqueline Vick writes the Frankie Chandler Pet Psychic Mystery Series about a woman who, after faking her psychic abilities for years, discovers animals *can* communicate with her. Her second series, the Harlow Brothers mysteries, features a former college linebacker turned etiquette author and his secretary brother. Her books are known for satirical humor and engaging characters who are reluctant to accept their greatest (and often embarrassing) gifts. Visit her at www.jacquelinevick.com

ALSO BY JACQUELINE VICK

Frankie Chandler Mysteries
Barking Mad at Murder
A Bird's Eye View of Murder
An Almost Purrfect Murder
What the Cluck? It's Murder
A Scaly Tail of Murder
A Scape Goat for Murder
Some Like Murder Hot

Harlow Brother Mysteries
Civility Rules
Bad Behavior
Deadly Decorum

Standalone Novels
The Body Guy
An Unhealthy Attachment
Family Matters